Chris Wiggins

BLOOD
FEUD

AmErica House
Baltimore

ISBN: 1-58851-929-5
PUBLISHED BY AMERICA HOUSE BOOK PUBLISHERS
www.publishamerica.com
Baltimore

Printed in the United States of America

Special thanks to Christen Beckmann and the rest of the gang at AmErica House publishing and to agents Caroline Carney and Debbie Fine without whose assistance and encouragement this work would never have seen print. Appreciation goes to editors Jaye Nelia and Leslie Kazanjian, who taught me, along with a lot of other things about writing, that it is best to spell all right as two words.

Feel free to e-mail me at: cewmd1@datasync.com.

To the nurses, the doctors--
the administrators, the technicians--
To all the dedicated health care professionals who spend their
lives to make our lives better

Prologue

Dr. Sharon Jackson knelt in the cave, carefully bracing herself to prevent the knee of her wet suit from sliding on the treacherously slippery stone floor. She blew into her regulator to clear it of any debris, then took two deep inhalations. The breaths came easily. She unclipped the rubberized underwater flashlight from her waist. With a reassuring click, a shaft of light cut through the gloom. She directed the beam into her duffel bag and rummaged around until she found the small canister of antifog spray. Two squirts and it coated the inside of her dive mask. Then she slipped the strap over her head and pulled it down to the base of her neck. The mask dangled around her chin. Only in the movies did divers set the mask up on their forehead--too easy to get it knocked off and lose it, and her life depended on her mask. Actually, she reminded herself again, in this business her life depended on a thousand such details.

For the third time she checked the safety line attached to her waist. Her gaze followed it past the crouching figure of Armand a few feet away at the cave entrance. Satisfied that the line had no tangles, she stood and studied her companion. The frown on his face and his quick, jerky movements, as if at any moment he might cut and run, left no doubt that he preferred the sunshine of his Caribbean island to following this crazy American into a cave--a cave whose only opening was exposed for just a few brief hours at low tide.

"Armand," she said sternly, "you must not leave me unless the water is up to your knees." He had satisfactory command of English, but for emphasis she tapped the location on the front of her leg. She needed as much time as possible, yet she also knew the incoming tidal surge would be swift. If the water reached knee level walking against its force would become impossible. Anyone so unfortunate as to tarry that long would immediately be trapped until the next low tide, when the body would be washed out, the victim's face frozen in the death agony of drowning, the corpse torn by sharp rocks and already attractive to hungry crabs.

In addition to the scuba tank on her back, she carried an emergency spare slung by a strap under her arm. The compressed air supply in each tank was good for an hour and a half at sea level, but if she were trapped in the cave an

7

extra tank would not provide enough air to last until the next tide change twenty hours later. But waiting out the tides was not her intention. She planned to be out enjoying the pleasures of the ocean breeze and a spectacular coastline view by the time the cave mouth next became submerged, and well before her tanks were empty.

"When you return, madame, I will be right here," said Armand, pointing emphatically to the stone floor beneath his feet.

Sharon started to say more but decided against it. She knew, and he knew, that unless he was there when she returned, he would not get paid, and jobs that provided hard currency in this poverty-stricken province were as rare as--well, as thirty-year-old blondes like herself. She smiled as she remembered the fascinated gazes of the villagers of remote Doúbe, who rarely encountered an American visitor.

The smile left her face just as quickly as it had come. She was not a tourist, and this was not a pleasure dive from one of the boats that worked that trade out of Port-au-Prince, boats offering vacationers a divemaster and twenty feet of clear blue water with plenty of pretty fish to gawk at. On such tame excursions the worst danger a diver might suffer was a splinter from sliding over the gunwale of the boat.

No, this was no pleasure dive. This was deadly serious. The old line about there are old pilots and bold pilots but no old *and* bold pilots came to mind—Sharon just substituted the word diver for pilot. But she had no choice. She had to be bold. This cave was her best prospect. She had made over a dozen trips to Haiti. She had pored over thousands of topographic maps, studied computerized projections of sea levels going back centuries, and personally explored by boat, motor vehicle, and on foot hundreds of miles of coastline, including five other caves. This one had to be it.

Her search had only recently focused on this stretch of coastline. Access was difficult, in part because the poorly kept dirt roads became quagmires during the rainy season, and during drier times, well, there was little reason for the villagers to travel. They lived on a subsistence level and had nothing left over to trade with in the larger communities. But there was another reason the area remained isolated--*la police de province*. The district law enforcement officers functioned with apparent autonomy and seemed more interested in keeping Dr. Sharon Jackson away from the region than in dealing with the myriad problems of their impoverished nation. *La police* had made it plain: tourists, visitors, any outsiders were unwelcome in this province. This area was poor. There was nothing of interest. Haiti had plenty of other far more intriguing sites to visit. Go there.

Recently two of the officers had been particularly obnoxious. She was stopped while driving alone on a dirt access road to the sea. One policeman stood at the front of her vehicle, his weapon pointing down. It didn't have to be up; AK-47s were menacing in any direction. The other man came to her window. His new uniform--and new was unusual for any Haitian official, particularly one in the provinces--was stained with sweat. He leaned through the window. His closeness was unnerving, and he spoke slowly in French-accented English.

He told her this was a dangerous area. He knew of others who had come, then were never seen again. The policeman turned one dark hand palm up and offered a shrug. Who knew what happened? The cliffs are high. He shrugged. There are bandits. And such a pretty lady... He started to reach in the car window, as if to touch her, then stopped. Sharon, rigid with controlled fear, stared straight ahead and told him she would be gone in a day.

She had lied. After they released her, she resolved to stay no more than three days and not to go anywhere without Armand by her side. Not that the slight and friendly little Haitian would be any real help in a showdown, but at least a witness might prevent *la police* from acting rashly.

A wave of fear now washed over her. She forced it from her mind. She had persevered and succeeded in other difficult undertakings. This would be no different.

Quickly she punched the final settings into her dive computer, then strapped it around her wrist. With mask and regulator in place, she slid off the ledge and into the darkness that was the underground river. Despite her wet suit, she shivered. The river was a subterranean run-off from the mountains, and it received no benefit of warming from the sun.

Sharon clicked on her dive lamp and was instantly surrounded by a yellow glow. If there were an underwater observer she would look like a giant firefly floating in a sea of blackness. But the only eyes turned her way were those of three fish who warily studied the apparition while maintaining a cautious distance with lazy beats of their tails.

A short distance beyond her underwater spectators loomed the back wall of the cave. In its center gaped an irregular black hole, seemingly ready to swallow her up. As she moved closer, the halo of light from her dive lantern revealed the interior of a tunnel. A tunnel whose entrance was guarded by daggers of sharp volcanic basalt that, like the teeth of some giant undersea eel, stood ready to rip her skin and slice her air hose. Carefully she pushed past them, then stopped suddenly as a wave of claustrophobia swept over her. She fought it down. Too much effort and planning had gone into this expedition to turn back now. She looked over her shoulder. The safety line lay in a smooth, rocky trough, pointing the way out. Momentarily reassured, she pushed forward.

Once she was past the tunnel's teeth, her progress was remarkably easy. This was slack tide and she moved almost effortlessly by alternately pushing along the tunnel wall with one hand and swimming with short arm and leg strokes.

The water was crystal clear, although she knew the sense of security that gave her was deceptive and instantly could change. More than one unwary cave diver had died as a result of wearing flippers--a single kick could raise a blinding cloud of sediment, obscuring the exit. Frantic attempts to find the way out only made matters worse, and subsequent rescue teams would find the unfortunate diver's body with air supply exhausted. Such occurrences had led to strict rules of cave diving safety. Today, except for leaving off her fins, and using a safety rope and back-up air tank, Sharon had violated every one of them, but she forced that thought from her mind.

The dull gray tunnel ceiling gave way to shimmering silver. Immediately her head broke the surface. She brought her arm out of the water, holding the lantern high. She would have shouted with joy if it had not been for the regulator still in her mouth. It was just as she imagined. The river had eroded out a series of caves that were as interconnected as a strand of pearls.

This inner cave was the size of a large room. Stalactites hung from the ceiling like giant stony icicles. Against the far wall, she could see the underground river flowing into this cavern and next to it a ledge cut by the running water over the eons and beyond that—only blackness.

Cautiously, she tested the air, ready to instantly resume breathing from her tank if she detected sulfur or any other noxious odor, but other than having a stale smell, like that of an empty athletic locker room, the atmosphere seemed harmless.

Sharon quickly pulled herself out of the water and shed her scuba gear. She was almost overcome with excitement. The dive lantern cast a cone of light which she swept in a full circle. Irregular masses of stone, with an occasional sparkle from embedded quartz, greeted her from every angle.

Suddenly she stopped. Something in the farthest recess of the cavern caught her eye. Backtracking with the lantern, she held her discovery transfixed in its glare. Her heart raced. Yet, what she saw was not that unusual, at least if it had been in a different setting. It was something she had seen a thousand, a million times over--but never before deep within the channel of an underground river.

She stood staring with rapt fascination at a brick wall. A man-made barrier built, no doubt, from ship's ballast and designed to protect whatever was on the other side. She took several cautious steps forward, moving slowly as if to do otherwise might make the centuries-old structure tumble down. The bricks were ancient. She could easily see that from their irregular margins, and the mortar, it was so old, that it flaked at her touch. Her heart raced.

She snatched her dive knife from its sheath. Dive knives were all-purpose tools, made for everything from cutting a trapped diver free of entangling fishnets, to prying up boat anchors wedged between blocks of coral. To hell with proper excavation technique. Her old archaeology professor at Tulane had taught her better, but she had little time, and if what lay beyond that wall met her expectations no one would care about a few scratches on the artifacts.

She began prying at the mortar, dropping loosened bricks onto the cave floor as she worked. Soon she had made a hole big enough to look through. The story of "The Cask of Amontillado" crept into her mind. In Poe's tale of horror, a man had sealed up his rival behind a basement wall, burying him alive. But, it was not a skeleton she hoped to find here.

She thrust the lantern through the hole and craned her neck to follow the beam. No glistening bones met her eye. Instead, she saw something far more valuable--pile upon pile of man-made debris, like the contents of a long abandoned attic. Slowly the images she was seeing began to take on meaningful shapes. The mounds were chests, old lockers, which once were stacked atop one another. But the organic material had decayed long ago, and now lumps of metallic gold and the mounds of multicolored jewels glimmered dully from beneath the shards of collapsed containers.

Adrenaline rushed through her veins. She raced back to her equipment, pulled out a spelunker's hammer, and returned to attack the wall with the crazed abandon of a jackhammer operator on speed. The dive knife became a pneumatic chisel; her arm moved at a blur. Bricks flew. Soon she had made an opening large enough to squeeze the upper half of her body through.

Leaning in, she brushed away the dust accumulation of centuries. The treasure was there! She found images of fertility goddesses, jade statues of grinning gods with emerald eyes and ruby lips, necklaces of gold and bracelets of pearls.

And there was yet another find. Tall glass jars stood in rows; the ancient wooden chest that originally had been their home had long since collapsed around them. One bottle was broken, its contents turned to moist debris. Carefully she removed an intact jar. Its top was sealed with pitch. She shook it and heard a dry rattle. Holding it in front of her light and straining to see through the green-tinted glass, she could see a roll of parchment inside. Her pulse raced. To an archaeologist, no treasure was more valuable than ancient documents. But to unseal this time capsule in a dank cave was to give its fragile contents a death sentence. The dry parchment would suck up the humidity like a ravenous sponge. Reluctantly she sat it aside and switched her attention to the next musty mound. But beneath a layer of decayed wood was only rusted metal. Corrosion had fused the objects into a solid mass.

Again using the dive knife to pry, she loosened a clump of metal, and with a heave, freed a short chain and attached to each end, ankle manacles. She felt disappointment. She must move on. Time was critical, and there appeared to be nothing out of the ordinary, archeologically speaking, in this pile. But suddenly a glint of yellow caught her eye. Another moment of prying and she pulled out a sword, or what was left of one. The blade of the cutlass showed the ravages of time, and the brass hilt was heavily corroded. But to an experienced archaeologist, an edged weapon tells its story as easily as a fine Bordeaux does to a wine connoisseur.

She sat cross-legged, like a little girl playing with toys, and examined her find. The weapon was European, definitely not English, probably Spanish or Portuguese, and fifteenth, maybe sixteenth century. All the signs, all the clues seemed right. This could be it. If so, the search was over. A dream first begun years ago when she was a beginning archaeology graduate student had now come true.

A chirping noise startled her. She looked at her watch. She had lost track of time. But she couldn't leave without something. This was only an exploratory dive; she had no way of bringing out anything sizeable. She turned back to the pile of what had once been a chest of treasure and quickly selected three items, which she stuffed into a thigh pocket of her wet suit. Then she raced to her scuba equipment. Pausing only to switch to a backup battery for her lantern, she pulled on her gear and leaped into the water.

With the safety line stretched ahead of her, she was able to pull along, and the return swim went much quicker. She broke the surface into the first cave, where Armand was waiting. He stood with one arm braced on the wall of the cave as water rushed past his ankles. But he was not alone! Two other figures stood just outside the entrance. Her eyes, still dark-adapted, could not make out the figures well, but she didn't need to. She knew who they were. Sharon pulled herself hesitantly out of the water and stood, one hand on the cave wall for balance. Armand made no move to help her.

"Armand, what's going on?"

He did not answer. As she stepped closer, she saw blood on his face and terror in his eyes.

One of the figures ducked his head and stepped into the cave. His silhouette was muscular. The uniform was familiar. So was the assault rifle.

The man advanced with head and shoulders stooped to avoid the cave ceiling, but his weapon was always pointed at the two of them. Armand remained frozen, his gaze darting side to side, like that of a trapped animal, from Sharon to the officer and back again. The other man, also armed with an assault rifle, stood blocking the cave entrance.

The policeman inside the cave spoke. "Did you find what you were looking for, Dr. Jackson?" His French-accented English did nothing to disguise the menace in his voice.

She waited, too long, before she answered. "No." She held out one hand empty, the other with the dive lantern. "Nothing."

"You are very persistent. Very troublesome."

"I've caused you no trouble," said Sharon, straining to keep her voice from trembling.

"You were told to stay away from this area. It is..." He searched for a word. "Private."

She started to say otherwise, that this particular stretch of beachfront belonged to no one, but she opted for silence.

"Why do you keep coming here?"

"I told you. I'm on vacation."

He cast a glance around the cave to emphasize he could imagine no drearier a place. "This is no vacation spot."

"I like to explore. It's my profession, my passion."

"For treasure, maybe?"

"No."

His next response was a menacing wave of the gun. Armand crouched closer to the wall. The water from the gulf was rushing in faster now. The gunman looked with annoyance as it splashed over the top of his boots. "If no treasure, then why are you here? To spy on us? From your government, your CIA?"

"No, of course not," Sharon replied. "I'm an American archaeologist on vacation. Call New Orleans, Tulane University. They'll verify I'm on the staff there."

"An excellent cover story, but even if it were true, you should still have heeded our warnings to stay away." He clutched the assault rifle closer to his waist, as if anticipating its recoil.

Armand's nerves could stand it no longer. He broke for the only way out. The man at the cave mouth had only to raise one booted foot, and Armand's headlong flight did the rest. The boot struck him in the chest, propelling the Haitian backward into the now-rushing torrent of water. There was a deafening burst of gunfire, and fountains of blood erupted as the high-velocity rounds stitched their way up Armand's torso. His face exploded into an unrecognizable mass.

Sharon screamed. The gunman who had spoken to her now swung his weapon in her direction. She spun to flee, but there was nowhere to go. Another five-round burst erupted from the assault rifle. Sharon felt the blow to her back, knocking her forward. Then came the slap of cold water on her face. She was no longer scared. She knew she was dead. Bubbles poured out of her buoyancy compensator, and without its counterbalancing effect, her weight belt pulled her straight down.

She struck the stony bottom ten feet below the surface, but death did not close over her. Suddenly she realized what must have happened. Her steel tank had shielded her from the bullets. But since there was no explosion of compressed air, it must have received only a glancing blow, while a second or ricocheting bullet had penetrated her b.c.

She felt like a death row inmate given a last minute reprieve. But it was not over yet. Her lungs burned. She needed air. Performing the emergency maneuver she had learned years earlier to locate a lost regulator in zero visibility, her hand went straight behind her head. By feel she located the valve at the top of the tank. Just below it was the regulator hose. She swept her hand down the hose, and there it was, the metal and rubber mouthpiece. She clenched the regulator between her teeth, then punched the purge button. A blast of compressed air blew the water out, clearing the way for Sharon to inhale deeply and ease her aching lungs.

Muffled reports and a series of rapid blurping sounds interrupted her second breath as gunfire struck the water. She crouched as close to the bottom as she could. She had read somewhere that the force of bullets was absorbed by the first three feet of water. Beyond that the projectiles were harmless. She hoped that was true.

She knew that her attackers wouldn't be there long. The cave would fill rapidly. Probably in another fifteen minutes the mouth would be fully submerged. She easily had that much air. All she had to do was wait them out.

Although her vision was distorted by the loss of her dive mask, she was still able to make out the light coming from the cave entrance and, in the opposite direction, the dark mouth of the underwater tunnel. She crawled toward the darkness. Inside the tunnel she would be shielded from the bullets if that three-foot penetration depth turned out to be a myth.

The flow of icy water irritated her unprotected eyes. She closed them and pushed forward, guided only by the feel of the cold current pushing against her face and an occasional peek to ensure that she was headed in the right direction. Suddenly, her hands struck something sharp--one of the rocky spikes that protected the tunnel entrance. As she pushed through them a second time, she felt a searing pain in her thigh as one of the edges sliced through her wetsuit and into her flesh. She forced it from her mind for the moment as she settled to the bottom safely inside the tunnel.

Now all she had to do was wait out her assailants, breathe slowly, and conserve air. Just hold on for fifteen minutes. Then the cave would be flooded and the killers forced out. She would count out twenty minutes, just to be on the safe side, then swim for the sunny Caribbean Sea. Open water did not cause her any fear. She was a good swimmer, and once she had ditched her tank and weight belt, her wet suit would make her positively buoyant. She could float for miles paralleling the beach before she came back on shore. By then she would be well away from these murderers.

Her count had just reached fifty-five when she heard three distinct plops, like the sound of large rocks thrown into the water. Puzzled, she paused for a moment, then resumed counting. At fifty-nine her underwater world exploded, and she saw only blackness.

Chapter 1

Brian Richards had been operating for four hours. Twice in that time the life of the man on the table had almost slipped from him; twice, with a combination of skill and luck, he had kept that from happening. The surgeon would stop the bleeding in one area, only to find it erupt somewhere else as a clot dislodged and another gusher began.

"You got it," said the scrub nurse as she expertly vacuumed blood away with the tip of the sucker. In her other hand she held a hemostat ready.

Normally Dr. Richards would have a first assistant helping, but the disaster at New Orleans International Airport had left every department of Beauvoir Memorial Hospital shorthanded, and the O.R. was no exception. There was no extra surgical nurse available to fill the role of first assistant. With a retractor in one hand, he held the free edge of the patient's liver up himself, but this maneuver still gave him only limited access. He twisted his neck at an acute angle to throw the beam from his headlamp deep into the dark recesses beneath the organ. He silently agreed with the scrub nurse. His gloved finger must have found the latest bleeder, because the flow of blood from under the liver had stopped.

Almost imperceptibly he released the pressure. Suddenly there was a spurt of blood timed to the man's heartbeat, but this time he could see the source of bleeding. "I see it! Clamp!" he barked. His gaze never wavered from its target as the nurse popped the hemostat into his extended hand; if he looked away, he might have trouble relocating the bleeder. That would mean more blood loss, and this man, critically injured, had lost all the blood he could tolerate. Unfortunately, the airport catastrophe had stretched the resources of the hospital blood bank to previously unimagined limits, and instead of the usual fifteen minutes to get a unit of replacement blood up to the O.R., it was now taking a lifetime. A lifetime in more ways than one, he thought grimly.

Brian worked the hemostat into the tunnel he had created, then quickly closed the clamp on the offending vessel. "Stapler." Instantly the stapler was in his outstretched hand. There was no way he could tie a ligature around a bleeder so deeply situated that he could barely see it. As he used the stapler, he was once again struck with its resemblance to the long-necked tools fishermen use to retrieve a hook from the throat of a fish. He slid it into the cavity, squeezed the handle, and stapled the wad of tissue at the end of the hemostat, applying two more staples for good measure. Then, still not daring to look away, he slowly unclamped the hemostat. Nothing. No hemorrhage. Not even an ooze.

He let out an audible sigh and straightened up. His eyes crinkled, his smile hidden beneath his surgical mask.

"Is that the last one?" asked the scrub nurse.

"Yeah." He paused. "At least if nothing else breaks loose. A chest tube, four small bowel lacerations, too many rents in the mesentery to count, a splenic laceration, and let's not forget that damn bleeder under the liver--that ought to be enough for now."

"Good job, Dr. Richards," she said.

Her compliment warmed him. The scrub nurse was a member of the old guard, and he was the new kid on the block, anxious to prove himself. A word of respect from her was like a vote of confidence from a battle-hardened sergeant to a young lieutenant after his first successful combat.

"Why, thanks, Vicki. I couldn't have done it without you."

"I know," she said.

This time eyes crinkled above the tops of both their masks. For the entire O.R. team it was now time to relax, stretch, and ease muscles too long held tense. A surgeon, an anesthesiologist, a nurse anesthetist, a scrub nurse, and a circulating nurse had all worked hard to save the life of this man.

Brian looked over the drape between him and anesthesia. This wasn't one of those nice elective cases where the anesthetist sat on a stool making occasional notes in the record and daydreaming. The constant attention of both anesthesiologist and nurse anesthetist were required at the head of the table for this major trauma case, and at one point it had seemed even those two might not be enough.

Gary Morrison, the nurse anesthetist, was now adjusting a knob on the anesthesia machine while watching a wavy line snake its way across the green screen of a multichannel monitor. In the background the rhythmic hiss of the ventilator could be heard forcing air into the unconscious man's lungs.

Dr. Dale Blevins was the anesthesiologist. He stood looking over the drape at the operation, his practiced eye assessing the degree of blood loss. In his six years at Beauvoir Memorial Hospital he had become the lead anesthesiologist, though not the department head. That position, of mostly titular importance anyway, went to an elder physician. Still, Dr. Dale Blevins was the physician whose steady presence made the O.R. function efficiently on a day-to-day basis. Seated on a stool next to him, Gary continued to adjust the flow rate of anesthestic gases.

Dr. Blevins once more checked the label on a pint-sized plastic bag, then reached up to hang it on the IV pole next to a half-dozen now empty blood packs.

"It looks like you've got things under control," he said.

"Yeah, it's as dry as a Baptist church social." Brian glanced up in time to catch a glare of disapproval from the scrub nurse.

"Sorry," he said, not feeling particularly regretful.

Blevins, not missing a beat, quickly interjected, "That's the way those boys from west Texas talk, Vicki, and it's going to take a lot more than eight months in the big city to change his ways. Although, come to think of it, lately I've heard a little Cajun creep into his Texas drawl."

Brian gave a short chuckle, then asked, "Everything all right up at your end, too?"

The anesthesiologist nodded. "We finally got another unit of packed red cells up here. So now we can start catching up." As he spoke, Blevins quickly squeezed the bulb of the blood pump several times to get the thick material flowing.

"I need a film to see if there are any more metal fragments, then we can start closing," said Brian.

The circulating nurse stepped to the wall phone, dialed a number, and quietly spoke. "X-ray to O.R. 6. X-ray to O.R. 6."

"While you're at it, Darlene, check with the E.R. to see if they'll need us when we get through here," added the surgeon.

"I already did, while you were elbow deep in intestines," she said pleasantly.

"I was elbow deep under his liver," he corrected, "wrist deep in intestines."

"I see," she said.

"Towel," Brian requested. The scrub nurse handed him a green sterile towel, which he used to cover his patient's incision while they waited for the portable X-ray unit to arrive.

"Anyway," continued Darlene, "there was an excellent response of doctors and off duty E.R. personnel to the emergency recall, so when you finish, we're through. The evening supervisor said that since we were the closest hospital to the airport, we were the first to receive victims. Once we reached capacity they started overflowing to Charity and Oschner's. At last count we got thirty casualties. About the same number went to the other two hospitals. Since we got started first, we got finished first."

"Sounds fair to me," piped up the anesthetist.

"I've never heard of something like this happening," said Dale Blevins as he fiddled with one of the many IV lines to get it to run better. "A jet skidding off the runway into a crowded airport terminal."

"When I was down in the E.R. I heard it was a private jet," said Gary as he adjusted the flow of anesthetic gases.

"Probably belonged to some rich executive," offered Brian.

"No, they said a cargo jet," continued the nurse anesthetist. "It slid underneath the concourse, clipping the building's supports like a linebacker taking out a row of freshmen try-outs. The whole thing came tumbling down carrying all those people inside with it."

"Including our unfortunate Mr. Moore," said Brian.

"Wrong place at the wrong time," said Dale.

"Not just that," said Brian. "I talked to his wife in the E.R. The reason he was at the airport was to fly to his mother's funeral."

"How tragic," murmured Vicki.

"Dale, we may have a problem," said Gary calmly, almost too calmly, to the anesthesiologist.

The room instantly fell silent. Any mention of "a problem" gets everyone's attention in an operating room. The anesthetist's finger pointed to the monitor displaying the patient's electrocardiogram. The numeric read-out to the right of the moving blip displayed 112, but the numbers steadily wound upward. As they crossed 120, a buzzer went off.

"Tachycardia alarm," said Dale, as he reached up and punched a button to silence the annoying sound. "Anything break loose down there, Brian?"

Brian figured his own heart rate was about 120, too, as he jerked off the surgical towel to expose the fourteen-inch incision that ran from the bottom of the patient's sternum to the pubis. Vicki instantly located the self-retaining retractors and passed them to Brian. He rapidly dropped them into place to spread the sides of the incision as he heard Dale tell Gary, "Check your lines! Make sure he's getting all his IV fluids!"

The surgeon probed inside the abdomen, pushing aside the intestines, looking for the puddle of blood that would signal the location of another severed and now hemorrhaging blood vessel--but there was nothing. "No bleeders down here," he announced.

Suddenly a second alarm, more shrill than the first, went off. "Desat alarm!" Gary said in a voice taut with terror. This one could not be silenced without correcting the problem.

"Check your tube!" commanded the anesthesiologist.

Out of the corner of his eye Brian saw the heads of both anesthesia personnel disappear behind the drape. An endotracheal tube placed in the patient's airway fed a mixture of anesthetic gas, air, and supplemental oxygen directly into his lungs. Brian knew they were checking to see that the tube had not become dislodged.

The desat alarm continued to whine. Blevins' voice came from behind the drapes. "How the hell can his blood be oxygen desaturated when we've got a clear airway and full O_2 wall pressure?"

Again Brian probed the deep recesses of the man's abdomen, looking for a hidden source of bleeding--some cause for the cardiovascular collapse. Again he found nothing. The surgeon stepped back from the table, watching the scene unfold as the anesthesia personnel struggled to save the patient's life--from what, none of them knew.

Brian felt confused and helpless, and these were foreign emotions for him. He was a surgeon, and he knew he was a good one. In medical school he had studied and struggled while many of his fellow students partied, and it had paid off. But, never satisfied, he continued to work hard in order to be the best. Now, his first year as a trauma surgeon in one of the largest, most medically sophisticated cities in the world, and he was at a loss.

The circulating nurse moved in closer to watch the monitor. "Pulse 130," she said. "Pressure down to 80 over 50."

"I don't know what the hell's going on," Dale exclaimed. "Everything seems okay except the patient's numbers." The anesthesiologist straightened up and grabbed the ribbon of gray paper that had been spooling out of the monitor. He shook his head. "It's not an airway problem. It's not a cardiac arrhythmia..."

Brian Richards stepped back to the table to look at the incision, and halted. Everything was dark-red, purple! The surface of all the organs was covered with a coating of blood. Even the walls of the abdominal incision, normally yellow from subcutaneous fat, were deep, dark purple--the color of unoxygenated blood. "He's bleeding everywhere!" he hollered. Although

Brian knew it was futile, he began cauterizing the bleeders. He worked rapidly, knowing it was a losing battle, with a lap sponge in one hand like a blotter and the electrocautery in the other, buzzing one bleeding point, then quickly moving on to the next. But by the time it took to cauterize three locations, the first had started oozing again. It was a cycle of hemorrhage that could not be broken. Richards' hands raced like a master pianist playing a *pretissimo*, but he knew he was falling behind. "He's not clotting anywhere!" he shouted.

Suddenly it came to him--a rare and often fatal condition in which the blood clots too much, but the clotting process is not seen. The clotting occurs at the microscopic level and uses up all the patient's clotting factors. Then the patient starts to bleed. It creates a situation akin to trying to put out a fire by spraying gasoline on it. The more clotting factors the body produces, the quicker the patient develops micro-clots, but, in turn, the faster the victim bleeds from the larger blood vessels because the clotting factors are used up. That had to be what was happening--Disseminated Intravascular Coagulation. "D.I.C.! It's got to be D.I.C.!" Richards exclaimed.

"D.I.C?" said the anesthesiologist. He froze at the pronouncement and stared with astonishment at the man's open abdomen, which now looked as if it had been sprayed with dark red paint. "By God, you're right." He jerked open the top drawer of the anesthesia medicine cart. "We need two amps of heparin in him! Where the hell is it?"

"Top drawer, far right!" shouted Gary, who was desperately occupied trying to bring the patient up from deep anesthesia. As soon as the desat alarm had gone off, the anesthetist had spun the valve to shut off the flow of anesthetic gas. Now he was running the man on pure oxygen while he squeezed the rebreathing bag to force even more oxygen into the patient's lungs.

The monitor on top of the anesthesia machine was now lit up like a Christmas tree. Every parameter outside the machine's preset normal limits was displayed in red: pulse, blood pressure, oxygen saturation, expired carbon dioxide concentration, even patient core temperature recorded from the probe inside the esophageal stethoscope. Brian had never seen that many red flashing numerals in his life.

"Heparin!" the circulator exclaimed. "Are you trying to kill him? He's bleeding already, and you want to give him an anticoagulant?"

22

"That's how you stop the bleeding," responded Brian, knowing the anesthesia team was too busy to answer. "The heparin stops the clotting process. It's the clotting that has used up the clotting factors, and without clotting factors, he bleeds."

"The man's hemorrhaging and you're giving him an anticoagulant..." The nurse's voice trailed off as she shook her head in disbelief.

"He's going to die if we don't do something," Brian said grimly. He knew that most cases of D.I.C. don't survive anyway, because the D.I.C. is just a manifestation of some deeper disease process. Even if the bleeding is stopped, whatever kicked off the D.I.C. is what usually kills the patient. His mind ran through the possibilities--cancer, drug reaction, massive trauma-- even as his hands continued to work automatically, burning each new bleeding point with the cautery. One corner of his mind struggled to remember every item on a list learned years ago, while the rest of his thoughts were occupied with trying to save his patient's life.

"The heparin is in!" shouted Blevins. He looked across at the monitor. "His pressure is down to 70 systolic, no diastolic recordable. Darlene, call the blood bank. Get every unit of fresh blood they've got up here as soon as it's cross-matched. We need to replace what he's lost."

"His blood still looks dark," announced Brian. "What's his O_2 sat?"

"Holding at 50%," said Blevins. "But it ought to be 100% on pure oxygen."

"What else could be wrong?" demanded Gary, his frustration evident in the shrillness of his voice. He continued to squeeze the bag rapidly with one hand. He used the other to reach up, grasp the swivel light, and direct it on the patient's face. Any piece of equipment can fail, including oxygen monitors, and the nurse anesthetist wanted to check his patient's oxygenation the old-fashioned way—by looking at the skin color.

He did a double-take. Giant blisters covered the face of Maxwell Moore. As Gary watched, speechless, another one began to form on the man's forehead. "My God! He's covered with blisters."

"Let me see," said Brian. "Drop the drapes."

The circulator scrambled to do his bidding. With the barrier down, Brian was able to see the face of his patient for the first time in four hours. "Those aren't blisters. They're hives. When they subside the skin will be undamaged--*and* they're always due to an allergic reaction, oftentimes penicillin." He looked to the anesthesiologist.

Dale spoke up immediately. "We gave him a broad spectrum antibiotic at the start of the case. It was penicillin-related, but if that was the cause, then the reaction should have happened hours ago, not now."

Brian's mind raced. If the D.I.C. was due to an allergic reaction, it had to be something recent. Then it struck him. "Blood transfusion reaction! A massive one!"

After a moment's, "You're right," shouted the anesthesiologist, reaching to the top of the IV pole for the last blood bag. It was empty.

"It has to be mismatched blood," said Brian.

"Give him Benadryl 100 mg IV and a c.c. of epinephrine, and what the hell, let's load him up with steroids, too--100 mg of methylprednisolone," ordered Dale Blevins.

Gary hurried to carry out the instructions of the anesthesiologist while Blevins hauled down the blood bags and began going through the requisition slips and bag numbers. "We double-checked each one before we gave it." The anesthesiologist addressed the room, as if offering a defense for an accusation not yet made. He quickly flipped through the requisition slips, then examined each of the empty blood packs still hanging on the IV pole. "All blood packs say *Maxwell J. Moore* and *A positive* and match the patient's name and hospital number."

Suddenly there was silence. The scream of the oxygen desat alarm had stopped. All heads turned to the monitor. It displayed 85%, and as they watched, it climbed: 86, 87, 88.

The phone on the wall shattered the quiet, causing the circulator to visibly jump, then hurry to the phone. After a moment, she said "Thanks" and hung up. "A runner's left the blood bank. He's bringing four units of fresh packed red blood cells."

The anesthetist sighed.

"Someone has fucked up and almost killed my patient," said Brian Richards, his face red with outrage. "And I intend to get him."

Not one of his startled colleagues doubted that he meant it.

Chapter 2

It was a weekly ritual, Dr. Thurston Walker strolling through the Durbane Pharmaceuticals building. He would start at the top of the four story Durbane building, one of the newest and most modern in New Orleans Industrial Park. Then he would work his way down a floor at a time, stopping in each department to ask questions, offer comments, and pay attention to the people who made his company what it was, the most innovative pharmaceutical house in the country.

Other corporate heads who heard of this ritual thought it a PR gimmick, useful to recount in the annual report, emphasizing the closeness, the empathy, that management had with its workers. The most pragmatic-minded saw it as a management technique to keep the workers pacified. Happy employees caused less trouble.

They were all wrong. Thurston Walker did it for himself. He was in charge, and he enjoyed letting others know it. He moved through his fiefdom confident in the knowledge that at the age of forty-three, he was the youngest C.E.O. of any pharmaceutical corporation in the world. Sixteen years ago he had begun as a research biochemist. Since then, his keen mind for management and inventiveness and a spirit that was never satisfied to just take orders had propelled him to the top of the company.

Walker handed the printout from the autoanalyzer back to the scientist. "Interesting," he said. "But do you think a fifteen-percent acceleration of T-cell induction will translate into a vaccine that's equivalently more effective?"

"We're setting up the animal studies now, sir," said the white-smocked man. "We should have an idea in about three months."

"Good," said Walker. The older scientist smiled at the display of interest in his work, and Walker turned to head for his last stop, the office of the medical director of clinical research.

* * * * *

Dr. Diane Gilmore was seated with her back to the door when Walker entered. With an annoyed flick of the wrist she tossed a sheaf of documents onto her side table and swiveled back to her computer.

"Is that your report to the board?" asked Walker.

"Oh," she said, surprised, "I didn't hear you come in. But no, my drugs in development report is already on your desk for you to look over prior to the meeting." She leaned back in her chair and sighed. "That," she said with obvious distaste, accompanied by an offhand gesture toward the documents, "is the latest nonsense from the FDA."

Thurston Walker talked to a lot of people on his rounds at Durbane, but Gilmore was his favorite. She was a class act, a sleek, smart professional whose smooth and lucid presentation could sway any dissenting board member.

Five years ago, Walker had lured her from another company to Durbane. Once, years ago, she'd had plans to be a bedside physician. Then had come the unfortunate oversight in her last year of training. Neither she nor her senior-attending physician had recognized the recently admitted man's complaint of back pain for what it really was--an aortic aneurysm subtly expanding. It blew out that night. The patient was dead in minutes, and a lawsuit followed just as quickly. The courts exonerated Gilmore; ultimate responsibility went not to the resident in training but to the attending physician whose malpractice carrier had to pay out two million dollars. But the event and its traumatic aftermath had convinced Diane Gilmore she wasn't cut out for the intimacy and intensity of the one-on-one practice of internal medicine. She opted for the abstraction of the laboratory and the corporate world and soon began making a name for herself in research and development. Thurston spotted her talent and offered to make her head of clinical testing for new drug development at Durbane. Doubling her salary brought her in and generous stock options for each new drug she helped to the marketplace insured her continued diligent performance.

Walker settled into a chair across from Gilmore and folded his hands across his abdomen, the classic psychoanalyst's pose. "Would you feel better telling me about it--the FDA nonsense I mean?"

Gilmore's quick smile showed perfect teeth. "A biochemist *and* a psychiatrist?"

"Most days a counseling degree would be more helpful," Walker admitted.

Gilmore smiled her agreement, then sighed. "The nonsense is the latest response from the FDA to the Phase II clinical trials of Toromycin. This time they want us to go back, pull out the subset of patients with liver disease, and redose them with Toromycin at twice therapeutic levels to look for signs of toxicity. We'll have to go through the whole rigmarole of getting the subjects' informed consent for receipt of experimental drugs, another week of blood and urine collections, physical examinations, documentation." She shook her head in frustration. "Do all that when I can get virtually the same information in less than a day by computer modeling the data we already have."

"They wouldn't go for it?"

"No. In fact, one of the asses on the committee actually said, 'This antibiotic is for people, not computers, Dr. Gilmore!'"

"Give it to them. Otherwise, they'll never let us go to Phase III testing."

"Of course," said Gilmore. "But it just seems like they have a never ending supply of hoops for us to jump through."

"That's why it costs four hundred million dollars to get one new medicine from the laboratory to the pharmacist's shelf." Walker was silent a moment. "Of course, if it's a hit, then the company makes its investment back overnight." A grin, more avaricious than amicable, crept across his face. "And along with the corporate profit, some generous bonuses for ourselves."

"That I wouldn't mind," said Gilmore. "I've been thinking about buying a place in the country." She took on a far-away expression. "Some place where I could see acres of grass and trees instead of a sea of cement and high-rises." She looked at her hand and examined the model-perfect nails while a grin, not dissimilar to Walker's, came to her face. "But I don't think I would take up farming--just a nice, restored two-story farm house, perfect for country-style entertaining--and with a cottage, where guests could stay." She let out a sigh of anticipated contentment. "So, a bonus would do me just fine."

Walker leaned closer and in a lowered voice said, "You'll be able to have that and a hell of a lot more if U.B.S. hits the market without competition."

Gilmore nodded.

Chapter 3

There is no substitute for preparation, Thurston Walker reminded himself as he sat at his desk reviewing the quarterly report, especially when dealing with the board of directors. Sales were level. Durbane had brought no new products to market in two years. Expenses, especially research costs, were up. Not the best report to offer, but he had explanations. Dr. Gilmore's section, Drugs in Development, as usual was excellent. It was particularly encouraging that six new medications were already well along in Phase III Clinical Trials, the final step before FDA market approval.

Phase III allowed--or, more correctly--required that the experimental substance be used on one to three thousand patient volunteers, with exhaustive reporting of all the drug's parameters: efficacy, safety, toxicity, side effects, metabolism.

Walker noted wryly that one drug was deliberately missing from the list. His stern military father had a phrase for such discrimination. It was: "a need to know basis."

A quiet buzz emanated from his desk phone followed by a soft voice through the intercom. "Karl's here."

"Send him in." Karl Dietrich never had to wait. Durbane's chief of security handled every aspect of his department with Teutonic efficiency, and that suited Walker perfectly. In fact, the less Walker knew about the specifics, the better. So the matters Dietrich did bring to his boss' attention were always of immediate concern.

Karl Dietrich had started with Durbane eight years ago as a security guard at their shipping facility in Frankfurt. His résumé had contained references to police work and time spent in South Africa doing surveillance and other security-related jobs. It was obvious that the Frankfurt position was only temporary. Soon, however, Dietrich was recognized as a man willing to undertake any task for his well-paying employer, and he rose quickly in the company. His street smarts, multilingual talents, and cultured European manner allowed him to deal skillfully with potential troublemakers whether they belonged to the rank and file or were among the wealthy and powerful.

Chief of security was a vitally important position for a worldwide pharmaceutical company where a breakthrough that led to more effective treatment for cancer, or AIDS, or Alzheimer's disease would mean not millions but billions of dollars in sales. In a business with such high stakes, security was paramount, and Karl Dietrich filled the need. He had no compunction about interrogating another company's dissatisfied employees or sneaking a peek at secret internal documents that might find their way from the vaults of a rival manufacturer to his desk and then, after the trail was appropriately covered, on to the scrutiny of Durbane's experts. Dietrich was adept at such tactics, but, equally important, his presence and ruthless reputation served as a warning to Durbane's own employees not to consider industrial espionage against their own company.

"One of our MD-101s crashed," announced Dietrich, his face tight.

"Where?"

"Right here. New Orleans International."

"When?"

"Twenty minutes ago."

"What happened?"

"Only a few details are in, but I have already placed several of my key people on it. The F.A.A. emergency center has called. They want our complete file on the flight crew

"Was anyone on the ground hurt?"

"Many. The airplane plowed into the terminal building."

"Jesus Christ! Was it on a Haiti run?"

"Returning."

Thurston Walker paled. "Any of the product on board?"

"No. I immediately checked with Doúbe."

"Get the specifics to me as soon as you have them. I suspect the news media will be calling any minute." Walker rose from his desk and started for the door. "I'll be in Perkins' office. Public Relations monitors the major broadcast networks and news services. That'll be the place to begin damage control."

Dietrich did not immediately follow. "When I called Doúbe I found out something else..."

Walker stopped abruptly.

"The good doctor has been treating more than just the locals."

Walker knew who the "good doctor" was. He turned. "Explain!" he demanded.

"An American tourist was seriously injured. Baptiste saved her life, then got her back to the U.S."

"Goddamn it! We don't want any attention drawn to that place."

"I am looking into this, too," said Dietrich.

Thurston Walker had no doubt that within a few hours Karl Dietrich would know all that could be known about both situations. The two men headed rapidly out the door.

Chapter 4

Cecil, Brian Richards' chocolate lab, ran ahead of him. Or to put it more accurately, Cecil was definitely chocolate and mostly Lab. When Brian was in surgical residency he had spotted the dog, at the time only a half-grown pup, abandoned on the side of the highway just outside Dallas. If a speeding car had not gotten the animal, then starvation surely would.

Brian had pulled over. The dog's ribs showed through his coat, and he had a tendency to slink from an extended hand. Brian lured him into his car with a breakfast biscuit left over from his swing through the drive-through. Then he'd turned around and driven the dog back to his small rental house. Brian, still in his residency, was criticized by his attending physician for being late to work that day. He'd apologized, said he had car trouble and never regretted that lie.

Cecil had entered his life at just the right time. Only a week earlier he had found out his recently ex- but previously longtime girlfriend, Cynthia Donald, had become engaged to a plastic surgeon fifteen years her senior. Although Brian had not really expected he would get back together with her, still, the suddenness of her new liaison had shocked him. They'd had some good times together, even though their goals were different. He still had one more year of residency followed by a lot of hard work before he could provide Cynthia with all the accoutrements of a well-heeled doctor's wife. The way she had chosen allowed her to avoid the wait. Helping Cecil back to robustness had filled Brian's home time with something other than disillusionment over a failed relationship.

Brian's thoughts returned to the dog working the field, staying twenty to forty yards ahead, proper shooting distance if any birds were flushed. But there was no shooting today. It wasn't hunting season, and even if it had been, Brian wasn't big on sport killing. This morning he just wanted to exercise his dog and clear his thoughts. But now it was time to head back.

Cecil, with tail wagging and senses alert, had covered ten times as much ground as Brian, but neither was tired. These, almost daily, excursions kept them both in good shape. Brian knew that some of his colleagues thought him a little peculiar--a single, thirty-four-year-old guy living out in the country with just his dog. Dale Blevins, his anesthesiologist buddy, had kidded him that he was unnaturally close to Cecil. But Brian countered that at least his association with dogs involved only the four-legged variety, unlike some tales Brian had heard of the kind of company Blevins kept back during his wilder days in medical school.

But Brian was hardly a hermit either. Since opening his practice in New Orleans eight months ago, he had gone to parties, met a few women, even dated some. But none had interested him for long and no lasting relationships had yet developed.

The phone rang while Brian was pausing at the back door; allowing Cecil to anoint his favorite bush. "Come on, beast," he said. The dog, in no mood to be rushed, continued to mark his territory. Brian went ahead and stepped into the house, knowing Cecil would eventually follow. He crossed the kitchen to the phone grabbing it on what must have been the twentieth ring. "Hello?"

"Out enjoying the pleasures of country life?" asked Dale.

"I would be except for the occasional colleague calling to harass me," Brian said.

When Dale next spoke, the jocular tone was gone. "Are you coming in today?"

"Yeah. I don't have any surgery scheduled, and I don't have to be in the office this afternoon, so I'll probably leave in about an hour. That'll give me time to make rounds and check on Moore in Surgery Intensive Care. Then I'm going to spend some time with Dr. Parker going over what happened yesterday. Why do you ask?"

"I can save you some trouble. Moore's lab reports are back. Parker called me about it."

Sam Parker was a pathologist and chief of the hospital laboratory. "What'd they show?"

"It confirmed the blood was mismatched. Maxwell J. Moore was blood type A positive. The last unit he got before everything went to hell in the O.R. was type B, not A."

"Damn! I knew a mismatch had to be the cause of his D.I.C."

"Parker's butt is the one in the sling," continued Dale, "so he's wasted no time in tracing the problem. It started with the technician who originally typed the donor blood at the blood processing center downtown. He recorded this particular unit incorrectly and put the wrong sticker on it. He's been fired."

"What about the cross-match? That's the fail-safe mechanism." Brian knew that the ultimate test of compatibility between two samples of blood was to mix a small portion of one with the other. If the red blood cells clump together, it's because antibodies are attacking them, and that test, in turn, predicts a transfusion reaction even if both blood types are the same.

"The unit we gave Moore was never cross-matched," said the anesthesiologist.

"What!" Brian yelled into the phone. "I can't believe that!"

"Believe it," said Dale. "When the victims from the plane crash arrived almost everyone needed blood. There was chaos in the blood bank. The screw-up on our end started with one of the victims who came in after we were already in the O.R. The man had been trapped in the wreckage and was *in extremis* on arrival--essentially no blood pressure, barely palpable pulse. I talked to the E.R. doctor. He didn't think the patient could wait the twenty minutes for a cross-match, so he ordered uncross-matched blood." The anesthesiologist paused, then continued. "It's rare to order uncross-matched blood, because of the dangers of reaction, but his patient had almost bled out. The E.R. doc made the right decision under the circumstances." There was another pause. "Unfortunately, his patient died anyway."

"Okay," said Brian into the phone. "That was *his* patient. What about ours?"

"The technician in the blood bank got confused. Too many orders from too many places at once--and most by phone." The anesthesiologist's voice changed from accusatory to analytical. "We need to look into that in the future. A written request is much less error prone."

"But much slower," said Brian.

"Anyway, a technician sent one of the uncross-matched units to us by mistake. It just happened to be the very same unit that was mislabeled downtown at the central blood processing center--a unit of B, that was labeled A."

"I thought uncross-matched blood was prominently marked as such."

"Well, there is supposed to be a sticker on the blood pack, but like I said, with all the trauma victims arriving from the airport, there was pandemonium in the blood bank. The technician forgot to put on the sticker. If it makes you feel any better, he got fired, too."

"It doesn't make me feel any better. It makes me want to kick some ass. What this really shows is a lack of foresight. The hospital should have been better prepared for a major disaster, and just maybe if that lab tech had had more help at the critical time, this never would have happened."

Dale's voice was concerned. "Brian, these things happen. No general hospital is fully equipped to deal with an emergency on that scale. You're my friend, but I want you to know you're getting a reputation as a troublemaker-- always fighting with Administration or Nursing Service."

"Every time I want a piece of equipment in the O.R. I've got to fight with somebody. They say budget cuts. Do you know any administrator whose salary has been cut? All I'm saying is that what happened to Moore in the O.R. was preventable. He's in the SICU right now as likely to die as live. I'm not going to let that slide by unnoticed."

"I know you can't ignore what happened. What I'm suggesting is that you tone it down. You've only been here a few months--"

"Eight, to be exact."

"And at one year your performance is reviewed to see if you can become a full staff member."

"Why would they keep me off? Because I've made a few complaints, all for the betterment of patient care?"

Dale chuckled. "A few complaints? There's a trail worn between the O.R. and the Administrator's office, and you're the one who made it." His voice turned somber. "Beauvoir Memorial is a private hospital with a board of trustees that answers to no one, Brian. They like team players, not rabble rousers--and they can be real mean if they think you're threatening the status quo. Just a word of friendly advice--keep your mouth shut until you're a full staff member--then they can only kick you off for some major blunder. After that, you can change the world. Okay?"

"I'll remember it." After they hung up, Brian stood thinking. What Dale was telling him to do was the smart thing. The only problem was, it wasn't his style to keep his head down and ignore a problem. As far as he was concerned, that was the same thing as seeing a patient dreadfully sick and addressing only the symptoms, not the source of the pathology. Unless you go for the cause, the problem only gets worse.

Chapter 5

For Sharon, reality had come and gone in the last two days--or was it three? The snatches of memory had finally linked themselves together into a somewhat coherent thread. In an undergrad sociology course she had read accounts of people coming off LSD, and at first it had seemed she was having a similar experience. It was hard to tell what had been real and what hadn't-- the assailants, the guns, Armand, a hazy view from underwater, and an explosion, a cot, Haitian nurses in white uniforms. Only one figure stood out among the shadows, a compassionate man wearing a stethoscope and speaking softly with a French accent.

Yes, the French doctor had been kind. Her memory of him and that last day in Haiti was pretty clear. She had been seated in a wheelchair on the veranda of a wooden building.

"Will they come for me?" she had asked.

"No. The police—" or had he said "guards"? "They do not know you are here. But even if they did, I do not allow them into the compound. Eventually they will find out you survived, but by then you will be gone."

The doctor handed back the waterproof pouch she had worn under her wet suit. "It is a good thing you had your passport with you."

On her first trip to the islands Sharon had learned to keep her passport and some money on her person at all times. Distrustful authorities were continually requesting her documents. Until now she'd thought the American seal on her passport would offer her a measure of safety, even if it opened no doors. For door opening--well, that was where the money came in.

"I took out only enough for your airplane ticket," he had said. "Martina will help you get on the plane at Port-au-Prince. I have prepared a letter for the airline officials explaining that you were injured and returning home for further medical treatment. Their assistance is requested to help you off the plane and through customs. Once you are in New Orleans, a colleague I have known for many years, Dr. William Penfield, will take over your care. He has arranged transportation from the airport to the hospital."

"Thank you," was all she could say.

"There were some other"--he paused--"personal effects. There could be a problem if you are searched and they are found."

Fear forced her from lethargy. "I need them... for my work," she said, trying not to sound too desperate.

The doctor's cheeks worked while he seemed to study the cracks in the wooden porch. Finally he spoke. "There are ways to carry items out of the country, as well as in, without attracting notice--but it must be worth the risk."

"You know these things?"

"I am also a priest. I hear confession."

"Isn't what you hear in confession kept secret?"

"Yes."

"Can your knowledge of my 'personal effects' be considered a confession, kept in confidence?"

"I... I suppose."

She reached out and grasped the Frenchman's hand. "Father, it is very important--not for me, but for many others. I have made a great discovery, and unless we can protect it, it will be stolen--lost to the world."

"Then tell me more, as a confession, and after that--Godspeed."

The vividness of the memory caused Sharon to sit up on the hospital bed. Instantly her headache returned with a throbbing vengeance. She reached a bandaged hand up to feel her temple. The soreness was slowly leaving. She had already seen herself in the mirror and knew the blue discoloration was advancing down the side of her face producing an impressive black eye. She looked like the loser in a prizefight—and felt like one, too.

A nurse, American this time, breezed into her room. "Dr. Penfield left word you could be discharged at ten unless there were problems, and everything seems okay."

The nurse's perky and impersonal manner was in such stark contrast to her memory of the studied concern of the missionary physician that Sharon was not sure she could tolerate it.

"I'll send an aide in to help you get ready," the woman added.

"I can make it," said Sharon.

"Do you have someone coming for you? You can't drive yet."

"A friend of mine is on the way, and she's bringing me some clothes."

"Fine," said the nurse, her smile still in place as she pulled the door closed.

Sharon's legs wobbled as she tried to stand up. Maybe she should have accepted the offer of help. But, she had learned a long time back that the only person she could count on was herself. Her mother, single and minimally educated, had worked hard at a succession of low-paying jobs that left little time for personally hand-holding her daughter through every one of life's travails. And Sharon's only father had been a stepfather. So, self-reliance had very early on become an integral part of her being.

Sharon clutched the bed rail and forced herself to an upright position. She swayed once, took a deep breath, then became steady.

She cringed at the thought of how she must look. A gauze pad over the sutured laceration on her right knee, the ugly ten-inch abrasion down the left leg, a black-eye, countless other cuts and bruises, capped off by two inch gap in her hospital gown from the nape of her neck to the bottom of her butt, all made for an interesting presentation. What if her graduate students saw her now?

There was a polite knock at the partially open door; then a familiar face peeked in.

"Darcy, come on in."

"My God, you look horrible!"

"Thanks," said Sharon.

"I mean, I expected some bumps and scrapes, but..."

"I told you, the tidal surge caught me and knocked me around. I had a concussion, some cuts and bruises."

"It looks more like a tidal *wave* got you." Darcy's hands went to her hips. "When are you going to quit roaming around those primitive islands?" she said with exasperation. "Come with me and research the Etruscans. After a day at the dig, we can eat in a quaint Italian restaurant, then sleep in a clean hotel room under a cool mountain breeze. Back when we were grad students you used to like that."

"Those were fun times," agreed Sharon. "Oh, to be carefree again."

Darcy continued enthusiastically, "So, seriously, you've got the summer off for research. You can come to Italy with me and recuperate in comfort."

"I wish I could, but you know I have my own project."

"Oh, yes, chasing after the early explorers of the New World." Darcy lowered her voice to just a stage whisper. "And just when are you going to tell me exactly what you're after?"

"I don't want some other archaeologist dogging my heels, or worse, getting there before me. Someday, when you see my picture on the cover of *Archaeology Review*, then you'll know."

"Well, when that happens, I hope you aren't dressed like that." Sharon looked sheepishly down at her hospital gown. Darcy held out a small valise. "I went by your apartment. You might prefer this outfit."

Chapter 6

"What do you mean, Mrs. Leathers, they came and got him?" exclaimed an incredulous Dr. Brian Richards to the director of nursing he had confronted in the Surgery Intensive Care Unit. "Nobody just comes and gets another doctor's patient and whisks him off to a different hospital."

"For the record, doctor, the decision was made late in the day. We checked with the doctor on call for your group. He said he had no objection since another physician had agreed to accept responsibility for the patient."

"Mrs. Leathers, nobody knew that man's condition like I did. Moore was critical, had just started dialysis for renal failure, and until yesterday required a dopamine drip to support his blood pressure."

"Would you lower your voice, doctor?" demanded the director. "We have some very sick patients here." They stood in the center of the circular nurses' station surrounded by several SICU nurses and technicians doing their best to look busy while soaking up the details of the argument.

"I sure as hell know how sick they are, and not a one of them is any sicker than my patient, Maxwell Moore." Brian threw up his hands in frustration. "At least I *thought* he was my patient."

The nursing director lashed back. "They aren't *your* patients, doctor. They are patients of the plan. Mr. Moore's insurance was with Consolidated Health Partners, and that company is well within its rights to transfer its patients to another hospital. They do this when another one of their contract hospitals can give less expensive care." The nurse director spoke as if lecturing a slow third grader. "That's why it's called managed care. It saves the patient, the insurance company, and the company's client, which is usually the patient's employer, money. It keeps the hospitals and the doctors cost conscious." She paused to add extra bite to her words. "We all suffer, doctor, when medical care costs too much."

Brian Richards stuck his finger in her face to emphasize what he was going to say, but his eye fell on her only article of jewelry. On the collar of her blouse was a pin. It was a small gold replica of a snake coiled around a staff, a caduceus. He lowered his finger from her face to the pin. "Have you forgotten that you were a nurse first, Mrs. Leathers? A nurse before you became a director, a member of the administration? Have you forgotten those nursing vows? Since when does the insurance company's profit margin matter more than the safety of the patient?"

The woman recoiled as if slapped in the face. "I've had enough of your insults, Dr. Richards. I never thought I would see this kind of behavior from a physician. I'm reporting what you said to Mr. Fendley."

"Well, you'd just better get going. Otherwise I might beat you there."

Mrs. Leathers squared her shoulders and stalked away, leaving Brian standing in the center of the nurses' station. He looked at SICU bed 6. Yesterday Maxwell Moore had been in there--and it looked like he might just live. Now bed 6 was empty.

Brian thought back over the last thirty-six hours. If there was anyone ever lucky to be alive, it was Maxwell J. Moore. He'd survived a blast injury when a crashing plane slammed into the concourse, only to suffer a near-fatal blood reaction. Amazingly, they had been able to resuscitate him after that catastrophe. But then, at the end of the first postoperative day, it became apparent that the reaction to mismatched blood was continuing to work its destructive process as hemoglobin leaked from his damaged red blood cells and began to plug up his kidneys. Moore had gone into acute renal failure and was placed on dialysis, which would keep him alive until, with luck, his kidneys repaired themselves. But what his status was at this particular moment, Brian did not know.

Brian felt someone touch his elbow. He turned to see a young student nurse.

"Dr. Richards, can I talk to you for a moment?"

She seemed unsure of herself. He waited for her to speak, then realized that what she had to say was not for all the ears around them. "Follow me," he murmured, leading her out into the hallway.

Outside the double doors of the SICU, the student appeared even more uncomfortable, nervously looking around at each passerby. But they were all too preoccupied with their own concerns to pay the two any attention. "I thought he was too sick to move, too," she finally said.

"You were assigned to Mr. Moore today?"

"Yes, sir. I came on duty at seven A.M. The ambulance crew arrived shortly afterward."

"If you felt that way, why didn't you say something?"

"I did, but nobody pays attention to what a student thinks, and anyway, everyone was in such a hurry. I asked that we page you, but Mrs. Leathers said it wasn't necessary. The patient's wife and the doctor on call had been notified, and all the details had already been taken care of."

"Mrs. Leathers was behind the transfer?" he asked incredulously.

"I don't know, but she did come up with the ambulance attendants, and she had all the transfer papers already completed. When I protested, Mrs. Leathers said the physician director for the insurance company felt it was safe to transfer Mr. Moore."

"He felt it was safe--without ever examining the patient!" Brian exploded. Surprised by the outburst, an employee from dietary, wearing a white cap and pushing a food cart, glanced Brian's way, then hurried on. Brian struggled to bring his temper under control.

"They review all the information by phone now. You know that, Dr. Richards."

He had to admit that he did. Many times lately, since the advent of managed care, a doctor representing an insurance company would call to coerce him into discharging a patient before Brian thought it medically wise. The doctor often lived in another state, had only rudimentary knowledge of the patient's case, and knew absolutely nothing about the patient's home situation. If Brian didn't acquiesce to the managed care doctor then came the threat: the insurance company might not pay any more on the hospital bill and the patient would be responsible. And with the current cost of medical care, a short hospitalization not covered by insurance could bankrupt all but the most financially secure individuals. Coercion it was but, until now, never outright abduction.

"What hospital was Moore sent to?"

"I don't know. I never heard them say." She looked confused. "I'm sure all that information is on the forms."

"Where are they?"

"With the chart," she said.

"Where's that?"

"I suppose down in medical records. Mrs. Leathers took it with her when she left."

"Thanks," he said and turned to leave again.

"Dr. Richards?" He stopped. "You won't mention me in connection with any of this, will you? I graduate in less than a month, and Mrs. Leathers has ways of getting back. I need her recommendation to get into nurse anesthetist school."

He smiled, realizing he didn't know her name anyway. "I'll never mention who told me--and thanks again."

* * * * *

Brian stalked out of the elevator. Thirty yards down the corridor an overhead sign read *ADMINISTRATION*. The white nonskid linoleum floor here became thick maroon carpet, as effective as an iron gate dividing this wing from the stainless steel and antiseptic environment that was the rest of the facility.

"I need to speak with Mr. Fendley," he said to the pretty young woman seated at the front desk.

"He's with someone at the moment," she said, flashing a dazzling smile. "Of course, if it's an emergency, I could try to interrupt."

"It's about a patient of mine who was transferred without my authorization." The tone in his voice left no doubt that this would not be a friendly visit. The woman's smile promptly faded.

Brian's pager buzzed. He plucked it from his belt and activated the display. The message scrolled across. 555-*6494 - level of response: urgent - 10:16*. Urgent. He frowned. Pulling his personal phone from a pocket of his white coat, he punched in the prefix for the hospital, then 6494.

A nurse answered. "Four West, Davis."

"This is Dr. Richards."

"Sorry to bother you, doctor. I'm the shift supervisor on Four West. I have a problem with one of Dr. Penfield's patients--at least I think--maybe, it's a problem."

It was unusual for a nurse with enough experience to be shift supervisor to sound so uncertain.

"Why are you calling me?"

"Central paging said Dr. Penfield was signed out to you."

As soon as she said it, Brian remembered that Bill Penfield had asked him a few days ago to cover while the surgeon flew to Atlanta for a few days for a seminar about new laser techniques. "I remember now. Go ahead."

"He has a patient, Miss--actually that's Dr.--Jackson, who is supposed to be discharged today, if she's doing well and all the tests are okay."

Brian, with phone tucked to his ear, moved away from the secretary's desk. "That's standard. So what's wrong?"

44

"I'm not sure anything is--or if it's the lab?"

Brian glanced over his shoulder. The administrator's secretary had given up waiting on him and had resumed some other task. "Is the patient in trouble?"

"No, not really, other than she looks very pale."

"So what *is* the problem?" His voice was now edged with impatience.

"Her hematocrit--it's nineteen."

Brian became keenly alert. "I'd say that's a problem. What's her blood pressure?"

"One twenty-two over eighty."

"Pulse?"

"Seventy-two."

"All normal? Are you sure?"

"Certain. I even double-checked it myself, and we used two different blood pressure monitors."

Brian relaxed. "Then it's lab error."

"No. The lab repeated the test on the same sample and even sent someone running up here to redraw blood." Brian could hear the nurse's bewilderment. "And it was still nineteen."

"That makes no sense. Normal hematocrit for a woman is at least thirty-two."

"I know," responded the nurse.

"With nineteen she has half the normal amount of blood, and her oxygen-carrying capacity is borderline for keeping her alive."

"I know."

"Is she short of breath, weak? Does she faint when she sits up?"

"Weak a little, but other than that she seems fine," said the nurse. "In fact, she's up walking around, packing to leave the hospital."

"I'll be there in a second." Brian strode rapidly from the administration office without looking back.

Chapter 7

"Tell the damn reporter I'm not here," said Thurston Walker.

"The gate guard already told him your Mercedes had come through," said Ellen Bumpers, the secretary. "They're not going to let up until they get a statement."

"Well, holy shit!"

"Dr. Walker!" she said with feigned shock. "The head of a company should watch how he talks."

"Get real, Sissy."

The secretary cringed. Since she had come to work here she had tried to forget every vestige of her earlier life, including the name Sissy. "I prefer Ellen," she said tightly.

It looked as if that was the only thing that would make him smile today--reminding Miss Bumpers about her previous existence, before she rose through the ranks to reach her current exalted status as private secretary to the Chief Executive Officer of Durbane Pharmaceuticals. She had a remarkable combination of good looks, great curves, and the ability to act sophisticated in public and behave like a slut in private, that made her so attractive to Thurston Walker. But there were always more where she came from, as he was apt to remind her.

Walker took a deep breath, then glanced at the wall clock, an electronic map of the world displaying the time zones in colored bands. "Tell him we'll have a news release at noon--nothing before then. It will be given to WXKL. Everybody else, and that includes CNN, can get it from them."

"Would you like Bill Perkins of public relations to start putting it together?"

"He's already on it, but tell him to have it ready by eleven so we can make any needed changes. In the meantime, I'll be in Dr. Gilmore's lab. She's got something she wants to show me. Oh, and fire the gate guard who talked to the reporter."

"Yes, sir." Sissy turned to leave.

Thurston Walker was too irritated to watch her exit, something he usually enjoyed.

Before he could rise, the door reopened. He motioned to Dietrich to have a seat. The security chief settled comfortably into the leather couch situated along one wall of the spacious office. With the efficiency of his Prussian forebears, he began his report. "Here is what happened. The pilot lost one engine while on final approach, apparently some mechanical malfunction. The situation would not have been critical except for a thunderstorm two miles north of the field. The Doppler radar reported intermittent wind shear, and the pilot told the tower he did not want to abort the landing and chance climbing into the thunderstorm." Dietrich shrugged. "Unfortunately, the thunder squall moved rapidly over the field. The MD-101 hit a solid wall of rain with a seventy-kilometer-per-hour shear, lost lift, and hit hard. The nose gear collapsed."

"The pilot did a good job?" asked Walker.

"From what one air traffic controller told me--yes."

"The landing gear collapsed," said Walker as he drummed his fingers on the desk. "So we might explain this away as a mechanical problem coupled with extraordinarily bad luck?"

"Yes."

"We might even blame the mechanical problem on the aircraft manufacturer or an outside maintenance company." An unpleasant smile crept across his face. "Pass that on to Perkins to incorporate into the noontime press release."

"There is one more thing," Dietrich said. "I spoke again with Doúbe--I have a supply officer there who gives me reliable information."

"And?" said Walker, his voice cautious.

"Our cover at Doúbe may have been compromised."

Walker's eyes became slits, his jaw rigid. "How?"

"The American tourist who was injured and treated by Baptiste--"

"He *knew* not to do that," interrupted Walker. "We want no attention drawn to that facility! All treatment was to be confined to locals."

"This tourist was injured because the local police, whom we pay to keep an eye on the facility, evidently tried to kill her."

"Jesus Christ!" Thurston Walker slammed a two hundred-dollar Mont Blanc pen onto the desk in disgust, irreparably bending its tip in the process. "They're not supposed to go around killing people--not Americans anyway. They're just supposed to scare snoopers away."

"Apparently this one did not scare off so easily."

"Apparently. Did she report any of this to the authorities?"

"Not that I can tell, and that is odd. Of course, the Haitian authorities are no cause for concern, and if some do turn up who are not already in our employ, it will cost very little to buy their silence. Our money goes a long way in Haiti."

Thurston Walker nodded his agreement, then paused as a thought struck him. "You don't think--surely Dr. Baptiste didn't treat her with U.B.S.?"

Dietrich shrugged. "I am looking into that now. But in any case, I think it only a matter of time before some U.S. government agency makes an inquiry."

"Then we have to close this matter--and quickly. Look into it, Karl. See if she is amenable to a settlement. If not..." Thurston Walker's eyes narrowed to menacing slits. "Encourage her. I know I can count on you to maintain the secrecy we need."

Dietrich had his marching orders. He rose to leave.

"And Karl," said Walker.

He stopped.

"There's a lesson here." Walker spoke softly as a father chiding a misbehaving, yet favorite, son. "The work you do is essential for the company, for me. But sometimes..." He paused. "You, your men, have got to know when to draw the line. There's been a few other times." Walker's mind went back to an interrogation of an employee thought to be selling company secrets--only a generous pay-off prevented serious problems.

Dietrich nodded his understanding.

"One thing still puzzles me. Doúbe is not a tourist area. What was that woman doing there?"

Dietrich shook his head. "No one knows."

Chapter 8

The screen projected an image above the microscope like a thought balloon over the head of a cartoon character. However, instead of words, a scene of microscopic detail was displayed.

Dr. Diane Gilmore was seated and staring into the eye tubes of a Zeiss research-grade light microscope. Walker stood close behind her, watching the view on the screen as she adjusted the slide to bring the area of interest into focus. He caught a whiff of her perfume and moved a little closer.

"There." Gilmore never looked up, but a movable pointer on the screen indicated a wavy blue line, a line that looked to Walker like some careless artist had marred his surrealistic landscape with a ribbon of dark paint.

"What is it?"

"According to our consulting histopathologist, it's a layer of abnormal tissue in the aorta."

"Diane, why did you call me here to see this? All hell is breaking loose over the plane crash, and I'm not a pathologist. A simple written report would have done just fine."

Gilmore turned from the microscope to face him. "Because it could delay U.B.S. still further, and if the new formulation has the same defect, the entire substance could wind up being abandoned."

Walker felt anger, then intense frustration, but he managed to fight down the emotions with a slow intake of breath. "Our company needs--the whole world needs--that product."

"I know."

"Explain," he said through clenched teeth.

"This tissue sample is from one of the aborted specimens. The spontaneous abortion side effect will be a serious impediment to marketing U.B.S., so I've had an entire team working on just that one problem. This is one of the results they've observed."

"You didn't tell them the reason for the investigation?"

"No, just that the samples were of human abortus tissue."

"And that blue substance is the cause of the abortions?"

"No. Unfortunately it seems to be another U.B.S. side effect. The red tissue is the aorta of the fetus. The blue stain is for proteoglycan." With her finger touching the screen above the microscope, Gilmore traced the blue line that lay just inside, and paralleled, the red one.

Walker nodded. Finally, something he was familiar with. "Proteoglycan, a long chain protein attached to a sugar molecule, a protein and a glucose."

Gilmore continued. "Proteoglycan is supposed to be there, but I'm told it should stain much lighter. There's something wrong with it. What that means is, if this fetus had not been aborted, if the pregnancy had continued, and the baby been born, then this defect would have been in its aorta--a weak spot waiting to give way under the pounding force of blood from the heart; in short, an aneurysm." Gilmore let out a long sigh. "Even if we substantially reduce the miscarriage rate for U.B.S. recipients who happen to be pregnant, our product could still create a serious health problem in their offspring."

Frustration overwhelmed Walker and he reflected back on Gilmore's past. "And you always scrutinize this thoroughly for aneurysms?" he said, his voice dripping with nastiness.

She glared at him. "Now I do," responding with a tone now icy cold.

"All right, what do you suggest?" said Walker his manner reverting back to that of the problem-solving C.E.O.

"Nothing for the moment," said Gilmore, her manner relaxing slightly. "I just wanted to alert you. The new formulation is almost ready. We've made some changes to affect the appearance and hopefully the abortion rate. If we're lucky, this side effect won't be in it."

"And if we aren't?"

"Then more modifications and more delays."

"How long will it be before you know?"

"Therein lies another problem. If the new formulation is as successful as the animal studies suggest, then the abortion rate will dramatically drop. But then we won't have as many samples of abortion tissue to examine. This defect, incidentally, is not universal. It's present in only about one in thirty samples. We were lucky to spot it. But if the side effect persists, then it means that one in thirty children of mothers who receive U.B.S. will have walking time bombs in their chests."

Long after Gilmore fell silent, Walker continued to glare at the blue line in the microscope.

Chapter 9

Like a panther lying in wait for its prey, Karl Dietrich reclined in his desk chair. His office was as different from Thurston Walker's as an underground combat bunker was from the captain's cabin of a luxury liner. The soundproofed walls, like the bulkhead of a submarine, were metallic gray and featureless. No decorative touches broke the monotony. His desk was bare of paper save for a solitary pad for short notes; which were quickly destroyed as soon as committed to memory. The computer and the telephone with its satellite up-link were all he needed to conduct his business.

The few visitors who came to his office would describe it as Spartan, but Karl Dietrich did not think of it that way. Compared to the East German orphanage where he had spent much of his youth, this was luxurious. For a moment he allowed a wave of self-satisfaction to wash over him. Yes, he had come a long way.

Hands folded behind his head and leaning back while he waited for Penfield to come to the phone, Dietrich remembered how he had felt years ago in that orphanage when he discovered his mother's brooch was missing. The brooch was his last memento of her. Only one other boy at the home could have taken it, a mealy-mouthed, sneaky child who Karl had caught once before going through his personal belongings. Apparently this time the little thief had found Karl's hiding place--inside the lining of the ragged stocking cap he kept in the bottom of his dirty clothes sack--and he had taken Karl's only treasure.

Karl remembered how he'd planned, and waited, then caught the other boy alone in the filthy room that passed for a water closet. The boy was a year older and twenty-five kilos heavier, but a piece of fence wire with rope handles on each end was all the equalizer Karl needed. The older boy struggled to the point of unconsciousness, his fingers unable to get beneath the wire around his neck, while Karl, desperate with rage, held on from behind. At last he loosened the makeshift garrote, long enough for the other boy to choke out his meager explanation. "I sold it," said the terrified youngster. "I needed money."

This time when Karl tightened the garrote it cut so deeply into the other boy's neck that blood flowed. He put enough twists in the two ends of the wire that there was no way the other boy would ever get loose. Karl climbed out the window never to return, leaving his victim on the concrete floor struggling unsuccessfully for his life.

Dietrich was still tilted back in his chair, both arms folded behind his head when the speakerphone crackled to life, jerking his thoughts back to the present.

"This is Dr. Penfield."

"My name is Evans," lied the security man. "The hospital gave me your name and location. I am sorry to disturb you, doctor, but--"

"Mr. Evans, this had better be an emergency to interrupt me in the middle of a seminar. Dr. Brian Richards is handling my calls while I'm out of town."

"I have only a few questions, questions that will help us quickly clear up a matter. I am an investigator of overseas affairs for the State Department." Dietrich trusted that his accent, although neither French nor Caribbean, would lend believability to his cover story. "A patient of yours, a Sharon Jackson, was injured in an accident in the Caribbean. We are looking into the case."

"I don't think I can tell you anything. Medical information is privileged, confidential. You know that."

Dietrich had anticipated that response. "In this situation, it would save a lot of time if you would help us. We, of course, can subpoena you as soon as you return to New Orleans, bring you down to the Federal building, and have you answer the questions here. It would just be more convenient for both of us if we did it this way."

There was a pause while the doctor absorbed the threat. "Uh, yeah, sure. What's the big deal anyway?"

"Our responsibility is the safety of Americans overseas. What type of accident was Miss Jackson involved in?"

"That's Dr. Jackson. She's an archaeologist and professor."

"I see," said Dietrich, intending to let slip nothing of what he already knew. "We need details. Was she at fault or was some other party? Did the government of Haiti act responsibly to protect one of our citizens?"

"I really don't know the details. It was some kind of diving accident, scuba diving. You see, she doesn't remember. She struck her head, a concussion with retrograde amnesia."

"Retrograde amnesia?"

"Yes, she not only has trouble remembering what happened after the accident, but also for a period of time before it happened. Anyway, I ordered

54

a CT head scan and an MRI. She was to be discharged if those are normal." He gave a strained laugh. "Insurance companies won't let us keep them very long in the hospital nowadays."

"You said she had trouble remembering. Is that a total loss of memory?" asked Dietrich as the hint of a grin crept across his face.

"Mostly. She has a few fragments of recall, but not much. Dr. Jean Baptiste, an old friend of mine--I met him years ago when I did a fellowship in France--treated her down there. Since he knew I was here and she was from New Orleans, he called and asked that I accept her as a patient. Of course I was glad to be of assistance. Dr. Baptiste put her on a direct flight. Beauvoir Memorial's transport service picked her up at the airport, and we admitted her overnight. Dr. Baptiste did not have access to the tests she needed, but he thought she would tolerate the flight without difficulty, and she did."

Dietrich placed both elbows on the desk to lean over the speakerphone. "Do you think her memory will return, Dr. Penfield?"

"Most probably."

"I see," said Dietrich slowly. His grin faded. "That is good news." The flatness in his voice belied his words. "When she is better we will ask her a few questions. Do you anticipate her discharge soon?"

"It'll be today unless something unusual turns up."

"And you expect nothing unusual?"

"Funny thing," said Penfield slowly, as if contemplating a puzzle. "*Unusual*, that was the exact word Baptiste used. He emphasized to me that Jackson did not have any infection or blood loss, and there was no need for me to get any blood tests on her, just A CT and MRI. In fact, he mentioned it twice, but then added that if something *unusual* did turn up, for me to call him first."

"That does seem odd," said Dietrich cautiously.

"Yes. Most blood tests are so inexpensive that we do them routinely. But this woman was so pale I decided to go ahead and get additional blood studies anyway."

At the word pale Dietrich sat upright. "And what did they show?"

"I don't know. They were to be completed this morning. I left her in the hands of a very capable young physician who will take care of any problems that might arise." He paused, then almost as an afterthought added, "You have piqued my curiosity though. I'll make it a point to check on her case."

55

"I would not be overly concerned," said Dietrich quickly. "These are just routine inquiries. Thank you, Doctor Penfield. You have been very helpful."

Dietrich punched the phone off. After a moment's thought, he entered a new set of numbers.

The woman in her white uniform from employee health arrived almost instantaneously. Dietrich did not bother waving her to a seat. She stood as fearfully stiff as a Marine recruit in front of an angry drill sergeant. Dietrich liked that with subordinates.

"There is a patient at Beauvoir Memorial Hospital named Sharon Jackson. I would like..." He leaned forward to emphasize his request, "very much, to know the results of her laboratory tests. Perhaps you would make a call and use your medical skills to extract that information without disclosing your identity. Also a Dr. Penfield. Is he someone of importance who can generate a lot of--attention? After you find those things out, can I count on your forgetting this entire occurrence?"

The woman's assurances were only too heartfelt.

Chapter 10

Brian slowed at the nurses' station just long enough to grab the chart with the label *416 Jackson*. Mrs. Davis fell quickly into step behind him, and together they rushed into Sharon Jackson's room.

Brian stopped short, his stethoscope halfway out of his pocket, the nurse almost colliding with him from behind. Unbelievably, the woman with a hematocrit of nineteen appeared in no distress. She stood upright beside her bed, fully dressed in a green knit shirt and tight blue jeans with brown leather hiking boots. Her blonde hair was neatly combed and did not quite reach her slender shoulders. In all, despite her recent injuries, she was pretty enough to be on the cover of an outdoor fashion catalog--except that she was pale, very pale, sported a black eye, and was visibly very angry. Sitting in a chair across from the bed was another woman, about the same age but a lot less upset.

"Dr. Penfield left instructions that I could leave this morning," the patient said, her arms crossed in an unmistakable gesture of annoyance.

Brian was frantically thumbing through the chart to familiarize himself with the case. Only two things were obvious: this woman was nowhere near death from anemia, and she wanted out of this hospital.

"My name is Dr. Brian Richards," he said. I'm covering while Dr. Penfield--"

"I know that. Mrs. Davis said you were coming. I also know my CT and MRIs are normal. Dr. Penfield left instructions that I could leave under those circumstances--and I *must* leave."

"Uh, yes, ma'am, but I'm afraid one of your blood tests is abnormal."

The woman's arms unfolded. Despite her thirty years, for a moment she resembled a little girl who had just been told that Christmas won't be coming this year. "What test?"

Brian looked uncomfortably at the woman seated in the chair, then back to his patient. "Would you rather discuss your condition privately?"

"Darcy is a friend."

"All right then. Your blood count is low. Extremely low. You're very anemic."

The patient thought for a moment. "If you read that," she gestured to the chart, "you would know that I was injured in a diving accident. I lost some blood, but now I feel fine."

Brian took a deep breath, stalling for time. Clearly it was going to take all of his patient-management skills to keep this woman here until he could find out what was wrong with her. He flashed his broadest smile. "Dr. Jackson, I'm sure you want to get home as quickly as possible," he said, "but please, give me fifteen more minutes to check something out, and then, I promise, you can leave. That way I will have done my job."

"Doctor, I have been out of the country for several weeks. My work was interrupted by--an untimely accident. I *must* get back to it. I do not care to hang around a hospital when I feel perfectly fine." She glared and refolded her arms.

"Do what he says, Sharon," said Darcy. "You've been through a lot. Don't take any more chances. I'll wait right outside."

Sharon reluctantly sat back on the bed.

Forty-five minutes later, Dr. Brian Richards had to admit he was amazed and mystified by the case of Sharon Jackson and, in addition, maybe just a little bit attracted to her. Once it became apparent to Brian that her vital signs were truly normal, and he finally admitted that there was no reason why she absolutely had to remain in the hospital, she dropped the hostile manner. Her attitude was lively, and other than a tendency for vertigo if she stood up quickly, her body was fit. But most of his questions about what had happened in Haiti went unanswered.

He turned his attention to carefully retaping the bandage on her forearm. Then he dismissed Nurse Davis, who was all too glad to leave this troublesome problem in his hands and return to her other duties.

An old expression came to Brian's mind: "an enigma shrouded in a mystery." That seemed to sum up the situation. For one thing, the lab had redrawn and retested Jackson's blood, and her hematocrit was still only nineteen. Yet she had no obvious symptoms. She claimed not to recall her accident in detail. She had been scuba diving, and something went wrong--an underwater tidal surge of some sort. She had no recall of the details of the accident, and although there was no doubt she had partial amnesia, Brian had the distinct impression that she was keeping something hidden. And although not exactly pertinent to the medical case, he had also found out she was single, an assistant professor of archaeology at Tulane, and lived alone.

"So, over all I'm in good shape."

"Well, yes, except that your blood count is barely compatible with life, and I would much rather you stayed for more tests."

"But I have no infection, no cancer, no broken bones?"

Brian had to assure her she didn't.

"Then I must be off." She stood, wavered slightly, then reached for her bag. She checked its zipper, then announced, "Thank you for your trouble, Dr. Richards. But I have important work to get back to."

Admitting defeat, Brian rose from the bedside chair. "All right, but if you start feeling bad, promise you'll call me. And, of course, keep your appointment with Dr. Penfield Monday."

She gave him a smile. "I promise. And I do appreciate your concern."

Chapter 11

"Nineteen," Dietrich repeated. "And that is low?"

The employee health nurse stood, once again, stiff and uncomfortable in front of his desk. "Very. I don't ever remember seeing a patient that anemic."

On the pad Dietrich had written: Jackson, Tulane, archaeology, an address on St. Charles Avenue, and the number nineteen. He circled the nineteen. "Yet the patient was well enough to be discharged?"

"That, in particular, I don't understand. Someone with a blood count that low would be near death. The person should be kept in the hospital and given blood transfusions."

"So, why was that not done?"

"The patient seemed in such good health that the personnel on duty thought her abnormal lab results were most probably lab error."

The barest hint of a smile crept across Dietrich's face. "You are certain of your information?"

"Yes, I spoke with both the hospital laboratory and the ward clerk of the floor on which she had been hospitalized."

"And you kept your identity secret?"

"Yes, sir. Each time I identified myself only as a home health nurse getting background information on my new patient."

The security chief stared at the pen he rolled in his fingertips, but his nod said he approved. "You recall the corporate secrecy agreement all Durbane employees sign? There are stiff penalties, from loss of your pension plan to legal action to..." His voice trailed off indicating there were other circumstances that could be added to the list. "For a company in the research business, our livelihood, the livelihood of hundreds of employees, depends on keeping certain privileged information secret." He lifted his gaze to stare intently at the nurse. "I would consider this information"--his gaze swept the room, searching for the right phraseology--"something best not to be spoken of. Do you understand?"

"Yes, sir," she croaked.

"However, we have a special fund to reward star performers such as yourself." The woman brightened. "Within the next few days you will receive a substantial bonus."

There were many human motivators, Dietrich reminded himself after the woman scurried away: money, praise, sex, fear. He had always found a combination worked best.

Now, a phone call to Walker. Then, if secrecy were to be maintained, several leaks would need to be plugged.

* * * * *

Thurston Walker threaded his Mercedes through the heavy traffic on Chef Menteur Boulevard, confidant that the plane would wait. After all, he owned it, or at least Durbane Pharmaceuticals did, and with the exception of occasional meddling by the board of directors, for all practical purposes he and Durbane were one and the same.

A jet was essential for a fast-moving executive in a fast-paced industry, and Walker made the most of the Gulfstream-45. It had twin engines, a ceiling of 55,000 feet, and could transport up to twelve people 500 miles per hour in luxurious comfort. Durbane had two other jets, both cargo carriers, or they did until two days ago, Walker reminded himself. Now they were down to one MD-101. The wrecked plane would need to be replaced as soon as the lawyers completed their obligatory dickering and the insurance company sent a check.

Strains of Johann Strauss filled the passenger compartment of his Mercedes. "Phone on," he said to the air.

The music winked off instantly, and an electronic voice said, "Number please."

"Call the Gulfstream."

"Dialing Gulfstream," responded the voice. There followed a series of clicks, beeps, and chirps.

"Dick Lane here. Go ahead."

"Hello, Mr. Lane. I'm running late. The morning traffic is unbelievable."

"That's all right, sir. I have filed only a preliminary flight plan. When you get here we'll update it with exact times."

Suddenly the pilot was interrupted by three beeps followed by the electronic voice. "Incoming message from Karl Dietrich. Will you accept?"

"Yes," Walker responded to the air.

"You have ten seconds before switch-over."

62

"I'll be there in about fifteen minutes--unless there's an accident ahead."

"We'll be waiting, sir."

"Goodbye."

"Switch-over to incoming message," said the electronic voice.

"Dr. Walker?"

"Go ahead, Karl."

"Are we in scrambler mode?"

"Always."

"I took care of the loose end."

"Good."

"There is another problem."

Walker sighed.

"Repeat please," said the electronic voice as it tried to convert a sigh into a command.

Walker ignored it. "And that is?"

"The young lady, the visitor to the good doctor..."

"Yes?" said Walker cautiously.

"I believe she was treated--that is--given the research medicine."

"What!" cried the C.E.O.

"Repeat please," said the electronic voice.

"Goddamn phone!" complained Walker. He slid into the next lane while glaring malevolently at an elderly man traveling at half his speed in a car that appeared held together only by rust and faith. Safely in the slow lane, he barked, "She was given the medication?"

"I believe so, sir."

"Okay, Karl," he said. "I'm on my way to visit Baptiste now. Meet me tomorrow in the office, nine A.M."

"Yes, sir."

"Phone off," said Thurston Walker.

"Phone off," responded the synthetic voice.

"That electronic son of a bitch has got to go," Walker muttered to himself.

"Repeat please," said the phone.

Chapter 12

Dr. Brian Richards entered the hospital laboratory with all the finesse of a recently defeated sumo wrestler determined to regain his championship.

"Can I help you, doctor?" said the technician.

"I want to find out about a CBC on Sharon Jackson," he demanded.

"Let me check." She turned to her computer console. After innumerable keypunch entries, the technician said, "Several were done--" and then she did a double take.

Brian looked over her shoulder and saw the value 19 followed by a series of symbols.

The technician explained "See the asterisks?" She pointed to the computer screen. "That means the value is so far out of normal range that the patient is in danger. We are required to call the charge nurse immediately to report the results." She peered closer. "Hmm," she said to herself. "They were also reported outside."

"What do you mean, *outside*?" Brian asked.

"That symbol--beyond the asterisks." He followed her pointing finger. "That's a verbal report given to an agent outside the hospital."

Brian thought for a moment. Who would want a lab report on Sharon Jackson? Then it came to him. "I'm sure that was from Dr. Penfield. He's in Atlanta today and probably was just checking back."

"No. We use a different symbol for a report to a physician. This was a nurse--like a managed care nurse or home health nurse."

"That's strange," said Brian. "She was a private patient not registered in any of those programs. Wonder who it was."

"Well, I wouldn't know. My shift just came on, and anyway, we have three data-entry technicians per shift, with hundreds of requests."

"Excuse me, doctor. Could I be of any help?" The voice didn't sound friendly. Brian looked up to see a stocky woman who could have been the coach for the women's international wrestling team. She wore a white lab coat and was armed with a pocket calculator.

Brian cringed. He knew of this woman. Emma Wilson, lab supervisor. Second in command under Sam Parker and responsible for the lab's day-to-day functioning. Nothing came or went without her knowing about it. She guarded her turf with the ferocity of a Rottweiler that hasn't had the opportunity to bite anything for weeks.

"I'm checking on a blood test result that's so far out of range it must be a lab error," said Brian.

Bristling, the laboratory director answered, "Abnormal results are always double checked." She, too, leaned to look at the computer screen. While using her small calculator as a pointer, she spoke with the offended sensibility of a teenager told on prom night that her boyfriend had just ditched her. "In this case I see that another blood draw was done with essentially the same results." She turned to face her accuser. "Why is it that when doctors don't know what's wrong with a patient they always blame the test results on our error?" The lab supervisor's calculator went to her pocket, her hands to her hips.

"It's not that, not exactly. It's just that it doesn't fit." Brian's mind ran rapidly through the possible explanations for unbelievable lab results. His gaze swept the lab--rows upon rows of serum-filled tubes. "Is there any blood left over for testing at a reference laboratory?"

"I'll check," said the supervisor icily.

"Fine," he said. Brian occupied himself by impatiently clicking the button of his ballpoint pen during the wait.

Eventually the woman returned with a handful of sealed tubes. "Do you want some of this sent out?"

"Yes--for a CBC."

Emma Wilson's manner went from icy cold to red-hot. "I have never heard of sending out a complete blood count. That test is so basic it's done in every lab in the world. Why would we, or the patient, want to pay extra for something like that?" She pointed to the computer they had used a few minutes earlier. "Right there you just saw that the test had been run twice and each was double checked. That makes four times, doctor." Her voice became louder. "There's nothing wrong with our equipment. The problem is with this blood." She held the tubes up, shaking them violently. "This is what's abnormal!"

Brian felt the gaze of the other technicians bearing down on him. He took a step back. He could see why this woman was kept in the lab--for the same reason a tiger was kept behind bars.

He threw up his hands in defeat. "Okay, you're right." He started to go. "Will you store the blood for a while, in case I order some other tests later?"

The supervisor recited from the laboratory policy manual. "All fluid samples will be maintained in refrigeration for seven days before being destroyed."

"Fine. Uh, thanks. Have a nice day," Brian said as he escaped.

Chapter 13

"*Comment allez-vous?*" said the doctor in the rumpled white smock. He bent over and placed his stethoscope on the chest of his patient. The man paused his rapid respirations to mutter a response, but the doctor did not understand him. The patient was too weak to speak above a whisper, and anyway, despite twelve years in Haiti, the doctor still had trouble understanding the patois used by many people of the back country.

As a young priest, Father Baptiste had struggled to mend the soul. Now older and a physician, Dr. Baptiste also worked to restore the body.

The doctor forced a reassuring smile, even though he had serious concern about the patient's prognosis. The man's skin did not have that healthy coal-black glow Baptiste liked to see. Instead, it was pallid, as if there were not enough blood coursing beneath. Dr. Jean Baptiste could glean a world of information from just looking at and touching a patient. He needed that ability. Until two years ago, the mission hospital had little equipment and almost no supplies. All he'd been able to do was drain abscesses, pull teeth, offer sacraments to the dying, and wait for the infrequent shipments of drugs and medical supplies. But now he no longer needed to depend on the minimal funding from churches and the vagaries of charitable giving. Now, by comparison, he was potentate of a medical Mecca.

His thoughts returned to his patient. As he held the stethoscope in place he could feel the heat that radiated from the man. There was a fine coating of sweat on the patient's body, which made the diaphragm of the stethoscope slide about. Dr. Baptiste withdrew the instrument and draped it around his neck. This patient's problem was not his heart or lungs. The stethoscope was just a way of laying hands on his patient--an action used by healers since time immemorial to reassure the sufferer that the physician was there watching, waiting, treating, and praying for improvement. In this case, Baptiste already knew what was wrong.

This man's problem was his foot. The foot was draining pus from a half dozen sinuses. By the time the man had appeared at the mission hospital, he was near death. Despite the ancient crutch borrowed from God knows where, and even with the help of his wife, who carried their meager provisions for the two-day trip, each time he had put his foot down he left a moist imprint behind--a stamp of blood-tinged pus. With each step of his journey, this patient had lost only a milliliter of blood--but it had been a long journey.

Baptiste slipped on a pair of rubber gloves and removed the dressing the nurse had applied to the wounds. A foul odor besieged his nostrils. He gently palpated the swollen tissues. Each time pressure was applied, the man groaned and pus exuded.

Dr. Baptiste leaned back. Sensation was present and the foot was not necrotic. Good, he thought--no gangrene. He knew that in times past this would be a dead man, but now things were different. Shortly he would begin a course of antifungals, but first the severe bacterial infection had to be brought under control. For that, he would use chloramphnicol, still the most powerful antibiotic available. It was only infrequently used in the United States because of its rare tendency to cause a fatal reaction, and when that unfortunate event did occur, a lawsuit against the physician was inevitable. That, however, was not a concern here. In rural Haiti, trained physicians with access to modern medications were so few that they carried the status of voodoo gods, able to dispense life and death at will. No one dared question such authority.

"Dr. Baptiste," said the nurse in her lilting Creole accent.

"Yes, Martina," he answered as he covered the man's purulent foot with a sterile towel, then peeled off his gloves and turned to face the nurse.

"The hematocrit is sixteen," she said, holding out a piece of paper.

"Thank you." Dr. Baptiste took the printout from their automated blood analyzer and read it himself. He looked up. Normal hematocrit for a male was around forty, although it was so seldom he saw a healthy male, he had decided that figure was almost imaginary. With a hematocrit of sixteen, the situation was fatal without a blood transfusion. But there was no such thing as a blood bank out here. Even in Port-au-Prince good blood was scarce. There, as in most crowded third-world cities, the AIDS epidemic showed no signs of abating. Thirty percent of sexually active adults tested positive for the HIV virus. Medicines were now available to dramatically slow the progress of the infection, but no cure was, as yet, in sight. "Give him two units," said Baptiste.

Martina had anticipated the order. She reached into a carryall and produced a half-liter plastic bag of milky white fluid. When the patient first arrived, he was so obviously debilitated that without asking she had started an intravenous infusion of glucose. Now, she expertly switched the IV line, plugging it into the port on the bottom of the bag of white fluid. She hung the new bag from the IV pole and adjusted the flow rate to 125 ml/hr. As she spun the bag to double-check that there was no air lock in the drip chamber, the writing on the bag was clearly evident: *U.B.S.*

"Piggyback the chloramphenicol into this same line," Baptiste commanded.

"Yes, sir."

Satisfied, the doctor reached down to touch his patient on the shoulder and said, "*Vous vivrez voir le lever du soleil et plus, mon ami.*" *You will live to see the sunrise tomorrow, and many more, my friend.*

Martina pulled gently on the physician's sleeve. "You must go and meet with your visitor now, doctor. Otherwise he will be angry with you."

Dr. Baptiste let out a long sigh and turned to go.

Alone with the patient, Martina needed no further instructions. She knew the doctor would not want the man to suffer, so she injected twenty-five milligrams of meperidine into the IV line. The medication, combined with his exhaustion, almost instantly closed the man's eyes. Martina slipped on disposable gloves and carefully redressed the infected foot. Then she elevated his limb on a pile of towels rather than risk soiling one of the clinic's pillows. Finally she rechecked the flow rate of the antibiotic and found it satisfactory.

Martina studied her patient. His respirations were rapid, driven by the fever. His sleep was fitful. One last thing remained to be done. She looked around. No one was at the door. Reaching into her pocket, she withdrew a small linen sack. It was one of several she had prepared a week earlier. It contained a small carved cross, two coins that had the word *God* on them, a dried chicken foot, and some secret herbs. She slipped it into a pocket of her patient's tattered shorts, then closed her eyes and murmured a prayer. When she reopened them, he seemed to be resting easier. Silently, she left.

* * * * *

A TWENTY-BED HOSPITAL, outpatient treatment clinic, warehouse, diesel generator, and packed-earth helicopter pad made up *L'hôpital des Anges--The Hospital of the Angels*. It was a short walk to his cabin on the other side of the compound. For some privacy, the doctor's home was set behind a screen of banana trees to separate it from the circle of buildings. He passed through the screened porch and stepped into the relative coolness provided by an overhead fan.

A middle-aged man dressed inappropriately for the tropical environment in a white dress shirt and dark trousers sat staring out the window at a gaily-colored bird in a tree. He pretended not to notice the doctor's arrival. Only the drumming of his fingers on a small side table telegraphed his annoyance.

"I am sorry I was delayed," said Dr. Baptiste in French-accented English. "A severe case of Madura Foot just arrived, and it was necessary to get the medication started."

"I'm sure," Thurston Walker responded brusquely. "I'm sorry to interfere with your work, doctor, but I am on a tight schedule."

"I understand," said the physician. "I have the records ready." Baptiste walked rapidly to his desk in the next room and returned with a stack of file folders. He placed them, like an offering, on the table beside the visitor. "In the past four weeks, thirty-one patients have received infusions of U.B.S. They all survived, with the exception of one elderly woman with metastatic uterine cancer."

"You were told not to use it on any terminal cases," Walker growled. "It skews the results."

"It eased her suffering," said the physician, stiffening.

"These clinical studies are very important," the man in the white shirt snarled. "Would the suffering of any of your other patients be eased if we had to move our Phase III program somewhere else because you would not adhere to the protocol?"

The doctor wanted to answer. He wanted to tell this man what he thought of him, but he knew, like Faust, that he had made a deal with the devil and could expect no compassion. He looked at the floor. "No, of course not."

"Just refresh my memory, doctor, what is the protocol?"

Like a guilty Boy Scout caught violating his oath, the physician recited, "Hematocrit under twenty-six, no terminal illness, age less than seventy."

"Anything else?"

"The subjects are to be local Haitians."

"Perhaps you want to re-count the number who received U.B.S.?"

The physician cringed. In that instant he understood that the other man already knew. How, he had no idea, but he supposed there were plenty in the hospital compound who would be glad to spy on him for a few American dollars.

But instead of sinking lower, Baptiste straightened and gazed directly at the other man. "Thirty-one were on the protocol--but there was another, a woman, who desperately needed the drug. She was a tourist. She would have died from her injuries without the medication."

"How was she injured?"

"A scuba diving accident. She was found washed ashore nearly dead. She had a concussion. She bled heavily. That is all I know."

"Doctor, this is not a tourist area, and most scuba divers practice their sport in groups. Did you ask what she was doing here?"

"My duty is to restore the body, not interrogate those God has placed under my care."

"Doctor, let me remind you--there are other physicians who would be glad for the opportunity to work with us."

"Yes, I know."

"All right," said Walker, "disregarding the tourist and the cancer patient, did the other thirty respond?"

"Yes."

"Were any of them pregnant?"

"Yes, two."

"And?" asked the visitor cautiously.

"They both aborted. One was at nine weeks gestation, the other about twelve weeks."

The man frowned. "What was the lowest hematocrit you encountered?"

"Fifteen. A boy with hemophilia. He had a nosebleed for--"

"It doesn't matter," said the visitor, smiling. "Fifteen."

Baptiste was reminded of a hawk that had spotted its prey and knew that soon the weaker creature would be within its talons.

"I don't believe there's ever been a documented case of recovery from such a severe anemia without blood transfusion," mused the visitor. "I'll have a computer search made of the medical literature to confirm that as soon as I get back." He picked up the stack of reports from the end table and started for the door, then stopped just before leaving. "That list of supplies and equipment you sent..." Baptiste stood meekly waiting. "We'll get that out to you in the next couple of days. And since you have so much paperwork here"--he hefted the bundle of reports--"we'll also send out someone to help you keep track of everything."

* * * * *

The pilot had been lounging outside, under the shade of a large tropical tree. As soon as he spotted the two men at the door, he climbed into the left front seat and began preparing for departure.

Dr. Baptiste stood on the porch of his house watching as the helicopter's engine spooled up and the rotors began to turn. Ducking to minimize the force of the rotor wash, the visitor hurried across the clearing and jumped aboard, securing the charts in a compartment behind his seat, then buckling in. The helicopter lifted off with an ear-throbbing roar, leaving Dr. Baptiste once again thinking of Faust and the deal he had made.

* * * * *

Inside the helicopter, flying at two thousand feet, the air was cooler. The man in the white shirt had already slipped on his suit coat. He had left his tie on the Gulfstream at Port-au-Prince. He would put it on during the flight over the Gulf of Mexico. It wouldn't look good for the C.E.O. of Durbane Pharmaceuticals to appear half-dressed when he arrived.

Thurston Walker glanced at his Rolex. He settled back for the thirty-minute helicopter ride to Port-au-Prince International Airport. After that, there would be a quick transfer to the Gulfstream, and he would be back in New Orleans for an early supper at his favorite restaurant. Tomorrow there would be the discussion with Karl, then it would be the security man's duty to find and convince that archeologist woman that her best course of action was silence. As for the specifics of how that was done, within certain limits, that was up to Karl. And the less Walker knew about the details, the better. That was called plausible deniability.

Chapter 14

A concussion rattles the brain; at least that was one explanation Sharon had heard, and she believed it. Her memory had returned, most of it before she left Haiti. It was her thoughts that remained jumbled. Her brain seemed like a dropped computer whose central processor was scrambled, but at least the hard drive was okay. Scenes of gold and immense treasure were interspersed with flashes of Caribbean squalor and a mission hospital. There was a soft-spoken, French physician, and later--she smiled to herself--a good-looking American doctor. Yes, the memory was there. It was just putting all the pieces together in the right sequence that was so difficult.

It was noontime, the day after she had left the hospital. The trip back to New Orleans International Airport to retrieve her possessions had been easy, and she was almost home. Her body made the drive automatically while her mind buzzed on.

She had spent the morning at her computer inputting every single piece of information about the trip, adding to the research files she had laboriously built up over the last three years. But something else happened when she worked at her computer. It helped clear her head. Mentally everything became better organized. It was that technique that had helped lead her to the discovery in the first place: keep throwing data into the computer, from every source, every level of reliability, and, if lucky, eventually some sense would emerge. Now that she had made her discovery she would need to keep her find a secret until she could accomplish its salvage, and feigning amnesia was not a bad way to avoid answering any troublesome questions.

Sharon consoled herself that despite the setback that had almost gotten her killed, her latest trip to Haiti had succeeded far beyond her wildest expectations. Better planning, more equipment, and perhaps someone else to help would guarantee that her next trip would bring her quest to its conclusion.

At least so far today two things had gone right: her Jeep had started after a lay-up of three weeks, and recovering her luggage and equipment at the airport had been uneventful. On that latter point she had been worried. When she returned to the U.S., airport personnel had delivered her by wheelchair directly from the plane to the hospital van. Her equipment, crated and checked for the flight, had taken the more circuitous route of going through customs for possible inspection, then to short-term storage at the baggage claim office. The crate, complete with the seal of the United States Department of Customs and apparently unopened, was readily handed over to her. Not that she expected any agent to find the hiding place that Dr. Baptiste had suggested. A scuba tank returning from the Caribbean is about as innocent a piece of baggage as can be found. Plus its steel is impenetrable to X-ray, and it is hard to get into without a large wrench. A wave of exhilaration rushed through her at the thought of what she would find. Nestled safely inside her tank were three items: a gold necklace with an icon of a warrior wearing a large headdress, a jeweled image of a macaw, and a large polished stone that could only be an emerald. Oh, yes, and a lot of straw. Compressed air is not supposed to rattle.

She rounded the corner into her apartment complex taking only vague notice of a nondescript white Ford parked on the opposite side of the street a few townhouses down from hers. What did catch her attention was a man dressed in workmen's dark greens and cap and wearing a pouch or tool belt. That, by itself, wasn't unusual, but the fact that he was walking out her front door was. The man turned and headed rapidly away from her.

Was this a hallucination--a weird response to her head trauma? She blinked her eyes. He was still there. What could be going on? She remembered locking the door. Was he a maintenance man summoned by the apartment manager? But in her three years here she had never known that to happen. The tenant was always the one who called maintenance and then had to wait interminably in the apartment to admit the repairman when he finally did arrive.

She was now only a few spaces from her usual parking spot, unsure whether to turn in and check her apartment or investigate further. In times past she would have just confronted the interloper, but since the assault in the cave she had come to realize her own vulnerability and caution seemed the better course of action.

Then from the corner of eye she saw something move. It was the white Ford sedan, cruising up slowly to stop directly opposite the passenger door of her Jeep. Had the occupant of the other vehicle seen something too and was cautiously checking the situation out? She strained to look inside the other vehicle, but the Ford's windows were tinted so darkly she could see nothing.

Gradually she pressed upon the accelerator pedal. Her Jeep crept forward. The man seemed to walk faster. She sped up slightly. He never turned his head to look at her and his cap was pulled down low. She could never see his face, but the skin of his neck looked black--and she saw one more thing. It looked like a cord was dangling from his ear to run down to his belt pouch.

She was so intent on following her quarry she paid no further attention to the white ford sedan until it was too late. It cut directly in front of her, then came to a sudden stop. As she slammed on her brakes to avoid a collision the man she had been watching jumped inside the car, and with a squeal of tires, the other vehicle shot forward.

What the hell! She wasn't going to let them get away with--with whatever they were up to. Flooring the accelerator, she sped after them.

Her apartment complex was a new one, two hundred-fifty units complete with all the amenities a gated community had to offer. There was a central swimming pool and fitness center surrounded by a warren of twisting streets and designer landscaping that gave the entire complex the appearance of a little well-kept private village.

The layout worked to her advantage. As they raced, the frequent turns kept the other car from outdistancing her. Then Sharon saw her chance. They were coming up on the automatic gate. They would have to stop and the gate was slow. That's how someone without a card could get in, just follow closely behind another car. But these folks would have to wait for the gate to crank out of the way, and then, even if she didn't choose to follow to try and stay with them until the police could be summoned, she could at least get a look at their license tag.

The car ahead stopped and Sharon pulled close. She grabbed her cellular phone to dial 911, but suddenly the other car roared backward. There was a crash of bumpers and her vision was instantly obscured by the rapidly expanding gray balloon that leapt from the steering column to smash her cellular phone against her head. Once again she lapsed into unconsciousness.

* * * * *

The laboratory supervisor was in no better mood this afternoon than she was yesterday, especially when the subject under discussion was the blood of one Sharon Jackson. She again recited the laboratory policy manual. "The

Laboratory Supervisor, under the direction of the Chief of Pathology, has the responsibility for the proper safekeeping and storage of all laboratory specimens. So, Mrs. Leathers," Emma Wilson said defiantly, "I cannot release the blood samples to you."

"The administration wants to verify some results by sending them to an outside lab."

"I understand that, and just as I told Dr. Richards--"

"Dr. Brian Richards?"

"Yes, he, too, wanted to send the blood out, although I think that's foolish, at least for a CBC. We've double-checked that result four times. If you want me to send a portion to a reference lab, well, that's a different matter than releasing the entire amount to you. Just give me the name of the lab you prefer."

"I can't do that. I wasn't told where the blood was going, only to pick up all the samples and Mr. Fendley would see that they got to the right place."

Emma Wilson's shoulders grew broad, her voice stronger. "All blood and tissue specimens are entrusted to my safe-keeping. Get the written release of the Chief of Pathology; otherwise I will send off only a portion of the Jackson blood for testing. The rest remains right here for seven days, although-" She paused. "On second thought, these blood specimens have attracted so much attention I think it would be better to maintain them indefinitely."

"I will relay that to Mr. Fendley," said Mrs. Leathers stiffly.

* * * * *

Dietrich hung up the phone. He used his pen to tap out his annoyance onto the notepad. First the girl gets away. Now, he is told that her blood samples exist, perhaps indefinitely, in cold storage ready to be trotted out at any time to cause problems. In addition, the hospital laboratory is always occupied and the samples can not be seized without attracting a lot of attention. He had suggested that it was in Fendley's best interest to find a way to solve the blood sample problem. It was his hospital and that blood had to disappear.

Then came the call from his "team." Nothing worthwhile had been found in the apartment of Sharon Jackson. Everett, the smarter of the two, had gone inside leaving the other to stand lookout. Although he couldn't get past the passwords on her computer, he had located her bank statement. Not much there. Certainly nothing to suggest payoffs in return for spying on Durbane. Maybe she really was an archeologist. Then why hadn't she gone to the Haitian or the American authorities after those fools had tried to shoot her in the cave? The only explanation--she had something to hide. And speaking of fools. His team had let themselves be spotted. They escaped only after blowing her airbag.

One loose end had become many. He tapped a while. Walker would have to be updated.

Chapter 15

Some people never give unfinished business a second thought, but that was not the case with Brian. Any details left dangling would surface and resurface in his mind, not so much as an obsession but as items on a to-do list, a list that must periodically be reviewed until all tasks were accomplished.

Early on in medical school Brian realized he had another special mental-processing skill. His brain sometimes seemed to continue studying a problem subliminally. On more than one occasion he'd been unable to solve a problem one day, but by the next, the answer was often apparent.

Sharon Jackson presented one such unsolved mystery, but at the moment, he still had no explanation for her unusual blood problem. He was still considering various tests to order on the remaining blood samples when he recalled the laboratory supervisor. Now there was a character. His mind ran through a potential list of occupations she might have enjoyed in past eras, ranging from whip hand on a slave galleon to a Nazi oberlieutenant. He had just completed his mental picture of a dumpy, middle-aged female wearing a black leather body suit, fishnet stockings, swastika armband, and holding a many-tailed whip when his beeper went off.

The message read: 555-6154 - *level of response: urgent* – *13:58.* By the end of his first week at Beauvoir Memorial that number had been committed to memory. Brian pulled out his personal phone and called the emergency room.

"A Sharon Jackson," said the E.R. nurse. "Motor vehicle accident and laceration. William Penfield is her doctor, but you're down to take his calls."

The emergency room was located on the opposite side of the hospital. Even though the nurse said that Jackson was stable, that the E.R. physician on duty had already taken a look at her injury, and that the police were interviewing her, Brian still made the trip in record time.

The clerk directed him to Trauma 4. Sharon lay on the treatment table in the center of the room. A nurse was seated at the small table that folded out of the wall, making chart entries. A city patrolman stood near the gurney asking questions.

"Excuse me," Brian said as he stepped past the officer to reach his patient. A moistened gauze pad lay on Sharon's temple. It was stained red.

Brian quickly assessed her appearance. Her skin still had that alabaster cast to it, but despite her new injury she did not appear as pale as yesterday.

"Are you all right?"

"I guess," she said, her voice quaking slightly.

The E.R. nurse proceeded with her report to Brian. "Dr. Thomas has already checked her. Some blood work has been drawn and should be back soon. The wound is relatively superficial but will need to be sutured, and Dr. Thomas is now tied up with a gunshot wound. Since you are covering for Dr. Penfield, do you want to suture it?"

Brian indicated that he would, then turned again to Sharon. "What happened?"

She turned her head to look at him more directly and immediately winced with pain. "I--got rammed," said Sharon meekly, cowed by her recent experience.

"What?"

"I caught somebody at my apartment."

"I don't follow," said Brian, his face twisted with incredulity.

When Sharon offered nothing more, Brian looked first to the nurse, then to the patrolman.

"She came back to find a man, apparently a burglar she'd interrupted, leaving her apartment. The guy had a lookout. They took off in a car. Your patient, trying to be a hero--"

"Heroine," corrected the nurse.

"Anyway, chased after them and almost caught them. That is until they threw their car into reverse, ramming her and blowing her airbag." The policeman shook his head in loathsome regard. "That's one of the latest tricks they use against us. At most the bad guy gets a dented bumper and can still get away while the poor cop is out of it until his head clears."

"That's incredible," said Brian studying Sharon and again wondering that there seemed to be a lot more to her than met the eye. "A burglary, in broad daylight."

"Happens more often than you think," said the patrolman. "People are at work in the daytime, their homes unoccupied. At least we presume it was a burglary. A detective team is already there." He nodded toward Sharon. "With her permission, of course, they got a key from the manager. So far nothing in the apartment appears to have been disturbed." Switching his attention back to Sharon, he added, "You'll need to check everything carefully yourself, though, and let us know if anything is missing."

Brian didn't know what to think. Did this beautiful woman somehow attract danger, or was she just the victim of a stupendous run of bad luck?

He looked again at Sharon. She did not appear seriously injured, mostly scared and shaken up. He wanted to put her at ease before he began the suture job, and one way to do that was with a little joke, variations of which he'd used on multiple occasions. "You sure lead a dangerous life," he said, shaking his head in mock dismay, "First Haiti, then here. If I see you coming, I'm going to run for cover."

"How's that?" said the cop. "Something happen in Haiti?"

"No," said Sharon hastily. "Nothing of any consequence--a minor scuba diving injury. Dr. Richards treated me for my injuries."

Brian watched her closely. She quickly rose from her reclining position even though the effort caused her discomfort. She was now supporting herself on one arm, anxiously returning his gaze.

"So, you were out of the country recently," said the policeman.

"Yes, but I go all the time. It's my work. I told you, I'm an archaeologist. I had just gotten back home."

The cop at first appeared to be disgruntled that perhaps a vital piece of information had been kept from him. But gradually a satisfied smile crossed his face, as if a problem that had been troubling him was now solved. "Well, that would fit in with a burglary. An unoccupied apartment is more easily spotted than you think. You just got back at the wrong time."

Sharon seemed visibly relieved at the explanation. She shifted back to a reclining position on the exam table.

"Sorry, officer, but I need to get to work here," said Brian.

"Sure, doc," said the cop. "I've got most of what I need." He handed a card to the emergency room nurse, who clipped it to the chart. "There's my number, Miss Jackson. Give me a call tomorrow. I may have some follow-up questions. It's probably safe enough to go to your apartment for a few things when you leave here--we have some officers there checking for prints and interviewing neighbors--but after that you probably ought to stay someplace else until you get the locks changed. And I suggest you get a security system installed, too."

"I will. Thanks," said Sharon as the policeman left.

Brian slipped on a pair of disposable gloves. "Now, let me take a good look at that," he said, his voice filled with concern. He studied the wound in detail, then announced, "Dr. Thomas is right. You won't have to go to the O.R. We can stitch you up right here, that is if you can put up with a few injections."

"Go ahead, Dr. Richards, if it will get me out of this place any quicker. I've had more than enough of hospitals" She cut her lively blue eyes and gave a quick smile. "But I guess you already know that."

"I would say you've made that pretty plain," he said, returning the smile.

He gently turned Sharon's head and motioned to the nurse who stepped forward to paint the wound with antiseptic. Sharon winced, but made no other movement. The nurse wheeled a mayo stand close by and began arranging a suture tray.

"Do you want me to stay and help, doctor?" asked the nurse as soon as her preparations were complete. "If not, I've got plenty to do."

"Uh, no. That's fine to leave. Just give me plenty of suture, mostly 5-0 nylon, and stay within earshot in case I need something else."

"Yes, sir, and I'll check back."

Usually Brian preferred to have a nurse stay in the room. Invariably something else is needed as soon as sterile gloves are donned. So why had he sent her away? Did he want to be alone with Sharon Jackson because of the attraction he felt, or because he wanted to find the answer to a medical mystery?

Brian draped the side of Sharon's face, gave the universal preamble of, "This may sting a little," and began injecting local anesthetic. She grimaced as the needle went in, but soon Brian was able to begin suturing. As he bent close to work, his face was only inches from hers. He could see her nose and one closed eye, the one that had the dark halo of a bruise around it, now only partly disguised by make-up. It gave her the pugnacious appearance of the pretty tomboy next door. He also caught a hint of a pleasant smell that was decidedly not boyish, and, although not perfume, was something more subtle, like powder.

Brian's hands moved with steadiness and skill, but all the while his mind was racing. What was going on with this woman? The blood abnormality was only part of the riddle. Now she had become the victim of a burglary followed by a car collision escape. She had been seriously injured in a diving incident, yet she had told the police officer it was minor.

84

"Sharon, something puzzles me--" For the first time he had called her by her first name, and she did not seem put-off by the familiarity. "Actually, more than one thing puzzles me, but for starters, why did you tell the cop it was only a minor accident in Haiti? You know it could have killed you. And apparently you never even mentioned to him that you had recently been out of the country until I brought it up."

There was a long silence before she spoke. "I--I just don't want to talk about that place."

"I don't understand. Why not?"

"I just don't want any attention drawn to my having been to Haiti."

"Why not? You said you go there often."

"Well, this time was different."

Brian had been seated on a stool, elbows resting on the stretcher to steady his hands while he placed the delicate sutures. Now he leaned back and held his gloved hands together while he studied his patient. "I get the distinct feeling your amnesia has cleared up remarkably since yesterday."

She turned her head so sharply, an instrument resting on the drape slid to the floor with a clatter. "Dr. Richards--"

"Brian," he insisted.

"Brian, I need your assurance that you won't say anything about this. "About what?"

Brian watched her jaw tighten. "My work in the Caribbean. I made a discovery, a very important one, I think, and if I don't keep it secret, at least for now, it most probably will be stolen."

"What kind of discovery?"

"I don't want to talk about it right now," she said, her voice now unmistakably edged with anger. "I just want your cooperation--your promise to give me some time to work this out."

"Okay, relax," he said reassuringly.

"Everything all right, Dr. Richards?" asked the nurse as she reentered the room. "Looks like you dropped your needle holder. Want another one?"

"Just getting clumsy in my old age. No, I'm about finished here," he said as he removed the drape and applied a square of gauze to cover the wound.

The nurse picked up the chart and poised her pen to make an entry. "Are you going to follow-up with Miss Jackson yourself or have her see Dr. Penfield?"

Brian looked to Sharon for some indication of how she wanted it handled.

"I'd like to see you, Dr. Richards."

Brian struggled to maintain his professional composure, but the warm feeling that poured through him made that difficult. "Fine," he said. "Thursday."

Chapter 16

Brian's sojurn to the emergency room to sew up Sharon Jackson had put him late getting to the office. Although the day had started with his appointment schedule only two-thirds full--actually a good testimony to his abilities as a new surgeon less than one year into private practice, still he was on call not only for Dr. Penfield's patients but his own group of six surgeons as well. Walk-ins and another trip to the E.R. to evaluate an acute abdomen case conspired to not only fill in the empty time slots but left him finishing one hour behind schedule.

Brian was the last to leave the office. He was locking the door when his pager went off: *operator 555-8000 - level of response: urgent - 17:22.* An outside call. At least it wasn't the emergency room. A call from the E.R. always meant more work. He decided to answer the message from his car on his way home.

"A Dr. Sharon Jackson," said the operator and gave him her number. He rapidly dialed it.

Twenty minutes later, Brian arrived at the address Sharon had given him. He thought back to her call a short while earlier when she told him her neck started bleeding after she accidentally jarred the dressing. With his phone advice of applying another gauze pad and constant pressure, it promptly stopped. From her description of the amount of blood loss, it didn't sound like there was a problem from that either. When she had first been admitted to the hospital two days ago her blood count had been abysmally low, a hematocrit of nineteen. But today in the emergency room, and despite blood loss from the neck wound, it had climbed to twenty-four. Her blood volume was rapidly replenishing itself, and it didn't sound like she had lost much from this episode. So, if there was no problem, why was he going to personally check up on her? Was he determined to take no chances or did he simply want to see her--or maybe a little of both?

Brian rang the doorbell.

Sharon let him in, explaining that the apartment belonged to Darcy, the friend he had met at the hospital. She had now gone back to Europe for a few days to supervise her graduate students at a dig.

Seeing Sharon in a domestic instead of medical environment blurred still further Brian's opinion of their relationship--she was both an attractive woman *and* a patient. Sharon was dressed in faded blue jeans and a yellow blouse with bloodstains on the collar. Before she had seemed a diminutive powerhouse, albeit somewhat challenged by the predicaments she had been in. But now she looked petite, a bit bedraggled, and vulnerable in way that brought out his every protective instinct.

"I probably shouldn't have called you," she apologized as she led him to the small living room. "But I wasn't sure whether it would keep bleeding through the night."

"I'm glad you did."

"You make a lot of house calls?" she asked, a bit of flirtatious probing in her voice.

"For special cases," he returned in kind. He checked the bandage on her neck. "It hasn't bled through."

"No, and it was probably my own doing that started it. The dried blood on my neck was gross." She crinkled her cutely upturned nurse, a maneuver Brian found particularly appealing. "And I was trying to wash it off."

"Well, let me take a peek, and I'll clean you up in the process. If it starts bleeding, I ought to be able to stop it--after all, that's what I do for a living." He was pleased to see her smile at his little joke. He then rattled off the supplies he needed and she went to scout them out in Darcy's medicine cabinet.

Sharon returned from the bathroom with the top two buttons of her blouse unfastened and the collar rolled in. Brian sat her on a kitchen stool while he used hydrogen peroxide to gently cleanse the wound. His eyes briefly drifted downward to her open shirtfront, but he forced them back to his work. Soon he announced. "That ought to take care of it." He stepped back to admire the completed work.

"Thanks for everything, both here and at the hospital," she said.

"Glad to help," said Brian. "But I don't want to have to keep bailing you out this way. We have to find a way to keep you safe," he teased, "or sooner or later something's going to get you."

This time she didn't like the joke. She rapidly stood; her face flashed anger. "Don't worry, I won't ask for your help again. I'm a big girl, and I can handle whatever I need to. And I was raised to take care of myself." Her words were spoken with bravado, but her expression was a mixture of exhaustion, fear, and uncertainty.

"Hey, that's not how I meant it," Brian said softly. I don't mind helping you--I want to, and everybody needs help sometime." He reached out and softly clasped her upper arms to reassure her, and gently sat her back on the stool.

She gazed up at him, almost plaintively--it seemed a far cry from the independent woman she evidently tried so hard to be.

"I want to know what's going on," said Brian, his words filled with tender concern, his face creased with worry. "You were seriously injured in Haiti, yet you tried to avoid mentioning any of that to the police. You claimed you made some important discovery in Haiti that you want to keep secret. Now somebody supposedly burglarizes your house. But that didn't sound like any routine burglary to me." Brian's grip on her shoulders unintentionally tightened. "Tell me. Please! What the hell is going on?"

She looked downward. "I--I don't exactly know, except that I think I need some help. Someone did try and kill me down there."

"What? And you don't know why. I find that hard to believe."

"It's true."

"Fine then. I'm not going to be a party to your death by stupidity. I'm reporting everything I know to the police." He made a move for the phone, but she grabbed his arm.

"No, Brian. Please. You promised!"

He turned slowly to face her. "Then you'd better explain. And you'd better start right now."

He could see her body sag slightly as the fight left her. She moved to the living room and sank into the couch. Brain followed and sat down next to her waiting.

"I--I do need your help," she said softly. "I've worked so hard, for so long. I can't have it all taken away from me now."

"I'd like to help you, Sharon," Brian said, "but I can't if I don't know what's going on or who's after you or why."

Brian reached to unroll the tucked-in collar of her blouse. She clutched his hand and drew it next to her cheek and held it there. Her skin was so unbelievably soft on the back of his hand.

Was he losing his mind--or his heart? He had never behaved this way with a patient before. The State Board of Medical Licensure had a way of expressing their displeasure over such unprofessional behavior, and if he didn't back away right now he might find himself with a year off to think

89

things over until he could get his license back. But he had done nothing--yet, and he pushed thoughts of the licensure board from his mind.

He noticed Sharon had a habit of biting her lower lip when thinking.

Finally she spoke. "Isn't there something about doctors keeping their patients' secrets?"

He nodded. "The Hippocratic Oath." He paused to search his memory. "Whatever I may see or hear in the lives of men which ought not to be spoken abroad, I will not divulge, as reckoning that all such should be kept secret." He smiled, pleased that he had remembered most of the relevant phrase. "Of course, in the two thousand years since that was written, laws and lawyers have added a few exceptions."

"I'm impressed," said Sharon.

"I got an A in oaths of all kinds. Do you want to hear me swear like a sailor?"

She laughed. "You're making me feel better, you know?" Then they both fell silent, she gazed into his eyes inclining almost imperceptibly toward him.

Taking the cue, Brian gave in to his longing, professional conduct be damned. He turned her chin upwards and kissed her, and then she was in his arms clinging to him.

It could have been an hour or only a minute, Brian couldn't tell, but it was still too soon when she pulled away. Sharon looked searchingly at his face. "If this is part of your treatment, I may need a second house call."

Visions of being guest of honor at a hearing of the State Board of Medical Licensure again jumped into his mind. "I'm not sure exactly how to handle this situation," he admitted.

"Do you have to handle every situation?"

Her question caught him off guard. He thought about it. "I suppose I do."

"Well, that could be a problem." A grave expression crossed her face. "Because I do, too."

They both laughed. Then Brian became serious once more. "You have to tell me what's going on, Sharon--the whole story."

Her merriment faded, and she let her hands drop into her lap. "This may take a while," she warned.

Brian leaned back indicating he had all the time in the world to listen.

Once again nibbling her lower lip, Sharon scooted to the edge of her cushion. Like a schoolgirl preparing to tell her closest friend a deep, dark secret. "I found Columbus' treasure."

A puzzled frown creased Brian's brow. "What are you talking about? Columbus who?"

"*The* Columbus--Christopher. You know, the one who sailed the ocean blue in fourteen hundred and ninety-two," she intoned.

Brian's frown dissolved into a cautious look he usually reserved only for hallucinating schizophrenics. "Maybe your head injury was more serious than I thought," he said.

She laughed again. "Sorry to disappoint you, but it's the truth. And I'm guessing the people who are after me might be from the Haitian government because they suspect I'm on to something of immense value."

"And they want to kill you for something they think you discovered?"

"I don't know," she said, her voice shrill with frustration. "I just don't know anything for sure."

Suddenly a low-pitched buzz sounded and the pager on Brian's belt began to vibrate violently. Brian punched the button and announced, "ER." He used the phone next to him to make the call. After listening for a moment, he said, "Well, that's a new one on me. Notify the OR and Anesthesia. I'm on my way."

"What is it?" asked Sharon.

"A man impaled on a tree stump," he said as he stood to go. "Sharon I have to hear your story, every crazy bit of it—but I can't do it now." He started for the door, then stopped when she called his name.

"Will I see you again?" she asked with uncharacteristic shyness.

"You can count on it," he answered. And he was out the door at a run.

Chapter 17

Admittedly, Brian was new to private practice, but that did not mean he was short on experience. Four years of college and four years of medical school had been only the beginning, like military boot camp. Then, came the real thing, a green lieutenant thrown into the trenches of big city medical warfare. He learned medicine by doing it, by watching, by reading, by going to lectures, and, in his spare time, by reading even more. When his sixth year of residency finally rolled around, he was a battlefield commander. When it came to medicine in general and surgery in particular, it seemed that he had seen almost everything. And what few things he hadn't run across, well, he had plenty of experience to fall back on.

But none of that had fully prepared him for what he saw when he stepped into OR 5 of Beauvoir Memorial. It was from a medieval torture. A young man, probably twenty, lay naked on the operating table with only a towel covering his groin. Arms were outstretched on arm boards and a tangle of lines fed IV fluids and blood into his pale body. The patient was already under anesthesia. An endotracheal tube protruded from his mouth and led to the anesthesia machine that was quietly cycling its ventilator. But none of that was unusual.

What caused him to stop and stare was a tree stump that protruded from the man's abdomen. It was old wood, like a homemade fence post that had been too long in the field, and looked to be eight inches in diameter and stuck upward a foot or more. The only good thing that Brian could see about the whole affair was his friend at the head of the table.

Dale Blevins spoke up. "He was in bad shape and a lot of pain. Didn't see any point in waiting on you." Dale cracked a grin. "Didn't think you'd want to take this splinter out in the ER. So, we rushed him up here so he'd be all ready for you."

"Thanks. Good job," said Brian as he moved to the operating table and began cautiously examining the wound. The timber protruded upward from the man's right mid-abdomen. Most of the victim's tee shirt had been cut away, but a ragged circle of bloodstained cloth remained where it had been pinned into his body. To all appearances this was some wretched victim of Vlad the Impaler, rescued only moments before death.

"Update me," commanded Brian.

"You ever been on the river and seen those fishing boats come flying by, you know light-weight fiberglass with a motor on the back big enough to propel an aircraft carrier?"

Brian only nodded.

"Well this guy was heading at full speed to his next fishing hole when either he looked off for a moment or lost control and hit the shore. He was catapulted up on the bank and skewered. The force of the impact broke off the old stump. Some other fishermen witnessed it. Fortunately one was an off duty fireman with a lot of emergency medical training. He knew better than to try and pull it out."

"Good thing," said Brian. His mind flashed back to an episode described to him by an old and experienced nurse. At the time of the incident she was working at a small west Texas hospital. A motorcyclist struck a chain link fence and the pipe that ran along the top went through his shoulder. The EMTs cut it off and brought the still skewered man to the nearest hospital. There was continued bleeding from around the pipe, the man's condition was rapidly deteriorating, and the hospital's only surgeon was tied up in the operating room. The doctor on call for the emergency room made the decision to pull it out so he could clamp off the bleeders. She told Brian that a fountain of blood six inches high followed it out. The pipe had torn through his Subclavian artery but had mostly compressed the vessel--until the pressure was removed. The doctor couldn't get deep in the chest to control the bleeder. The cyclist died and the doctor was sued.

"So how are you gonna get it out, old boy?" said Dale Blevins.

"Carefully, Dr. Blevins. Very carefully."

While washing his hands at the scrub sink Brian issued orders to the circulator. In addition to the basic laparotomy instrument tray, we need the large vascular set. From the direction of that stake and how firmly it seems seated, I think it must penetrate all the way into the retroperitoneal wall. The ER doc couldn't find any foot pulses even with the doppler. That means his aorta may be crushed. If so, it's a major vascular case."

After the surgical prep, Brian made his incision. It went from the rib margin to the pelvis. Gently he worked around the stake, cutting, tying, dissecting, always taking care not to dislodge it and risk an eruption of blood that would instantaneously exsanguinate.

Forty-five minutes into the procedure he announced. "Yeah, it's got his aorta pinched down like a garden hose under a car tire, and there's probably a hundred holes in it."

Dale Blevins had just walked back into the room. For a while he had left the anesthesia in the capable hands of the nurse anesthetist while he started another case down the hall. It was now 9:30 on a Friday night in New Orleans and the trauma cases were beginning to roll in.

"So it's going to be a big case?" Dale intoned, a hint of weariness in his voice.

"It was already a big one. Now it's going to be a long one," answered Brian. "I'm going to have to cross clamp the aorta, then get this timber out of him, then--" he was silent for a few moments while he probed inside the man's abdomen. His blood-coated surgical gloves pushed the intestines aside for a better look. "I'm sure I can't repair the aorta. It's too crushed. We'll have to put in a graft."

Everyone in the room had been in on those vascular cases before. The aorta was the vessel that carried all of the blood from the heart down to the rest of the body. An aortic graft was made of nylon mesh and had had to be sewed in with sutures strong enough to hold against the forceful pounding of the blood pressure, yet fine enough and close enough together that there was no leak. Magnifying lenses, skill, precision--and a lot of time were needed.

It was three-thirty in the morning when the last skin staple went in and Brian was able to peel off his gloves and flex his sweat-soaked and fatigued fingers. "I'm going to talk with the family, then I'm too tired to drive home. I'll just crash in the call room," he said to the circulating nurse who was, at the moment, involved in taping down the dressing on the patient's abdomen. "Sometimes I don't hear the beeper, so if I don't answer you'll still know where to find me."

"I hope they won't need us again tonight," said the circulator. A chorus of agreements rose from the anesthetist and the scrub nurse.

Two hours later, Brian was jangled alert by the bedside phone. "Time to get up and make a living, sleepy head."

Brian was in no mood for Dale Blevins' foolishness. "Damn it, Dale. Doesn't anybody ever sleep in this city."

"No rest for the wicked," continued Dale ignoring Brian's foul mood. "I'm down here in the ER getting someone else's case ready, but there's also one for you. Gun shot wound to the chest. A burglar had the double misfortune to be both noisy and to choose to enter the home of one of our well-armed citizens."

"Shit!" Brian rubbed his eyes. "You said something about making a living--burglars now got insurance?"

"Of course not. But, he'll probably sue the homeowner for shooting him, then maybe we can get a piece of that action."

Brian dropped the phone on the hook and slowly got to his feet.

The burglar was a drug addict--they all are. And Brian took great care during surgery not to nick himself or the nurse since they usually carry the hepatitis virus and occasionally AIDS. So it was midmorning when he finally finished sewing up the nick in the guy's Pulmonary artery and inserting a chest tube.

While waiting on the elevator Brian thought of Sharon and her blood situation. Well, he had the rest of the day off and could sleep later. He might as well swing by the lab and see if they had gotten any results back on the blood sent out to a reference laboratory. He hoped to avoid the lab director.

Like the burglar he had just finished operating on, he was unlucky. He immediately ran into the lab director, but this time it was a more contrite Emma Wilson that he faced.

"Her blood sample is gone."

"Sent off?" asked Brian even though he suspected that wasn't what she meant.

"Gone. Missing."

"How did that happen?"

"I don't know," said the lab director shaking her head with dismay. "I found it missing yesterday. I had been keeping a close eye on it, since the Jackson blood was getting so much attention."

"What do you mean?"

"Shortly after you wanted some of it sent out, Mrs. Leathers came and requested the samples herself to send off to have it tested."

"That's unusual," said Brian.

"I wouldn't release the blood. Only the Chief of Pathology can authorize that."

"So it was stolen?"

"I interviewed every employee that had been on duty since it came in. No one admits to taking it, and no unauthorized personnel were seen near the clinical refrigerator."

"Someone has to be lying?"

"Maybe," said Mrs. Wilson, "but there is one other possibility. There is always someone in the lab--except for a short while yesterday. Every laboratory employee was required to attend a meeting with the administrator. It was about that mix-up on the cross match with your other patient Maxwell Moore. Mr. Fendley wanted to personally impress on everyone the gravity of that problem and insure that it never happened again." Mrs. Wilson lapsed into reflective silence for a moment, then continued. "The entire laboratory was unattended. I suppose the Jackson sample could have been taken then."

"Did any of the blood get sent off to the reference lab?"

"No. I was going to do it later."

The crestfallen expression on the lab director's face told Brian that she was undergoing her own private rebuke. There was no point in him adding to it. "I need some vacuum tubes and a phlebotomy set," he said.

Chapter 18

"Good shot," said Thurston Walker. Clarence Durbane's ball sailed two hundred yards in the air, easily cleared the water hazard, and landed on solid ground to roll an additional thirty yards. Of course, as chairman of the board of Durbane Pharmaceuticals and the only son of the late, great Theodore Durbane, the man had plenty of time to play golf. His official duties required him only to chair the directors meetings twice a year. The rest of Clarence's time was spent "protecting the company's interests," especially those that required his personal attention on the French Riviera. This suited Thurston Walker fine because it allowed him to run the company without interference.

Walker stepped into position, teed up his ball, and, waiting barely a second to fix his stance, took swing. With a metallic crack, the ball sailed over the water hazard. It came to rest twenty yards short of Clarence Durbane's shot--a respectable feat, considering the other man outweighed him by a hundred pounds. Apparently Durbane had enjoyed a lot of fine dining while in Europe, too.

Walker slid onto the cart seat and announced in a voice loud enough to reach their opponents, "Let's go, partner, and take some easy money from the Huns."

Sitting in the other cart was Adam Duncan, a CPA with an MBA in finance. He was in charge of accounting for Durbane Pharmaceuticals. Beside him was an older man, George Barclay. Barclay was the company's legal advisor.

Duncan, Barclay, and Karl Dietrich, along with Walker, comprised the usual Wednesday foursome. Walker liked to think of the group as his war council. These men were the ones he trusted for advice to guide the company in the right direction, *his* direction. But today since the chairman of the board was making one of his rare visits back to the home office, Clarence Durbane was invited in Dietrich's place.

The accountant and the lawyer were not ones to ignore the gauntlet their grinning opponents had tossed in their direction. "The only time I've been called *Hun* was by adoring females—and that's because they knew me so intimately they didn't have to be formal and say honey," said George Barclay.

"Let's go," said Walker to his cart partner. "We ought to associate with a classier group."

"A classier group wouldn't associate with *you*," came the response.

Walker floor-boarded he golf cart, and soon they were well separated from the other two men. When time came for his next shot, Walker chose his club with exaggerated care so he could pump Clarence Durbane.

"Well, are we going to get a new supply depot in Rome?" he asked, although frankly, he didn't give much of a shit whether they got a supply depot there or not. He was searching for some clue why Clarence had come back a week early for the board meeting and then spent much of his time in his usually unoccupied office going over books and making phone calls. "Or is there something else?" He peered at the son of Theodore Durbane.

"We'll get the supply depot, and there is something else," said Clarence.

"Oh?"

"My presentation at the board meeting will be different this time, and I don't think you're going to like it."

"I see," said Walker, his voice growing cold. "Why don't you just try me right now?"

"All right, there's concern about our expenses," said Clarence Durbane carefully. "Deep concern. Our debt-to-equity ratio is approaching the highest in the industry. Some fear that if there's anymore encroachment on our profits by managed care, the company won't be able to meet its interest payments. On top of that nobody quite knows where all the money goes."

Walker had no ready response. Never in his life had it been necessary to engage in a substantive discussion with Clarence Durbane. Maybe Clarence had paid more attention years ago in business school than Thurston had thought--or perhaps he had received a backbone transplant while he was overseas. "Is that strictly your opinion, Clarence, or do you have... supporters?"

"I do, and the 'supporters,' as you put it, were the ones who brought the problem to me."

"And just who might they be?"

"I don't think I should say," answered Durbane.

Walker rolled his club in his hand, as if examining the feel of the implement, while he pondered the situation. Usually the board of directors let him run the show without interference, but now it looked as if a meddling few wanted to change things. They were wise to remain anonymous. Although Walker knew he did not have the authority to dismiss another board member, he did have ways to *encourage* cooperation. They all had their golden parachutes: a base salary of six figures to continue for three years after they left the company, and a separation bonus of ten thousand shares of Durbane stock--certainly enough to cushion the blow of looking for another job, if any of them wanted to even bother. "We'll see how bold your backers are when it comes time to vote," Walker said somewhat smugly.

"There's talk of making the vote by secret ballot this time."

Walker, poised over his ball, swung with all his force. The tungsten filament alloy three wood, the acme of the club maker's art, struck the top of the ball, causing it to perform a ground loop followed by three short hops. The ball came to rest twenty yards away next to the trunk of an oak tree. He steeled himself against the whoops of joy from his opponents on the other side of the fairway.

"Son of a bitch," he said.

"Perhaps we should talk later." This time Durbane sounded smug.

"Goddamn club is nothing but an overpriced fly swatter," Walker grumbled, then slammed the club into the bag and threw himself behind the wheel. "Yeah, we'll talk later, but you don't need to worry about the company, Clarence. I've got plans, big plans. I haven't been able to update you before because you've been so busy with your overseas work and all." Walker almost choked as he said that, and then he lapsed into sullen silence for the six-second ride to his ball.

Walker forced other thoughts from his mind, then with focused gaze and firmly planted feet, he let swing. There was a resounding whack, and his ball lifted cleanly out from beneath the canopy of the tree to sail a hundred and ninety yards down the fairway and roll onto the green. Walker looked satisfied as the other golf cart came bouncing up.

"Not a bad shot," said George Barclay. "But it wasn't worth the wait."

* * * * *

Three hours later, eager attendants dressed in green knit shirts and color coordinated pants had pulled the golfers' bags off the carts, wiped the clubs clean, and hauled them to the locker room. The four men stood in a small knot in the parking lot.

"Clarence is going to catch me up on the latest from Europe," said Walker as he accompanied his comment with a dismissive wave.

101

The two men took the hint. George Barclay climbed into his Cadillac and left, and Adam Duncan followed in his Miata.

The country club bar was all dark paneling, cigar smoke, and elderly black men in white jackets serving cocktails. No money changed hands. Since the waiters knew all the members on sight, the patrons had no doubt that although their monthly bill would be exorbitant, it would be correct.

A small group of golfers was clustered around the bar watching television. The usual topic of club conversation was sports, with the perennial favorite being arguing the merits, or lack thereof, of the New Orleans Saints. But on this occasion everyone's attention was riveted on a golf tournament in progress. Walker and Durbane paused for a few moments to watch while one of the leaders made a long putt, then triumphantly sheathed his putter as if returning a sword to its scabbard.

The two men turned to the bar, placed their order, then Walker indicated an isolated table at the back of the room.

"Let me tell you where we can take this company," began Walker. "You know of Beauvoir Memorial Hospital here in town..." Clarence Durbane said nothing and Walker continued. "Lately it's been on shaky financial ground."

"It's always done a lot of business with us. Are you suggesting they're going to go under and stick us with a big debt of unpaid pharmaceuticals?"

"No," said Walker smiling slyly. "I've been considering Beauvoir for acquisition."

Durbane's face, normally plethoric anyway, assumed an even more violaceous color. "What do you mean *acquisition*, Thurston? We're in the pharmaceutical business."

"It's just something I've been looking at--we're doing a feasibility study. I was going to bring it up at the board meeting."

"You see, that's exactly the kind of thing I'm talking about--spending money rashly," exhorted Durbane. "When you're not out trying to buy hospitals we don't need, then you're funding research that has nothing to do with our drugs."

"All our research is pertinent," protested Walker.

"What about that stuff in England, that guy working on some kind of esoteric germ that's never infected more than a dozen people, and all of them were overseas. Why Thurston--why are we pouring funds into his research with no prospects of any gain to Durbane?"

Walker replied in carefully measured tones. "So, you do have your sources, don't you? Well, I wouldn't be so sure that research will prove fruitless. Prion-related disease may be the next medical frontier pharmaceuticals will have to deal with."

Conversation stopped for a moment while Walker received his vodka martini and Clarence a dry white wine. Then Walker leaned forward to press his case. "Look, Clarence, you have to spend money to make money. Anybody with your business acumen knows that. I have plans already in place to form an international consortium of pharmaceutical companies." Walker flushed with excitement. "We're going to be the largest manufacturer of medicines in the world, and the company name--your name--will become a household word."

Walker sat back to observe the effect of his pitch on Clarence Durbane. To his surprise, the fat son of a bitch seemed unimpressed.

"Thurston, I want my company to be the best, not the biggest. The Durbane reputation--"

"That's where you're wrong," Walker interrupted. "The biggest is the best. What people respect is power--power and money. I didn't get where I am by sitting around letting others take the lead, and I don't intend to let this company stagnate from a lack of nerve."

"Does that 'nerve' include marketing a drug that hasn't been adequately tested, a product that may well be dangerous? We've heard speculation that work is being done on such a drug, one not mentioned in our Drugs in Development report."

Walker frowned in angry surprise. "Just who is 'we,' Clarence?"

"I needn't tell you that."

"I see," said Walker, letting his tongue probe the inside of his cheek while he ran through a mental list of potential enemies. It didn't matter. He would ferret them out soon enough.

"Very well. Even though you won't answer my question, I'll answer yours. I cannot disclose the details of this new product yet because our competitors will attempt to reformulate it and market it themselves. But I can tell you," he said, his voice deep with fervor, "it is revolutionary. It will generate income beyond our wildest dreams. With this one product and the worldwide marketing consortium I'm putting together, Durbane Pharmaceuticals will be the single greatest factor influencing health care for decades to come."

Walker couldn't contain the pride he felt as he finished his pronouncement. He watched Clarence's face for the effect of his words, but the fat man's response was only a troubled frown.

"Sources close to new drug development say it has a troublesome side effect--a problem that's going to prevent its approval by the FDA."

"Just how do you know all this?" demanded Walker.

"Some of the board members keep a closer eye than you may think on the running of the company."

Walker had endured all he could tolerate. "Well, you sure as hell aren't one of them," he said so loudly that a couple of the TV watchers glanced at him. He stood, signaling the meeting was over.

Clarence Durbane remained in his seat. "That's where *you're* wrong. I'm prepared to take a managing role in the company to preserve its integrity, and my friends on the board will support me. Your policies, your borrowing, are going to put us in receivership, and I'm not about to let that happen."

"I am chief executive officer. *I* run this company," said Walker hotly.

Clarence waggled a stubby finger at Walker. "And I am the chairman of the board. Don't forget, you can be replaced by a majority vote. My father believed in quality and safety, Thurston, and I won't let you take Durbane out on a limb any further than you already have with your shady projects. Whatever this drug is, if it isn't safe, then we can't promote it. Cancel it, and let the researchers go."

"You have no idea how big this product could be."

"Very well. The board of directors meets Thursday, Thurston. I'll expect your resignation at that time. But don't worry," he added snidely, "you'll still have your golden parachute." With that Durbane heaved his bulk from the chair and stomped out of the bar.

Chapter 19

The building was one of the older ones at Tulane, imposing and built of gray stone with the intent to last centuries. Sharon walked briskly up the wide, white cement steps. It was Saturday and the summertime so none of the department offices were officially open. That suited her perfectly. She was still in turmoil over all that had happened and preferred not to have to talk to anyone. She was here only to check the mail in her departmental mailbox and then leave.

"Dr. Jackson."

So much for keeping a low profile she thought. She stopped and turned to see a black man rising from one of the benches to walk toward her. He was casually well-dressed, appeared aerobically fit, and looked like any of a thousand older students on campus who had come back to supplement their careers with more education.

"Yes?"

The man folded the newspaper that he had been reading. "Can I talk with you?" She hesitated. "It is very important," he added and gestured back to the bench. "And will only take a minute."

"I suppose," she said.

The man took his seat and, reluctantly, she followed.

"I'll come straight to the point, Dr. Jackson. I am aware of what happened in Haiti."

"What do you mean?"

His eyes narrowed. "What really happened."

Sharon felt a flash of fear that she had not experienced since the cave. "Just who are you?"

"I'm sorry. I can't say, but I can tell you that I represent some very important people who want to make it right with you."

She looked around. Where the hell were the campus security people when you need them? She managed to speak, forcing her voice not to quaver. "Go on."

"What happened was an accident. No ultimate harm done. We would not want any bad..." the man seemed to search for a word, "...publicity to come from this."

"Are you from Haiti, the government?"

The black man ignored her question. "I'm prepared to offer you some money--fifteen thousand dollars for your silence."

She stared at him, not really believing this was happening.

"And, if you agree not to come back to that area for three years... say another fifteen thousand dollars."

A thousand thoughts ran through her mind. The treasure, they wanted it. But that didn't seem right. The treasure was worth far more than that. If they knew it was there they would offer a lot more. Maybe they were just guessing or maybe it was something else entirely."

"I don't think so. My life's work is in that country."

"We're not asking you to quit, just postpone it for a while and keep silent in the process."

Sharon shook her head.

"Then, I must warn you *Miss* Jackson..." He hissed the word *Miss* as if to emphasize she was a single female and, by necessity, vulnerable. "The people I work for take this matter very seriously. I wouldn't want you to have another accident."

She stood abruptly. "You can't threaten me."

He stood too. "No threat, a business proposition. If you change your mind, run an ad in the personals of *The Times Picayune*, saying 'I've thought it over. Come back.' Sign it Sharon and give the number where you want to be reached." His eyes became thin slits. "I would advise you not to wait long." With that, the man turned and walked rapidly away.

Sharon stood there alone. She had lost all interest in checking for messages in her departmental mailbox.

Chapter 20

Maneuvering in midday traffic in New Orleans was like competing in the Indy 500, but with fewer rules. It was all Brian could do to concentrate on the road. The combined effects of an all-nighter of feverish activity and concern over Sharon's situation had left him with the alertness of a depressed zombie.

When they had last spoken--it seemed eons ago--Sharon said she wanted to see him again. He would have to call her, but he was tired, hungry, and dirty. A trip home to check on Cecil, then a shower and a few hours in the sack were essential to be at his best to deal with Sharon and her problems.

He was jerked to full attention when a rusty pickup abruptly switched into his lane. The other vehicle was so close he could easily read the sticker in the rear window: *JESUS LOVES YOU* including the fine print below it: *but I think you're an asshole.* It was rare for him to be cut off like that. His Honda was so battered-looking that most vehicles gave him a wide berth.

His infatuation with old cars had begun when he was a teen. He'd always been good with his hands, and he enjoyed the challenge of fixing machines that had broken down. That combination of skill and interest led him to occupy his spare time by rebuilding old cars. It was in high school biology class that he realized that the ultimate machine was the human body--and the ultimate challenge to understand it, and if broken, to fix it. From that point on, his career path was to medicine.

Nevertheless, he continued to enjoy working on old cars, and as a teenager, he found there was an added attraction in driving a clunker. His father owned the largest automobile dealership in Abilene. Brian could have had a new car every year if the elder Richards had been so imprudent. But his father, a self-made man, was not one to set his son on the road to becoming a wastrel, nor Brian one to openly flaunt the family finances. So, at a time when his companions were thumbing their nose at convention with scruffy beards, tattoos in generally inconspicuous places, or piercing various body parts, Brian, by nature a straight arrow, expressed his individuality by driving a clunker. Surprisingly, his parents didn't mind. His father, simply, and with a bemused smirk, requested that when Brian was at home he keep his car parked in back of the house lest the neighbors think they had fallen on hard times and, of necessity, taken in a down and out boarder.

Brian smiled, making a mental note to check in with his parents one day soon. He hadn't talked to them in the past couple of weeks.

A series of short rings snapped Brian out of his reverie. He scrambled for his white coat on the seat beside him, all the while struggling to keep the car steady as he searched one-handed through the pockets. After pulling out stethoscope, pens, notebook, and a pack of peanut butter crackers, he located his personal phone. "Hello?"

"Hi." The voice was Sharon's.

His heart sped up a dozen beats. "Hey!"

"You sound surprised to hear from me."

"I am, but I expected you to page me. How did you get this number?"

"Easy. I called your office and identified myself as Dr. Jackson."

"And they gave you the number without checking?"

"Sure. To get anywhere within the medical system just tell them you're a doctor, and doors instantly open. No one ever thinks to ask what kind of doctor you are."

"It's never worked that well for me," he said laughing.

When Sharon next spoke, all levity had left her voice. "I need to talk to you--in person. Can you come by?"

"Now? I've been up all night." He glanced down at his green scrub shirt that was covered with dark stains; some were blood, others were less readily identified. "And I'm sort of"--he searched for the appropriate term--"cruddy."

"I can't imagine you any worse than I am after a few days in the back country. So, *please* come by."

That *please* was all it took. Brian switched lanes so fast that the driver of a brand-new Cadillac had to slam on his brakes to avoid a ding that would likely have cost more to repair than the worth of Brian's entire vehicle. "I'm on my way," he said.

Chapter 21

Sharon answered the door. Brian's professional opinion was that she looked rested and her complexion now even hinted at a rosy glow; but the personal side of him would have pulled her into his arms if not for his disreputable state.

As if on cue, she eyed his rumpled and soiled scrub suit, then took in his wreck of a car parked behind him. With an exaggerated arching of the eyebrows, she opened the door wide.

"You look like something the cat dragged up," she announced.

"Thanks," he said, and came in.

Immediately Brian began peppering her with questions about her welfare, but she insisted he slow down, wash up, and get some food into him first.

After a beer and a good portion of the eighteen-inch pizza she provided, Brian announced that he was beginning to feel human again. He pushed himself back from the kitchenette bar. "So tell me, what's really going on?"

Sharon stood leaning against the sink, marveling at his appetite. "I'm not sure where to start," she replied.

"It seems there's any number of places: your burglar, apparently there was an attempt on your life in Haiti, something about Columbus' treasure. You pick where."

"Okay, the burglar. I'm not so sure he was one. At least, he didn't take anything."

"Then what was he doing?"

"I don't know, maybe checking up on me." She shivered. "And I had another visitor..."

"What do you mean?"

"Some man was waiting for me outside the department at Tulane. I guess he hadn't been able to trace me here to Darcy's. He said he was representing some important people, and he offered me money, a lot of it, to not tell what happened in Haiti--and to stay away from there."

"Because of that treasure? He wants it?"

"I don't know. I don't see how he could know I found anything."

Brian pushed the few mortal remains of his pizza away, then used his fingertips to knead his brow, as if that technique might help her comments make more sense. It didn't. "Jesus, Sharon, apparently somebody has tried to kill you. And you've got some blood condition the likes of which I have never seen. You claim to have discovered a treasure belonging to Christopher Columbus. On second thought, don't start anywhere. Begin at the first."

She hesitated, then pointed to the living room. "Let's go in there."

Brian chose an overstuffed easy chair decorated with large cabbage roses, intentionally keeping a distance to better concentrate on Sharon's revelations.

Sharon fiddled with the stereo, eventually settling on a quiet classical station. She turned around but remained silent, as if reluctant to part with a secret that had long been hers alone. Finally, as if casting off a weight, she went to a bookcase across the room. After a moment's search, she located the volume. "Darcy has some of the same textbooks I do," she said as she thumbed through it. "This will probably help," she said as she handed it to him. "Read this section."

Brian took the book from her, and Sharon seated herself on a large floor cushion. He used one finger to save the page while he turned the volume over to see the cover. *The Americas, Volume II,* by Anthony Tudwell Braxton. It looked to be thick, dry, and, without doubt, a required reference book for a graduate student in history.

The pages she had indicated looked well worn. He read: *Columbus was a devoutly religious man. He named the island Trinidad after the holy trinity. After obtaining fresh water, he sailed across the Gulf of Paria. The next landfall was on August 14, 1498, at Hispaniola*--he paused in his reading--"exactly where is Hispaniola?"

"It's the island that now consists of two countries, Haiti and The Dominican Republic," said Sharon.

Brian returned to his reading. *"The next landfall was on August 14, 1498, at Hispaniola. The governor, as well as the monarchy in Spain, were disappointed with the amount of gold he had obtained from the New World. Arriving in Santo Domingo, Columbus found that the colonists had revolted in his absence, and the new governor would not allow Columbus' crew to disembark. The small fleet set sail again, but they were unable to obtain adequate provisions for the transatlantic crossing, and, of necessity, returned to Santo Domingo four days later to bargain with the governor. Columbus was forced to agree to humiliating terms. Ultimately, Francisco de Bobadilla, the royal commissioner, placed Columbus in chains and returned him to Spain in October 1500.*

The narrative then continued on about a fourth voyage.

Brian yawned, his exhaustion catching up with him. "Interesting, but perhaps you could cut to the chase."

Sharon let out a small laugh. "I suppose you have to be into this sort of thing." She scooted to a more upright position. "My old professor, Dr. Sewell, was the one who really got me fascinated with Columbus. Dr. Sewell is dead now, but he took me on my first two field trips to the Caribbean. No one knows with certainty exactly what island Columbus first landed on when he discovered the New World, and that was Dr. Sewell's quest, to discover archeological evidence of that historic arrival. He never found it, but I continued his work, and, in some of my related reading, I found something else--missing days."

"Missing days?" Brian echoed.

"Yes. You see, those seafarers kept careful logs. They were modestly accurate in terms of latitude, and longitude was at most only an educated guess, but they never missed daily entries into the ship's log--weather pattern, current direction, water depth from soundings. Their survival depended on this record. It was their map back home."

Sharon's voice and manner grew more intense. "There are no journal records to be found from the time of Columbus' first run-in with the new governor of Hispaniola on August 14, 1498, until he returned four days later."

"Those old records are that complete?"

"Remarkably so. We think modern society has a bad case of bureaucracy, but I tell you it's nothing compared to the early days of European colonialism. No self-respecting administrator in the New World wanted the wrong conclusion drawn about how he was managing the king's affairs, especially when summary execution was the usual means of handling any misdeeds. So everybody covered themselves--and in writing."

Brian was now so caught up in the narrative that his enthusiasm matched hers. "Go on."

Sharon continued. "I'm not the only one who's noted missing records. Two subsequent accounts also make reference to missing ship's log entries on Columbus' flagship, but both scholars sadly assumed that they were just lost over the intervening years. But I think they were lost back then--and on purpose."

"Why?"

"To conceal where Columbus had been." Sharon shifted closer to him. "Columbus was absolutely compulsive about his journals. But on this particular voyage, poor record keeping was cited as one of his many shortcomings." Her sparkling blue eyes radiated her excitement. "Of course the main reason the governor was mad was that there wasn't enough gold."

"Hang on. I think I need another beer for the rest of this." He raced into the kitchen and returned in record time.

Sharon continued the story. "So, where could Columbus go for four days, when he knew the governor wanted his hide? And remember"--she pointed at the book--"he had been sailing around making stops in the New World for three months, *but* the administration was 'disappointed with the amount of gold.'"

"You think he had the treasure all along and stashed it somewhere?"

Her eyes danced with excitement. "I know he did. I want to show you something." With that she jumped up, disappeared into the bedroom and returned a moment later. She handed him a gold object.

Brian studied it. It was a necklace, and from it dangled a pendant the size of a large coin. On it was the carved image of a warrior wearing a headdress and holding what looked like an axe in one hand. The workmanship was less than perfect, yet its roughness was appealing. He had never seen anything like it. He looked up to see Sharon grinning broadly.

"That's from Columbus' hoard. I found where he hid it!"

"For real?" Brian asked in astonishment.

She nodded. "Or at least I'm pretty sure it was Columbus'. I found gold, gems, weapons, and what might even be the missing records from the ship's log! Wouldn't that be fantastic? Authentic documents from one of Columbus' voyages never before seen by the world. But I didn't have a chance to go through it, much less retrieve more than a handful before--" She stopped.

"Before the other attempt on your life--the one you didn't tell the cop about?"

"Yes," said Sharon looking downward somewhat guiltily.

"I had already suspected there was more to your diving 'accident' than you let on," Brian said. "With you, there's always more than meets the eye."

A puzzled expression flashed briefly across Sharon's face.

"But go on. Clear up that particular mystery for me."

She began haltingly to explain. "I'd found a cave that looked promising to explore. It's below sea level much of the time now, although exposed at low tide. A local guide, Armand, was with me, waiting while I made my dive in the cave's underground river. When I came up, two of the thugs who serve as provincial policemen were there." She covered her face for a few moments, shuddering. Then she dropped her hands and grimly continued. "They shot and killed Armand--" A sob escaped, Sharon paused for a moment, then continued. "And tried to shoot me too, but my scuba tank shielded me. I was knocked into the water. They threw something in after me. It exploded, and after that all I can remember are fragments. I was told some locals found me washed ashore and carried me to a nearby mission hospital. I was pretty much out of it for a couple of days, but a doctor there helped me, and as soon as I could travel, shipped me back to the States to-- and you know the rest." Her lips quivered; a series of sobs racked her body.

Brian leaned to put his put his arms around her. Her slim frame had grown rigid as she relived the terrible events. But he couldn't stop questioning her; for her protection, he had to get to the bottom of this. "Were those policemen trying to steal the treasure for themselves?" he asked.

She shook her head. "There's no way they could have known it was there." She raised both hands palm up in frustration and confusion. "The treasure had remained untouched behind a wall built centuries ago, and I had only just then discovered it. Sure, I had been searching for years, but as far as anyone knew, it was a routine, boring archeological investigation."

"So, if those policemen didn't know about the treasure, why were they there? Why try to kill you? It makes no sense."

"I don't know either. Except that those two had already been hounding me, telling me to stay in the city, away from this province. They said they couldn't 'protect' me out in the "provinces." And it's true, I was in a remote area that rarely sees any tourists. But there was no misunderstanding what they wanted." Sharon stared intently at Brian. "They were not interested in my welfare. Their only concern was to run me off. And when I wouldn't go..." Her voice trailed off and she shivered slightly.

"So," said Brian with even more insistence. "What were these men protecting?"

"I have no idea! The only thing out of the ordinary around there is that medical facility. The police seem to be especially zealous in keeping foreigners away from the place."

"What's so special about a medical facility?"

"Well, I think it's quite advanced for such a poverty-stricken area, and I've heard they do some research there. That same missionary doctor, Dr. Baptiste, runs it."

"You were there. Did you see anything suspicious, anything--nefarious going on?"

"No, people came and went, mostly patients. It seemed fairly normal, except maybe for being so well-equipped. Haiti is poor and there are shortages of everything--food, building materials, and I'm sure that especially goes for expensive medical supplies." She thought a moment. "And there was one other odd thing. Something the doctor said."

"What was his name again?"

"Baptiste. And he said he didn't allow those guards into his compound. Guards. That's exactly what he called them, not policemen."

"Guards, huh?" said Brian, also thinking. "So he has some control over them? But why would he save your life if he'd ordered them to get rid of you?"

"I know it makes no sense. Besides, Baptiste is a priest as well as a doctor. A very gentle man. Those other guys, they seem to be a law unto themselves."

Brian shook his head. This was all difficult to ponder, not at all like a nice easy, medical problem of life or death. "So, how do you explain what happened with your intruder yesterday? Do you think the killers, regardless of why they were after you in the first place, found out you were still alive and followed you to this country. Maybe their intent was to cover up their original deed by--" Brian paused. "I don't know, maybe threatening you, setting a trap to blackmail you, stealing any evidence you might have; only you surprised them before they could do it." Brian had to admit to himself, though, all that seemed pretty far-fetched.

"Well, something like that crossed my mind. But I got to wondering that maybe the guards, or the man yesterday, are acting under the orders of someone else."

"Like who?"

"Like somebody else who wants the treasure. Maybe somebody knew I was getting close."

"You said nobody knows about it!" exclaimed Brian, going through another ritual of brow massaging.

"I wonder now." She reached out to the table and picked up the gold necklace with the icon pendant. "Dr. Baptiste saw the few objects I brought out of the cave. He said that, as a priest, he was sworn to secrecy, and I trust him. But there are others who even if they don't know exactly what I'm working on, they may suspect."

Sharon rolled the object in her hand, examining it as if it might offer a clue. "For one, there's Dr. Ethel Stern, who works in the Virgin Islands. She's given me a lot of information about Columbus' presumed routes through the New World. And there's an expert in Mesoamerican antiquities in Mexico City who's been helpful to me for years. In fact, I e-mailed him a scan of this ornament as soon as I got home, before the intruder incident. Last night I used Darcy's computer to check back with him. He thinks the image is Tilequatyl."

"I knew I recognized it," Brian said dryly.

Sharon glared at him. "Don't be droll. This god was worshiped only in a small region of Central America, an area easily visited by Columbus, and civilization there disappeared shortly afterward, thanks probably to disease introduced by the Spaniards. So, that's still another reason I think there's a good chance what I found was Columbus' hoard. But it also means there's another person out there who knows I'm on to something. Of course, he didn't know about the necklace until after the intruder incident. And then there's Ethel Stern. She's at a dig in the Virgin Islands sponsored by the University of Texas, but she used to be here. She's been almost like a mother. I trust her with my life."

"This stuff you found--is it worth a huge fortune--huge enough to kill for?"

Sharon nodded. "Columbus' lost treasure—the value is incalculable." She paused, then continued, "And I thought I'd been very careful at keeping my real objective secret, so the world could have the treasure before it had a chance to get plundered. Even Darcy doesn't know exactly what I've been doing. But someone very curious, some other archaeologist in the same field, might have figured it out." Sharon became more animated as her line of reasoning started to make sense. "It wouldn't be that difficult to track me, I suppose. Once in Haiti I wasn't exactly hiding. And on each trip I narrowed my search area. Maybe some other researcher was watching, figured I was close, and decided it was time to take over and get the credit--or the goodies, for himself." She sighed.

"So you think this guy in Mexico City might be behind it?" said Brian.

"No, not necessarily. He's certainly a reputable authority, or I wouldn't have used him myself. But I was continually doing research, probably leaving a trail both by computer and in the library, if someone wanted to pursue it. I guess it could have been any one of a dozen people." She sighed again.

"Even Darcy?"

"I don't think so. She's my friend, remember? I kept her in the dark only so she wouldn't slip and inadvertently tell someone I couldn't trust."

Brian stood up. "Well, then it's time to go to the police. Let them run down the list of suspects."

"No!"

The vehemence of her response surprised him. "Why not?"

"Well, for one thing, the police are already involved, at least with that intruder."

"But they don't know about the first attack in Haiti, or about your theory of why all this is happening."

"And they're not going to. At least not until I can arrange to protect that treasure."

"What the hell do you mean? Just tell the authorities in Haiti where it is. They'll protect it."

"They're the ones it has to be protected from. Most of the officials on the island are totally corrupt. Or if not, they're just one step from it. One little jewel from that hoard would set a person up for life in that poor country."

"So what do you think you'll be able to accomplish?"

"I've given that problem a lot of thought. I'd love to bring the treasure out and get it promptly to a reputable institution for verification and cataloging, but I can't. Underwater salvage is difficult. It requires too much manpower and equipment to pull it off surreptitiously. But what I can do is go back in and get as much of the treasure as I need to prove it belonged to Columbus, like those documents I saw. Then I can go public with the find. No one would dare to pilfer it then."

Brian fought off the urge to simultaneously massage both his brow and the back of his neck. "Why not? Is Christopher Columbus' treasure off-limits to bad guys?"

"No, because the story would be too big then. The media attention would be unbelievable. Money and assistance would pour in as historians and archaeologists the world over converged on the discovery. I could immediately arrange a recovery expedition and go in with plenty of muscle as well as with the focus of world opinion on what we were doing."

"I don't know, Sharon. I still think we should go to the police with this." Brian leaned back wearily.

Sharon moved to sit beside him on the arm of his chair. "We already have. Even now they're investigating my intruder, and as for the murder attempt in Haiti, there's nothing they can do about that."

"Surely if the State Department--"

"Trust me. I know Haiti. Nothing will happen to those two unless some higher-up wants it to, and that's not likely. And in the meantime, the Columbus treasure, the archeological find of the century, would evaporate into thin air."

"I still think for your safety we ought to involve the authorities. I've just got a feeling there's more to this than some old pirate treasure."

"Christopher Columbus was hardly a pirate," She said indignantly.

"Oh, he merely borrowed those things from another civilization?" retorted Brian. He ignored her glare and continued. "Anyway, the connection of the treasure and the attempts on your life still seems tenuous to me, especially since the first attack came only minutes after you made your discovery. There's no way they could have been sure enough that you had found anything valuable to risk killing you off and loosing their trailblazer. I hate to say it, but maybe the attack and then the intruder were only coincidental after all." Brian paused, his brow wrinkled in concentration. "But if not, maybe it's something else entirely."

"Like what?"

"I don't know." It was his turn to be frustrated and confused. "Maybe your blood," he said almost haphazardly, mentally flailing about for answers. "That's another mystery that I need to check out."

"But you said I was getting over that problem--whatever it was."

"You are. Your blood is replenishing itself."

"So that problem is solved. Brian, I called you here because I wanted to see you again, but also because I... because I need you. I need you to keep quiet about this whole Haiti thing, and I need you to help me go there one more time."

117

"Sharon, you have lost your beautiful but obviously deranged mind, and if you're not careful, you're going to wind up losing your life!"

"Not if you help me. I've thought out every step." She made a grasping motion with her right hand. "In one swift move we can be there, make the retrieve, and get out." She dropped her hand to her lap, and waited, but Brian said nothing. Sadness filled her voice. "Then, if you can't help me, at least remain quiet about what I've told you and I'll go by myself."

He looked at the earnestness in her deep blue and beautiful eyes, and he knew she would do what she said--or die trying. Foolhardy as it might be, he couldn't possibly let her go alone. "Well, I'm overdue for a vacation, and now is as good a time as any to take it. My partners can cover for me." He sighed deeply, wondering if he had lost his mind--or maybe his heart. So, I'm all yours." He put on his most charming smile and hoped she took it all the ways he intended.

Sharon grinned broadly. "Great! Do you scuba dive?"

"Uh no, but I'm real good at carrying heavy stuff--you know, like gold, diamonds."

"Let me get you another beer--to celebrate, and I'll have one with you." Sharon leapt up, filled with excitement.

"One more will do just fine." He looked around the apartment. "But I'm about twenty-fours behind on my sleep. Do you think I could just crash here for a couple of hours? It doesn't take me long to get my stamina back."

"No problem," Sharon said as she disappeared. In a moment she returned to sit on the chair arm beside him. "Why the long face?" she asked as she handed him his beer. "We're going to take a trip to the Caribbean, discover treasure, and become famous."

"I was just thinking about something I said earlier--about you attracting trouble."

"And?" she said cautiously, her gaiety fading.

"There was another murder--your previous helper, Armand."

Reminded, Sharon's pretty features dissolved into grief as she began to cry.

Brian reached out and lowered her into his arms, cradling her with his body, cocking her, trying to ease all the sorrow and trauma and fear that was finally catching up with her. Gradually her sobs gave way to silent weeping. Her cheek pressed closely to his chest.

Then she turned her tear-stained face upward for his kiss. Her lips were desperate, hungry. Her breasts pushed into him. Brian felt her need, felt the same urgent need stirring in him, a primitive, deep, animal need.

Together they slid to the floor. Her hands were all over him, clutching madly, tugging at his clothes. His kisses moved greedily over her face, taking her salty tears, savoring the softness of her neck. It was all he could do to be mindful of her injuries as he nipped lightly at her throat, when he really wanted to devour her. She pushed him backward. Surprised, Brian feared he had hurt her. "Sharon, I'm sor--"

She took his head in both hands and whispered, "Don't talk." It took only moments for her to undo their buttons and belts, to rip off their clothes, and to throw them aside. Then she lay back again, pulling him to her.

Chapter 22

"It certainly looks better than the old version," said Thurston Walker as he held the IV fluid bag aloft and inspected it.

"Yes," agreed Diane Gilmore. "I think the appearance problem is solved. But since the gestation period of a rhesus monkey is six months, we have no idea whether the abortifacient property persists into primates. We have, however, been running it through rats and rabbits by the gallon, and there the spontaneous abortion rate has dropped from fifty to six and one-half percent."

"Excellent," said Walker. "Rush it to Baptiste."

"I'm making personal delivery of the first batch of the new formulation later today."

Usually Walker went to special pains to be courtly with Diane Gilmore, but this time his voice carried a stern edge. "Don't remind Baptiste about this abortion business. Such things worry him out of all proportion to the problem."

"He's well aware of that problem already, and he refuses to use U.B.S. in pregnant females except in life or death situations." A troubled frown crept across her face. "But even if we are lucky enough to solve the abortion problem, the aortic wall defect may persist."

The two were standing in the Quality Assurance laboratory, the site of final processing before a product was packaged for shipment. Gilmore had arranged for them to be alone, but Walker looked around anyway to insure no employees had come in unnoticed. "Aortic aneurysms?" he said with annoyance.

"Yes. If the proteoglycan abnormality persists in this new formulation, then some of the fetuses, those not aborted, will have the defect and will likely blow out their aortas at a later date."

"What do the animal studies show?"

"No help there. We found the abnormality only in human aborted fetuses, and only about one in twenty of those. If the new formulation induces fewer abortions, then we'll have fewer specimens to examine." Gilmore took on a pained expression. "Consequently, we may have saved a pregnant woman from death due to blood loss, and even avoided miscarriage, but the child she's carrying may be heading for an early death."

"Diane, are you just looking for things--"

"That's my job," she retorted, the flush of anger readily visible on her face beneath the delicately applied cosmetics.

"No, your job is to prepare reports for the FDA--reports that will get our drugs to market. Need I remind you of the healthy stock bonus you get for every product you shepherd to market? And that's the operative phrase--*to market!*"

"I am well aware of that," she said icily.

"Don't you want that house in the country?" Walker said in a more conciliatory tone. "Is your husband's new boat paid for?"

"Look, Thurston, don't pull that crap with me. You know we're getting a divorce, and you know I'm facing a lot of expenses."

"Then help U.B.S. along," he pleaded.

"I can't help along a bad product."

"It's not a bad product!"

"I know," she said, her voice growing quieter as she struggled to gain her composure. "I didn't mean that." Her back was turned, her hands braced on a counter. "It's a good product, a life-saving one. But it's got problems."

"Diane..." Walker reached out. He wanted to touch her. She was so unlike other women he had known, so much better, yet so unobtainable. Slowly, he placed a hand on her shoulder. She seemed not to notice.

"It has problems," she said resignedly, and she turned to face him. His hand dropped to his side. "But they can be overcome with more research, more changes--more time."

"Diane," Walker began cajoling, "you know we can't afford more delays, or we'll lose our competitive advantage. Lose everything. We already have plans to introduce U.B.S. into underdeveloped countries where AIDS and Hepatitis C epidemics render most blood unsafe for transfusion. Their national authorities will be a lot less picky than the FDA. And once the new medication is available--and successful--elsewhere, demand from both the public and medical sectors here will build, putting pressure on the FDA to expedite its approval. Never underestimate the American public's craving for a quick fix. Nor those deep-seated suspicions over the safety of our blood supply--" Walker stopped and smiled thoughtfully. "We might even tap into those groups opposed to blood transfusion on religious or moral principles."

"I know the plan," said Gilmore, "but it's predicated on the product being reasonably safe." A pained expression crossed her attractive face.

"The only way U.B.S. will hit the marketplace here without years of more research and testing is if there is some instantaneous and overwhelming demand for the substance, some public panic that will push it through the FDA regardless of its current side effects."

"Like an outbreak of prion-related disease?" Walker asked cautiously.

"Well, the thought crossed my mind," Diane said. "I know we've been funding Peter Obrien's research on prions."

"Yes, those undetectable little things that are neither viruses nor bacteria," said Walker. "We've been funding his project as a side issue with the thought that perhaps U.B.S. can be used in situations where there is concern about the safety of the blood supply because of possible prion infection."

"Yes," agreed Gilmore. "Many authorities in the infectious disease community fear prions may be the world's next biggest health threat. Not that we haven't had fits with Ebola virus, Hanta, and resistant T.B., and the like. Fortunately there's only been a few isolated outbreaks of prion disease in humans, like Britain's Mad Cow disease scare."

"But if a more widespread event did occur, then demand for U.B.S. would go ballistic," said Walker. "But that's not highly likely."

Yes, thank God," Diane said.

"Still," Walker mused aloud, "you never know. And we wouldn't want Durbane to be behind the eight ball in such an event--especially when we already have as excellent a product as U.B.S. just about ready to go. So, do what you can, Diane. This drug needs to be released--for everyone's benefit."

"I'll try, Thurston. That's all I can say. I'll try."

"Fine," Walker said, smiling appreciatively.

"As a matter of fact, I need to get to work on *our product* right now. The Gulfstream is supposed to leave"--she glanced at her watch, its rosette of small diamonds sparkling in the bright fluorescent lights—"in two hours. Oh," she added lowering her wrist. "I've been thinking that an ob-gyn doctor would be a great help at Doúbe. Since we need to identify whether the aneurysm problem will show up in the new formulation, while, at the same time, trying to avoid pregnant women, the number of abortus specimens available to be examined will be drastically reduced. But there will always be those pregnancies that slip by. Patient ignorance, false negative tests, or occasional life-threatening situations that need U.B.S. will see to that. So we'll need to make the most of any material we do get. An ob-gyn doctor in the compound would be helpful."

"I'll see what I can do."

On the walk back to his office Walker pondered the options... and the odds.

* * * * *

The physician trudged wearily across the compound, his fatigue due not so much to the nocturnal interruptions of nurses requiring his medical advice as to the loathsome necessity of resuming the discussion with his visitors from Stateside.

Dr. Baptiste went up the hospital steps, past the six treatment rooms, the nurses' work station, and the X-ray facility. Just outside the door to his office he spotted a syringe on the floor. One of the nurses must have dropped it. He bent to pick it up. At least this was a clean, linoleum-covered concrete floor, he reminded himself. Until two years ago it was old wood planks, with cracks big enough for Geckos to crawl through. He took his time disposing of the syringe, before proceeding on to his office. But when he finally stepped back into the room--they were still there.

He tried to ignore the man in black who sat quietly against the wall. Baptiste always tried to avoid him. Dr. Walker was not here today, but when he was, Baptiste sometimes thought of him as evil, although he knew that was not the case. Dr. Walker was not immoral, just amoral. This man however, the one they called Dietrich, Baptiste knew was the devil incarnate.

Baptiste apologized to the well-dressed woman in the room. "I'm sorry to keep you waiting, Dr. Gilmore, but a man was admitted last night with continual seizures, almost impossible to control. He just had another one which my nurses could not stop with my standing medication orders." Baptiste shook his head in dismay. "I am not sure what is wrong, and I fear I will never find out. It is doubtful the patient would survive the transfer to Port-au-Prince government hospital, even if they would take him."

Baptiste stole a glance at his desk. The plastic bag filled with clear intravenous fluid still lay exactly where Dr. Gilmore had placed it a short while before.

"That's quite understandable, Dr. Baptiste. I know your services are desperately needed here."

Baptiste needed no reminding of the miserable plight of the Haitian poor. He knew, better than anyone, that the people of this remote province were dependent on him and his small facility for their medical care and that if for some reason he lost his funding or source of supplies or government approval, then he could not continue to operate, and his people would be left without a doctor.

"You were telling me the formulation has been changed," Baptiste said, taking his seat behind his desk and looking at the plastic bag but not deigning to touch it.

"Chemically only in some minor ways, but aesthetically"--Dr. Gilmore smiled broadly--"our new formulation, producing a clear fluid, is a major advance. As you yourself have already observed, the milkiness of the old U.B.S. temporarily altered the patient's coloration, especially in massive transfusions, say after six units or more. The appearance was very noticeable in Caucasians, but in darker-skinned individuals"--she shook her head--"the effect was positively ghastly. That, of course, doesn't hurt anyone," she said, "and their natural color returns when the patient's own bone marrow replenishes his red blood cell mass. But that can take three weeks, and it doesn't make for a very pretty ad: a smiling face with a hue previously unseen on a human being."

Baptiste finally reached out to pick up the IV bag, hefting it slightly in his hand. "This fluid is clear, but after six units any patient is still going to look pale. If you are going to change the color why not make it red?" His brow wrinkled. "Or are you concerned about gaining approval from the American Food and Drug Administration? They are quite the stickler about any additives to medications that are not absolutely essential."

"No," said Dr. Gilmore emphatically. "That's not the reason. It would be easy enough to add an inert red colorizing agent, and I think we could talk that through the FDA. Our concern has to do with the planned marketing approach. We want to emphasize the difference between U.B.S. and human blood, and our advertising experts think that would be a lot easier if they don't look the same."

"I see." Baptiste had given no thought to visual appeal of the new product by either patient or physician. He thought only that if it was effective and saved lives, that would be enough. He placed the IV bag back on his desk. "You brought more?"

125

"Four cases--on the helicopter. The pilot is unloading them now. The rest should arrive by ground shipment from Port-au-Prince in a few days. The trucks will take back your supplies of the older formulation."

"Has anything else about it been... improved?" Baptiste asked slowly.

"What do you mean?" said Gilmore.

"The problem--the side effect—the... abortions."

"Dramatically so," she assured him. "But we are still advising against its use in pregnant females, except, of course, for life or death situations. Our research people continue to look at every aspect of that problem. The rhesus monkey studies, however, are not yet complete."

Dr. Baptiste kept his gaze on Dr. Gilmore. His patients--and he had lived here so long he now also thought of them as his people--needed the drugs, the equipment, and the money that this big rich American company could bring. It was not merely a matter of a better life; for many it was the difference between life or death. But where did he draw the line? When would he say the trade off was too much? "I am not talking about tests on monkeys. What about the other human studies?"

Dr. Gilmore seemed puzzled. "What studies?"

"The ones in Europe. Dr. Walker said U.B.S. had been used on volunteers there first."

Gilmore was slow to answer. Then, like someone struggling to remember the specifics of a lie, she replied. "Yes. Of course. It has been thoroughly tested there, as far as we can up to this stage."

Baptiste was not going to be put off this time. "Yes, but isn't this latest formulation being tried on volunteers first?"

Dr. Baptiste studied the face of this woman who was also a physician. Could he trust her? Did she hold the first maxim of medicine--*Primum non nocere; Above all, do no harm*--as sacred as he did? Or that company called Durbane, was it truly working for the betterment of the human race? Or was it instead a cabal, and it's employees all hand-maidens of the devil? He tried to keep his anger in check. He did not want to endanger his work here in Haiti, nor jeopardize the lives of his people--but he had to know. "You told me my people were not being experimented on. You told me the preliminary clinical trials had already been done. You told me the data from our cases was needed only for final approval to market your medication."

"Calm down, doctor. Clearly, you are working too hard lately. If you collapse from exhaustion, it will do no one good. Remember, your people

126

need you." Baptiste struggled to gain control of himself. "We realize how much there is for you to do here," Gilmore continued on in a soothing tone. Durbane is going to send you another physician to relieve you of the stress of dealing with every affliction that passes through your doors. He will be a highly trained man--an obstetrician."

The offer caught the physician by surprise. "That would be a help, but another general physician or a pediatrician would be much better. The women here have been having their babies for many years, rarely with medical assistance."

"Doctor, I can only do so much." Gilmore spread her palms up, her face a study in sincerity. "You know better than I how hard it is to get someone to come here, so far from anywhere. I have approval from Dr. Walker to hire an obstetrician for you." She gave a short laugh. "He, too, is concerned about this miscarriage problem that occurs in some patients."

"Some!" snorted Dr. Baptiste. "At least one-half of my pregnant patients have miscarried."

"That was the old formulation. We are all working to minimize that side effect, yet still get U.B.S. out to all the people who so desperately need it. Paying an obstetrician whatever it takes to get him here is a financial investment Dr. Walker is willing to make."

Baptiste looked about his office as if some of his books or, more likely, the crucifix hanging on the wall, might offer him the help he needed. "I guess any doctor would be of assistance," he said softly. "Thank you," he forced himself to add.

A few minutes later, Dr. Baptiste sat alone at his desk, his head in his hands. The sound of helicopter rotors turning up to speed easily penetrated the thin walls of his tropical clinic. Baptiste knew by now that each time the visitors left, he felt worse. It was like a visit to a prostitute--a need was fulfilled, but afterward there was a shameful feeling in its place. Today, had he done the right thing, the best for the most? Or had he once again sold out?

* * * * *

Inside the helicopter, Diane Gilmore buckled her seat belt, then slipped on the head set that allowed for conversation despite the noise of the rotors as they escalated up to take-off power. Dietrich, too, silently strapped himself in.

127

"How did your visit go, Dr. Gilmore?" asked the pilot.

"Okay," she said. "Except now we need to hire an ob-gyn doc to come to this godforsaken place. You don't happen to know of one who wants to relocate, do you?"

The pilot looked away from his engine controls to see if his passenger was kidding. Dr. Gilmore's wry smile gave him no clue. So he turned his attention back to the engine r.p.m. gauge.

"Well, no matter. Mr. Dietrich can get it done," she said. She glanced at him in the seat behind her. "You can handle anything Thurston Walker wants, can't you, Karl?" she said enigmatically.

Chapter 23

Brian washed the last of the shaving lather off his face. There were only two nicks on his chin, probably not too bad for shaving with a woman's razor. He smiled into the mirror as he thought about the night before.

He cracked open the bathroom door and looked at the bed. A pillow covered her head, but the tousled sheets revealed a shapely leg. He enjoyed the view for a moment before he spoke. "I've got to go."

Sharon groaned under the covers in response. "I thought you didn't have to see patients today. You were going to take a few days off, helping me get ready to leave."

"There's one patient I want to check on. He was stolen, and I've got to find out what happened to him."

"Stolen?" said the pillow-muffled voice.

"Yes, for all practical purposes. An insurance company spirited him away to another hospital.

"And you have to check on that now?"

Brian grinned. "Yes, now. But, there *is* something I'd like to do before I leave..."

"Oh?" she said in a voice that sounded both hopeful and not too surprised.

"I want to draw some blood."

"What?" Only one eye peeked out from beneath the pillow, but there was no mistaking the frown of displeasure.

"I brought some vacuum tubes from the hospital. I want to find out if you're still anemic."

"I feel fine, and anyway you're not going to see me until I've brushed my teeth and done my face."

He stepped to the bed and stood over her, hands on hips. "I'm a doctor. I've seen a lot of terrible things in my day."

"Well, count this one out, Buster," she said, pulling the pillow back over her face. "At least go make some coffee while I get up," she commanded.

Twenty minutes later, she wandered into the kitchenette where Brian sat eating a piece of toast. She wore a white terry cloth robe sashed at the waist, but with enough cleavage showing to cause him second thoughts about leaving right away.

She poured a cup of coffee and sipped it in silence. Brian was about to ask her what was wrong when she finally spoke.

"I--I enjoyed last night," she said slowly. "But I'm... confused."

"Me, too. That's why I think there has to be more to this than just someone after the treasure."

"No, that's not what I mean. What's confusing is--" She searched for words. "It's you being here."

"Why is that?" Brian said with surprise.

"I'm a big girl, but I don't generally sleep with men I've just met."

"I hope the hell not. And we haven't just met."

"But it's... it's more than that. I wasn't looking for a relationship right now. I've got my work to do. And this"--she waved her hand in the general direction that included not only Darcy's apartment but Brian as well--"it's so complicating."

Brian smarted from her comment, even though he realized it was not intended to hurt. The intensity of their coming together had stunned him, too. And Sharon had reason to feel far more vulnerable than he. No wonder she was confused. "Sharon, a lot of things happen that we don't intend--but not all of them are bad. From my standpoint, I wasn't looking for a relationship either. But I've never met anyone who's affected me the way you do. So, from where I stand, you could be the best accident that's ever happened in my life."

Sharon's face, still somewhat bruised, had been tight as she struggled with her emotions. Now she smiled. "Why, aren't you the romantic."

Brian beamed back. "Whether you wanted a relationship or not, you've got one now, and it's going to work. I'll see to that."

She took three steps to where he sat and leaned into him. Brian put his arms around her waist. She ran her fingers into his hair, then took her time smoothing it down. "You do have a way of changing a girl's mind," she said. Then her gaze fell on the syringe and purple-stoppered tubes lying on the counter. She moved away from him. "You were serious about the blood test."

"Absolutely. I need to get another sample for analysis before your body has totally replenished your blood supply."

"You don't get enough for that when I was in the hospital?

"Oh," said Brian. "I forgot to tell you. Your blood is missing from the hospital."

"They lost it?"

"I doubt it. I think somebody took it."

Sharon's brow wrinkled as she puzzled over the new information. "Why would somebody want it?"

"I'm not sure, but I think your blood condition may be the key to this. First, though, I've got to find out exactly what wrong with you."

"You don't think I had just lost blood due to my injuries?"

"No. For one thing, your blood profile wasn't typical of Thallasemia, Sickle, or a host of other anemias I'm familiar with. But, more strangely, your anemia was so unbelievably profound, yet you had virtually no symptoms, other than pallor and a little fatigue, to go along with it." He peered across the bar at her as if to reaffirm that she was the picture of good health. "I can't figure it out, and it's driving me nuts."

"I never did feel sick," Sharon agreed. "I felt like I'd ridden the inside of a washing machine on spin cycle, but never sick."

"I know. That's the strangest part." Brian continued to ponder the situation out loud. "I've been rolling this around in my mind. Your blood picture is most like that of someone who has been exposed to a toxin and is getting over it."

"A toxin?" Sharon repeated.

"Yes, for example: chemotherapy, radiation, certain chemicals. Maybe you came near something like that at that Haitian clinic." Brian's face brightened with a new idea. "Maybe they were doing some military research there, like CBW--chemical, bacteriological warfare. I thought our country had outlawed that research, but then, that isn't our country, is it. Maybe you were exposed."

Sharon nodded in an almost zombie-like fashion. "I guess I thought you were overreacting."

"Overreacting? Sharon, you were under-reacting. You were going to just ignore this whole thing and hope it would go away? I call that the ostrich-with-her-head-in-the-sand approach."

Sharon's eyes flashed. "I've had a few other things on my mind, like finding and keeping safe the discovery of the century, not to mention having to periodically dodge murderers and burglars."

Brian's second piece of toast, buttered but uneaten, lay limp in his hand. He replaced it on his plate, then stood placing his hands on her shoulders.

"Sharon, you mean a lot to me. And I'm going to make damn sure nothing happens to you."

Sharon drew back. "I don't need a man to take care of me," she said sharply.

""Hey, hold on a minute," Brian said, surprised at the outburst. "I didn't mean to imply that you couldn't." He drew her gently into his arms and urged, "Now, why don't you tell me what nerve I just touched?"

She slowly wilted as his kind words and soft embrace defused the anger. "I--I'm sorry. I know you didn't mean anything by it, but I guess all I've gone through lately has made me"--she thought for a moment--"overly sensitive."

The side of her face pressed against his chest. He felt a shudder run through her body. Brian spoke softly. "Something I've found, from practicing medicine and just talking with people, is that we're all sensitive on the inside. So, tell me what upset you--so I won't do it again."

Sharon was slow to answer, then, "I guess I take offense if someone assumes that, because I'm a woman, I can't take care of myself. I don't need anyone to 'help out' the little lady."

"Sorry, Sharon. I didn't mean anything like that. God knows you're about the most self-sufficient female I've ever met."

"I'll tell you something, Brian," Sharon said, her face still buried next to him. "My real father never would marry my mother. He left when I was a baby, so Mom always worked. Sometimes I would go for days seeing her only for an hour in the evening before I went to bed. So I know how to take care of myself."

"I don't doubt it for one second. You're a Ph.D. You're a college teacher. You go all over the world. You can scuba dive."

"I can shoot too," she added straightening up, her attitude visibly brighter. "Mom did marry and my stepdad owned a pawn shop. I loved hanging out there if nothing else was going on. And when I got a little older, he'd let me mind the store for short periods if he had to run out on some errand." Her face clouded over. "But he died when I was sixteen and life went back to the old way. Mom worked really hard to make sure I had what we needed. But there was no way she was going to be able to afford a college education. Since she didn't want me to wind living the way she did, she encouraged me to study. I did and I got good scholarships." She shrugged. "And here I am."

"I had it easy compared to you," admitted Brian. "My father built a successful automobile dealership in Abilene, so we had a big house, I suppose plenty of money, and everything that went along with that lifestyle. Sounds like the only thing our parents had in common was their values-- wanted their kids to study hard and find happiness and success, too. I could have joined my dad's business, but I wanted to do something else." He shrugged. "So here *I* am."

Sharon smiled. "You make it sound simple," she said. "But all those years of medical school and interning around the clock couldn't have been a piece of cake. I'd say *you're* pretty strong and self-sufficient, too." Suddenly she giggled.

"Something strike you as funny?" he asked, wondering if she had snapped under the stress.

"I saw your car when you drove up."

"Yeah?"

"You mentioned your dad?"

"Yeah?"

"He must really be mad at you if he couldn't give you a better car deal than that."

Brian laughed. "Believe it or not, this *was* the best deal--at least the best deal he had on his used-car lot at the time. I've always driven a clunker. I like to fix them up, when I have the time."

"I think that one still needs a little work."

"Yeah, when I visited Mom and Dad last month, they still insisted I park out back."

Sharon laughed.

"Feel better?"

"Yes," she said. "I have to admit that, despite your shortcomings"--she eyed the syringe and tubes--"and your obvious inclination to cut and poke people, you do make me feel better."

Brian followed her gaze. "I've got a friend I think may be able to help--a hematologist at L.S.U. Medical Center. She was one of my professors--the smartest one on the faculty. I want her to analyze your blood."

Sharon studied the medical implements suspiciously. "Are you any good at drawing blood? I've always seen nurses do that."

Brian grinned. "I'm the best."

"All right." She sighed. "Where do you want me?"

133

He indicated a stool at the counter. While Brian readied his venipuncture apparatus, Sharon took a thoughtful sip of coffee. "Can you come back tonight?" she asked.

"I will every night until I know you're safe--or you throw me out." His tone sobered. "I can't risk anything else happening to you. Before I leave we're going to call the police, arrange for you to have some protection, and let them find out who's after you."

She jerked her arm back, leaving him holding the rubber tourniquet. "No!"

"Don't be ridiculous, Sharon. People are trying to kill you."

She stood up. "What I told you last night was in the strictest confidence. The treasure I found in Haiti is the archeological find of the century. It needs to remain hidden until it can be salvaged and protected." Her chest heaved with passion. "I already told you about the corruption in that country. As soon as the site is known, it'll be raped. All those priceless items with their incredible history, scattered among every dishonest official who can get a piece of the action. That's why I have to be so secretive"--her fists were balled, her body rigid with resolve--"until I can arrange some protection for the treasure."

Brian slung the rubber tourniquet onto the counter. "Your life means a hell of a lot more to me than some ancient trinkets."

"I appreciate that, Brian," she said. "Really. But this is my life's work. Let me finish it." She reached out to touch his arm. "Help me finish it. And then we'll go to the police."

* * * * *

Brian slammed the door to his locker with such force that the metal frame bent and the combination lock fell to the floor. "What killed him? Moore had renal failure on top of everything else, but he was on dialysis and showed signs of improvement when he was transferred."

"All I can tell you is what I was told," explained Dale Blevins, as they stood alone in the surgery dressing room. "Since I was attending anesthesiologist, I was required to complete the report of an adverse reaction in the O.R., and for that, I needed to know Moore's status. He'd been sent to West Parish Hospital. Their medical records department had only a death certificate signed by a Dr. Abbas. I called him. At first he was reluctant to talk, but finally he loosened up and blamed it on pneumonia, generalized sepsis, massive trauma, and, of course, renal failure."

"Who the hell is this Dr. Abbas anyway?" demanded Brian.

"I gathered he was just some H.M.O. doc on duty the day Moore was transferred over to them."

Brian reached down and picked up the lock from the floor but the frame was bent so badly he had to push his knee into the door to get it to close. He gave a disgusted spin of the combination dial and said, "There's going to be hell to pay on this one, Dale. With Maxwell Moore they've finally gone too far. Someone's been out and out killed as a result of their goddamn *cost effective* policies."

Dale put a firm hand on Brian's shoulder. "You better hold on there, old buddy. Accusations like that can get you into deep trouble."

"If the man had received decent care, he would have lived."

"You don't know that, Brian."

"Oh, I think I can prove it. I'm going to go over Maxwell Moore's chart with a microscope. I'm going to graph every parameter, record every vital sign, and I know I can show that while he was very sick when he was here, he was steadily getting better--until they transferred him--a critical patient, and to a substandard hospital, at that."

"West Parish has a history of financial difficulties and it's smaller than Beauvoir, but that's a far cry from saying it's substandard. Besides, haven't you ever had a patient die before?"

"Of course."

"When you didn't expect it?"

"A few times," Brian reluctantly admitted.

"I rest my case. It's happened to everybody who treats sick people. You'll never prove anything against the hospital or the insurance company. You'll just wind up getting yourself kicked off this staff. Hell, the scuttlebutt in the doctors' lounge is that you're already slated to appear at the next credentials committee meeting."

"Don't worry. I can take care of myself."

"No other hospital will take you if you're forced out of here with a black mark on your record. Look, Brian, you've been working too hard. Take some time off. Get yourself collected," Dale pleaded.

Brian sighed. "That, you're right about. I've already called my office, and signed out for some vacation time."

Dale smiled with relief, and Brian headed out of the dressing room. Before the door could swing shut, Joel Brentstone, an orthopedic surgeon, came bursting through.

"Dale! The goddamn surgery schedule is running three hours behind! Can't you do something about it?"

"Surgeons!" exclaimed Dale and he stalked out the door toward the operating rooms.

Chapter 24

The sign on the door read *Medical Records*. Brian entered and went straight to the doctors' transcription room. In the center of the room were a dozen carrels, each complete with dictation equipment and an ample supply of pens. Over half were occupied as physicians and other hospital functionaries did their part to add to the growing volume of documentation that consumed more and more of the business of medical care.

Brian sought out one particularly friendly clerk. She was carrying a stack of charts that reached from her waist to her shoulders. "Hi, Becky."

"Hi, Dr. Richards." She looked surprised. "I didn't know you were coming, otherwise I would have had your charts ready for you."

"I need only one chart today."

She sighed with relief. "Let me get loose from these, and I'll be with you in a sec."

He followed her to her desk. As she unloaded the charts, the uppermost ones began to topple. He quickly reached out to halt the avalanche.

"Thanks," she said gratefully. "Now, what was the file you wanted?" she asked as she seated herself at the computer keyboard.

"Maxwell Moore," he said quietly, glancing at the carrels. Only the tops of a few heads showed above the partitions, and everyone seemed engrossed in the minutiae of their paperwork or engaged in muffled dictation.

Becky returned to her keyboard. "Middle initial?"

"J."

"Date of birth?"

"I don't have it, but his age was forty-five."

Becky made rapid entries into the computer while watching the screen. "There it is, chart number 276-582999. I'll go get it," she said as she made to leave her desk.

"On second thought, I do have another case I need to check on. Could you get me the chart on Sharon Jackson, too."

"Middle initial?"

Brian inwardly winced. He'd slept with the woman, yet he didn't know that. "Uh, I don't remember."

"Date of birth?"

"Sorry," said Brian, wincing again. Maybe he didn't know as much about her as he thought. "But she is around thirty years old."

"I'm coming up with nothing," Becky said.

"What do you mean?"

"See for yourself." The clerk pointed at the screen. "In the past we've had three Sharon Jackson's, one with birth date in 1999, one in 1946, and one in 1932."

"Maybe data processing hasn't had enough time to list her yet?" he said pointing to the computer screen. "She was discharged only three days ago, and spent just one night in the hospital."

"This is the central database. Her name would be entered immediately on admission."

Brian stared over the clerk's shoulder. A column of Jacksons filled the screen. Near the bottom were the three Sharons as Becky had said--none with birth dates even close. His mind quickly sifted through various explanations. Someone--or more than one someone--had tried to kill Sharon. Her back-up blood samples had disappeared, and now her name was nowhere to be found in the hospital central database. It was almost as if someone was trying to do away not only with her but also with all evidence of her existence--at least her existence here at Beauvoir. "How would you go about erasing a name from the computer?" he asked.

"It can't be done," said Becky as she swiveled around in her chair to look at him. "All the information that's entered is delete-proofed. We can make additions and corrections, all of which are documented, but we can't take data out." A grin crept across her face. "Otherwise employees would all delete their own hospital bills."

"Could someone higher up do it?"

"Well." She thought for a moment. "I'm sure Mr. Fendley, the administrator, has access to the delete codes, and Mr. Netherland, the chief financial officer, and maybe Mrs. Simmons, the head of computer services."

Brian's thoughts raced. "Let's just say for some reason the computer record of this person did get deleted. There's still a hospital chart. Could you find that woman's chart without its number?"

"As I said, I don't see why that would happen, but the charts of all discharged patients are brought to our inprocessing department, where they are checked for completeness." She grinned again. "That's where we catch all those orders you doctors call in and forget to countersign."

"Would you go check, Becky, just on the off chance?"

"For you, Dr. Richards, anything."

"And don't forget Maxwell Moore's."

"Sure," she said.

The wait seemed interminable. Brian paced about the room. His surgical training was his greatest problem-solving skill, and he knew the drill. First, the problem must be clearly identified; then there were always options to explore. In Sharon's case, there were two problems. A someone might be trying to eliminate her. B she had a blood disorder.

B was easier. Always take the easier first, and Brian had. As soon as he'd left her apartment this morning he'd driven to L.S.U. Medical Center and was waiting when Dr. Jeanette Edwards arrived at her office. She was surprised by his unexpected visit but glad to see her former student. Brian presented her with three tubes of blood and explained all he knew about Sharon's condition, taking care to leave out any references to discovered treasure or attempted murder.

The story had immediately intrigued his one-time professor. The scientist's first thought was that while Sharon was in Haiti she might have picked up some type of hematologic infestation, perhaps similar to Malaria. In that well-known condition the parasite lodges inside the victim's red blood cells, then ruptures out to infect many more cells. The cumulative destruction of red blood cells ultimately makes the patient anemic.

Brian had reiterated that even more confounding than the severe unexplained anemia was that the patient was otherwise healthy with no physical symptoms of the condition. By the time Brian had finished the story, Dr. Edwards was enthusiastic about exploring the medical mystery saying she had some time after her morning lecture and would be glad to test the blood samples on her personal laboratory equipment. When Brian had left for Beauvoir Memorial, she was holding one of the tubes to the ceiling light and slowly rotating it.

Now back to problem A. The more difficult one. The presumed-- attempted elimination--of one Dr. Sharon Jackson, archaeologist. The treasure provided the likeliest motive. Yet she had spoken to no one about it, except in veiled allusions to that missionary priest-physician and that was only after the murder attempt had already occurred. Were the murder attempt and the burglar incident coincidence? Or was Sharon's theory right? Had another researcher or treasure-seeker on the same trail figured it out and wanted to eliminate her as competition? But perhaps the treasure had nothing to do with it, and there was another reason.

"I'm not sure what's going on," said the returning Becky, breaking into his reverie.

"What's that?" said Brian, turning to face her.

"One of the girls who does records inprocessing remembers Mrs. Leathers asking for a chart about three days ago. She's not one hundred percent certain the patient name was Jackson, but she thought it might be. As you can imagine we get hundreds of requests a day, but that visit did stick in her mind because Mrs. Leathers is the director of nursing, and she never comes down here. If she needs something, she sends someone for it."

"Did Leathers take the chart?"

"The clerk didn't know. New charts are put on the rack by the door, and Mrs. Leathers said she would look herself." Becky stopped as she remembered her second mission. "Oh, and I can't find any chart for a Maxwell J. Moore either. It's like it was never brought here." She gestured with bewilderment. "We rarely have missing records. It's strange to have two in one day."

Brian knew what had happened: Leathers, Darrell Fendley's number one flunkey, had taken them. "Thanks, Becky." He grabbed her shoulders. "You've been a big help." Then he was gone, leaving Becky to stare wistfully after the retreating surgeon.

Too impatient to wait for the elevator, Brian took the stairs two at a time, and with each his fury rose. The dazzling smile of Fendley's personal secretary did nothing to defuse it.

"Well, it's Dr. Richards again. What can I do for you?"

"I need to see Fendley."

"Can I tell him what this visit is about?"

"Tell him it's about missing charts, a stolen patient, and one very pissed-off surgeon."

"I see," she said, and, remarkably, only the corners of her smile wavered. "I think I will let you tell him yourself." She picked up the telephone receiver, tapped a number, and spoke into the mouthpiece briefly. Then she looked up. "You may go right in, Dr. Richards."

Brian was familiar with the administrative sanctum sanctorum. During his tenure of less than a year in private practice, he had been here at least once a month. At first the visits were cordial--a suggestion on how the operating room could run more efficiently, requests for equipment he felt would improve the quality of medical care but which he couldn't get past purchase committees. As his pleadings on behalf of patient care went unheeded, his tolerance diminished.

On his most recent trip, sharp words had passed between him and Darrell Fendley when he complained that the hospital's two-tiered pricing structure for X-rays and laboratory tests was unfair. Outpatients had a variety of places they could go for X-rays or lab tests, so the hospital had to lower its prices to compete with these other facilities. An inpatient had no options. And the very same test performed inside the hospital cost three times as much if the patient were lying in bed rather than visiting the outpatient clinic. Mr. Fendley had argued that this reflected the overhead of providing care inside the hospital. Brian had acknowledged that some cost increases were understandable, but it was pure bullshit to charge three times more for the same test, not to mention two-dollar Band-aids and six-buck Tylenols.

"Good afternoon, Dr. Richards," said the administrator. With his short stature, bald head, and pinched face, he always struck Brian more as a penny-watching accountant than the caretaker of a sophisticated medical establishment.

"I'm not so sure it's good, Mr. Fendley," said Brian without ceremony. He sat without being invited. "I believe some patient records are missing, or I should say, *all* the records are missing for two of my patients."

The administrator looked puzzled. "Well, doctor, remember this is a large hospital, with four hundred and eighty beds. Occasional misplacements can occur."

"No, I don't think that'll fly. One of these *misplacements,* as you call it, was a patient file completely deleted from the hospital's central database. And not only are the computer records missing; but the patient chart is gone as well. And I have reason to believe your Mrs. Leathers is behind these particular *misplacements.*"

Fendley was on his feet. "I don't know who you think you are, Richards, but you can't come barging in here making unfounded accusations."

Brian laced his fingers and let his hands drop comfortably into his lap, enjoying, for the moment, Fendley's discomfiture. "Oh, there're not unfounded. Your Mrs. Leathers participated in the risky transfer of a critical patient solely for the hospital's financial benefit. You lost the gamble, and Maxwell Moore died." Brian felt like he was loosing control, but he didn't

141

care. This was too important. "No, I'm not going to let anyone else die as a result of your misguided policies. There may even be a cover-up here. The records on that patient, as well as another patient of mine, Dr. Sharon Jackson, cannot be located. And speaking of missing--Sharon Jackson's blood is missing, and Mrs. Leathers was down in the lab trying to get it. I think Dr. Penfield would like to know about all that. Jackson was his patient too. He swings a lot of weight with the medical staff."

For a moment Brian thought the man was coming for him, but the administrator, his face red and fists balled in rage, stalked across the expanse of his office to stop before the window that filled almost one entire wall of his office. Even seated across the room, Brian could see that the view was magnificent. In front of the hospital were vast green lawns and manicured shrubs, a man-made pond complete with elegant geyser, and a host of smaller brick and glass buildings that served the mother structure.

Brian watched the little man survey his fiefdom. Gradually the tight fists relaxed, and the administrator turned to face Brian.

Fendley strode to the credenza behind his desk and shuffled through a stack of cream-colored folders to select one. "This, Dr. Richards, is your missing chart on Maxwell J. Moore." He let it drop onto the edge of the desk, so that Brian could see that he spoke the truth. "Mrs. Leathers brought it to me for review. Indeed, we review the charts of any patients who have died within seventy-two hours of discharge. Although the quality assurance committee will make the final assessment, I have seen nothing in here that is the slightest bit improper."

The smile on Fendley's face was almost more than Brian could tolerate. The man continued. "As for the second patient, what was the name?"

"Dr. Sharon Jackson," Brian said through clenched teeth.

"I have never heard of that particular patient and have no idea about her chart. But you will have the opportunity to explain your concerns to others, because the next meeting of the credentials committee will be in one week, and the first item on the agenda will be whether to continue your staff privileges. Your constant agitation has reached the point where it is damaging to effective hospital routine." He paused to observe the effect of his words.

Brian gave him a gaze of intense hatred, but the cagey veteran of many a hospital battle maintained his composure.

"You see, doctor, it has also been brought to my attention that your performance in the operating room has been substandard of late."

"You'll never make that stick," said Brian.

"You may wish to avoid the unpleasant and inevitable outcome by resigning beforehand," Fendley continued. "It might save your reputation and enable you to find a position at some other, more tolerant and less exacting, institution.

This time Brian kept his anger in check. When he spoke, his voice was as steady as the crosshairs on a sharpshooter's telescopic sight and--he wished--just as deadly. "No, Mr. Fendley, I'll be there at the credentials committee meeting, but it is you who'd best come prepared to answer charges." With that, he stood and stalked out.

* * * * *

As soon as Brian left the room, the administrator returned to the window. The view always helped him put things in proper perspective. He was up here. They were all down there. After a period of reflection, Darrell Fendley returned to his desk, settled in his leather chair, and punched the intercom button "Hold any interruptions please, Kathy."

"Yes, sir."

He dialed a number from memory. An electronic voice advised him to be patient, as his call was being processed by satellite. After a short wait, the voice asked for a verification code. He punched in more numbers and was rewarded with a series of beeps that informed him the remote system had accepted his call. A voice, this time unquestionably human with its German accent, answered. "Yes?"

"Are we on scrambler?" asked the administrator.

"Of course," said the German.

"I think we may have found a contact with the girl. One of our younger surgeons claims to be her doctor and has expressed an interest in her records"

"His name?"

"Dr. Brian Richards."

"Gather what information you can on him and get back to me," the German directed.

143

Chapter 25

"Problems?" asked Dr. Thurston Walker as he placed his vodka martini in the holder in the Gulfstream's armrest.

Karl Dietrich had just closed his personal phone and was regarding it thoughtfully. His was one of the bulkier models. Not only did its thallium hydride battery have enough power to run for several days without recharging, but it could project its signal through the shielding of all but the thickest concrete and steel buildings to lock on to the nearest private communications satellite. Here at 40,000 feet, shielding was not a problem. But one other feature the phone boasted was useful enough to cause Dietrich and others with a need for privacy, to forego the usual models that were smaller than a deck of cards. And that was the scrambler circuit which generated a carrier wave of constantly changing frequency. With appropriate access codes this mobile unit could receive the signal of another scrambler-equipped phone without fear of interception.

"No problems, sir," Dietrich answered. "Actually, a solution may be at hand."

"Oh?"

"That woman traveler Baptiste treated and sent back to the U.S., the one we have been unable to locate..."

"Yes?" said Walker cautiously.

"A physician has surfaced, claiming to be her doctor now, and he seems to have taken a special interest in her case."

Walker took another sip of his drink, and rolled it slowly in his mouth as he thought. "Use the physician to find her, but beyond that, he's not the problem. A doctor can do nothing without the cooperation of his patient. She's the problem. She's a walking exposé of our research, and that we can't have, especially this soon."

"I know."

"Buy her off, intimidate her."

"We have tried, but without success--then she went underground."

"I know I can count on you, Karl. Do whatever it takes to keep this entire matter quiet."

"I will take care of it as soon as we land."

"But I can't spare you right now, Karl. This meeting is too important. I need you with me."

Dietrich nodded his understanding. "My best men will be on it, and if the problem is still there when we return, I will take care of it myself."

Thurston Walker smiled and raised his glass. He appreciated Karl's quiet efficiency. If Dietrich said he would solve it, the C.E.O. had no doubt the matter was as good as taken care of. He took a long pull, finishing his drink, then closed his eyes.

Dietrich reached up and punched a small button on the screen before them to change the display from the alphanumeric read-out to a Global Positioning System map. He always liked to know exactly where he was. At the moment the blinking cursor that was the Gulfstream was crawling across New Mexico. He settled back to watch their progress toward San Francisco.

* * * * *

Brian was so mad he kicked the side of his car. Then looked around, shamefaced. Not the way for a doctor to act, even though another dent made absolutely no difference to the resale value of this wreck, and kicking something sure as hell made him feel better.

It had been naive of him to think that Darrell Fendley, when confronted with evidence of his own malfeasance, would wag his tail sheepishly like a dog caught eating out of the baby's dish and promise never to do it again. No, Fendley was an experienced hospital in-fighter, a man who knew how to stack the deck in his favor.

Brian remembered Dale's warning. The administration would take a run at revoking his staff privileges. Was he foolish enough to think that being a good doctor would be all the defense he would need? No doubt Leathers, nurse from hell, would testify at the committee meeting that he had slandered her, and Fendley could probably dredge up a couple of doctors willing to say Brian had been derelict in some aspect of his performance. These days almost sixty percent of the physicians worked for the hospital, which meant the hospital signed their paychecks. Fendley would have no trouble coercing one or two of the younger, more vulnerable, hospital doctors to testify against him.

The administrator had a lot of tactics at his disposal. He could threaten, as he had done in Brian's case, or even reward a cooperating physician with a lucrative directorship of some department. In return, the physician could point out some error in judgment Brain had made in a particular situation. Medicine was complex enough that in many instances the proper course of action was controversial, and in critical situations, decisions had to be made immediately. Since Brian worked in trauma, some of his patients, not unexpectedly, died. So, there were plenty of cases to look at for "errors."

But he wasn't going to give up. Silence about critical issues affecting patient care was not something he would trade for the continuation of his hospital privileges. He hadn't gotten where he was by crumbling when the going got tough. He didn't go into an operation unprepared, and this battle wouldn't be any different.

An essential part of the preparation would be to marshal his forces. Dale Blevins would speak for him as would a few others, but what he needed was the power of William Penfield. That man was well-respected, independently wealthy even without his medical practice, and wouldn't shy from a fight with the administration if he thought it was in the best interests of his patients or the hospital. Penfield was due back tomorrow. Brian would just go ahead and give him a call so the man could get appropriately worked up before he arrives.

Suddenly his beeper went off. The display read: *Dr. Edwards via BMH operator −555-2612 - Level of response: routine − 15:20.* He unlocked the Honda's door and sat inside to make the call.

"I've never seen anything quite like this," said Brian's old mentor, Dr. Edwards, as soon as she recognized Brian's voice. "Most unusual."

"Is it neoplastic?" Brian stated the ultimate fear of every doctor and patient alike.

"Oh, no, nothing to suggest malignancy. And my original guess about parasitic infestation was wrong, too. I thought I might just show you my results if you care to come by."

The evening rush hour made the drive across New Orleans an exercise in frustration. Brian even called back to assure Dr. Edwards he was still coming. Eventually he reached her lab on the second floor of the research wing of L.S.U. Medical Center. Although he was a physician with a science major's background, he didn't recognize half the equipment that filled the room. Dr. Edwards' laboratory gave evidence of a lifetime dedicated to research. He knew there were medical investigators who would give a decade's worth of grant money to be able to work in her facility. A rare disease even carried the eponym of Edwards Lymphoma.

She handed him the printout from a standard blood profile autoanalyzer. "To start with, and to put your mind at ease, your patient is in no danger from her anemia."

Brian's eyes ran down the printout while she talked. The hematocrit leaped out at him: 27.

"You can see her hematocrit is twenty-seven, a vast improvement over the nineteen you said it was three days ago," Dr. Edwards continued.

Brian knew better than to ask if she had double-checked the autoanalyzer results. This woman left nothing to chance.

"So her bone marrow is in great shape, strong enough to pour out that many red blood cells in such a short time," he said.

"Exactly," responded Dr. Edwards. "Even without performing a bone marrow aspiration, we can feel sure she has no space-occupying lesions, such as metastatic cancer, within her blood-forming system. Secondly, if she had an iron or vitamin deficiency, such as folate or B-12, it would take longer than it has for her marrow to gear up and start pouring out the red cells." Dr. Edwards was running through her differential diagnosis, the list of possibilities that had to be proven or refuted. "Hemolytic anemia crossed my mind--maybe your patient had gotten exposed to some substance, an industrial chemical, for example, that caused her red blood cells to lyse. Of course she probably would have been sicker than you described, but I went ahead and checked anyway."

Brian moved to a stool while she talked, reminded of his medical school years and this woman's brilliant lectures.

The professor handed him more paper, this time a single continuous sheet folded to make a pile one-half inch thick. He unfolded it on the countertop to follow a squiggly blue line that worked its way the length of the paper. Below the line were cryptic symbols in the arcane lexicon of the chemist.

"You'll recognize the printout from the mass spectrometer."

Brian thumbed through the report. He had last seen one of these in biochemistry class. The blue mark jumped upward in several places. *Hgb*, hemoglobin; *O*, oxygen; and *Fe*, iron; they were all expected components of blood.

"Go to the very end," she said.

He did as instructed and there the line continued across its zero station past *Br*, bromine; *Cl*, chlorine; but at *F* it jumped to the top of the page. "Fluorine?" he asked.

Dr. Edwards smiled and nodded.

"Her blood contains fluorine?" Brian mentally ran through the possible sources of fluorine. "Has she been swallowing too much toothpaste?"

The professor laughed. "I wondered something similar, although the value is many times what you'd expect for that to be the cause. I actually thought she might have been intentionally ingesting sodium fluoride. Some people do that expecting to strengthen their teeth and bones. A more likely source of exposure is from areas where the drinking water is unusually high in that substance. Anyway, I prevailed upon a colleague down the hall who's the closest thing to an inorganic chemist that we've got."

"Was it a fluoride?"

"No, It's fluorine wrapped in some complex organic matrix. It'll take an analytical chemistry lab to carry the analysis further. I have two tubes left if you want me to send a sample out." She pointed to the purple-stoppered tubes in a metal rack. "That, of course, will take days, but I was sure you wanted to know something as soon as I had it."

Brian was crestfallen. She didn't have an answer yet, at least not a complete one. He reached out and picked up one of the tubes, studying it. Finally, he slipped it back into the rack next to the other and looked into the lined face of Dr. Edwards. "Are you telling me she's been poisoned?"

"No, I don't think so. Fluorine is not a recognized component of most toxins."

"If you have no ideas, then I guess we have no choice but to send it off to a reference lab and wait it out."

"I didn't say I had no more ideas." Her eyes danced with enthusiasm. "There is one other experiment--I've already done it, but I thought you'd appreciate the results more if you performed it yourself."

Brian's disappointment vanished instantly. He had forgotten that Dr. Edwards' teaching skills were as accomplished as her research ability. She never told a student the answer. She led him to discover it himself. "Show me," he said.

She plucked one of the tubes out of the rack and handed it to him. "Let's go over here where the light is best." She indicated a spot on the bench directly beneath a large fluorescent ceiling fixture. "Place your arms on the countertop so you don't jiggle."

He did as instructed.

"Watch closely. Don't let your eyes move from the tube."

There was nothing out of the ordinary to see--dark blue-black venous blood in a purple-capped vacuum tube.

"Now carefully remove the stopper."

He held the tube in one hand, inches from his face, and with the thumb and index finger of the other hand, he slowly began uncorking the tube. As he cracked the seal, the blood instantly lightened to crimson. He did a double take. It had happened so quickly. There was no gradual color change as oxygen from the air diffused down the column of blood.

Venipuncture, drawing blood, was the first procedure a medical student learned to do. The blood was drawn straight out of the venous circulation of the patient into a vacuum tube without ever being exposed to air. It was dark purple, unoxygenated. When the tube was opened it took at least a dozen seconds for a crimson coloration to descend the column of fluid as oxygen diffused downward and was absorbed by the blood.

His eyes were wide with incredulity, his voice low, when he spoke. "The sample--it was instantaneously oxygenated. I've never seen anything like it."

"Neither had I," said Dr. Edwards. "I repeated the same experiment in a somewhat more sophisticated fashion, but each time the results were the same." She pointed to the tube he was holding. "That blood has twenty times the oxygen gathering and carrying capacity of normal blood. That means, Dr. Richards, that either your patient is really an extraterrestrial, or else she has been transfused with artificial blood--a substance that if you had asked me yesterday, I would have said doesn't exist."

Chapter 26

"Penfield is not someone to be taken lightly," whined Fendley.

"I did not have any trouble with him," retorted Dietrich. He had taken the call in his hotel room on his scrambler-equipped personal phone.

"How's that?"

"Never mind," said Dietrich shaking his head with annoyance. "You run the hospital. Tell him it is no longer a concern of his. Tell him that other doctors are on the case. Threaten to not allow him to work at your hospital. Do whatever it takes. We have invested a lot in you. It is time to show your appreciation."

"I'll have you know that I've done plenty for you all, for example that last contract for hyperalimentation solution--are you sure we can't be overheard?"

"This the latest technology. If you followed procedure..."

"I did. But you still don't understand. Penfield is one of the 'senior' doctors."

"So, what if he is old."

"Not old, well he is but what I mean is that he's one the others listen to. Senior in hospitals means powerful. He was chief of staff two years ago. If he confirms the records are missing he'll make a stink, and then we're going to have a real problem. He has already been on his high horse about a screw up in the blood bank. And I'm pretty sure he's suspicious about most of the pharmacy contracts going to Durbane. He was asking the head of purchasing some questions about that. Penfield would like nothing better than to see me canned."

"And he told you he is coming back to look into all this?"

"He told me," said Fendley slowly repeating what he had already said, "that Brian Richards had called him. Their patient, Sharon Jackson, both her blood and records are missing. Richards thinks I'm behind it. Penfield said that when he got back he was going to look into this personally, as well as some other matters that concerned him."

"And you can't do anything to prevent it."

"He's got too many friends."

"I will take care of it."

For a long time after he hung up, Dietrich sat there. The situation was like a drop of ink on fabric; the stain was spreading, and soon, the entire garment would be ruined. That is, unless he employed a stain remover. Yes, a more interventional approach would be required. His man could be in Atlanta in a few hours. It would be necessary to update Walker, but as far as the details, well, it was best the C.E.O. not know certain things. They both preferred it that way.

* * * * *

The midafternoon break was clearly posted on the placard outside the meeting room. From 3:00 until 3:30 was time enough for a trip to the men's room and the hotel gift shop before the next lecture began. The subject was laser ablation of intrabdominal tumors, and Dr Penfield did not want to miss it. He just needed some antacids first.

Bill Penfield straightened the front of his jacket as he exited the restroom and headed toward the bank of elevators. The mezzanine floor of the Peachtree Hilton was lined with large conference rooms, all named after Roman emperors. The American Academy of Laparascopic Surgeons was meeting in the Constantine room. The corridor outside the meeting room hosted a steady stream of passersby. The hotel functionaries moved at the fastest pace. A waiter hurried by, pushing a cart littered with used coffee cups and saucers. A young man wearing the green blazer of the hotel staff and carrying a clipboard scurried past. Hotel guests were more easily identified by their slower gait and, in the case of meeting attendees, by their plastic nametags clipped to their lapels.

The physician stepped onto the elevator noting that the ground-floor button had already been punched by one of the two other occupants. No one paid any attention as a casually dressed black man carrying a folded *USA TODAY* pushed onto the elevator at the last instant.

It took only a moment to reach the ground floor. The physician headed for the gift shop.

"Dr. Penfield?" The voice came from behind.

"Yes?" the doctor answered. He turned to see the black man from the elevator approaching him. The stranger scrutinized Penfield's face, then his nametag.

"From New Orleans?"

152

"That's correct. Have we met?"

The answer was three gunshots. The first two tore into Penfield's chest, leaving a gaping hole as the hollow-point bullets expanded. The impact propelled him backward. The third bullet struck him in the abdomen, but he did not feel it. Dr. Penfield was already dead.

The hotel entrance was only twenty yards away. With a gloved hand the assassin brought out a small canister and tossed it behind him as he raced through the revolving door.

Screams instantly erupted. One patron, at the sound of the first gunshot, had flattened himself on the lobby floor. Others dived behind anything that would shield them or else scattered out the closest exit.

A doorman hollered, "Get him!" and pointed to the fleeing man. A clerk with the sinewy build of a jogger vaulted the chest-high counter to give chase. Thick smoke billowed from the canister as it scudded across the floor. Within moments cries of distress were everywhere, and a fit of coughing brought the clerk-jogger to an abrupt halt.

Outside, as the building's fire alarms activated, the assassin made a turn into a nearby alley and disappeared.

Chapter 27

Dr. Edwards' conclusion that Sharon had received artificial blood became the final component in what had, until then, been just a hodgepodge of confusing facts and suppositions. As if he had found the critical missing puzzle piece, Brian now felt ready to assemble the picture. He was driving slowly back to Darcy's apartment, giving himself time to put it all together when Dr. Guess' call came. The Chief of Staff asked him to continue looking after Penfield's patients, because the physician would not be returning. Brian although shaken by what he was told and wanting to help, still had to say that he was leaving immediately on a vacation. However, he would arrange for his partners to cover.

* * * * *

"Artificial blood!" Sharon exclaimed for the third time. "Is it harmful?"

"I doubt it, but how would I know? I've never heard of it before. Oh, sure, there's been talk and some hope, but to my knowledge no company is even close to producing it."

"It seems to be available now, at least in one place," Sharon said wryly.

"Apparently, and that explains those guards at that Haitian clinic. That must be where whoever is making the product is doing their testing. Although killing someone to protect an industry secret seems a little extreme," Brian mused aloud.

"Maybe those Haitian thugs knew they'd lose their job, or worse, if the place was exposed through their negligence." offered Sharon. She pondered a moment. "That also explains the attempt here in the States to buy me off-- or scare me off. They want to keep their research secret, no investigation about what happened to me in the cave."

"I bet they can't figure out why you haven't gone to the police already," said Brian. "Which is something we're going to remedy right now."

"No, we are not," said Sharon firmly. "You promised. I have to make arrangements to protect my discovery first."

"Well, Sharon, I take back that promise, because this whole situation is becoming deadly serious. I just found out--Dr. Penfield was murdered."

Sharon's hand flew to her mouth. "My God. How? When?"

Brian shook his head. "I don't know any details, just gunned down in his hotel in Atlanta. No obvious motive. The police are working on it."

She stared into space. "I didn't know him that well, but he was nice with me, a good doctor."

"Sharon, I had talked with him about what was going on at Beauvoir: missing records, your missing blood, that patient of mine who was transferred and then died right afterward, a lot of stuff. He was going to come back and get to the bottom of it."

Sharon snapped out of her reverie. "Do you really think he was murdered to prevent him asking a few questions?" Her tone of voice suggested that she seriously doubted it.

"I don't know, but I do know this. There is currently only one proof that artificial blood exists, and I'm looking at her."

"Brian, I think you are getting ridiculous."

"You said that man threatened you at Tulane."

"Yes," she reluctantly admitted. "But now I'm in hiding. No one knows where I am."

"You hope."

She pondered that for a moment. "If what you say is true, and I don't think it is, then who could behind all this?"

"That's for the police to find out."

Sharon slowly paced the room with her arms folded tightly to her chest. "No, no," she murmured, "there has got to be some other way." She stopped suddenly and held out two fingers an inch apart. "I was this close, Brian. This close. What I found, I know, is truly the discovery of the century."

"It's not worth your life!" Brian protested.

"It's worth more than my life! It's a window into the past for millions of people. Brian, I can't help the people who may have gotten hurt or lost their lives over this weird blood stuff in my veins." Sharon shook her head in dismay. "Life is important, but so is knowledge. Brian, you've just got to help me get to Haiti one more time."

"You actually still want to go there?"

"It doesn't seem a whole lot more dangerous than here." She pointed him to a chair, then sat on the couch. "Look, do this. Let me go alone if you won't go with me. Give me two days. I've thought out every move."

Brian fought to control his frustration and concern, because he knew, without a shadow of doubt, that this stubbornly determined, strong-willed woman would do what she had to do, with or without him.

"I need only to arrange some equipment in Port-au-Prince, then I'll go straight to the cave. No fooling around, no exploring. I'll be on the lookout for the guards now, so they'll never know I'm there. One dive, and I've got what I need. I'll come straight back to this country. Then you can tell the cops about your theory--and Brian, it is a theory. You don't know any of this for certain, except that something is wrong with my blood."

"Did I neglect to tell you about your medical records?" said Brian, his manner now more than a little sarcastic. "They've all been removed from the hospital, deleted. You don't exist there."

"Brian, you're carrying this too far. You don't think you've gone paranoid over some missing hospital charts?"

What she said struck home. Brian pondered the situation, then answered with a dejected air. "No, I don't think I'm carrying this too far. But you are right. I don't know anything except that there has been one attempt on your life and you have, or had, some abnormality in your blood."

"Good," Sharon said, leaning back into the couch with relief.

"But," he said, "you're not going to Haiti by yourself. I've already signed out on vacation. So, I'll just go with you. Before I leave, though, I'm going to tell my suspicions to the police."

"No, Brian. If you tell the police, then they'll keep me around for interrogation, or whatever it is they do. I wouldn't be able to leave the country. If you feel you must get them involved, then at least wait until we leave. Let someone else explain your theory to them. But leave me time to make my dive."

"I guess you'll only do it your way," said Brian, his voice heavy with resignation. "Well, maybe I can do some exploring on my own--in that clinic--while I'm down there."

Sharon rose from the couch, crossed to him, and settled into his lap. "Thank you, Brian. You're a darling."

Chapter 28

This was almost fun, thought Sharon. The last time she had been in costume was as Joan of Arc, for the Mardi Gras ball during her second year at Tulane. Of course, that occasion was different, all gaiety and alcohol. Now her safety, even her survival, might depend on her disguise. Talk about dressing for success.

The clothes came out of Darcy's closet. Sharon's taste ran to blue jeans and shirts, Darcy's to skirts and color-coordinated twin-sets. So much the better, for Sharon looked utterly unlike herself. She put on a ton of eye makeup and tucked her long blonde hair beneath a hat. Now she could go with little likelihood of being recognized.

She needed some things before leaving for Haiti, but she couldn't return to her own apartment and risk another encounter with the black man who wanted to make her a deal or else. Her options were to venture out on her own or stay in hiding and let Brian gather what she needed. Earlier, she had given in to Brian's concerns and agreed to stay put until he got back. However, with her concussion now faded, she had recovered her equilibrium and her self-sufficient style and now was impatient to once again do things for herself. She had shared her bed and her secrets with Brian, but she wasn't ready to relinquish her independence. She would get what she needed while he was out making his own preparations for their trip.

Her first stop was the bank. Repaying her education loans still ate up a big part of her paycheck, and after her latest trip to the Caribbean, she had just enough money remaining for a plane ticket and a few extras. She and Brian had discussed that either her enemies or the police could trace them through credit-card purchases which meant making the trip on a cash basis. She withdrew all her savings, leaving in only a hundred dollars to keep the account open. Brian was to go to the bank today, too, having agreed to help out financially as well as physically on the trip.

Sharon's next stop was at a place she knew well, Gulf Divers, Inc. The store was tended by a muscular young man wearing a T-shirt that read *DIVERS DO IT DEEPER*. She had seen him here several times in the past, so she was pleased he didn't recognize her. She would obtain the heavy equipment--tanks, weights, and regulators--in Haiti, but the underwater communications gear she needed was too sophisticated to find there. She paid in cash.

She saved the most difficult purchase for last. She pulled up to Westside Pawn and Gun but did not get out right away. The neon sign brought back memories of a similar place of business years ago. With her mother always working long hours, the time a stepdad entered her life offered Sharon a glimpse of a more normal life, the kind, it seemed, most of the other kids enjoyed, with two parents and a mother whose one job left her time for her family and home.

Orville Sawyer, her stepfather, hated the name Orville, and insisted everyone call him Rusty. He was a good-natured man, and he welcomed Sharon's presence and help at the pawn shop. On Sundays, he took the family on outings, and on a few of these, he even taught her to shoot. She chuckled to herself; if there was one thing a pawn shop owner always had, it was access to a lot of used firearms.

To a sixteen-year old that had never had a father, it was an idyllic life. But that life was only an interlude and ended when he died. Rusty's Pawn Shop was sold to cover debts, and it wasn't long before her mother resumed a second job. Her mother was dead now, suffering a fatal stroke four years ago. Sharon closed her eyes and pushed the memories deeply. When she reopened them, the garish sign of Westside Pawn and Gun was there.

The door closed with the jingle of a bell, and the place was empty except for a man behind the counter who eyed her approvingly. He wore a gaudy gold chain, and when she made her request and he reached out to tap the glass countertop, the back of his hand featured an amateurish tattoo. "This here twenty-five caliber snub nose is ideal for a pretty lady like you. Nickel-plated with white plastic grips. If you have to pull it out of your purse, say if somebody's trying to take advantage of you, they can't miss seeing it."

Sharon rejected it with a shake of her head. She moved down the counter. Across the display case from her the man followed sideways like a crab stalking its dinner. "These are automatics. They're a little trickier. Some ladies don't have enough strength in their fingers to work the slide." He gave her a patronizing smile.

She pointed. "That one."

"That's a nine-millimeter Smith and Wesson," he said with a hint of incredulity in his voice.

"I know," she said.

160

He raised his eyebrows.

"How many cartridges in the clip?" she asked.

"Fourteen. The government don't allow them to be made like that anymore."

"I'd like to see it." He hauled on the ring of keys attached to his belt, unlocked the cabinet, and produced the weapon. Sharon inspected the gun, then expertly punched the clip release. The clip popped out. "Good," she said in a barely audible voice, "high capacity magazine." With a finger she checked the spring tension. She worked the slide and found it to be smooth. Inside, the gun seemed to be well cared for with no evidence of abuse or neglect. "I like it." The proprietor watched with the awe of a paleontologist who had just spotted a *Tyrannosaurus rex* alive and well on downtown Canal Street. She flashed him a grin, and said, "I need it today."

The man snapped back to reality. "No can do--we have to Brady it."

"It would mean a lot to me." She leaned across the counter, close enough to smell the garlic on the man's breath; the prominence of her breasts were not inconspicuous. "I've got to make a long trip all by myself, and without it I won't have any protection."

"It's the law, ma'am. I got to--"

Sharon already had her wallet out. "I know you could do the paperwork now if you wanted to." She slid her driver's license across the counter, and leaned farther. "I really need to take the gun with me. It'd be worth an extra two hundred to me." A wad of twenties followed the license.

The man glanced first one way, then the other while he pondered. The store was empty. Sharon put on her best feminine "please-help-poor-little-ole-me" smile. Grumpily, the proprietor finally answered. "There's a garbage can behind the store. The gun will be in there inside a box." He frowned. "But if you do anything with it in the next three days, I'll swear you stole it."

"I understand," she said. "And there's just one more thing." He glowered. "I want three boxes of ammo, steel-jacketed, of course," she said.

"Of course," the proprietor sighed.

* * * * *

Brian whipped into the doctors' parking area, and he mentally ran through the office schedule. As he slammed his car door shut, it bounced back, unlatched. A quick inspection of the problem revealed that the rubber door seal hung loosely from the top of the doorframe. Age and the heat of the sun had combined to convert the glue that held it in place to ineffectual dried flakes, and the rubber itself had taken on the consistency of old leather.

He fiddled with the seal to force it back into place. It wouldn't cooperate, so he began pulling on the dangling seal. The remaining adhesive suddenly turned loose, and Brian staggered backwards, like a fisherman who'd just caught a six-foot eel that now vengefully flew out of the water to wrap itself around him. Cursing, he hurled the length of rubber into the back seat for reattachment at a later date and headed into his office.

On his desk was a list of his inpatients. He dictated a short note to his partners about each one and added the information that most of them probably already knew about Dr. Penfield and that their practice would be covering the deceased man's patients until other arrangements could be made. Then Brain carried the tape to one of the transcriptionists to get it out to the doctors who'd be covering for him in his absence. His last stop in the office was to see the appointment clerk to confirm his appointments were canceled. Then he was out the door.

His Honda, a good vehicle for years, had, like a bored forty-five–year-old man facing a mid–life crisis, evidently decided to act up before it was too late. For the vehicle, a new wife or job change was out of the question, but it could still find other ways to express its independence. Apparently pulling loose the dangling door seal had in turn caused a terminally attached headliner to give up the ghost and the car's interior fabric ceiling now hung down like, if not a sword, then a blanket of Damocles.

"Shit," Brian announced. If he ripped it out, he would have to order a whole new one, which was the devil to install. It would be easier to glue this one back up without removing it. With all he had to do before leaving the country, what would have normally been a fun repair challenge, was now a frustrating inconvenience.

Once in the car, he had no choice but to back out with one hand on the steering wheel and the other extended overhead, holding the headliner up so he could get at least a glimpse through the rear-view mirror. A sudden squeal of brakes alerted him that his view was not good enough. He had backed directly out in front of a moving car. A minor crunching sound instantly followed, and Brian winced. The apology and amends were his to make, but that was hard to do with one hand in the Statue of Liberty position.

He clambered out with an apologetic grin, bringing both hands palm-up to signal that he was sorry. But before he could complete the gesture the doors of the white Ford flew open and two men leaped out, each to crouch behind a door as if using it for a shield.

The surprise of it all froze the image in his memory. One man was black and appeared to have something in his hand as he ducked behind a dented door, the other man heavy-set and swarthy, crouched likewise behind his door. Almost simultaneously a van with a man and woman inside rounded the building and stopped short behind the white car. The driver honked in annoyance at the developing miniature traffic jam. The two crouching men looked around, then jumped back into their own vehicle and roared off, all the while Brian watched in open-mouthed astonishment.

Shaking his head, he got back into his own car and pulled it out of the way. The van moved on. Brian's first thought was that he had scared two extraordinarily jumpy motorists. Maybe they'd thought they were going to experience some road-rage first hand. His second thought as he drove away to continue his preparations for leaving town was that his twenty-year-old Honda was getting to be far too much trouble. A nice ten-year-old pickup truck for him and Cecil might make a fine replacement.

* * * * *

Several hours later, after Brian had ripped out his headliner, made rounds at the hospital, picked up his laundry and a box of fried chicken, he was now stepping out of his car in his driveway.

"Cecil. Did you miss me?" The answer to that question was obvious. The dog's happiness at his master's return was evident in every inch of his wagging body. Brian squatted down to vigorously rub the dog's flanks. "You don't look too skinny. Mrs. Thompson always feeds you well." The dog responded by making a short run away, then tearing back to Brian. "Okay, I'll take you for a hike in the woods, but it's got to be a quick one."

Living in the country couldn't have been better for the two of them. His father had been an avid hunter, and although Brian didn't enjoy sport killing, he had always liked the outdoors. Now that the time-consuming years of medical training were over, he was glad to get back to what he enjoyed. And for Cecil, there were smells to investigate and wild creatures to chase, pleasures the city could never equal. And there were enough surrounding woods to satisfy them both. Mrs. Thompson's frame house was four hundred yards away on the other side of their rural road. The next neighbors, the Fletchers, were a quarter of a mile farther on. When nighttime emergencies kept Brian away, with only a phone call Mrs. Thompson was glad to provide her favorite dog with enough food for an entire kennel of Labrador Retrievers.

After his walk with Cecil, Brian was in the kitchen wading through the messages on his answering machine when he heard a familiar voice calling from his open front door. Mrs. Thompson stood there. Sixtyish-plus, she was somewhat on the heavy side and dressed in blue jeans with an untucked short-sleeved shirt. To Brian, she was the neighbor from heaven. She, in turn, considered Brian the son she'd never had. "Come on in, Mrs. Thompson," he said, holding the screen door open.

"You have been working hard lately," she said, "spending your nights at the hospital."

Brian nodded. "Oh--many thanks for looking after the hound."

Cecil, with the special sense peculiar to pets, knew he was being talked about and responded by cocking his head to pay closer attention.

"Well, I have decided to take some time off--for vacation," he added, "but I'm not leaving for a day or two."

With the back of one hand she wiped a loose wisp of grayish hair away from her face. Brian started to ask her if she wanted coffee, but she spoke first. "Brian, are you in any trouble?"

He froze. "Why do you ask?"

"A couple of men were out here, asking questions about you."

Brian's search for the coffee can went into slow motion. "What do you mean?"

"They said they were investigators doing routine checks on doctors and medical credentials, making sure who they said they were, that sort of thing."

"They asked about me?"

Mrs. Thompson nodded. "I was in the yard when this car came by, driving real slow. I paid no attention even when it came back by again, but then they pulled over and stopped. A black man got out and did all the talking. He said his name was Bradley. The other fellow stayed in the car with the window rolled down." Brian stood motionless, a container of Maxwell House in his hand. She gestured at it. "I think I will take a cup if you don't mind," she said.

"Sure," he said. "Tell me, what color was the car?"

"White, but it had a scrape down one side and a big dent in the door. I remember thinking that a government car ought to be kept up better than that, but maybe it had just happened."

Brian's hands began to tremble. "What else did you notice?"

"The black fellow was clean cut. White shirt, no tie, like maybe he'd taken it off. The other man in the car was a Cajun." She laughed. "You couldn't miss that thick accent when he called for the other fellow to hurry up."

"A black man and a Cajun?"

"Yes."

Brian's body was rigid. This visit was no coincidence. Clearly, it was the same car and the same men he had seen in his office parking lot. Sharon wasn't the only one being trailed. "They asked you questions about me?"

"That's right. They asked if I knew Dr. Brian Richards. Of course I said I did. The black man, Mr. Bradley, said it was a routine check to make sure the information you'd given them was correct."

"That *I'd* given? What did they want to know?"

"Nothing special--if you were a surgeon, whether you had a girlfriend, that sort of thing. I didn't really tell them anything new. They already knew it all. Then the Cajun guy grumbled about sitting there, and Mr. Bradley got back in and they drove off."

Brian poured water into the drip chamber of the pot. "Who did they say they were again?"

"Government Investigators."

"What branch?"

"I don't recall them saying," said Mrs. Thompson, struggling to remember.

"Did they show you a badge?"

"No," said Mrs. Thompson, now looking apprehensive.

"When was this?"

"Less than an hour ago." Her face was a study in concern. "You're not in any trouble, are you?"

"No," he said, hoping he sounded more convincing than he felt.

"I told them not to worry," she said reassuringly. "I said you were a fine young man, a true-blue American, and as far as I knew didn't even have girls staying over at your place like so many of the young folks do now."

165

Brian was dumbfounded. "How did *that* come up?"

"Oh, the man asked if I had seen you with a woman, about thirty, with shoulder-length blond hair."

Sharon! That's who they really wanted. These men were no more federal agents than he was. But they had known where he lived. How? He wasn't listed in the phone book. They described Sharon. She was somehow the key. Again, though, how? He had only recently met her, and he hadn't spoken to anyone about her, except, of course, at the hospital. He'd made a lot of inquiries there.

That must be it. The connection must be through the hospital. He'd made a lot of noise there about Sharon's missing chart and computer records, annoying the ever-pesky Mrs. Leathers and her vengeful boss, Darrell Fendley. The same men following Sharon were now looking for him. If they couldn't find her on their own, then maybe her new doctor would lead them to her. And the hospital knew where to find the new doctor.

"Brian, is something wrong?"

"Uh, no," he said, snapping back to the present. "I was just thinking."

"You looked so far away."

Over their coffee, Mrs. Thompson made conversation about the weather, the state of her garden, and what the Fletchers were doing to their house. Brian offered just enough comments to be polite, but his mind was occupied elsewhere. Eventually she announced that she would be off. Before the screen door shut, Brian told her that he had some business that required him to stay overnight in town, and since he hadn't seen Cecil much lately, he would take the dog with him.

Brian stood at the door watching his neighbor walk down the road to her house. It would be so much easier to go to the police, he thought. But he had made his promise to Sharon, and he didn't want to violate that. Sharon and her dream to recover Columbus' lost treasure were one and the same. If he wanted her, then he had to make sure her secret stayed that way, at least for a few days, until she was ready to tell the world.

His decision was made. A few changes of clothing went into a duffel bag, and in the top drawer of his dresser he found his passport. He glanced at the gun case in the hall, eyeing the two shotguns and the Remington 0.30-0.30 his Dad had insisted on christening Brian's rural house with. He'd look just a little conspicuous carrying a long gun around New Orleans, he decided.

No, to protect Sharon, he'd have to rely on his wits until they got their mission done in Haiti.

He went to the door and whistled for Cecil. The dog was there in a flash.

* * * * *

Mrs. Thompson didn't know what to make of Brian's sudden decision to leave and take Cecil with him. And Brian hadn't seemed sure how long he'd be gone. Even though he hadn't asked outright, Mrs. Thompson thought she should keep an unofficial eye on things, not that she didn't anyway. She flicked off the security light and walked outside. It was a pleasant night. The stars were out, and Brian's porch light burned in the distance. She wondered if in his haste to leave Brian had remembered to secure the tops of his garbage cans. The raccoons around here were expert at getting into anything that didn't have a combination lock, and she'd rather he not find garbage scattered all over his yard.

In less than ten minutes she was at Brian's house. The place was deserted. She went around back. Sure enough, the tops were off his trash cans, but there was no mess. She realized that Brian probably hadn't been around enough in the last few days to generate any garbage. Since she was there, though, she thought she might as well check to make sure he had locked up.

His back porch served as a mudroom, storage room, and general catchall for whatever he didn't want to put away. She crossed through it, walking carefully to avoid tripping over anything. Successfully reaching the back door in the dark without breaking an ankle, she reached out and twisted the knob. It turned easily. He had forgotten to lock up. She pushed the door open and flipped on the light to check that all was well.

A creature with telescopic eyes stood in the kitchen. Mrs. Thompson screamed. The creature slipped into the crouch of a professional shooter and ripped off its goggles. Too late, she saw that the creature was a man, and that the man held a gun with an unusually long barrel. The weapon coughed three times, but she only heard the first two.

The noise as her body crashed backward onto Brian's porch brought another man at a run. He was black, with night-vision goggles in one hand and an identical pistol in the other. "Goddamn, you stupid shit!" he said after inspecting the body. "It's that woman from down the road."

167

"She surprised me. I didn't expect company," the shooter whined in a Cajun accent.

"We were only supposed to snoop around. Find out where else he might be staying," interrupted his companion. He shook his head. "When we report back, your ass is going to be in big trouble."

"What was I supposed to do?" said the Cajun, still staring at the body. "Say 'scuse me, Ma'am, just inspecting for rats?"

"We'll see how funny you are when you tell Dietrich about this." The black man disappeared into another room and returned a moment later with a bedspread. "Let's get her out to the woods and into the Landrover. We'll take a ride up to Point aux Chenes. You got your knife?"

"Yeah."

"A few cuts to get some blood in the water, and by daylight, if there are any fisherman up that way, all they'll find is a bunch of well-fed alligators."

Chapter 29

The guests were all well-dressed. Many held drinks in manicured hands as they stood in small knots talking while a coterie of waiters ferried them tasty morsels and more drinks. Other guests preferred to work their way around the hors d'oeuvres table for an even greater selection of edibles.

The sound of a dozen different accents echoed off the high ceilings. Thurston Walker forced himself to appear absorbed in the dialogue between an older gentleman speaking with enthusiasm about his recent trip to Africa and a much younger woman who appeared more interested in her third glass of Dom Perignon.

"Excuse me," said Walker, feigning disappointment, "but I must leave this fascinating conversation. As host, I have certain duties..."

The two guests smiled their sympathy and the Englishman returned to his discourse, the lady her champagne.

Walker sidled up to Karl Dietrich who stood in an out-of-the-way location against a wall, far enough from the door so as not to be obvious, yet close enough to intercept intruders. Uninvited visitors were not expected, but in a large hotel anyone wandering around could easily be a competitor's spy or even a government agent sniffing for a potential indictment.

"What do you think, Karl?" Walker asked as he surveyed his guests.

"All thirteen are here. They seem to be enjoying themselves." Dietrich spoke without looking at his boss. His gaze remained fixed on the small crowd, alert for any occurrence out of the ordinary.

"The Hilton gives good service," said Walker as he continued to scan the group.

"But it is too open for my liking," responded Dietrich. "Any number of people could have spotted us in the lobby."

"Yes, but there's also anonymity in a crowd. Only if we're seen together as a group would an outsider realize that a meeting is going on, and that's not likely, considering the guests were all given different arrival times, and some stayed at other hotels. And what's the likelihood of someone being here who'd recognize any of these overseas pharmaceutical C.E.O.s anyway?"

"Admittedly," said Dietrich, "very small, but with so much governmental concern about price fixing of late, it would take only one person to make one call, and the antitrust people would be down our throat in seconds."

"It's not the antitrust people I worry about," said Walker. The C.E.O. of Durbane Pharmaceuticals looked at his wristwatch. "It's time."

Dietrich nodded and began to move through the crowd as silently as a submarine on deep-water patrol. Each waiter was quietly intercepted and dispatched from the room.

To maintain their privacy, Dietrich, using the name of a fictitious company, had booked all the rooms on this corridor. He had then chosen the one farthest from the elevators for Durbane's reception. Dietrich now returned to the doorway and looked into the corridor. It was empty except for two men. He beckoned to the man who was lounging on a settee and looking bored, as if waiting for his wife to return from the ladies' room. Instantly the man arose, stepped inside the reception room, and began closing the ornate twelve-foot high doors. Simultaneously the other man moved to stand guard outside them. Dressed as a hotel waiter, this sentry stood six foot four inches tall and had an impressive girth to match, giving the impression that he was doing this work in his off-season from the N.F.L

"Ladies and gentlemen," said Dr. Walker, "if I can have your attention." Although the group was neither loud nor large, it took a few moments for the chatter to die down. Once the room was quiet, he continued. "Please move this way." He gestured toward a second double doorway. "We have a short presentation which, we hope, you will find entertaining, informative"--he paused to flash a gleaming smile--"and profitable. It should take no more than an hour. There's a self-service bar in the meeting room and some additional refreshments."

There was a general murmur as the guests moved through the second set of doors. Thurston Walker joined the procession, but instead of taking a seat in one of the velvet upholstered chairs, he continued purposefully to the center of the room and waited there.

The chairs were arranged in a semicircle, much as they might be for a gathering of a chamber music society. But instead of an ensemble of musicians and stringed instruments, there were three large, flat, black cases, similar to footlockers, each with a dome-shaped lens projecting from the top. The cases were arranged in a triangular configuration with cables connecting them to the electrical access panel on the wall.

Walker watched an old colleague, Sergeyev, stop at the small bar to pour himself another drink, a double vodka with ice. Next to him waiting for his turn was Charles Tipton, Jr., the man who had just taken over the reins from his father of the small Australian pharmaceutical house, Tipton and Quarles. The rest of the guests headed directly to their seats. Dietrich closed the double doors and continued his vigil from the back of the room.

"On behalf of Durbane Pharmaceuticals I want to thank you all for coming," Walker said.

"We'll go anywhere on your money," said the red-faced Russian, holding his vodka tumbler upright in a toast. A short burst of laughter filled the room.

"It's not your transportation bill but your liquor bill that's got me worried," Walker responded. His comeback was greeted with even more laughter, and the Russian held his glass up a second time.

Walker waited for silence to return. He was at his best in these circumstances, close to his audience and without the podium or lecture notes that so many speakers liked to hide behind. His air of easy command was just one of many skills that had helped propel him to his current position. His part of the presentation would appear as relaxed and off the cuff as if he were the host of a Saturday evening barbecue chatting with his neighbors.

"First, a few necessary details. We do not wish to hurt the feelings of our competitors or any representative of a government agency who may have been left off the invitation list..." There was another chorus of laughter. "So after the presentation, I must ask you to leave not as a group but separately at three-minute intervals. Our security chief"--he pointed to Dietrich in the back of the room--"will assist you. After you return to your room in this or the other hotels, you are free to do whatever you indicated as your preference in our pre-meeting planning. To those returning home immediately, I wish you comfortable flying, and for those going with me tomorrow on the company Gulfstream to Jackson Hole, Wyoming, I encourage you to bring your best hiking boots. Everything else will be provided at the lodge. I have already checked, and the weather in that beautiful area is perfect."

"I want to shoot a moose," said the Russian loudly.

"Sorry, Sergeyev, but it's not hunting season. Our game wardens might have the hide of a Russian bear to tack to their wall if you try to take one of their moose." Again laughter filled the room. "For the four golfers, I hope you enjoy your trip to Pebble Beach--and I sure hope you're good."

"Good enough to take you, Thurston," said Nigel Thatcher. "Unless, of course, you have improved a lot since we last played." The Britisher chuckled, accompanied by knowing smiles from those who planned to assault the difficult golf course with him.

"I haven't, Nigel, and that's why I'm going to fish for trout at the Wyoming lodge."

Walker smiled, then grew serious. "This meeting never occurred," he said abruptly. The guests stopped laughing, their eyes focused on the speaker. "You will not speak of it even among your closest advisers." His gaze moved steadily from one guest to the next, to imprint upon each of them the importance of what he had said. "You thirteen are a select group, providing pharmaceuticals on every civilized continent on the globe. But in addition, you elite few are aggressive in your marketing, innovative in your thinking, and willing to take risks for substantial profit. And each of you has complete control of your own company."

With that he took from his pocket a cordless remote control, pointed it at the center trunk, and pressed a small button. He waited, his nerves concealed beneath a façade of calm. A team of electronics and video technicians had worked around the clock fine-tuning this equipment, but an improperly aligned laser projector or a mistracking CD-ROM could still destroy his presentation. The room lights began to dim automatically, and the opening strings of a Mozart concerto came from unseen speakers. Thurston Walker let out his breath, gave silent thanks, and took his seat.

The room grew steadily darker until total blackness descended on the group. Extra seals around the doorway ensured that not one photon of stray light would enter the room. There was only the sound of the music within the void.

Gradually a suggestion of light appeared, at first like a trick the retina was playing. But the speck of light enlarged until it became a spinning globe floating unsupported in midair. The three dimensional image had been created by computer enhancements of photographs made from earth-orbiting satellites, giving the spectators, who were murmuring in amazement, a view of their planet as if from 22,000 miles in space. The apparition rotated as multicolored laser beams, each almost invisible until their intersection point, produced the holographic image.

With each revolution of the globe a letter appeared, centered over North America, until the name *DURBANE* was spelled out. Then the letters became smaller, centered in the southern United States, and red lines radiated out to other sites. Soon the spinning globe was webbed by connecting pathways to

London, Moscow, Sydney, and Riyadh, each bearing the name of the pharmaceutical house located there. Dr. Walker stole a glance at his guests, their faces showing pleasure in the reflected light as the names of their companies appeared.

Next the slowly rotating globe faded to nothingness, replaced by the head and shoulders of a professional actor chosen for his scholarly appearance and deep, pleasant voice. "Since the beginning of time mankind has fought against disease and injury." The image of the professor gave way to a view into a sick room of the 1700's. A child, pale with illness, lay in bed, the mother beside him, her hand tenderly on his brow. A physician in black waistcoat and knee britches sat on a nearby chair, his medical bag at his feet. His expression of helplessness matched the mother's.

The now-invisible speaker continued. "Sadly, many times, the battle was lost. But now, through the efforts of thousands of dedicated scientists and physicians the world over"--the scene dissolved away to be replaced by the image of a modern laboratory facility. In the foreground was a smiling black woman in a white coat holding up a vial of clear liquid for inspection by an older Asian man and a young Caucasian woman. "A new chapter is about to be written in that struggle. One in which humankind will at last be victorious."

The image of the speaker returned. "To understand, we must go back to the beginning. Even in earliest times it was known that to lose blood was to lose life. But the first attempts to do more than apply tourniquets to control bleeding came in 1655, with the transfusion of blood directly from one dog to the other. Although the donor dog died of exsanguination, the recipient lived, proving such an undertaking was possible."

The holographic professor continued his lecture. "The first recorded attempt to reproduce this feat with a human recipient was by Jean Denis, physician to Louis XIV. He transfused nine ounces of lamb blood into a young man suffering from madness. Unfortunately, the patient passed black urine and thus became the first recorded victim of a transfusion reaction. The physician continued the treatment but his patient died of a hemolytic reaction after the third transfusion. As an aside, the deceased patient's wife charged Denis with murder, and although he was acquitted, the medical faculty of the University of Paris forbade him from transfusing again."

Another murmur arose from the audience at the interesting tidbit of history.

The speaker's image dissolved again, replaced by a Confederate infantryman crouched behind earthworks, clutching his rifle. "By the time of the American Civil War, direct human to human transfusion was being performed with some success. In 1914, with the discovery of the A, B, and O blood groups, it was recognized why one in three transfusions resulted in a major adverse reaction. With further research into the minor blood groups, such as Rh, Kell, and M,N,S, as well as greater understanding of infection control, transfusion became routine."

Now came an image of an emaciated boy, about ten years of age, lying in a modern hospital bed. "However, the emergence of the AIDS virus in the 1980's brought home to us the dangers of medical complacency. Unintentional introduction of HIV into hemophiliacs was the horror that, too late for some, focused attention on an entirely new problem in blood transfusion--the transmission of viruses." The hologram of the boy disappeared, and in its place appeared a scene of a family, lighthearted and carefree, hiking across a country hillside.

"Durbane Pharmaceuticals, a leader in innovative research, has helped carry us into the next century of blood replacement." The professor's image returned. He was holding in his outstretched hand a plastic intravenous bag, filled with fluid and marked boldly, *U.B.S.*. "Transfusion without blood."

The room erupted into sound as a dozen amazed guests begin talking at once. Slowly they quieted as the supernatural speaker continued, oblivious to the hubbub. "Although the exact chemical composition of universal blood substitute is complex, the essential ingredient is Fluorine. This atom can, when wrapped in a blanket of organic molecules, trap and hold oxygen just as hemoglobin does."

The image of the speaker's head dissolved away to be replaced by a symbol. A red *F* appeared in place of the speaker, and a thread began progressively wrapping around the letter. The symbol O_2 floated by and became entrapped by the threads. More and more O_2 came by to be ensnared until the *F* was obscured from view by a giant cloak of oxygen molecules. Nearby, the letters *HgB*, the universal symbol for hemoglobin, appeared. Soon an O_2 drifted by and promptly became attached to it. A second O_2, then a third and fourth encountered the same fate, but after that, no more. Yet a host of O_2's continued to parade past, all to be caught up by the ravenous Fluorine molecule. There was no misunderstanding the demonstration.

"Not only does Durbane Pharmaceutical's universal blood substitute have oxygen carrying and release capability, but the new compound has twenty times the oxygen capacity of human blood." The floating symbols disappeared, and the professor was back, holding up the intravenous bag. "U.B.S. comes in a standard half-liter bag, the same volume as a unit of human blood. It has a shelf life of five years, and it is *preoxygenated.*

Since U.B.S. already contains oxygen, in addition to its obvious importance in treating acute blood loss and chronic anemia, it offers a new form of therapy for other life-threatening conditions. A quick IV of U.B.S. will save the life of a person with carbon monoxide poisoning, breaking the nearly irreversible bond of carboxyhemoglobin. It can save a near-drowning victim whose lungs are filled with water. U.B.S. can even save a patient with severe trauma to the airway preventing air exchange, or one with an airway blocked due to an inhaled foreign body. All these cases can be successfully treated with U.B.S. A rapid infusion of U.B.S. provides approximately fifteen minutes of available oxygen, *without the need for an airway.* This is enough time to suction out lungs filled with seawater, to perform a tracheostomy, or remove a deflated balloon from a child's throat--enough time to save a life. *And* our research still continues, as we search for even more uses for U.B.S."

"Fantastic," said the representative from Australia.

"Amazing. A miracle in a bag," offered another voice in the room.

Thurston Walker's voice cut through the darkness. "Hey, I like that--a miracle in a bag--I'll pass it on to marketing."

The holographic image of the professor was still holding up his IV solution for everyone in the room to see. "There will no longer be a need for expensive blood collection, storage, and transportation programs. There will be no danger of disease transmission. There will be no delays in transfusion due to blood typing and cross matching. No blood transfusion reactions." The speaker's image finally dissolved, leaving only the letters U.B.S. floating in the air. "There will be only U.B.S.-universal blood substitute, a product of Durbane Pharmaceuticals and their authorized distributors." The sound of the Mozart concerto swelled again as the room lights gradually returned and the final hologram faded away.

The audience sat stunned. The visual display had been a marvel of marketing technology, but the product they had seen--that was the real miracle. The Russian clapped, and instantly others joined in. The swell of applause carried Thurston Walker to the center of the room.

He waited for silence, his manner not unlike a victorious general preparing to address his troops after a great triumph. "There are at least five thousand blood transfusions a day in this country alone. That figure can be multiplied a dozen times over for the entire world. Add to that the newfound applications for our product, and you can foresee that the demand for U.B.S. will be astronomical.

We intend to market this product for the same cost as a unit of whole blood, which in this country, with processing fees, is over two hundred dollars. I will save you the trouble of doing the math--a million dollars a day in the U.S. alone." He became more excited. He raised a hand pointing to heaven. "But price will not be an issue because no one will want real human blood anymore. The market will be ours to command." The audience went wild with applause.

Walker looked from one company executive to the next. In their eyes, he could see the greed that was part of the make-up of any good C.E.O. "Durbane is already stockpiling U.B.S. in depots around the world, but there's no way we will meet the initial demand." He surveyed the excited faces. "Therefore, Durbane is offering each of you the opportunity to form a partnership to manufacture and dispense our artificial blood solution within your own territory." The faces became rapturous. "The cost for each franchise--one hundred million dollars, plus fifty percent of the profit you make from the sale of U.B.S."

A moment of stunned silence turned to an uproar of indignation. "Are you crazy?" growled Terrence from South Africa.

"I doubt my company could even borrow that amount of money," murmured Sergeyev.

Walker knew this would be the critical moment. He directed his response to Sergeyev. "Durbane will take letters of credit drawn on international banks using your own company assets as collateral. You can pay us the franchise fee out of your profits."

"Out of our fifty percent," complained Nigel Thatcher. "Durbane gets the other half."

"True," said Dr. Walker. "After all, Durbane has incurred considerable research expenses, as you can well imagine. But each of your companies will not only make more money than you have ever dreamed possible, but those who choose to sign on will immediately become the pre-eminent pharmaceutical manufacturers in their territory." He pointed to his security man in the back of the room. "Our accountants have prepared for each of you an individual prospectus of your anticipated income based on the historical blood usage in what will become your marketing part of the world. Karl will hand those out as you leave. My people will check with you in a week to determine your level of interest. Again, I request that there be no discussion of this information outside this room. The risk of government intervention is too great. I especially caution any of you who decide not to partake of this offer"--*always have a stick to back up the carrot*, Walker reminded himself-- "Should any company choose to create problems, have no doubt that it will be instantly swallowed up by a competitor that does choose to market U.B.S."

He smiled graciously. "Now, I want to thank you all for coming, and for those who are not immediately returning to their homes, I trust you will enjoy the recreations you've chosen for your visit here."

"One question, Dr. Walker," said the man from England.

"Yes, Mr. Terrence?"

"Does your product have any side effects?"

Although Thurston Walker had been standing under small floodlights, for the first time he felt sweat break out. He hesitated, but there was no avoiding it. "The only troublesome complication is that U.B.S. can sometimes induce pregnant recipients to abort."

"But that's unacceptable," said Dickinson of Chilton Laboratories as he jumped to his feet. "The Food and Drug Administration would put severe marketing restraints on us. Human blood may still wind up being more frequently prescribed in females."

"First," said Walker. "Our researchers are making progress on this problem even as we speak. I have a plan for dealing with the problem in the United States. Second, regulators in many other countries may not be so fussy as our FDA."

"I'm not so certain," said the woman who represented a consortium of pharmacy houses in southern Europe. "We have a large proportion of Catholics in our area. Many would not want to risk abortion even if the medication were given with the best therapeutic intent."

"And the Right to Life piranha would eat us alive," interjected Dickinson.

A tall figure stood. Davidson from Ireland, a man recognized for his business acumen and respected for his good judgment. "Dr. Walker, your company has made an outstanding medical and scientific breakthrough that will accomplish much good, not to mention be well worth our financial investment. However, that can only be after you have solved the abortion problem, *and* if no new side effects turn up." The man sat down, and the room fell silent.

Thurston Walker's hands tightened into fists. "We are assiduously working on this problem, and, as I've said, making great strides. But in the meantime, the longer we delay getting U.B.S. to market, the greater the likelihood another company will get there ahead of us."

That will give the grumblers something to think about thought Walker, as he walked from center stage.

Chapter 30

Sharon stopped cutting the tomatoes to scrutinize Cecil. The dog was happily curled up in Darcy's kitchen as near Brian's feet as he could get. "I had no idea that you and your furry friend were thinking of moving in with me for the duration."

She went to the refrigerator and brought out some hamburger meat. Seconds after the plastic wrap was opened Cecil raised his head to sniff the air.

"Actually, Sharon, we can't stay at my place."

"Why not?"

"Because I'm being followed, too."

Sharon froze.

Brian continued, "Two men came by asking my neighbor, Mrs. Thompson, about me. They told her they were government agents investigating my medical credentials, making sure I was who I said I was, or some such malarkey. But when she described them, I realized I'd seen them outside my office, and they didn't appear the friendly type. I accidentally spooked them by backing out in front of their car, and they must have thought it was an ambush. They came piling out in combat mode, one, I think, with a gun out. I didn't tell any of this to Mrs. Thompson--I didn't want to worry her—but I'm sure these guys are lying."

Sharon's hands moved slowly as she molded the meat into patties. "How do you know?"

"For one thing, they said they were checking up on what I'd already told them—but I haven't talked to them. For another, these guys asked about you. I haven't mentioned you to anybody except at the hospital when I was working up your case and trying to locate your records. So someone at the hospital has to be in on it."

"In on what, Brian? What?"

"Sharon, you are a unique commodity--the only known walking reservoir of artificial blood--and somebody wants that covered up."

"I guess, I still don't understand why it has to be such a big secret—big enough to kill for."

"That's a major part of the puzzle for me, too. Much of modern drug development is kept secret. Fortunes turn on who is the first to market a new class of drug. But to go to this extreme to cover it up?" Brian shook his head. "I don't understand it. But there are two things I do know: I want to talk to that doctor at, where is it?"

"Doúbe."

"Yeah. The doctor there has to be aware of what's going on."

"What's the other thing?" asked Sharon, nervously shaping and reshaping the beef.

"We have to go to the police."

"I knew that's what you were thinking." Sharon stopped her kneading to look him in the eye. "You know how I feel about that."

Brian stood and went to her side of the countertop to gather her into his arms. "Sharon, I don't want anything to happen to you. We have to tell the police."

"Tell them what, Brian? Just what would you tell the police. That I'm some kind of walking medical mystery, and I happen to know where Columbus' treasure is located? That's going to sound wild enough, and everything beyond that is just supposition."

"Then what do we do to end this madness?"

"We go to Haiti tomorrow as planned," said Sharon firmly. "That's where all this started, and that's where we'll find the answers."

Brian capitulated with a long sigh and a nod.

"Fine," said Sharon smiling. She glanced at the meal fixings spread out on the counter. "I don't cook you know. This is a rare exception for my--" She eyed the dog again, "guests. Now, how do you like your hamburgers?"

* * * * *

After supper, there was more wine and a mutual decision to pretend to watch TV and relax before their big trip the next day. But soon they were stretched out on the couch, wrapped in an embrace.

"Do you get the feeling we're being watched?" Sharon suddenly raised her head and asked.

Brian startled in alarm, then heard a scratching sound from the floor near the foot of the couch. He craned his neck to see what was going on. "Nah," he said, dismissing her mock concern. "Cecil's not paying any attention. He's working on an itch."

Sharon giggled. "Well, if you don't want to be left with an itch yourself, I suggest we move to the bedroom. Mr. Cecil can stay out here."

The deep bond between dog and man notwithstanding, Brian opened his mouth to instantly acquiesce, but before he could speak a beeping sound cut through the quiet of the room.

"Damn it!" he exclaimed.

"Don't you ever turn that thing off?" said Sharon.

"Not usually, but I'm beginning to give it some serious thought." His plucked his pager from the coffee table and punched the button to read the display. "It's the hospital operator, outside message." He sat back on the couch, one arm around Sharon while he dialed the number.

"You said you were taking some time off. Don't your partners cover for you?"

"Yeah," he said, "but sometimes someone still needs to reach me."

Sharon crossed her arms, scooted a couple of inches away from him, and glared at the television set.

"This is Dr. Richards." He listened, then asked, "What's her number?"

Sharon made an exaggerated show of raising her eyebrows at him and mouthing, "*her*?"

"Thanks," he said to the operator. "It's Dr. Edwards," he told Sharon excitedly, "the hematologist. And it must be important for her to call me at this hour."

"You doctors all seem to keep strange hours," Sharon observed.

She could only hear one side of the conversation, and her curiosity had reached a fever pitch by the time he finally hung up.

"Well?"

"She did a literature search on artificial blood," recounted Brian.

"And?"

"As she thought, most of the chemical approaches have been done using fluorine compounds. Interestingly, much of the early research was carried out by scientists at a company called Durbane Pharmaceuticals."

"I've heard of them," said Sharon. Her brow furrowed as she tried to remember why.

"They're a worldwide company, but their home office is right here in New Orleans Industrial Park." He added, "I'm familiar with them since they manufacture some of our hospital supplies. We get quick service because they're local."

181

"And Durbane makes artificial blood, but you didn't know about it?" Sharon asked.

"Not exactly. Currently nobody makes--or, I should say, markets--the substance. *And* Durbane stopped publishing data on the topic over two years ago."

"What does that mean?"

"Possibly that they gave up on that line of research, but Dr. Edwards thinks it's more likely that they made a major breakthrough and they wanted to keep it to themselves for the moment."

"And they're giving it out in Haiti?" said Sharon, puzzled.

"What better place to do research on artificial blood than in a country with plenty of 'volunteers' and a pressing need for a blood substitute?"

"How do you figure that?"

"Well, AIDS is rampant in Haiti. The C.D.C.--Centers for Disease Control--is constantly sending us flyers reminding us of countries where a traveler could easily have been exposed to the AIDS virus. Haiti is always on that list."

"That's true," interjected Sharon. "All the tourist guides have warnings about that, too."

"So you see, that country's medical system probably has very little whole blood available because of a lack of healthy donors. Plus, the country is so poor, I suspect human guinea pigs can be purchased relatively cheaply."

"All the more reason for us to get to Haiti, Brian. I went ahead and picked up some scuba equipment when I was out today. And this." She walked to the bookcase and from a high shelf produced the nine-millimeter Smith and Wesson."

Brian whistled. "The way your luck has been going lately, you'd better be careful you don't shoot yourself."

"Funny," she said dourly. "But you may be glad for some protection when we get to Doúbe."

"I'm more interested in checking out that clinic and the mysterious doctor."

"Not until after we recover the treasure," Sharon said, her voice now stern and her hands on her hips.

Brian raised his hands in surrender. "All right, all right. But I have something to do here before we leave--and that's pay a visit to the Durbane home office."

"And just what do you expect them to tell you?"

"Nothing. If Durbane is behind this, sticking my head up will just get it shot off. So I'm not going to ask."

"But we leave for Haiti tomorrow."

"I agreed, for now, not to go to the police, Sharon," Brian said. "In return, grant me one extra day to find out what I can about Durbane--from the inside. Then maybe the police will have something to work with besides just my theories."

"I suppose one day won't make a huge difference," Sharon conceded. "But there's one more matter you have to take care of." She grabbed his hand and pulled him toward the bedroom.

"With pleasure," he said in response.

"But first turn off that damn beeper."

Chapter 31

Thurston Walker stood on the balcony. San Francisco seen at nighttime from the twenty-seventh floor was impressive. The penthouse suite would have offered an even more spectacular view, and the corporation would have not minded paying the $2500 a night bill, but he did not want to attract the attention that went with the price tag.

He took another sip of his vodka martini. It tasted good, a restorative against the bite of the wind. Wasn't it Mark Twain who had said the coldest winter he ever spent was a summer in San Francisco?

Walker tried not to think about the unexpected attack on his presentation, but his mind kept coming back to it. Partnering with other pharmaceutical houses would not only have helped Durbane get large quantities of U.B.S. to a world-wide market thereby making an instant fortune, but also by pulling off such a coup he would've been shown as an innovative and successful C.E.O. His position would remain secure from Clarence Durbane's ouster attempt. But, the presentation had been a failure.

After the meeting, a few supporters had come to express their interest in U.B.S. Most, however, had slunk off to resume their trivial discussions with old colleagues or competitors. Earlier in the day, he thought he would be returning to this room like a lion after the hunt retiring in satisfaction to its lair. He had not imagined more than one or two of this hand-picked group turning down the opportunity to make billions of dollars for their company and probably millions for themselves. But rebuff him they had, and he had returned to his lair only to lick his wounds.

And back in his hotel room, there had been more upsets awaiting him. Karl told him that that troublesome Jackson woman who had been transfused with U.B.S. had not agreed to work with them and had even disappeared into hiding. Although he left the details of his plans unsaid, he indicated he was pulling out all stops to find her and coerce her into silence. Sometimes Karl was a little too aggressive, but in this case... if they could just keep U.B.S. under wraps a while longer, a fortune would be made. So Walker had chosen to say nothing to reign Karl in, a tacit go ahead, yet one which he could always deny later.

But the other upset was equally troubling--a coded message from Diane Gilmore. Using the appropriate passwords, he'd typed it into his laptop to retrieve the translation. Gilmore, through her contacts, had learned that MedUniversal Pharmaceuticals was well along in developing an artificial blood product. The substance was produced not by chemical methods but by genetic engineering. Even though it was still in the preclinical testing phase, she expected the company to move rapidly to request FDA permission to begin Phase I clinical trials. Her estimate: three years before the product was on the market.

He turned to lean against the balcony while the wind whipped his hair. He had earlier ditched his tie and now the unbuttoned cuffs of his white shirt flapped in the breeze.

Yes, this last cut was deep. What had earlier been unlimited potential was now only a window of opportunity--a three-year window--and that only if he survived the coming clash with Clarence Durbane.

The security man waited in the plush living room. He stubbed out his cigarette as Walker re-entered the suite through the sliding glass doors. "Do you need anything?" Dietrich asked.

Walker did not look him in the face but stared into the depths of his drink. "Yes. Put in a call to England, Dr. Peter Obrien. Tell him I want him here immediately. Send the Gulfstream for him. Tell the man--" The C.E.O. paused. "Tell him to bring his latest research with him, that his lab, the finest of its type in the world, is ready."

"It was already planned, as soon as we returned to New Orleans tomorrow, for me to take the obstetrical doctor to Doúbe."

"Oh, yes," said Walker. "Where is the man?"

"South Carolina."

"Dr. Obrien needs to get started on his work here, so take care of that matter first." Walker was silent for a moment while he pondered. "And this doctor from South Carolina..."

"Yes?"

"I had not planned to talk with him, but I've changed my mind. Bring him to the plant before the two of you leave for Doúbe."

"Very well," answered the security man as he turned to leave.

Walker stopped him. "One last thing. It would be a waste to spend an evening alone in this enchanting city, don't you think?"

Dietrich nodded. He had suspected that the C.E.O. might be in the mood for female companionship tonight. For that eventuality he had already arranged for two ladies whose beauty was matched only by their willingness to please. They could be here in fifteen minutes, and if his boss chose only one, Dietrich would be fortunate. They were both already paid for.

* * * * *

"This is not the time--"

"Nurse Connors," interrupted the bearded man in a tweed suit. He made a show of looking at her I.D. badge, as if to remind her that he would not forget her. "The situation is critical. I must examine that patient."

The nurse, with arms crossed and jaw set, stood steadfast. The other ward personnel had made themselves scarce as soon as it was apparent this confrontation was going ballistic. "Dr. Gilchrist, who just happens to be the boy's doctor, left very explicit instructions. They are not to be disturbed." She stood sentinel in the hall outside the nurses' station, her body a physical barrier between the interloper and those she was sworn to protect. "And you are not the child's doctor."

"Nurse Connors, there is not much time. You have seen the documents." He indicated the papers lying on the desk. "I have the authority of the Ministry of Health to pursue investigations of communicable diseases anywhere within the U.K. That includes this--" He looked around as if unsure what word to use for such a third-rate establishment and finally, after considerable thought, spat out, "--hospital." He pointed to the phone. "Shall I summon the magistrate?"

The nurse, whose responsibilities had aged her far more than her forty years, lowered her voice. "This is most likely their last night together."

"I will be brief," said the man. "Leave me to my job, please."

Room 1016 was at the end of the hall in the isolation unit of a hospital so old that some of its original wings had sustained damage during the blitz. Before entering, personnel had to go through an anteroom complete with scrub sink and dressing facilities.

During the thirties and forties, scarlet fever victims were the unit's most frequent residents, but the availability of penicillin brought that era to a close.

In the early fifties the ward accommodated poliomyelitis cases. Many a young person was wheeled through its doorway and into an iron lung, emerging later with paralysis of a foot or arm as evidence of the battle they had fought. With the advent of the Salk and Sabine vaccines, the iron lungs were moved into permanent storage. After that, the second floor was

187

remodeled, gone were the large wards and amphitheater atmosphere, replaced by smaller rooms better suited to the modern demands for privacy and to the latest concepts in isolation.

The eighties saw these rooms filled with AIDS cases, until the medical profession finally accepted that, as long as direct transfer of body fluids was avoided, AIDS was no more contagious than a heart attack. In the nineties the emergence of multi-drug resistant TB again filled the infectious disease unit to capacity, but newer antibiotics ultimately brought that modern plague under control, and the unit, once again, fell dormant.

Nigel Cunningham was the first patient to be in room 1016 in four months. He had Creutzfeldt-Jakob disease, the human equivalent of what the popular press termed Mad Cow disease.

In the isolation anteroom the visiting doctor pulled off his tweed jacket and tie. It was always hot under the protective garments. From the cabinet he took a one-piece jumpsuit and stepped into it, struggling to work his feet, still in his shoes, down the pants legs and into the attached booties. After zipping up the front, he put on the disposable hood. Then he donned a pair of rubber gloves and topped off the garb with a surgical mask that sported a glassine splash-shield for the eyes.

He pushed the inner door open. The room smelled of death. The lights were low, and a soundless TV flickered. A woman in protective clothing identical to his sat in a nearby chair. A comatose form lay in the bed.

"I am Dr. Peter Obrien from the Ministry of Health."

"I know," said the woman. She pointed to the wall intercom. "They told me."

"I need to examine your son to confirm the diagnosis. I must take a few samples." He indicated the small valise he carried. It too was covered with a disposable protective cloth. "Perhaps there is still something that can be done." Of course, that last statement was a lie, but it might make it easier for the mother to submit her son to more medical probing. The son, of course, would not mind.

"I would rather not leave him, doctor," said the woman. "We may not have much longer." She spoke in a resigned tone, as if too weary to even cry.

"I will only be a few minutes. If you go to the dining room, the nurse will come for you the moment I am finished. Doubtless you could do with some tea," he said firmly.

She rose slowly, and he noticed that in her hand was a small book embellished with a cross. She placed it in the seat of the chair.

As soon as the woman left Obrien flicked on the overhead lights bathing the frail body on the bed in brightness. He moved to the bedside and began his examination. One could never trust the reports sent in by the local physicians, even if confirmed by a neurologist. Most doctors went a lifetime without seeing a case of C.J. Disease, and there were no laboratory tests definitively diagnostic of the condition. Imaging studies of the brain were useful. An M.R.I. showing vacuoles, or holes, making the computerized slices of brain look like Swiss cheese, supported the diagnosis, but even that test was nonspecific. Electron microscopy of brain tissue, revealing the unbelievably tiny infectious particles, was the only way to be certain. There was no time to schedule a brain biopsy now; he'd just have to wait for the postmortem.

He leaned over the bed. The patient's stated age was fifteen, although the child was so emaciated it was difficult to tell. The chart indicated that the boy had been unable to eat for the past six weeks. Dr. Obrien believed it. Intravenous hyperalimentation feedings never fully replaced the body's caloric needs.

The cheeks were flaccid, the mouth open. He unsnapped the valise and removed a small penlight. The boy's tongue was dry and cracked from mouth breathing. A fetid odor came from inside, and the doctor recoiled slightly. He pulled apart the eyelids. The surface of the eyeballs was dry and lifeless. He shone the penlight directly into the pupil. No reaction. The optic-ciliary nerve pathways were gone.

Obrien continued the examination. When he picked up the boy's arm, it was like rubber. He let it drop. He produced the reflex hammer and tapped at the appropriate points. No deep tendon reflexes. He pulled the sheet down. The boy was catheterized to drain away wastes. The lower extremities were as fleshless and flaccid as the upper. He supposed there was no reason to doubt the boy had the new and rapid variant of Creutzfeldt-Jakob.

From his valise the doctor removed a rubber tourniquet, applied it to a skeletal arm covered with blue splotches, and began his search for a vein that might have survived countless encounters with other needle-wielding medical professionals. Eventually he located one on the palmar side of the wrist. Taking no chances, he donned a second pair of protective gloves. Made of tightly woven Kevlar, they were stick-proof but almost impossible to work in. The vein was fragile and rolled whenever he tried to stick it. The boy never reacted to the probing. After three attempts, Obrien finally managed to fill several tubes with the blood he needed. He pulled the sheet back up, then busied himself double-sealing the blood tubes in plastic and storing them in the valise. The venipuncture needle went in the sharps container that was attached to the wall at the head of the bed.

Obrien closed his valise pleased his efforts had not taken long. He had plenty of time to get back to his lab, freeze this specimen, and pick up the others before the Durbane jet arrived.

Suddenly he noticed that an intense silence had descended on the room. There were no more rasping respirations from the patient. Dr. Peter Obrien looked at the boy. The jaw hung slack; the chest no longer moved. Just as well the mother was absent, he thought. Such a moment is always so traumatic with a family member at the bedside.

He left to tell Nurse Connors.

Chapter 32

After the phone call from Dr. Edwards, Brian and Sharon had retired behind a closed bedroom door. The unfortunate Cecil had no such luck and found himself shut out. He chose to exact his revenge by ignoring the prohibition against dogs on the furniture. Jumping up onto the couch, he engaged in a short bout of scratching, followed it with a canine sigh, then settled deeply into the cushions for the night.

As Sharon slept--Brian lay awake thinking about what must be done--and whether he was the man to do it. The people after Sharon seemed to be everywhere. Could the police really protect her if there was a determined assault, one that could occur anytime, anywhere? Was Durbane responsible? Possibly, but with the resources at their disposal, would they ever be found out? Probably not. A large, multinational company would have many ways to conceal unethical, even illegal, practices. What he needed was evidence, something the police could work with. He could just picture an N.O.P.D. detective, armed with a search warrant, knocking on Durbane's front gate. How would the police even know what to look for? They wouldn't, but he would. The answer was obvious. He had to get into the plant and find the evidence himself--something to connect Durbane Pharmaceuticals with the Haitian medical clinic. And where was the best place to look? He would have to talk to someone on the inside.

Clearly, Sharon thought he was the one to turn to, to trust, and he couldn't bear to disappoint her. He'd already taken the risky leap, from her physician to her lover, and now to protect her he'd need more than just his medical skills. He'd need to be a bodyguard and a sleuth. Brian could only hope that the investigative techniques he'd honed for searching out hidden illness or injury would stand him in good stead in the work that lay ahead. Because, otherwise, he had a lot to lose. Dale Blevins had as much as told him that his career at Beauvoir Memorial was hanging by a thread. And losing that would be nothing compared to losing Sharon.

As if receiving his thoughts by telepathy, Sharon turned and murmured in her sleep, clinging to his shoulder. He had no choice but to press on with their plans. Because to hesitate now might be to lose this fierce, brilliant love he had found. And then he would have nothing.

* * * * *

Brian arose the next morning with a new sense of purpose. His mind had been processing the situation even as he slept, and now, as he showered and shaved, he plotted his next moves. There were so many ways to go wrong, to blow his cover, but in a sense what he had to do was no different than plotting a successful solution to a tricky surgical problem--take it one step at a time, make each move count, and *be careful*.

He began with a series of calls while Sharon was still asleep. The first was to Mrs. Thompson to find out if anyone else had been by asking about him. She didn't answer her phone, but he knew she was an early riser, and perhaps she was outside doing the yard work she so enjoyed. He'd try her again later.

The next call went to the shipping and receiving department of Beauvoir Memorial Hospital. The day shift began at seven A.M., and the one person he knew, Warren Hewitt, had just come on duty. The man had helped him a few months earlier by tracking down a piece of surgical equipment that had been ordered but never arrived. Warren again was helpful. He verified that Durbane was one of Beauvoir's major suppliers, although he knew little about the inner workings of the pharmaceutical plant. He did, however, have a contact there and gave Brian the man's name.

For the call to the Durbane plant, Brian adopted the title of supervisor of purchasing. He had decided an aggressive approach would work best, and it did get him past the first two levels of functionaries. Finally he was speaking to the supervisor of shipping.

"Beauvoir is down to a twenty-four hour supply of lactated ringer's solution, and instead of that your company has sent us some kind of intravenous fluid I've never heard of."

"I don't see how that could happen," said the supervisor. "Are you sure your people didn't make a mistake with the order numbers?"

"Would they make a mistake about our location? The routing slip says Haiti, not New Orleans." Brian heard a choking sound come from the telephone.

"Haiti?" the supervisor said in a much subdued tone.

"That's right."

"Oh, shit."

"Problem?" said Brian innocently.

192

"A big one. Security will have my butt if I don't get that shipment back."

Brian was all ears. "Security?"

"Uh, that's not exactly what I meant. It's just that we've got a special department that handles consignments to Haiti, and they don't like any slip-ups. They take 'em real personal."

"I might be able to help you out of the jam," said Brian conspiratorially. "If I send this stuff back, then they'll know your department screwed up..." Brian let the man hang for a moment before he continued. "But if it just disappears, no one will know anything, providing, of course, you can cover any paperwork at your end."

"Great idea, but will you be sure it disappears?"

"No problem. It's only three cases. I'll have them sent directly to our on-site compactor and then out for incineration with the biohazardous waste."

The man's sigh of relief came through clearly over the phone. "If there's ever anything I can do?"

"Think nothing of it. But I do have a few questions. Maybe if I know how your department works, then, we can avoid these mix-ups in the future."

Soon Brian had a fairly good picture of how Durbane's deliveries were handled, the location of its shipping and receiving department, and even whether a gate pass was required.

When he hung up, Brian also had the good feeling of knowing that Beauvoir Memorial Hospital would receive a hundred free cases of lactated ringer's solution. And, doubtless, at Christmastime Beauvoir's supervisor of purchasing would be pleasantly surprised by a most generous gift from his opposite number at Durbane Pharmaceuticals.

Brian looked at his watch. Nine o'clock and Sharon was beginning to stir. Which left him just enough time to dally a bit before he searched out the bar nearest the Durbane plant for a couple of lunchtime beers and to ask a few more innocent questions.

* * * * *

It was late afternoon. Wearing neatly pressed gray work clothes he had purchased for only a few dollars at the Army-Navy store, Brian strolled up to the Air Cargo Terminal desk at New Orleans International Airport. This was not a ticket counter staffed with attractive sales reps in their designer uniforms. Here a duo in rumpled service overalls were occupied checking routing numbers on shipping crates.

Brian waited until the female member of the team looked his way, then he gave his most appealing smile. The workers here had not been through an airline-sponsored course in public relations, but the woman stopped what she was doing anyway and asked if she could help. He placed his hands on the counter to reveal the thick, red and blue striped package he carried. "I'm with Rapid Courier Express," he explained. "Do you know where I can find the trucks going to Durbane Pharmaceuticals?" He pointed over his shoulder. "My truck broke down, and they told me to ask here."

She indicated an exit sign. "Go past the gate to the metal hangar, but don't cross the fence onto the runway taxi area."

Brian followed her directions and soon encountered delivery trucks of every description. He wandered among them until he began to wonder if the information given him from the supervisor of shipping at Durbane was incorrect and their delivery truck left earlier for the plant. Then he rounded an eighteen-wheeler and saw a smaller truck with *Durbane Pharmaceuticals* in blue lettering on its side. The driver wore the same dark green work uniform he had seen on the other lower-echelon Durbane workers in the bar. The driver, who bore a striking resemblance to Telly Savalas, stood talking to a man wearing a floral print shirt that looked like it came straight from a tourist trap in Honolulu. Brian hoped the refugee from the tropics wasn't planning to take the passenger seat he wanted to get for himself. Both men stopped talking as Brian approached.

"Sorry to bother you," Brian said, speaking directly to the Durbane driver. "I'm Brian with Rapid Courier Express." He nonchalantly flipped the identification card hanging from its clip on his shirt pocket. It swung back into place with only the blank side showing. He talked quickly, hoping the driver wouldn't pay attention to the card, because closer scrutiny would reveal it was actually his Beauvoir Memorial Hospital I.D. "This came in on Delta." He held out his package. "I need to get it to Durbane, but my van won't start."

The man with the floral shirt said to the driver, "I've got to go, Nick. Catch you later."

The driver nodded his goodbye and returned to Brian. "Want me to take it for you? This is my last run, and I'm going straight back to the plant."

"Thanks, but I'm supposed to hand deliver it." Brian shook his head and accompanied it with a smirking grin, as if this were just another example of corporate idiocy. "It's a company requirement. But the office did call your dispatcher, and they said to try to catch you here for a ride in. They'll come get my van later." He made a point of looking at his watch and seeming peeved. "I don't care if they ever get that damn van fixed. It drives like a rattletrap, and this is the second time this month it broke down. And I had big plans with my girlfriend tonight," he added with a lewd grin.

The truck driver leered back. "I know how you feel. Climb aboard."

By big-city standards the airport was not far from town, but in rush-hour traffic the trip could take three-quarters of an hour--a long time, in close quarters, to keep a lie going. Brian said something to Nick about staying out too late last night, then pretended to doze. The driver made a few unsuccessful attempts to engage him in conversation, but finally he, too, lapsed into silence against the background of music from an oldies-but-goldies station.

Brian pretended to rouse as the truck slowed at the Durbane gate. He had a story prepared if he were challenged, but they were waved through without a second glance. Once inside the plant, the trucker let him off and asked if he knew where to go. Brian said he already had directions and thanked the man.

The main building was obvious. Brian recalled what the Durbane shipping supervisor had told him, and it took only a moment to locate the side entrance. He walked in as nonchalantly as any Durbane employee who had done this every day for ten years.

Just inside was the employee cafeteria, a giant room used as gathering place and dining hall. At the vending machines he studied the choices, made a purchase, and then settled at a corner table to nibble on his Fritos and, he hoped, avoid attention.

The room filled rapidly as workers stopped in to grab a snack or trade talk prior to going home. Some gathered around the wall-mounted television set to watch a few minutes of the evening newscast while waiting for their carpool members to arrive.

Brian feigned interest in the TV. One particularly garrulous worker kept offering his opinion on local affairs, first to the television, then to anyone nearby. Brian wanted no conversation, so he retreated behind an abandoned

newspaper. Suddenly the newscaster's droning voice tore into Brian's consciousness.
"The body was identified as that of Mrs. Inez Thompson." Mrs. Thompson! Brian jerked the newspaper down to stare incredulously at the T.V. The newsman's face was impassive as he read from the teleprompter. "Two fisherman discovered what remained of the body shortly after daybreak. The victim was a sixty-five-year-old resident of north Orleans parish. Prompt identification was possible through the newly established National DNA Databank. The Chief Deputy said foul play is suspected, but no motive has yet been established. Anyone with any information that might help in the investigation of Mrs. Inez Thompson's death is asked to contact the N.O.P.D. detective squad at the following number."

Brian stared, open-mouthed, while the newscaster recited the phone number on the screen, then turned and said, "Now Spencer Davis will tell us what's coming up for the weekend weather."

Brian was in shock. Another innocent bystander—his friend--cut down in cold blood. He wanted to rush to the authorities, tell them what he knew--what he suspected, the thugs behind this were on Durbane's payroll, men who wanted to protect a secret at all costs.

But what could he do right now? He was deep in enemy territory, and if discovered, there was no way he could make it past the gate guard and out of the plant. He would be apprehended by plant security, and--what was it that the Durbane shipping clerk had said? All Haiti consignments went through a special department overseen by Security, and they take anything that goes wrong real personal. No, he couldn't get away now. He might as well do what he'd come for.

And what about afterward? Would he be safe with the police? Would they believe that there was a giant conspiracy to protect a pharmaceutical secret, or would they consider him a lunatic? Sharon's blood was rapidly replacing itself, and whatever product had been in her body might now be completely eliminated. All her medical records at the hospital were missing. And even if he did convince the police to search the plant, the chances were that only spotlessly clean laboratories would be found, devoid of any incriminating evidence.

No, for the immediate future, he had to proceed on his own. Find the damning evidence here or in Haiti. Help Sharon retrieve her treasure. Then pass everything on to the authorities, and in one single crushing strike this entire snake pit could be cleaned out.

With renewed determination, Brian grabbed his courier package off the table. He asked directions from a man waiting for a vending machine to brew a cup of industrial-grade coffee. As the thick black fluid spewed into the container, the worker answered his question but added that all the departments were already closed. Brian responded that he was only dropping something off, and he headed out the door.

It was a long hike through deserted hallways. Just as he was about to conclude this giant building was a labyrinth like the Pentagon, where one could walk the interconnecting corridors forever, he encountered a metal rolling door and a plastic sign announced *loading dock*.

Brian looked around for a place to hide.

The adjacent glass-doored office was lettered *Shipping and Receiving*. That was too exposed, even if he could get in. A door on the opposite side of the hall said read *Utility*. He tried that knob--unlocked. He flipped the light switch. Mops, brooms, and buckets filled the closet. He slipped in, made a space for himself in the cramped quarters, and shut the door.

Ripping open the package he had used as a prop, he extracted the other uniform he'd purchased—one in the same green color worn by the Durbane workers he'd first seen in the bar. He quickly donned the outfit, stuffing the one he'd just removed into a refuse bag attached to a utility cart. Then he flicked off the light, leaving only the illumination from the crack under the door. Now all he could do was wait.

Time passed slowly. Thoughts of Mrs. Thompson, who had showered her kindness on him and Cecil, nearly overwhelmed him. The person responsible for taking her life deserved a fate worse than what had befallen her--and if there was some way he could tend to that personally, he would.

He settled back against a carton of toilet tissue and tried to concentrate on the matter immediately at hand. He wasn't really afraid of being discovered. His visit to a bar near the plant entrance had paid off well. All he had hoped for was a close-up look at their uniforms and some information about Durbane's work shifts, but a dedicated drinker just off the night shift and already sitting at the bar was glad to be helpful in return for a few beers and a sympathetic ear. There were not many nighttime workers, he told Brian, mostly security guards and a few people in the warehouse where stock checks and such went on around the clock in readiness for instant shipment of Durbane pharmaceuticals to anywhere in the world. That's where he worked--the warehouse.

Brian had asked about shipments to Haiti. The man nodded and lowered his voice, saying those were strictly hush-hush and always overseen by security. Lately there'd been a lot of activity requiring the attention of the security department, especially at night, when special shipments left the plant to go to the airport and then on to distant parts via Durbane jet. The drunk boasted that he had been with the company thirty-one years and so was trusted with such assignments. To Brian's cautious inquiry about what was being transported in the dead of night, the warehouse man said he only knew it was medicines so new they were still secret. Brian left the man gazing fondly into his fifth beer.

He had been told that lately the shipments went out most nights, shortly after midnight, so if he were lucky, he would get to see one tonight. Then he might have some proof positive of what Durbane was up to.

At the moment, though, the main problem he had to deal with was restlessness. After another thirty minutes, Brian decided he was wrong. Restlessness was no longer the main problem--slow death by asphyxia was. Unless something happened soon the morning janitorial crew would probably discover his oxygen-starved body--stiffened by rigor mortis into a bookend for a box of Charmin.

He had just made up his mind to crack the door open for some ventilation when he heard the rumbling of heavy equipment, the sound of voices, and a racket as the metal door rolled upward. He waited until the noise died away, then stood, shook the kinks from his legs, and cautiously peered out of the closet. The rolling door was still up. He inched out into the hallway, to hide in the shadow cast by the metal doorframe.

A tow motor idled on the concrete loading dock. Attached to it were two flatcars, each stacked high with cardboard boxes lashed to wooden pallets. A truck waited on the loading dock. Beside it were four men; one in a white lab coat, one leaning on a forklift, and two were clearly laborers.

The loading went smoothly as the forklift transferred the pallets off the first cart and into the waiting truck. Brian wondered if his beer-drinking buddy was on the forklift, but he couldn't be sure at this distance, especially in the glare thrown off by the overhead lights. He watched and waited hoping for a chance to get closer. Then the white-coated man went down into the bay to talk with the truck driver, while the laborers climbed into the truck to arrange cargo. The forklift driver dismounted and walked into the darkness. Brian saw the flare of a cigarette. It was now or never.

A quick sprint and he was beside the second cart, hidden by the stacked boxes. He searched the cartons' exterior for a label or description of the contents but found none. After digging into his pocket for his knife, he began Brian sawing into the shipping carton nearest him. The cardboard was sturdy, requiring considerable effort, but suddenly the blade pushed through and a gush of fluid poured out. Brian jumped back as clear liquid covered his hands and ran down the side of the stacked boxes--thoughts of toxic chemicals and caustic acids ran through his mind. But he felt no pain. He cautiously sniffed his drenched hands but detected no smell. Carefully he peeled back the cut cardboard. Inside were tightly packed bags of the same clear substance. He worked a hand into the box, grasped a bag, and pulled it out.

So this was the big secret--a one liter plastic bag with a loop on one end and a rubber-sealed nipple on the other. He had seen this type of container a thousand times over--IV fluid. He turned it over. There print read simply *U.B.S.* He knew thousands of medical abbreviations, but not this one.

A quick glance around the loading dock confirmed he was still alone and unobserved. Clutching the IV bag like a football, he sprinted for his closet.

Once he was safely hidden, his heart rate gradually slowed to normal. In a few minutes, when the workers discovered the torn box, he hoped they would conclude the forklift had done the damage during loading. And if the rest of his expedition went as well as it had up until now, he would be back at the apartment with Sharon in time for breakfast. All he had to do was wait in the closet until 7:00 A.M. Then, with his stolen IV fluid in a paper sack disguised as leftover's from his meal, he would mingle with the night shift workers as they left.

Chapter 33

Dietrich fixed himself a rum and water from the small bar in the Gulfstream. With disappointment he noted there were no lime wedges. The copilot must have forgotten. He added two ice cubes and settled back, then cast a glance at the man in the seat across the narrow aisle. It was amazing how a thirty-five million-dollar jet could have less room in it than a small motor home, he thought.

Dietrich spoke to the other man. "Are you sure you don't want something else? The bar is well stocked, except for lemons and limes." He carefully watched for a reaction--a wavering of resolve that might indicate the temptation was too much. The man was thirty-nine, recently divorced. He had the smooth hands of a physician but the jittery temperament of a newly recovering alcoholic within reaching distance of a drink.

"No thanks. I'll stick with this." The doctor held up his soft drink.

"Fine," said Dietrich, twisting to look out the small cabin window. "We're above a heavy cloud cover. Not much to see." He turned back. "You might find this entertaining." He reached toward the small video panel on the bulkhead. He pressed a button, and a print display sprang to life showing ground speed, 495 miles per hour; outside temperature, a disconcerting thirty degrees below zero; and altitude, 38,000 feet. "I prefer this screen," Dietrich said as he punched another button. The digital display was replaced by a green map. A wavy line represented the coast of Florida, dotted with the three-letter designations of airports. Dietrich pointed to the blinking cursor. "You can see we are just now crossing into the Atlantic to swing east of Cuba."

The doctor put an elbow on his armrest and leaned to take a closer look. As he did, his gaze fixed briefly on Dietrich's drink perched in the holder of the armrest. But he quickly looked away.

Dietrich smiled to himself. So far, so good.

"How long before we're there?"

"Less than two hours until we land," said Dietrich, "and after that we have a short helicopter ride."

For a while the doctor watched the cursor's slow crawl, then he settled back to stare out the window at the white cotton floor below.

Dietrich pressed the lever to tilt his seat back. He took a sip of his drink and closed his eyes, savoring the alcohol as it slid down his throat.

This particular task was progressing satisfactorily. Once Dr. Walker had given him his orders, the search had taken no more than a day. In fact, thanks to computers and the recent demand for medical accountability, it was amazingly easy. All Dietrich had needed was someone to help him access the files of the medical licensure boards, an easy enough task for Darrell Fendley's organization. Fendley had been part of Dr. Walker's network for years. Durbane's public relations department worked hard to establish such useful business liaisons. Fendley never had to do anything overt, merely drop a word here, a suggestion there, and Durbane products were favored in nearly every bid. In return, favors found their way to Mr. Fendley: big-game hunting trips in Colorado; gift shipments of prime cuts of beef and expensive wines for Christmas; the latest personal computer for his home, and a few other things that the wife didn't know about.

Dietrich scrutinized the doctor across from him and reflected on how simple it had been to get the right man for the right job.

Two days ago, when he called Fendley, the administrator had transferred him to a Mrs. Leathers, Beauvoir's director of nursing, who seemed only too eager to please; no doubt she already knew that working with Durbane had its perks.

By late afternoon Mrs. Leathers had called back with the information Dietrich needed. Posing as a member of the hospital credentials committee, she had checked with the medical licensure boards of Louisiana and of other nearby states, surreptitiously searching out records on any physicians whose licenses had recently been suspended.

It was amazing the number of doctors who were in such trouble. In Louisiana alone, it amounted to at least ten a month. A few lost their medical licenses permanently, usually because of a serious felony, but most licenses were suspended only until the errant physician had successfully completed a substance-abuse program, made restitution to Medicare, undergone psychological counseling, or performed whatever penance the board deemed appropriate.

Dietrich had methodically searched the list of potential recruits, over a hundred names. He decided he preferred someone who had lost his license due to alcohol abuse, a not insurmountable problem.

The next step was to query the National Practitioner's Data Bank. Of course, access to that physician database was limited to those with demonstrable need-to-know such as government agencies, hospitals, and medical insurers. Once again Mrs. Leathers was utilized. From the National Practitioner's Data Bank she obtained the additional information Dietrich required: number and type of malpractice suits and the amount paid out on each claim. A physician who had recently lost his medical license and had enough suits against him would be at the rock bottom of his professional life, Dietrich had concluded, ready to grab any opportunity. And the final selection criteria: the doctor had to be single and, most importantly, an obstetrician.

Armed with a list of prospects, it took only three calls before Dietrich thought he had the right doctor. An offer of half a million dollars a year, frequent rest trips back to the U.S., and an agreement that Durbane Pharmaceuticals would provide his malpractice insurance coverage when he returned to private practice was sufficient inducement to get Dr. Robert Taylor on the plane immediately.

Dietrich had considered simply supplying Dr. Taylor with an airline ticket--after all, unfinished business with one very slippery female archaeologist still required Dietrich's attention, but he decided it would be best to personally escort the physician to his new job. It was not that Dr. Baptiste would pose any problem; the French medical missionary's over-developed sense of responsibility allowed him to be easily manipulated. Dietrich's concern was that Dr. Taylor might avail himself of the all too convenient Haitian rum and forget the main reason he was here. As a matter of fact, Dietrich himself once had to spend the night in Port-au-Prince because of a problem with the helicopter. A goodly part of his wait took place in the hotel bar where he developed a certain fondness for Barbancourt Rum. Hopefully, the new physician would not fall prey to old weakness.

Dr. Walker had already instructed the new recruit on his responsibility to find more of the right kind of experimental subjects for U.B.S. Dietrich smirked. An obstetrician who had worked with a family-planning clinic in Columbia, South Carolina, and was listed with the pro-choice agencies as willing to perform abortions should have no difficulty with that aspect of the situation. The only concern was whether the new doctor would feel ethically compelled to tell his patients that they were also test subjects. Dietrich's initial impression of Dr. Taylor was that the man would probably not mind keeping that little fact to himself.

Chapter 34

"The face"--Sharon pretended puzzlement--"I think I recognize it. But the clothes? Did you give up doctoring and take up honest employment?"

"Very funny, Sharon." Brian stood in the living room of the apartment wearing his fake Durbane work uniform, now soiled with a sticky fluid and a prodigious amount of closet dust.

He walked straight to the kitchenette and opened the fridge. "What's for breakfast?" he asked hopefully.

"Whatever you fix," she retorted.

He hung from the refrigerator door, a forlorn expression on his face. "You haven't prepared a welcome-home feast for Sir Galahad, who has been out risking death in his search for the truth? Which, incidentally, I found."

Sharon's teasing attitude evaporated. "You found something at Durbane?"

He nodded. "At least I think I did." He explained. "They're making secret shipments out of the plant--at night. I got into one of the crates. It was IV fluid, labeled U.B.S."

"What does that mean?"

"Beats me. I've never heard of it, so on the way here I called one of my hospital pharmacy buddies. He tried to look it up, but it's not listed anywhere. But I had a lot of time to think in the closet."

"In the closet?"

"Yeah. That's where I hid. Anyway, I'm going to look up U.B.S. in a directory of trademarked names, though I doubt that'll tell us anything other than that the name belongs to Durbane, which we already know."

"If this stuff is so secret, why would they publicize it with a trademark?"

"The chemical formula would remain a proprietary secret. They'd just obtain the rights to the name so somebody else can't use it. These big drug companies have entire departments sitting around thinking up names to save for the time when the right drug comes along. But I do have a way of finding out if that stuff is what they gave you." Brian grinned as triumphantly as if he had discovered a cure for the common cold. "I stole a bag of their U.B.S. and dropped it off with Dr. Edwards this morning. It won't take her long to analyze it. Of course, I didn't tell her how I got it. Wouldn't want my old professor to think I was a thief. Now, did I at least earn a piece of toast?"

Sharon padded across the kitchen in her socks, got out a loaf of bread, pulled the toaster forward on the counter, and pushed it in his direction. "Somebody smart enough to pull off an escapade like you just did ought to be able to figure out how to work one of these."

Resigned, Brian made his own toast. He remained silent, lost in thought, while the toaster worked. Then, quietly, he asked, "By any chance, did you watch the local news last night?"

"No," said Sharon.

The toast popped up, but Brian simply stared at the machine. "Remember my telling you about Mrs. Thompson, my neighbor, the lady who looks after Cecil?"

"I remember."

"On the news, they said her body was found in a swamp up by Point aux Chenes."

"What? What happened?" Sharon asked, her voice filled with dread.

"She was murdered," he said, his tone flat and emotionless. After a moment, he went on. "It had to be the men who were out there asking about me. Christ," he blurted out angrily. "She was an innocent old lady who never hurt anyone. Whoever did this to her doesn't deserve to live."

"They must be everywhere," Sharon moaned.

"I wonder," said Brian as a thought struck him, "where's my pager?"

"On the dresser in the bedroom."

He located the pager and returned. As soon as Brian activated it, messages began scrolling across the screen. There were two from Dale and a half dozen from the hospital operator. He called the hospital first.

"We've been trying to reach you," said the operator as soon as he identified himself. "A detective Bennie Touchett with N.O.P.D. wants you to call him. He left his number." She read it off.

"Thanks," Brian said.

"What was that all about?" asked Sharon as soon as he clicked off the phone.

"It's not just the bad guys who're after us. Now the police want a piece of the action, too."

Sharon gave him a puzzled look.

"Some N.O.P.D. detective has been calling for me. I'm sure it's to question me about Mrs. Thompson. It only makes sense, right? I'm her nearest neighbor, and I've been missing since about the time she died. I'm probably number one suspect on their list."

"But Brian," Sharon gasped, "if they interrogate you, it will lead them to me, and that could lead to Haiti."

Brian slammed a fist down. "Jesus Christ, Sharon. You can't let people keep getting killed for the sake of a few old doubloons. We've got to tell what we know so the murderers can be caught."

Sharon trembled from his sudden ferocity and her own horror, but after a moment she regained her composure and pointed out the obvious. "And just what *do* we know? Two men were asking questions about you. The neighbor lady they talked to wound up dead. We think Durbane is making artificial blood and their evil organization is out to destroy me?" She stood with angry stance and fading black-eye, every bit a prize fighter ready to take on all comers. "It won't work, Brian. From what you say, Durbane is a very reputable company. There's not even grounds to search the plant--just our suspicions."

"So what do we do?" Brian shouted in frustration. "Keep hiding and wait for more murders?"

Sharon dropped her head. Her tone was conciliatory. "No. You're right. This thing has gone too far." She looked up at him, her expression bleak. "Tell the police before somebody else gets killed."

"It's the right decision, Sharon," Brian said quietly.

Then her attitude brightened slightly. "I've got our plane tickets out of here for late this afternoon. Maybe if you don't say anything about my discovery, I can still pull off my plan." Brian saw the hope in her beautiful blue eyes.

"It's a deal."

The microwave timer went off. Sharon removed a plate of perfectly done bacon and turned to the range to pour an egg mixture from a bowl on the counter into an omelette pan. "I thought you said I had to make my own breakfast," Brian said.

"I lied," she replied softly.

Chapter 35

Detective Bennie Touchett was not a happy person, thought Brian. In fact, the man might derive substantial benefit from an extended course of psychotherapy. If nothing else, it might help him get over his pathological dislike of doctors. Brian had seen it before. Not only in reluctant patients but also in insurance claims adjusters suspicious that every doctor was out to rip off the company or the patient. The same attitude could pop up anywhere. Distrust, no doubt, went with a police officer's job, but in Touchett's case, it seemed as if he took particular enjoyment in making what he took to be an overpaid and usually mollycoddled physician squirm. Then again, maybe Touchett simply disliked people in general.

The paunchy, detective with a head of thick, black hair had been at the apartment within an hour of their call, bringing a mostly silent sidekick along with him. Brian unfolded their tale, from Sharon's injury diving in Haiti to Mrs. Thompson's murder. He left out everything about the cave and the Columbus treasure, and he studiously avoided any mention of his sneaking into the Durbane plant and carting out a pack of their IV fluid. Somehow he didn't think this detective would take too kindly to the revelation of his breaking, entering and theft, especially if it turned out that what Brian stole had nothing to do with Sharon's problem.

"We're about through--for now, doc," the detective grumped.

The sidekick asked no questions. Evidently it was his job to scribble continually on a pad, leaving Touchett to take his full pleasure with the interrogation.

"Only a few more points to go back over, doc. Now, your alibi at the time Mrs. Inez Thompson was murdered was that you were making a house call with"--he looked over his glasses at Sharon and paused--"your friend."

"It's not an alibi."

"Don't be so touchy, doc. It's just a term."

Brian thought of a few terms, too, but kept his temper under control. "Yes," he responded icily.

"Were there any other witnesses to this 'house call'?"

"No, we were alone," interjected Sharon from beside Brian on the couch.

"Look," Brian said. "I returned your call and have tried to explain what I think is going on here. I have no proof yet, but I believe Durbane

Pharmaceuticals is behind all this. You need to interrogate them, not me. There are two guys, a black man and a Cajun man, I think."

Brian saw Touchett's eyes narrow when he said Cajun. "They drive a white Ford sedan, that's probably two or three years old. They have been at my office and my home. Mrs. Thompson described them."

"I'll check all that out, too."

* * * * *

During the drive back to the police station, the detective's partner spoke up. "Do you believe them?"

"Their story has more holes in it than my favorite pair of yard-work shorts," said Bennie Touchett. "Which, incidentally, Gloria threw away last week," he added with unmistakable annoyance.

"What do you make of that stuff about Haiti?"

"They're covering something up. For one thing, why didn't Jackson or the doctor over there request the assistance of the American Embassy? It sounded almost like she was slipped out of the country."

"Slipped out--why?"

"Don't know," said Touchett. "Smuggling maybe. She goes down there several times a year--plenty of opportunity to pick up something besides old fossils to bring into the country. Maybe she and her boyfriend kept something for themselves this time instead of sharing it, and now they're running scared."

"Richards did seem a bit edgy to me," observed the partner.

"And Richards says that people around Dr. Jackson are being killed," added Touchett. "Hell, she doesn't even know Inez Thompson. The target, if there is one, may be Richards himself. Maybe he crossed somebody not used to being crossed."

"Should we put them under surveillance?"

"Not right now. If they were going to run, they would have done it before now."

"Satisfied?" asked Sharon.

"Assholes," was Brian's response. "I try to help the police, and they make me out to be the mad murderer of Orleans Parish."

"I guess he was just doing his job," said Sharon smoothing Brian's hair in an attempt to soothe his frustration. "Look, we only have four hours to go, Brian, and we're all packed."

"Then let's get the hell out of Dodge. I've done my bit with the authorities, not that they believed me, and I'm ready for a change of scenery." Cecil was in his sitting-alert-and-maybe-something-fun-will-happen stance. Brian clasped the dog's head so he could look into his eyes as he spoke. "Sorry, Cecil, you've got to stay here. My good buddy, Dale, and his wife are going to look after you for a few days. They have a nice yard and a girl Cocker spaniel." Brian made his gaze more intent. "Remember you're a guest in their home. Don't take any liberties with her."

Behind him, Sharon spoke up, "Don't count on it. Like father, like dog."

Chapter 36

Dusk fell quickly in the Caribbean. As the sun dipped behind the low mountain, it seemed to suddenly wink out. Dr. Baptiste sat at the end of the hospital bed, leaning forward, peering between a woman's legs.

"Move that lamp closer please, Martina," he said. There were two ceiling fixtures for this six-bed hospital room, but they were insufficient for close work, especially since he and his assistants were working in the shadow of portable screens set up to provide some privacy during the pelvic exam. This girl was sick, very sick, and he didn't want to move her to an examining room, so he'd had Martina bring a gooseneck lamp to the bedside and connected it with a long extension cord to the nearest wall socket. "Tilt it down."

Martina moved the gooseneck so close he could feel the heat from the bulb burning his neck. He looked at the sheet under the girl's perineum. A creeping red flow oozed closer to where he was sitting. He hoped for his sake as well as hers that she was not HIV positive.

His gloved hands held up the speculum. The nurse squeezed a clear jelly onto the instrument while he rotated it so both blades were lubricated. Gently he spread the girl's labia, but before he could insert the speculum he saw tissue hanging out.

His patient moaned, as much from fear as pain. She had little acquaintance with medical care, and now she was bleeding to death. Dr. Baptiste had no doubt the girl knew it. She had seen sufficient hogs and chickens slaughtered to know that when they lost enough blood, they died.

A nurse's aide sat at the head of the bed. Her job was to hold the patient's hands and to calm her so the other two could work. Other than keeping the frightened girl from reaching down, she was not accomplishing much.

"Get Dr. Taylor!" Baptiste ordered the aide. "We need him." Maybe the ob-gyn man was finally going to earn his keep, thought Dr. Baptiste. The aide, new to her job, looked up at Baptiste in terror and mute appeal--she had never seen anyone bleed to death before.

Baptiste barked at Martina, "All right, you go. Now!"

"He cannot come," said Martina.

"What do you mean? Is he not here in the compound?" Dr. Baptiste asked as he spread the speculum to look farther inside the girl's womb.

"He is in his room," she said.

"You mean he is with a woman there? I do not care. Get him anyway!" the physician demanded.

"No, it is not that," said Martina.

Suddenly he knew. "Did someone get him rum?" Baptiste cried out so loudly that his patient jumped and the aide cringed.

"I think he paid one of the workers," Martina said quietly.

"Damnation!" He would deal with Taylor later. "Forceps!"

Martina peeled open a clear plastic bag.

He grasped the handles of the twelve-inch instrument and began pulling out tissue, which he discarded in a metal pan between the girl's legs. As he evacuated her uterus, the bleeding began to slow. "Get me two units of U.B.S.," he ordered. He glared at the useless aide. He wanted her to be the one to fetch the medication because he could not spare Martina.

"You want two more units?" the young aide asked.

"Two more? What do you mean? She has already had some U.B.S.?" The aide nodded. "Yesterday."

"Was she bleeding then?" Baptiste asked in shock. If his patient had been bleeding for two days, she might be so anemic that she could die before they got enough U.B.S. into her.

"No, doctor," said the nurse's aide, keeping her gaze averted.

"Then why did Dr. Taylor give her the U.B.S.?" Dr. Baptiste asked softly--but even as he said it, he feared he knew the answer.

* * * * *

Dr. Baptiste stared with disgust at the sorry specimen of humanity before him. Taylor lay motionless in a pool of drying vomit. His deep snoring was the only indication of life.

Baptiste felt closer kinship with the illiterate poor who scraped out a meager existence on this dismal island than he did with this educated man who had so much to give but gave so little. The priest in Baptiste said to judge not. The doctor in him had been taught that alcoholism was a disease. But Baptiste was a man, too, and his personal sense of justice said to let

214

Taylor lie there, perhaps to aspirate his own vomit and die of pneumonia. But compassion won out.

With some effort, he rolled the obstetrician onto his side so any material in his mouth would run out.

"Taylor! Taylor!" he shouted, shaking the man. His action produced a paroxysm of coughing and sputtering, followed by a streamer of mucus from the corner of the inebriated doctor's mouth. Taylor flopped back and mumbled something incomprehensible, but at least he looked as if he was going to live. Dr. Baptiste went to the bathroom and returned with a moist towel to wipe the man's face. Taylor sputtered again and tried to pull his head away.

"You are awake?" Baptiste demanded.

"Yeah," growled Taylor, eyes only half open.

"The girl lived."

"What girl?"

"The one you were too drunk to attend."

The man's eyes wavered as he stared up into the face of Dr. Baptiste. He blinked hard; as if that would help him focus better. "I don't know what you're talking about."

"I could not help her baby, though," Baptiste continued. "She aborted."

Taylor's eyes opened wider.

Baptiste rose and left the room to stand on the screened front porch of the small hut. He breathed in the night air. It was clean and light, not heavy with the smell of alcohol and unwashed human presence like Taylor's bedroom. He wanted to get even farther away, out into the tropical evening, find a place unmarred by the taint of man.

He pushed the screen door open and went down the two steps to the packed earth. Behind him, the door swung shut. Out of the corner of his eye he saw movement. He jerked around. There were climbing snakes here in Haiti. But he saw no serpent. Something was tied to Taylor's door handle. While Baptiste watched, the rope's swinging slowed. From it dangled a cross, an upside down cross, and on it was no Christ image, nor anything remotely holy. Rather it was a skeletal figure made of straw resting inside an open coffin. Baptiste grabbed the offensive object, jerked it off the door, and flung it, like a hot coal, into the night. He had worked hard to help the modern church eradicate these ancient symbols and rituals. Yet there were still those who believed.

Chapter 37

There were a dozen flights a day from the U.S. to Caribbean capitals, many connecting with Haiti. Brian and Sharon had caught theirs and by the end of the day were watching the sun set over the right wing of their aircraft. The throb of the engines, the low lighting, and the realization that they were alone, out of the country, and, for a while, untouchable; all combined to put Brian in a relaxed, contemplative mood. He sipped a beer, Sharon a white wine, and, holding hands, they looked so much the part of newlyweds that a flight attendant had even asked if they were on their honeymoon.

"It's odd, but somehow I feel free for the first time in"--Brian shrugged--"in days. Weeks. Months. I didn't tell Dale much when I dropped Cecil off--certainly nothing about you and what all has gone on--just that I was taking a vacation. Dale said that my case will be brought before the credentials committee in two days whether I'm there or not. I told him that my record and my colleagues will just have to speak for me." Brian let out a long sigh. "But I got to wondering--years of rigorous training to wind up charged with behavior disruptive to hospital routine? And surgical incompetence? Oh, and after the visit from Detective Touchett, I wouldn't be surprised is suspicion of murder isn't added to the list."

Sharon elbowed him lightly in the ribs. "Brian, snap out of it. You don't sound free--at least of your worries--to me."

Brian made a half-hearted smile. "You're right. I'll try not worry about that stuff until we get back." Brian tilted his seat back the few degrees allowed on modern tightly packed passenger planes and turned his head to her. "What about you? You ever have second thoughts about what you're doing?"

A smile crossed her lips, and Sharon closed her eyes for a moment; then slowly reopened them. "I did. Until that day in the cave. Then I knew all the hard work was worthwhile."

"From what you had said about your days as a youngster, it must have been tough to get where you are now."

Apparently, the isolation from earthly affairs had put Sharon in a meditative mood as well. "My early life wasn't so bad, Brian. I had all the essentials. I just didn't want to end up like my mother, slaving away at dead-end jobs and seldom making ends meet. I wanted to work at something I loved and I knew an education was the key."

"So you studied hard for an archaeology scholarship?"

"Not exactly. I always liked history. When I was a junior in high school I won a writing competition." Sharon chuckled to herself. "I wrote about a slave in early Louisiana, from her point of view--what life was like, her misery, her baby that died. Although she was sick after the delivery she was sold to a planter who lived in another state. The implication was that she probably wouldn't survive the journey, whether from sickness or loss of the will to live, but I left it up to the reader to imagine the ending."

"Interesting!"

"Presumptuous of me, actually. But my essay did get attention and was forwarded up the line until I won second prize at the state level. The prize helped me get a special scholarship sponsored by the history department at Tulane for needy students with an aptitude for both history and writing. But reading and writing was so sedentary and I craved more activity, so my second year at Tulane they let me switch to archaeology as a major and keep the scholarship as long as I maintained a minor in history. Then I began studying under Dr. Sewell, and here I am." She gestured around the aircraft.

"Well on your way to riches and fame," Brian said.

"No!" Sharon responded adamantly. "That's not why I'm in this. Riches mean little to me. But all the years I was growing up, I was a tenement girl. And whenever I had a date, and he asked where to pick me up, his face would fall when I told him, because he assumed that if I came from nothing, I was nothing. What I've always wanted was to be somebody, amount to something, become a person of accomplishment."

"Well, I think you've already achieved that, and you've got a hell of a lot more on your horizon." Brian pointed out. "But, you've never married. No time for it for a girl on the fast track?"

Sharon laughed. "Bingo. No way I was going to lose my momentum, tailor my life to someone else's, and end up miserable under some man's thumb."

This time Brian laughed. "Sharon, I can't imagine a girl on the planet less likely to lose her independence to any male of the species."

"Thanks--I think," she said.

He slipped an arm around her shoulders, and she nestled in comfortably.

Chapter 38

Their first night in Port-au-Prince, where they could enjoy the luxury of relative anonymity as just another tourist couple, Brian and Sharon savored a romantic supper on the veranda of the finest hotel in the city.

The following morning Brian was awakened by a disconcerting clanking. He peered over the edge of the bed to see Sharon sitting on the floor with her scuba tank as securely clamped between her legs as the head of a wrestler pinned by his conquering opponent. She had a wrench on the valve at the top of the tank. Her second heave was successful, and the valve loosened. She unscrewed it, then reached inside the steel tank. After removing wads of crumpled newspaper, she produced her disassembled nine-millimeter automatic, a box of cartridges, and a small leather pouch.

He watched in amazement as she quickly and expertly assembled the pistol. "Not bad for a girl," he said.

She momentarily glanced in his direction, but continued on with what she was doing as if his comment were to boorish to even consider a response.

"You always carry a wrench with you?"

"Any self-respecting scuba diver keeps a tool pouch handy," she answered.

Brian tried again. "I thought you liked to sleep late."

"Only when there's nothing to do, and we've got plenty. Besides, life in Port-au-Prince always starts early. Whatever work there is, people try to get done before the mid-afternoon heat and doldrums."

Brian still made little effort to get up. "I've been thinking," he said.

Sharon was now screwing the scuba tank's valve back in place. "About what?"

"Your treasure."

"And?"

"How many voyages did Columbus make?"

"Four."

"And he hid his treasure in your cave on that last voyage?"

"No, the one before."

"That's it!" he said, abruptly sitting up in bed. "That's what bothered me. You couldn't have found Columbus' treasure."

"What do you mean?"

"That textbook you showed me, *The Americas*. I remember now. It mentioned that fourth voyage. Don't you see? If Columbus made another trip back to the New World he would have retrieved his booty. What you found must be the leavings from some other pirate or conquistador."

"You should have studied the text more carefully," she said in a tone he sensed she had used on more than one occasion in the classroom. "I suspect Columbus did plan to pick up the treasure on that voyage, most likely secretly with a small, select group of helpers. And probably he didn't intend to share that particular cache with the governor and king. But he didn't get a chance to pull off his plan because his fourth voyage ended in disaster. His fleet was beset by storms and hostile Indians. All the ships sank, and he was even marooned for seven months. He and the other survivors were rescued and returned to Spain, and he died shortly afterward."

"So we'll get it for him," Brian said.

"Yes, dearest, and in order to do that--we leave bright and early."

Brian had not even finished his second go-cup of coffee when Sharon had him at the Caribbe Dive Shop. They arrived just in time to see a group of tourists boarding a boat with the shop's name printed in faded blue letters on the side. Slowly it chugged away from the pier as they went into the dive shop.

Inside they found a Haitian storekeeper who beamed with pleasure at the appearance of more customers.

"Good morning," he said in English, his accent tending more toward British than American. "I am Morris. How may I be of assistance, but if you have come for the reef dive, you have just missed it. We will have another at one o'clock." He pointed to a hand-lettered schedule hanging on the wall.

"That's okay," Sharon said. "We just need some equipment. We want to go diving on our own."

The proprietor tilted his head, studying her. "You look familiar. You have been here before?"

"Yes," said Sharon.

"Good. Our waters can be dangerous for the inexperienced. It is best you know your way around."

"I'm also a certified divemaster."

"I see. Well then, how can I help you?"

"Our small sailboat sank. We need to salvage some of our personal belongings."

"How upsetting for you."

Sharon waved off the concern. "Yes. That's why we need salvage equipment: ropes, three fifty-five gallon drums, an air compressor, a generator to power the compressor, and several dive tanks." Sharon ticked off the items on her fingers. "I have my own personal dive gear."

"It seems a large undertaking."

Sharon was prepared for this. "Not really. It's just that the items we're retrieving are heavy. I'm a marine biologist, and we had coral samples on board it took us three months to collect. I don't want to start all over again."

The Haitian's gaze went to Brian, then returned to concentrate on Sharon like a coiled cobra fixing on its next meal. "I do not have that kind of heavy equipment," he said. "My business caters to sports divers. You should go to Dummond. He is a commercial diver and has done underwater salvage."

"We want to do it ourselves."

"I understand, but he can help you."

The proprietor wrote down the address, then with avaricious pleasure sold them what supplies he could. When they left to find a taxi in the crowded waterfront street, Brian's money belt was lighter by several hundred dollars.

* * * * *

As soon as they were safely gone, the proprietor lifted his phone and dialed a number. Dummond's woman answered the phone. "Quickly, get me your husband," he said in rapid Creole. After an interminable wait, the man came to the phone. "I am sending two Americans your way," he told Dummond. "They want to rent some salvage equipment."

"I am not in the business of rental," growled Dummond.

"You will be when I tell you this," hissed Morris. Then he proceeded to tell Dummond what he thought the pair was really up to.

* * * * *

Eric Dummond was of indeterminate ancestry. He appeared to be in his middle years and walked with a limp. Brian thought perhaps the worn-looking man had suffered one too many cases of the bends. The visit, however, went smoothly, almost as if the commercial diver knew exactly what they wanted even before they asked.

When it came to the fifty-five-gallon drums to bring up "the coral samples," Sharon was very specific. They must be of heavy-gauge steel, not plastic, have tops that screwed on and off, and be absolutely watertight. She insisted on inspecting them herself. Dummond showed her out back to a collection of cast-off items that would have done any stateside junk dealer proud. Eventually she located three drums that met her requirements. They seemed solid enough, well preserved by a thick coating of bright blue rust-resistant paint.

Once her shopping list was complete, Sharon negotiated with Dummond on a price that seemed exorbitant to Brian. Sharon told the salvage diver someone would return in a day or two with a truck to pick it all up.

Chapter 39

On their second morning in Haiti, Brian and Sharon again arose early. Brian complained that if he had wanted to get up early every day, he could have stayed home and done his usual seven-thirty surgery cases. Sharon told him to quit bellyaching; they had important work to do.

Brian considered the change that seemed to have come over her, then quickly realized that he had never truly seen her in action before, completely in her element. As she had promised, she had every step mapped out in her mind, and the closer they got to their goal, the more efficient, even zealous, she became.

He was still in bed when she exited the bathroom, already dressed in khaki shorts and matching shirt with her blond hair pulled back in a ponytail. She poked him in the ribs. "Get up, lazy."

He rolled over, groaned, and announced, "I've got an idea. Let's just not bother going to bed. That way we can get started even earlier, like the night before."

She ignored him. "We've got a big day ahead of us. We'll leave in thirty minutes."

He groaned more loudly. "What about breakfast?"

"You can grab a beignet at the hotel restaurant."

In the Landrover they had rented the sixty-kilometer drive took four hours. The road, which started out as blacktop, worsened progressively until Sharon turned off onto what was barely more than a dirt trail.

Brian had tried several times to engage her in conversation, but she was unusually taciturn. All she said was that she was going to visit the family of Armand, her guide who had been killed by the police. They drove slowly through a village of homes made of white stucco and stone. It looked to Brian like a bit of old Mexico, except that the peasants lolling about were black and tended to wear baseball caps, instead of brown-skinned and topped with sombreros.

Sharon stopped the vehicle at a little house with flaking paint and an almost grassless dirt yard, that still seemed to be cared for better than most of the others on the street. She instructed Brian that while she was inside he was to stay put and avoid talking with anyone, but if he did, to stick to the story that they were American tourists.

She had no need to worry. All Brian got were cautious stares from the few villagers on the street. He turned on the radio, but all he could find were French broadcasts. Too bad Spanish had been his choice to fulfill his foreign language requirement in college. A surprisingly cool breeze wafted through the open car window, and in a moment he was asleep.

"Brian Richards, I'd like you to meet Philipe Dubuisson."

Brian jerked awake. The sun was hot, and it took a moment to get oriented. Then he became aware that Sharon and a young black man were standing at the open car window.

"He scooted to an upright position and ran a hand through his hair. "Sorry, I missed your name."

"It's Philipe Dubuisson," Sharon said. "He's Armand's brother. He doesn't speak much English."

Brian extended his right hand through the open window.

The man shook it. "Hello," he said in accented English.

"Philipe will be our driver and guide, and he'll get a few other things we need," said Sharon.

"I see," said Brian.

"Philipe," she said to the Haitian, her voice now somber. "I have something to give you." She reached into a pocket, and extracted a small leather pouch, and handed it to him.

He opened it. The large uncut emerald caught the sun's rays and reflected them back in iridescent green.

"This is for you and your mother and your sisters. It is very valuable. You must promise to keep it hidden until we are gone. Armand would have wanted you all to have it, to make your life easier."

"*Merci*," the Haitian said quietly. "I will give it to my mother." And he slipped the gem back into its pouch.

"Was that what I thought it was?" Brian asked Sharon.

"Yes, and there's plenty more where that one came from. It'll do a lot more good here than in some museum."

Brian nodded his agreement.

"Now, I need five hundred dollars." Sharon stuck her hand palm up through the car window.

"I thought this kind of thing only happened after you got married."

Sharon merely rubbed her thumb and fingers together to reinforce her request.

"Okay." Brian unfastened two lower shirt buttons, dug into his money belt, and came out with five bills, which he handed over.

She turned to Philipe and passed him the money. They had a short exchange in French, then Philipe started walking toward the center of the village.

"Where's he going?" Brian asked.

"He'll get us a truck, pick up the heavy equipment, and make transportation arrangements to leave the country. After that, he'll meet us at the straw market in Port-au-Prince tomorrow," Sharon explained.

"That was five hundred dollars. Are you sure he's reliable?"

"He knows the authorities were responsible for the death of his brother. His only way of getting even is by helping me defy them. Yes, he'll be there."

* * * * *

Once their arrangements with Philipe were complete, they returned to Port-au-Prince. After the hours spent on roads bumpier than a roller coaster, Brian was glad for the cool and restful atmosphere of the hotel lobby. "I'm going to grab a drink from the bar before we go upstairs. Do you want anything?"

Sharon flopped exhaustedly into a rattan chair underneath a slowly turning ceiling fan. "See if they have a glass of iced tea so large it will take two porters with a handcart to bring it to me."

Brian headed for the lobby bar and its friendly Haitian bartender.

The man greeted him first. "Monsieur Richards, two policemen were here asking for you and the lady."

Brian froze. "What did they want?"

"I did not ask. They have just now gone upstairs to your room."

"Thanks."

Brian slid a twenty across the counter, then walked rapidly across the lobby to grab Sharon by the wrist. "Let's get out of here, now."

"But I'm dying of thirst."

"The police are here looking for us," he hissed. "That New Orleans detective, Touchett, must have realized we were gone and traced us here."

Sharon was on her feet in an instant. "Our luggage is in the room, and--"

225

"Forget it. We don't have time. All we need are our passports and some cash, and we have those on us." With his forearm against his side Brian felt the reassuring presence of his money belt, even though it was decidedly less full after Sharon's transactions of the day. He motioned toward the exit.

"Do you think your friend Philipe can hide us for the night?"

"Without a doubt," she responded. And they were out the door.

Chapter 40

"This is the latest in security technology," said the technician. He placed his palm on a flat panel. A small screen lit up, and a message scrolled across- *-Jerome Weber, security/computer, 13:24, ENTER--*and a buzzer sounded. The technician made some rapid entries on the keypad beneath the panel, then announced, "Doctor, if you would place your hand on the panel."

In his left hand Peter Obrien carried a heavy black satchel. Obediently he raised his other hand and did as instructed while Thurston Walker and Karl Dietrich watched. The technician entered a few more keystrokes and stepped back. The panel display read: *Peter Obrien, Ph.D., M.D., 13:25.*

"Your print is now in the computer and you are cleared to enter." The technician turned to the group. "That makes a total of ten people with access to this laboratory, counting you three gentlemen, of course."

"Thank you," said Dietrich. The three men stepped past the door, which slid silently shut behind them leaving the security technician outside.

"Unbelievable," said Dr. Obrien as he gazed about in amazement.

Research C was a two-part facility. The large, outer laboratory through which they had just passed did innovative work on several programs of vital interest to Durbane Pharmaceuticals. As such, the workers were used to a secretive atmosphere equally appropriate for a military installation doing weapons research. They were highly skilled, extremely well paid, and extraordinarily close-mouthed.

The second, innermost, sanctum, termed "Special Projects" by Dr. Walker, was actually a biocontainment facility. Behind the high security door was a sealed unit intended not only to prevent the escape of lethal microorganisms but also to keep knowledge of the work being done there from spreading to the outside world.

The Special Projects laboratory was entered only through the single, unmarked, security-controlled door. Immediately inside, next to the monitor, were the environmental controls. With its own electrical generators, internal air recirculating system, and multiple other self-contained operating systems, the laboratory could isolate its organisms and its workers from the outside world as effectively as if they were on a space station.

The biological research laboratory was filled with every scientific instrument imaginable. Electronic instrumentation lined three walls from floor to ceiling. The fourth internal wall was glass, allowing a view into another, smaller room that held three gleaming stainless steel vats.

Obrien was amazed at the sheer volume of sophisticated equipment. He had never seen a laboratory so compact yet so well equipped: mass spectrophotometer, gas chromatograph, equipment for electrophoresis and X-ray diffraction analysis--it was all here. Off to the side was a small cubicle labeled *Electron Microscope*. He moved like Alice in a scientific wonderland from one instrument to the next, stopping to give each a light caress and a murmur of appreciation.

Thurston Walker stepped ahead of the group and led them through another door to a small room filled with row upon row of animal cages. From within could be heard the scurrying of small and frightened beasts.

"We haven't set up for primates in here yet," said Walker, "but if you think they're essential, I'm sure Dr. Battley, who's in charge of our veterinary research program, could get you some without any trouble."

"I shall require no primates. My cultures were all taken from proven infectious cases."

"Very well," said Walker. "But just in case you want to check their efficacy, the room beyond is environmentally isolated for any infected animals. Oh, yes," he added, "knowing of your dedication to your work," pointing to another closed door, "we've included a convertible couch and small lavatory in your office should you choose to remain here overnight to oversee the project."

"You have thought of everything. Not even at the National Institutes of Health or *L'Hôpital National Faire des Recherches* in Paris have I seen so much state-of-the-art bioscience instrumentation in one place."

"A man of your stature deserves an equally advanced workplace," said Dr. Walker.

"As if the generous salary you have provided me was not enough," said the beaming Dr. Obrien.

"And now for the *pièce de resistance*," said Walker, gesturing toward the spherical tanks beyond the glass wall. Each globe was made of stainless steel, with myriad elaborate pipes and tubing. A small glassed anteroom served as the airlock into the chamber. A row of environmental isolation suits hung on a wall rack like discarded skins molted by larger-than-life humanoids.

Dr. Obrien stood motionless, his gaze transfixed by the gleaming vats. "Beautiful," he murmured.

"Your little beasties need a place to grow and flourish," said Walker.

Peter Obrien looked down at the black case in his left hand, raised it, and patted it with his right. "You know, these are the best of the lot--very fast, incubation period of only a few weeks." He lifted his gaze again to the stainless steel tanks. "Yes, they should like it here."

* * * * *

Thurston Walker smiled to himself. Dr. Obrien had been at work for four hours. No doubt he had already inoculated the vats with his prion cultures and probably wouldn't come out of his lab until driven out by hunger or pressure from his small group of technicians for him to bathe.

Walker's phone rang. "Yes?"

"I apologize for bothering you just before your meeting, but I thought you should know this."

"What is it, Karl?"

"A police detective called. His name was Touchett. He said he had to check out a report that Durbane may have been involved in the abduction and murder of a local woman--a neighbor of Dr. Brian Richards."

"Well, were we?"

"Of course not," lied the security chief.

"I hope you satisfied him."

"I believe I did--on that matter. However," continued Dietrich, "somewhat more disturbing was that the same informant expressed the opinion to Detective Touchett that Durbane was making artificial blood and was going to extremes to cover it up--such as threatening the archaeologist, Sharon Jackson."

"God damn!" Walker exclaimed.

"Touchett wants to meet us personally and perhaps tour the plant."

"That doctor you told me about has to be behind this, and also that woman, Sharon Jackson. What did you tell the detective?"

"I offered my opinion that Durbane was being slandered by someone who sounded mentally unstable. The detective said he thought the allegations were absurd, too, but he had to check them out. I assured him that we would, of course, be eager to cooperate but would want our attorneys present at the meeting."

"I guess that's the best you can do in this situation--damage control, Karl. Go ahead, arrange a visit by the detective, and, as you said, have George Barclay, and whoever else George wants, there as legal counsel."

"Yes, sir."

The phone clicked off, followed immediately by a rap at his door.

Sissy stuck her head in. "It's time."

Walker nodded and mentally ran through the major points of his presentation. He would be totally prepared this time. At last he rose and marched out of the office.

"Good luck," his secretary said as he passed her, her breast lightly touching the sleeve of his jacket.

"Thanks, Sissy," he said.

She sucked in a breath and said with annoyance, "I prefer--oh, never mind."

The boardroom was just down the hall. As Walker made the trek, he knew that Clarence wouldn't try this ouster on his own. No doubt the board chairman had a couple of backers who thought that once he was in the C.E.O. seat and Walker was out, things would be even cushier for them. It really didn't matter who Clarence's cronies were, because when this meeting was over Walker would be in an even stronger position, and Clarence Durbane would be lucky if they let him keep his corporate American Express card.

Thurston Walker entered the boardroom, his gait purposeful, his manner resolute. Sitting in the premier position at the head of the table was Clarence Durbane. Official meetings of the board of directors called for the chairman, not the C.E.O., to preside. The seven other members were already there. George Barclay and Adam Duncan sat together. Walker acknowledged their presence but did not smile.

Clarence shifted, then raised his prodigous bulk from his chair. He cleared his throat and began. "This meeting will be held by the rules of executive session, which means the only minutes kept today will be of any resolutions approved by majority vote." He waited. No one spoke.

He scanned the people seated around the table, then continued. "I find it necessary to dispense with the usual agenda and go directly to a matter of major concern--this company's swelling indebtedness, as well as its"--he paused to glare at Thurston Walker--"misguided direction." With the blame now assigned, Durbane took a deep breath and returned his gaze to his audience.

"In the last two years Dunn & Bradstreet has lowered their opinion of Durbane Pharmaceuticals corporate bonds from 5A to triple B." The fat man leaned forward on his knuckles. "Gentlemen, Durbane Pharmaceuticals is now considered no better a credit risk than your corner supermarket. This is because our debt is the highest it has ever been in company history." Durbane's face tightened with dramatic intensity.

By God, thought Walker, the man must not have been lazing on the Riviera the whole time he was in Europe; somehow he'd squeezed in acting lessons.

"Something must be done, some changes made." Durbane's gaze moved around the table, pausing on each person to impress the gravity of the situation before moving on. "There is only one item on today's agenda. We are here to consider replacement of the current chief executive officer." With that, he sat down.

Throughout the short but impassioned diatribe Walker's head remained upright, his gaze fixed on an imaginary spot on the opposite wall. Now his attention flicked, almost unnoticed, to George Barclay.

On cue, his old friend and counselor made a show of taking the unlit cigar from his mouth and looking directly at Durbane. "Well, Clarence, that's some mighty strong language about a man who has moved Durbane from being a regional supplier of generic pharmaceuticals to a company whose innovative research rivals that of corporations many times our size which, in turn, allows us to now market our own name-brand drugs throughout both North America and Europe." Barclay paused, then turned to look at Walker. "I, for one, would like to hear what Dr. Walker has to say."

"I agree," said Adam Duncan, nodding vigorously as two other members of the group murmured their assent.

Durbane made as if to say something more, but he let it pass and gestured to Walker that he had the floor.

Walker rose slowly. All faces turned to look at him. Most were carefully neutral, but Walker knew each and every board member of them was calculating where his loyalty should lie. He smiled at Adam Duncan, and Duncan grinned back. He and his wife drove matching Miatas and had two children at expensive prep schools. Duncan wouldn't benefit from a toppling of the status quo. George Barclay was looking decidedly gray, and well he might, thought Walker. They had buried a lot of bodies together, he and George. So, at least two definites were on his side. Now, with a little work on the undecided... Walker forced himself to appear impassive even as he felt the thrill of battle run through him.

Walker was glad Diane Gilmore was here. Although a woman of confused goals, Leopards rarely change their spots and so far she had not let her concern over the safety of their new product win out over her desire for the material advantages of life. She spoke well, and her opinion could swing the tide. But since she was an employee and not a board member she could be present at the director's meeting only if specifically invited. Walker had seen to that.

He moved to the wall behind Clarence Durbane, where the company name was displayed in polished brass letters. He punched a button, and with a barely perceptible whir a media screen slid down. Stepping to the side, Walker produced a remote and aimed it. The lights dimmed, and the beam from a multimedia projector cut through the darkened room. Clarence Durbane was caught full face in the glare. Looking foolish, he scooted his chair aside. Pleased, Thurston Walker moved forward, effectively blocking Clarence from the scene.

"Before I begin my presentation, I want to make only one personal remark. I apologize if any of the board members think I have been too"--he appeared to search for a word--"aggressive in developing Durbane Pharmaceuticals. But these are highly competitive times. My motives have been what is best for *our company*, not what is best for myself. Some people may desire more immediate income to support a more lavish lifestyle"-- Walker glanced ever so subtly toward Clarence Durbane--"but my only interest is in moving our company forward, and that requires investment in the future, not income for the present. Walker took a deep breath, as if that unpleasant disclaimer was now completed and he could continue with the business at hand. "I had planned to make this presentation a few weeks from now," he began, "but under the circumstances, perhaps now is more appropriate."

A slide appeared. "This is our company today." He indicated the Mercator projection of the world with red stars highlighting the main Durbane plant in New Orleans and its overseas facilities. There was no star in the Caribbean.

"We manufacture the following medications." Another slide appeared, listing an impressive roster of best-selling pharmaceuticals. "Some of you may have heard rumors of another new, even revolutionary product in development. What I am about to tell you must be kept secret. Our scientists have made a breakthrough that will do more for us than all these other products put together."

Another slide flashed, this time with only three letters on it: *U.B.S.* "Universal blood substitute," said Walker. "The first artificial blood. It will save millions of lives, and it will change Durbane from this"—he returned to the original slide of the world--"to this." The same slide was now covered with hundreds of red dots. The slide winked off and the room lights came back on.

Now Walker was the one at the head of the table, not Clarence Durbane. "But it is time to move beyond being just a supplier. In this era of managed care, price controls and competition insure that any profits are barely enough to cover the cost of development of new medication. If we really want to achieve preeminence, we must move beyond simply the supply side."

Walker surveyed his audience. He had their interest. "The first step has already been taken. We have acquired a respected New Orleans hospital, Beauvoir Memorial. That hospital will be the first in Durbane's new health-care-provider division. A few more such acquisitions and we will announce the existence of our own hospital chain. And how will this new operation be managed?" He paused, but there was no response to his rhetorical question. "Consolidated Health Partners, an insurance company with considerable experience in health-care management, will merge with us to form Durbane Enterprises."

Walker continued. "Our new conglomerate will offer managed-care insurance, which will funnel patients to our new cost-efficient hospital system, where we will provide the drugs and supplies. Add to that our profits from U.B.S"--Walker spread his arms wide--"and we will control every aspect of health care from cradle to cremation. In a few months, my friends, we will be the dominant force in world health care."

Applause filled the room. Only Clarence Durbane refused to join in.

The first to speak up was Ed Sheldon, the only member of the board who was a physician. "I was told that research on this product was shelved two years ago due to concern over side effects. Am I to take it that those problems have been solved?"

Beverly Powers piped up before Walker could answer. As a pharmacologist she was the most medically well-informed non-physician in the group. "Thurston, I have some friends in the overseas pharmaceutical community who, although you pleaded for secrecy, told me of your recent attempt to franchise this very product. They were concerned that it still causes spontaneous abortion in pregnant patients, among other possible side effects, so they turned you down."

Outrage flooded Walker at the leak; he thought he had screened the San Francisco meeting participants sufficiently. At least the leak had been to a Durbane board member and was probably only an attempt to get more information about the drug--a far cry from a public broadcast of proprietary secrets.

Walker fought down his irritation at the unknown persons who had violated his confidence. There was nothing he could do about them right now, but he could do something about disloyalty in his own ranks. And he just might start with these two. Sheldon and Powers must be Clarence's people. They would definitely have to go in the near future--a new project for Karl, who was very effective at helping people decide it was in their best interest to resign.

Walker looked to Diane Gilmore, on hand to address medical questions. Could he trust her now? His instincts had gotten him this far without failure, and he had to have faith they were still on target. "I'll ask Dr. Gilmore to field your question."

Diane looked at Walker, as if weighing her decision, then began. "All drugs have side effects," she said. "What is important is the risk-to-benefit ratio. We have substantially improved the formulation of U.B.S. and its ratio is now satisfactory."

Not the most ardent endorsement, but adequate thought Walker as he let out a silent breath.

"Unless you happen to be pregnant," said Dr. Sheldon.

"I'm well aware of that," Gilmore replied easily. "We will require a pregnancy test on all females of child-bearing age and exclude U.B.S. from any positives."

"But the test may not be positive in the very earliest stages," countered Sheldon.

"If you run the math on that, Dr. Sheldon, and we have, the likelihood of giving U.B.S. to a pregnant female with a false negative is one in eight hundred. Factor in the projected miscarriage rate from the drug, and you have a one in eight thousand risk. Weigh that against the countless thousands of people saved from death and disease by all that U.B.S. has to offer."

Dr. Sheldon looked to his compatriots for help, but none had the expertise or fortitude to argue the position. Forced to retreat, Sheldon muttered, "I suppose, but if any more side effects turn up, the marketability of U.B.S. would be seriously hampered."

Walker cast a surreptitious glance at Gilmore, but to his relief, she appeared unmoved and made no response.

Walker rose to his feet and surveyed his audience. The voices of doubt and dissent had been silenced for now, but the squeamishness and faintheartedness were still there, ready, at any moment, to erupt and destroy U.B.S. He had worked out the fallback scenario in his mind, and all the preliminary steps, save one, had been laid. The time for desperate measures had now arrived.

"Gentlemen and ladies," he said, "what I am about to tell you is so classified that only a few people at the World Health Organization and a handful of pharmaceutical researchers are aware of. For fear of creating worldwide panic, they have pledged secrecy until--" He stopped, as if it was too painful to continue. Then he cleared his throat. "Until a way is found to combat the coming pandemic."

"What the hell is a pandemic?" muttered George Barclay.

"A pandemic is a worldwide epidemic," said Dr. Sheldon. He turned back to Walker. "A pandemic of what?"

"Prion disease," said Walker. His distressed expression indicated that no graver pronouncement had ever been made. "*Human* prion disease."

"Rapid variant Creutzfeldt-Jakob disease?" gasped Gilmore.

"That's right," Walker said.

"We presumed U.B.S. would be most readily welcomed in areas of the world where the blood supply wasn't safe. Since prion disease, theoretically, would be the most insidious, we even supported some research..." Diane's voice trailed off.

"Prions? Isn't that Mad Cow disease?" asked Beverly Powers.

"An unfortunate term," Walker responded. "'Mad Cow' conjures up images of Bossie tearing around the farmyard in a fit." A short burst of laughter came from one member of the group but was immediately cut short when no one else joined in. "Bovine Spongiform Encephalopathy is the correct term. In short, holes develop in the brain tissue. The victim, be it cow, sheep, or human, becomes demented, experiences seizures, looses control of bodily functions, and dies in a coma."

George Barclay looked like he would be sick all over the table. As a lawyer, the worst ailment he had ever encountered was his own case of the flu. He swallowed hard, then asked, "What causes it?"

"Prions," said Walker. "Proteinacious Infectious Particles. They are undetectable in the bloodstream. They have no DNA or RNA. Many people don't think they're even alive."

"Jesus Christ," said Adam Duncan, the accountant. "How can something that's not alive kill you?"

"A bullet can kill you, and it's not alive," said Dr. Sheldon, with more than a hint of irritation at such a stupid question.

"You know I didn't mean it that way," retorted Duncan.

Thurston Walker explained. "Prions multiply, possibly by a chemical reaction, *AND* spread, just as they did in that outbreak in British cattle some years ago. At that same time, Cruetzfeldt-Jakob disease, which is essentially the identical process in humans, started showing up in beef and dairy farmers who had contact with those products, perhaps even ingested them in undercooked or unprocessed states."

"But that epidemic was brought under control," Sheldon said.

"In cattle, yes," responded Walker. "But, sporadic human cases continued, and for the past year there has been a rapid upswing in occurrence for what has traditionally been a rare disease. A mutation has apparently developed producing a new variant of C.J. disease, one that is highly infectious, runs a rapid course, and, most pertinent to the problem at hand, has been spread by blood transfusion."

George Barclay spoke up again. "Well, why don't they just do a test to see who or what has got it so blood banks can screen them out as potential donors?"

"Therein lies a major part of the problem," said Walker. "There is no test to diagnose C.J. disease, except of course a brain biopsy when the victim is nearly gone."

"Hold on! Hold on!" clamored another board member as he tried to cut through the racket of individual conversations. Gradually the noise level subsided. "What does all this really mean? What does this have to do with

Durbane, or U.B.S.? There's no test for C.J. disease, and no treatment once someone has it."

"Besides, it's very rare," added Dr. Sheldon.

"Not for long. Prions are in the human blood supply chain in a half dozen countries. Thus the coming pandemic."

"Oh, my god."

"Holy shit!"

Diane Gilmore had remained silent during the initial hubbub. She now spoke. "The World Health Organization's Council on Prion Diseases has identified over one hundred fifty cases proven to occur from blood transfusion."

"I haven't heard that," said Dr. Sheldon.

Walker jumped back in. "That's why we went ahead and instituted a research program on prions, with the idea that U.B.S. could be the ideal way to prevent its spread. A program that some of you," he added with a glower, "took to be an example of wasting research monies."

Gilmore continued. "Those of us in the field feared that if there were a widespread dissemination of prion disease, as with the AIDS virus, then no one could be sure they had received a safe blood transfusion--and U.B.S. would be the only option." Gilmore leveled her gaze at Dr. Walker. "Are you telling us, this has now happened?"

Walker reluctantly nodded. "Several hundred more cases have been detected."

"I didn't know that," said Gilmore, "and I would have thought..."

"It's being shrouded in the deepest secrecy." *So deep,* thought Walker, *that she'll never find out it's not true--at least, not true right now.*

"Where are the cases?" asked Beverly Powers.

"Almost half were in England, which is where the disease first mutated," said Walker. "The rest are now scattered everywhere--Europe, Sumatra, and over forty cases in the United States. Remember, this is the era of global travel. Someone infected can carry the disease to the other side of the world in twelve hours. Soon, every country will be forced to realize that their blood supply is tainted with a lethal and undetectable organism."

The room fell deathly quiet, each board member lost in individual thought.

Finally, Thurston Walker broke the silence. "As of now, the only way to get an absolutely safe blood transfusion is with artificial blood. And we are the only ones who make it."

Chapter 41

"Congratulations," said Dietrich.

Karl Dietrich and Diane Gilmore had followed Thurston Walker back to his office after the board meeting. Everyone else had promptly filed out, leaving Clarence Durbane sitting alone. "Thanks, Karl. I guess this means both of us get to keep our jobs for now. But while Clarence will likely tuck his tail and run, I'm uneasy that his chums who backed him up in this are still around. Do a little digging on Dr. Sheldon and maybe Beverly Powers, too. I would bet those two are his cronies. See what you can find--girlfriends, boyfriends, too much drinking, too much spending--everybody has something. Then pay those two a visit. It's time to pull the rip cord on their golden parachutes."

"Files already exist on each board member."

Diane Gilmore shook her head in horrified awe. "I suppose your files include employees, too," she said.

"It is necessary to protect the interests of the company," said the security chief matter-of-factly.

"Something concerns me more," said Gilmore "than the Big Brother files you two keep." She looked squarely at Walker, the intensity of her gaze exceeded only by the tightness of her otherwise beautiful mouth. "How did you know about this coming pandemic? I'm the medical director here. I have contacts with all the major national and international health organizations. If something like that was beginning to occur, I should have heard before you."

"Diane, this is so dangerous, so frightening, that only a few people at the very top of the World Health Organization know the true extent of the outbreak. They, in turn, privately contacted only the heads of the major pharmaceutical houses to request acceleration of any work relating to prion disease."

"And Dr. Obrien, that's why you brought him over from England now?"

Walker hesitated a moment. "Yes, to expedite his work. His facilities were very limited compared to what we could offer. But even he doesn't know the full reason--"

Diane interrupted him. "You said over half the cases were in England. His own country, where he is one of the leading prion researchers; and he doesn't know?" The rising tone of her voice said that she found that hard to imagine.

"This matter is being handled with near-military secrecy. Obrien is"--Walker searched for a word--"peculiar. No one knows what he might say to the public. So he is to be kept in the dark. I would have not told anyone, but I had no choice. If I had lost my position here and U.B.S. became sidetracked, the entire world would suffer the consequences."

Diane lapsed into silence, as if pondering his words--or his candor.

"Dr. Gilmore brought me some information immediately before the meeting," said Dietrich, "but we did not have a chance to discuss it with you." Dietrich looked in Diane's direction.

"A Dr. Jeanette Edwards called me," she said.

"Who the hell is she?" Walker asked.

"A hematology professor at L.S.U. Medical Center," Gilmore replied. "She's well respected, almost retired."

"What did she want?"

"She was asking about artificial blood," said Dietrich.

"God damn it! How did she find out?"

"She said somebody brought her a bag of U.B.S.," Gilmore answered. "She tested it and recognized its properties. She then ran a computer search of the medical literature. My name came up as the co-author of several papers on artificial blood."

"I thought we decided to put a cap on publications two years ago when the breakthrough was made?"

"We did," Diane said. "But she went back several years before that, and of all the facilities reporting work on the topic, we were the closest and easiest enough to call, I suppose. But I did get the impression that she didn't realize the bag of U.B.S. came from us."

"What did you tell her?"

"Nothing--the usual party line. After a lot of money and no progress, we abandoned research on artificial blood and went on to other things."

"Did she believe you?"

"I suppose so. From her standpoint, why would I lie?" said Gilmore, her voice quavering slightly."

"Thanks, Diane. I know it's sometimes difficult to be a team player when there are personal reservations." His voice was genuine. "It's hard to decide what's best. But we have to take the broad view. In this case, what's good for Durbane is also good for the world." He hoped she would agree. She was one of the few women he had ever met that he both desired and respected.

"I suppose, Thurston," she said wearily.

"Diane, get away. Shake some of this off, and come back refreshed in a day or two." In his heart he wished he could go with her--*and he* wished that she wanted that, too.

She just rose and said," Maybe I won't come in tomorrow," and left.

Alone now with Dietrich, Walker paced about his office while he fretted. "How did this Dr. Edwards get a bag of U.B.S?" he demanded.

"One of our latest shipments to the European warehouse had a carton broken into."

"Why wasn't that reported?"

"When the damage was discovered, the supervisor assumed it was due to an accident, that maybe the forklift operator had inadvertently punctured the carton. In any case, the supervisor did not give it much thought at the time. Only when I started checking did it become apparent that one bag was punctured, but an additional bag probably was missing."

Walker leveled his gaze at Dietrich. "I thought you kept a tight rein on internal security."

Dietrich shifted his stance and, for once, looked uneasy. "I think I know who is behind this, and I am already investigating. Dr. Edwards would not tell Dr. Gilmore who gave her the U.B.S., but she did ask him if any trials had been done in Haiti. She had found the same material in the blood of a patient who had been injured and treated there."

"That must be the archaeologist woman."

"Yes, Sharon Jackson."

Walker's voice became almost menacing. "Then, Dietrich, I would say your first order of business is to recover that bag of U.B.S. After that, you find the missing woman and her doctor friend who got all this started in the first place, and clean this mess up. It's too soon for U.B.S. to go public. At the current level of testing, it won't even get past the FDA. And knowledge of its existence will only give more impetus to MedUniversal and any other company working on a similar product."

Walker resumed pacing about his office. He had dodged Clarence Durbane's bullet of attempted ouster, and he intended a mopping-up operation to rid the board of Clarence's supporters, but that would not be the end of it. Clarence was right. The company was overextended, and as long as that situation existed, there would likely be other attempts to remove him from leadership. If the banks recalled their notes, Durbane Pharmaceuticals could even go into receivership. It was like a poker game in which he had let his winnings keep riding. Now he held a full house, but the other gamblers still left in the game were savvy, and if any one of them had a better hand he, or Durbane, or both would be wiped out. Yet, he could still win--especially if the game were rigged. All the preparations were done, the cards were marked, and the dealer worked for him. All he had to do was to give the nod, and the final hand would be dealt.

Walker stopped walking as a sudden calm descended over him. Yes, desperate times called for desperate measures. "Karl, go ahead and begin final plans for distributing Obrien's cultures. Tell him nothing. I'll deal with him. I think we can keep U.B.S. under wraps for another couple of months, and by then the first reports on the widespread occurrence of human prion disease will be surfacing. Then the worldwide demand for U.B.S. will be astronomical, and it will roll right through the FDA approval committees on a wave of panic."

Dietrich nodded once and rose to leave. He had his orders.

Chapter 42

The number stenciled on the door was 2E09. The two men stopped and listened. One was black, of medium height, and well dressed. The other man was shorter and had the rough complexion that came from spending a lot of time outdoors. It was shortly after five, and the building was beginning to empty out. The only other person in the hallway was an elderly housekeeper, occupied with organizing the cleaning materials on her janitorial cart.

The black man put a hand on the knob and waited. No sounds came from within. The other man gave a quick nod, and he pushed the door open.

The room was a small laboratory filled with scientific equipment. A woman, her hair heavily streaked with gray and wearing a white lab coat, was seated at a desk studying some reports. She looked up with surprise. "Can I help you?"

"Dr. Edwards?" asked the black man.

"Yes?"

He flashed a smile. "Oh, good. We've been all over. These big old buildings sure are confusing."

Dr. Edwards said nothing. She remained poised with computer printout in one hand and pencil in the other.

"We're sorry to bother you," he explained, "but we're investigating the theft of a chemical product—one that may have come to your attention."

Dr. Edwards put her papers aside. "I'm sorry, but I have no idea what you're talking about."

The black man waved his hands as if to shake off any misunderstanding. "Of course, of course. You had nothing to do with it. We feel certain you didn't even know the solution was stolen."

Dr. Edwards had by now pushed her chair away from her cluttered desk and turned to face the intruders. The Cajun moved sideways, putting distance between himself and his partner. He stopped to lean nonchalantly against the counter, a bored expression on his face and his left hand in the pocket of his baggy trousers. The Cajun was left-handed.

"You might remember better," said the black man, "if I tell you it came in a plastic bag, like they use in hospitals, for patients."

The bewilderment on her face dissolved away. Her response was cautious. "Exactly what kind of solution?"

The black man smiled again. "I'm not supposed to say. You see, the ingredients are a company secret."

Dr. Edwards involuntarily glanced at the laboratory bench to her right. The movement was not lost on either of the two men.

"You're not in any trouble, Dr. Edwards--yet," said her visitor. "But possession of stolen property is a criminal offense."

"Are you police?"

"No, private investigators. But the police can easily become involved, although my employers would prefer the matter be settled in another manner."

The hematologist nervously shifted her position and looked with apprehension across the room to where her work was spread out on the counter. The Cajun moved nearer that location. "I don't know what you mean," she said.

The black man's voice took on an edge. "I must remind you, the material you've been studying is not yours." His impatience was beginning to show. He moved closer to Dr. Edwards. "I'm sure the owners would pay you just to recover their property--a reward, so to speak, for doing the right thing."

Before Edwards could answer, the man across the room spoke for the first time, and it was with a thick Cajun accent. "Here it is." In his hand was a plastic bag filled with clear fluid. He held it up.

The silenced Glock in the black man's hand was only inches away when it went off. With her head turned, Dr. Edwards' temple presented a perfect target. The force of the projectile snapped her head sideways. Although she died instantly, her body convulsed as millions of dying neurons gave off their last electrical discharges. It was obvious to the black man that, despite Dietrich's recommendation, on this occasion it was unnecessary to pump second and third play-it-safe bullets into the target's chest.

The Cajun's pistol had appeared instantly but was not needed. He slid it back into his pants pocket, quickly stepped to the door, opened it, and signaled out into the hallway.

Instantly the "custodian" wheeled the janitorial cart into the room and shut and locked the door. Heavy duty black plastic bags were handed around. The first object to go in was the IV pack of U.B.S.; then the trio combed the rest of the room for all glassware containing fluid. In less than two minutes the collection was complete, the bags sealed with twist ties and loaded onto the cart.

On the bottom shelf of the janitorial cart was a large box of the type used for contaminated waste. The Cajun knelt down and removed from inside it a contraption of beakers, flasks, and tubing. It looked like a miniature distillery, and an aroma of pungent chemicals leaked from the containers. The Cajun carried it to the countertop with more care than an alcoholic with impending D.T.s guarded his final bottle.

The black man and the janitor slid a plastic trash bag over the bloody mass that was Dr. Edwards' head and sealed it at the neck with duct tape. Then the dead woman was folded like an accordion and her arms and legs taped together. The empty box received the trussed corpse, and after being sealed with more tape, the heavy package was wrestled back onto the cart.

The Cajun finished tinkering with the apparatus he had brought and cast a final glance around the room to see that everything was complete. Directly overhead was a water sprinkler. Climbing on a stool, he used a pair of pliers to disable the mechanism. As he stepped down, the custodian, her cart now heavily laden, was wheeling out the door.

Satisfied, the Cajun uncapped a small bottle and poured its contents into the beaker. Immediately the liquids began frothing and a column of warm fluid began to rise in the tube, which led to the other flask. The chemical reaction was underway. In about ten minutes the temperature would reach the flash point, and the acetone would ignite. The larger beaker, filled with volatile hydrocarbons, would follow almost instantaneously. The room would become a giant fireball, incinerating all evidence of the doctor's research. *About* ten minutes--that's why the Cajun hated chemical timers. They were so imprecise. Still for this particular case, they were useful. What better way to disguise arson than in a laboratory filled with chemicals?

As soon as the two men stepped outside room 2E09 they surreptitiously removed their almost invisible latex gloves and went down the stairs. The janitor had taken the elevator and would already be in the basement and heading toward the panel truck waiting out back.

Chapter 43

A cave that was underwater most of the time was not Brian's idea of the perfect Caribbean vacation spot. In fact, he concluded, it would be a very easy place to get killed. He crouched just inside the cave mouth and looked around nervously, picturing how his final moments would be spent, swimming about, gasping for breath from the last remaining air pocket until it, along with his life, was extinguished.

He had asked Sharon if it were possible to swim out against an incoming tide, and she had assured him, in explicit detail he could have easily done without, that it would be like trying to escape a car sinking into water. The doors can't be opened until the pressure is equalized. Ergo, once the cave was filled, if one were able to survive that tumult, then scuba gear could be used to swim out.

Unfortunately, Brian wasn't a scuba diver.

He wondered if Sharon would be interested in putting her project on hold while he went back to Port-au-Prince and took a crash course. From the zeal with which she and Philipe were unloading and checking out equipment, that wasn't too likely.

Of course, drowning wasn't the only calamity to fear. Being trapped by a cave-in was another. Brian edged closer to the opening and shined his flashlight at the cave roof.

"*Pardon moi*," said Philipe as he edged by carrying a giant coil of rope over one shoulder.

"Sorry," said Brian as he wriggled aside to allow Philipe to pass, then resumed his inspection of the rocky ceiling. Yes, a cave-in was a real possibility. If rocks fell and partly blocked the entrance, water would get in, but they couldn't get out. Then it would be both a cave-in *and* drowning!

"Brian?" Sharon's voice came from the path that led down from the ledge.

"Yeah," he said as he ran his flashlight beam along a particularly worrisome crack.

"Would it be asking too much for you to carry some of this heavier stuff?"

He looked around. Sharon had a duffel bag in each hand and an expression fit for a mother dealing with a recalcitrant three-year-old. "Sure." He scrambled out of the mouth of the cave to where she was standing.

"Not these," she said with mild exasperation. "I've already got these down here." She tossed her head in the direction of the steep incline. "It's going to take both you and Philipe to bring those drums."

Brian set off but stopped after ten feet. "Uh, Sharon, do you really think this is safe?"

"Of course it's not. Safe is with buddy divers, a back-up team, cables attached to the wall with pitons." Seeing his distress, knowing most of it was worry over her safety, she began to soften. She put down the bags, walked to him, and took his hand. "Look. I know what I'm doing. Once we make the recovery, then we'll pay a visit to the Doúbe clinic. After that, you and I are going back to good old U.S.A. Then I'll make my announcement to the world about finding Columbus' lost treasure, and you can hound the authorities about Durbane and their artificial blood."

"That treasure has been in there for four hundred years. Don't you think that's a safe enough place for a while longer?"

"Five hundred," she corrected. "And no, it's not. The police who caught me here may right now be planning their own dive just to see what I was up to." Her grip tightened on his hand. "That cave is not what we've got to fear. It's the discovery. That's why we've avoided every person and every village in this province. If the police find me here a second time, they'll know this is no longer an unsuccessful archeological search. They'll know we've found something--and they'll go for it, and they'll make doubly sure this time that they get rid of me, of us, in the process."

"We went into Philipe's village. What if we were reported."

"We couldn't avoid that. We had to have some help. And that was pretty remote from here anyway. Besides, most of the local people hate the police--they're the most visible part of a corrupt government that keeps them in poverty. The villagers won't give us away."

Brian stood motionless, considering her words. "I guess we'd better get to work," he said resignedly.

Sharon smiled and let go of his hand. "Yeah, let's do that." She looked at her dive watch. "The tide will start turning before long." She looked up the steep hill, then pointed. "When you get through unloading, back the truck out of sight into that grove of trees."

* * * * *

"The woman is pointing this way," said Morris the dive shop owner as he peered through the binoculars.

"Does she see us?" asked Dummond, who squatted beside him.

"No. We are too far away. I believe she is just giving instructions to the man."

"If she were my woman, I would be the one telling her what to do," said Dummond.

"Which is why you are on your fourth wife," said Morris as he passed the binoculars.

"That is not the reason," said Dummond, his voice filled with indignation. "I require a young woman. When they reach their third decade, it is time to get a new one."

"And each one you get is uglier than the last."

Dummond did not answer. He was engaged in focusing the binoculars. "The white man is heading back up the hill. Their hired man is coming with him."

"Let me see," said the dive shop owner as he roughly jostled his companion's shoulder. He took the binoculars and watched for a long while. Finally he spoke. "They are unloading the oil drums and carrying them into that crevice in the rock face." He turned to the other man with a self-satisfied smile. "There can be no sunken sailboat in there. I was right."

"I think it is time we make our way down the other side of the ledge," said Dummond. He picked up the AK-47 on the ground next to him and slung it over his shoulder. The dive shop owner grasped his weapon and did the same. Keeping their heads down, they backed carefully away from the tree line.

Chapter 44

Dietrich thumbed through the campus directory. College people were so trusting, he thought. The students haven't been away from home long enough to realize the deception and danger that lurks for the unwary. And the professors were so accustomed to their protected little environment of neatly landscaped walkways and campus security force armed with nothing more dangerous than parking tickets that they, too, felt safe from the depredations of the outside world.

Dietrich stood at the Tulane information desk looking through the campus register for a name. There it was: Jackson, Sharon, Ph.D., Assoc. Prof., Arch., followed by two sets of phone numbers; home and office. He knew there would be no answer at home. He had tried many times over the last few days. He wrote down the office number.

"Thank you," he said politely as he slid the directory back across the counter. "I can't believe I lost my niece's telephone number," he said, but the clerk, who without doubt was on a work-study program, paid no attention. A rather good-looking young man sporting a cap with an Ole Miss emblem on it was asking directions to the Rathskeller, the on campus pub. The young lady was overly enthusiastic in accommodating.

Back in his car, Dietrich called the office number. He got Sharon Jackson's voice mail and immediately hung up. He pondered the situation for a moment, then dialed information and got the number for Tulane University. The on-campus operator promptly connected him with the Archaeology Department office.

"Hello," he said, exaggerating the German inflection in his speech. "I would like to find Dr. Sharon Jackson. I have brought a specimen from Europe for her, but she does not answer at home or at her office."

The department secretary explained that Dr. Jackson was off for the summer.

"Do you know where she can be located?"

"No, not really. We have fifteen full-time members on the archaeology faculty, and since we have few classes during the summer, it's hard to keep track of the staff.

"That is too bad. I have a relic she has wanted. It is of some value. Does she have a friend or some family member who knows where she can be reached?"

"Well, she does have a close friend on the staff, Darcy. That's Darcy Flemming. Although she is gone a lot, too. The secretary helpfully provided the number, and after Dietrich said he might just leave the package there, Darcy's address as well. He recorded the information, then dialed the new number.

* * * * *

Darcy had just set down her bags and made a quick inspection of the apartment when the phone rang.

Dietrich identified himself as Gustav Erikson, then quickly ran through the same routine he had used with Tulane's archaeology department secretary. Unfortunately, it did not work as well. Darcy Flemming seemed immediately suspicious.

"I didn't know Sharon had any interest in European relics."

"It was a side interest," Dietrich attempted to assure her. "She has long been seeking a specimen of this type. I was lucky enough to locate one and, because of its value, I need to give it to her personally."

"What kind of specimen?"

Dietrich did not like the way this was going. "An amphora. But no mind, I suppose I can bring it on my next trip to the United States." He made one last try. "Do you not know of a way to reach her?"

"Sharon likes to keep her business and her whereabouts to herself. Now, give me your name again and how you may be reached. I'm sure I'll be able to get a message to her eventually."

"Gustav Erikson." Then Dietrich rattled off a fictitious address in Austria, followed by a hurried goodbye.

This woman was close to Miss Jackson, knew her habits, and apparently would sooner or later make contact with her. He looked down at his hand-written list, the last entry being Darcy's address. He would simply have to use more persuasive techniques. But first he would find out a bit more about Darcy Flemming. Everyone had a soft spot, an easy place to set a hook. He had only to discover it. Dietrich redialed the archaeology office.

252

"I apologize for bothering you once more," he said after falsely identifying himself again. "Darcy Flemming. I couldn't reach her, and I must return to Europe. Do you know exactly where she does her overseas work? I might be able to reach her there. I have some many contacts in Europe."

The deep voice and Continental accent of the caller worked to intrigue the secretary. And Dietrich suspected she would like to meet the man behind the fascinating voice. She was all too helpful.

* * * * *

Darcy studied the note she had found next to the phone.
Had to stay at your apartment for a few days--with a friend!!!
If anyone is looking for me, DO NOT hazard a guess where I might
be found. I'll be in touch.

Love,
S.

Chapter 45

Sharon's heart raced, more with anticipation than exertion. She had made it a point to let the men do the heavy labor, saving her own strength for what lay ahead. And there had been plenty of laborious tasks--lugging the equipment down the hill, filling the drums with sand until they attained neutral buoyancy, and laying safety and communication lines in loose coils on the cave floor. It was all ready now, and she was suited up. She blew into her regulator and took a deep breath. It worked fine.

The glow from her lantern cast pale illumination on the two men standing in the cave. She tried to overlook the worried expression on Brian's face. She knew it was no longer due to fear of the cave, because once he set to work, that had seemed to evaporate. But as her departure time neared, he spoke less and seemed to watch her more.

"Cheer up. We're about to make history."

"You'll be all right?"

"Yes. I know every inch of the way, every move to make. I've reviewed it a thousand times."

"Okay," he said without conviction. "One other thing..."

"Yes?"

"I was wondering," he said, "did Columbus have scuba gear, or were his men just unusually good at holding their breath?"

"Probably neither," answered Sharon with a chuckle, pleased that at least he wasn't asking another gloomy question. "Haven't you heard of global warming, the polar ice cap melting, and rising sea levels?"

"I suppose."

"Sea level is at least five feet higher than it was in Columbus' time. In fact, that's what led me to look for a submerged cave mouth. I suspected Columbus and a select few loyal comrades rowed in at low tide to hide the treasure and let the rising tide conceal much of the entrance." She grinned. "I was right. Back in Columbus' day they probably had a good twelve hours to get in and out. Of course, the rising sea level has altered the situation until now we have only a two-hour window."

"Speaking of high tide, don't you think you ought to get going?"

"It's a short swim," she said. "Don't fret." She flicked a black cord. "This communication system has a throat mike. It works almost as well underwater as out. I'll stay in touch."

"Hurry back," said Brian, his voice taut. She stood on tiptoes and gave him a peck on the cheek, then waded into the water.

The swim was just as she remembered it--the razor-sharp teeth of the underwater entrance, the cave fish, the tunnel, but almost before she expected it she was into the second cavern. No sooner was she out of the water than she flashed her lantern around the cavern. In the farthest recess her light reflected off a jumble of bricks and the ancient wall.

She had thought her excitement was at a fever pitch already, but she was wrong. She unsnapped the communications line from the throat mike and dropped the utility belt with its attached ropes. Her eyes riveted on the wall, she unbuckled her tank straps and let it and her buoyancy compensator slide to the rocky floor. Then she raced to the wall and shone her light inside. The chests, the rusted weapons, the gleam of gold--it was all still there. No one had gotten here ahead of her.

She returned to plug her microphone back in. Instantly Brian's alarmed voice was in her ear, begging her to answer. "Everything is here, Brian, untouched," she said breathlessly, as she pushed the mike tight against her throat for better transmission.

"Where were you?" his voice crackled.

"Sometimes I have to disconnect to work. Let's get going. Are you ready with the ropes?"

"Yes."

"Okay, I'm bringing them in." She unhooked a nylon line from her utility belt and started pulling. It wasn't difficult. In less than five minutes, a large metal clip appeared. She attached to it a heavier rope and announced, "I'm ready for the drums," she said.

"Go ahead and pull," said Brian's static-filled voice.

This was more difficult. The drums attached to the rope, although weighted for neutral buoyancy, still provided some resistance. Sharon had feared that they might get hung up at the entrance to the underwater tunnel, and, in fact, she did feel a sudden jerk at one point. But she waited like a patient fisherman, gently pulled again, and the rope started coming. Before long a blue drum popped into view, and she rolled it up onto the ledge, then kept pulling on the rope until the second drum appeared.

By the time all three drums were in the cavern, her arms were aching. She spoke into the mike. "Brian, I'm going to disconnect now. Don't get nervous. I estimate thirty minutes to load the barrels." She pulled the plug before he had a chance to argue.

The hard part was over, the barrels unsnapped from the rope, their tops unscrewed and sand poured out, and rolled up to the wall. Sharon worked quickly and efficiently by the light of her battery-powered fluorescent lantern.

Into the first drum she would put the contents of what had been the document chest, but first she just had to have a look at what was inside. With shaking hands she carefully removed one jar, examining its glass top sealed with pitch. She smiled. Columbus was a crafty fellow. He knew he might not be back immediately and that any written material would quickly deteriorate in the damp cave. She knew she should wait to send all the artifacts to a specialist in ancient documents, but--life was short, and lately there were indications hers might be shorter than most. She had to know.

Out came her dive knife. She scraped the tar away, then, with a twisting motion, freed the top. Inside were parchment sheets, curled with age but otherwise perfectly preserved. The hermetic seal and darkness of the cave had combined to safeguard them for over five hundred years.

A dozen pages were covered with the fine script she had seen photocopied in the library many times before, but never in the original. It was the handwriting of Christopher Columbus--the missing pages from his journal.

Breathless, she opened a second bottle. Inside was an ancient map, its edges decorated with fearsome and fanciful beasts. Her heart raced, but she knew detailed study would have to wait. Carefully she returned the documents to the glass bottles, and replaced the glass tops. The bottles were no longer air tight, but she had provided for that eventuality. From an inner pocket of her wetsuit she extracted folded plastic bags. The opened bottles went into these, then the bag tops folded and sealed securely with twist ties. If necessary, document restorers would always work their magic later. For now, speed was essential. She placed all the jars into the first drum and using the sand remaining in the bottom to pack each bottle and hold it in place. The drum was still too light, so she placed some gold ingots into it one at a time, estimating their weight as she went. Too heavy and the drum would drag along the bottom, but if it were too light, it would float and bob and be impossible to pull out of the submerged tunnel. Finally satisfied, she screwed on the watertight top and dragged the drum to the edge of the underground river.

Loading the other drums went more quickly. The gold and gems could stand up to less delicate handling. The last barrel was finally sealed and dragged to the water's edge. Exhausted, Sharon stopped to rest. Six heaps of artifacts remained: the edged weapons, the leg irons, what had once been a cask of silver now fused by corrosion into a giant mass. But this and other material from Columbus' secret cache would have to remain for another day.

Sharon's excited breathing slowed as she realized the end was in sight. Her ultimate career quest had now been fulfilled. She plugged the communications line back in. "Brian? Brian, are you there?"

"Where have you been? Why haven't you called?" He sounded frantic.

"What's wrong?"

"It's been over an hour!"

"Sorry! I've been busy." She had been sitting on one of the drums to regain her strength, but now she stood up. "One more second to hook the ropes up, and I'll push the drums into the water. Then you two can do some work."

"Hurry," he urged through the static. "Tide change is in forty-five minutes."

It took only a moment to connect the snap shackles on the rope to the lug on each drum. One by one she pushed them into the water. She was gratified to see each one slowly drift downward. Sharon pulled on her b.c., then opened the valve on her tank, checked the air supply, and slid into the straps. Quickly she dropped over the side and grasped the rope. "Ready," she said into the throat microphone. "Start pulling."

The trip back was so easy it was like a Disneyland ride. All she had to do was hold on to the rope and keep track of the progress with her underwater light. Only once did a drum hang up. The third barrel caught at the basalt teeth that guarded the underwater entrance. She communicated with her shore hands to slack off the tension. Then she followed the rope back, freed the barrel, and told them to haul away. When she broke the surface in the first cave with all drums with her, she whooped almost as loud as Brian did.

It was a simple matter to pull the barrels out into the sunshine but more difficult to get them partway up the hill to higher ground. However, by the time the tide first spilled over the lip of the cave, all three barrels were safe.

Exhaustion now claimed Sharon, and she could barely move. But Brian was as excited as a birthday boy in front of his presents. "Go ahead," she said.

He quickly unscrewed one drum's lid and looked in. The afternoon sun was reflected back in sparkles of yellow and green and red. He dipped his hands in and came up with gold, emeralds, rubies. Philipe gasped. Amazed, Brian dug in again, examining the treasures in each hand. Although some of the gold had been molded into beads, most was in the form of preColumbian jewelry: stylized warriors, fat goddesses, birds, and panther-like animals. Jewels decorated the images.

"Beautiful," Brian gasped. "Let's see inside the others," he said, starting for the next barrel.

"No," said Sharon, "there's time for that later. Philipe, get the duffel out of the cave. Our lives would be worth nothing if anyone found out what we have. From now on, we'll keep our weapon close by."

The two men managed to move the drums about a hundred feet from the cave mouth, safely above the rising water. Philipe scampered back down the slope, showering rocks with each step as he returned for their equipment. Sharon hollered after him in French, "Dump the tanks and scuba gear into the ocean. I won't be making a second dive, and we don't want to leave evidence of our visit."

She turned to find that Brian, from some secret repository, had produced a pint of rum, a can of Coke, and some paper cups for an impromptu toast. They touched cups and drank. Sharon could imagine nothing better than this.

"I think you have had enough," said a strange voice from behind them. They turned to see two men carrying assault rifles, Philipe their prisoner. Brian immediately recognized the man from the dive shop and Dummond, the commercial diver. The two must have followed them all the way from Port-au-Prince.

Anger at his own stupidity flooded over Brian. If he hadn't been so occupied with having a celebratory drink, he would have seen them coming. Of course, with Sharon's gun still in the duffel, there was little he could have done anyway, especially against modern military assault rifles.

Dummond's giant hand held Philipe by the neck of his shirt. With an effortless heave, he slung the much smaller man toward Brian and Sharon. Philipe took several staggering steps and fell at their feet.

"Let me see what you have. Back up!" ordered the dive shop owner, gesturing with his weapon. Philipe crawled to his feet to join Sharon and Brian as they moved several feet up the hill.

Brian stole a glance at Sharon. Her face had the look of a trapped wild animal that might at any moment spring murderously at its captors. But against rapid-fire assault rifles, they both knew they stood no chance.

Morris reached into a barrel and came out with a dazzling gold necklace from which hung a jeweled pendant.

"*Jésus et Saint Mary*," exclaimed Dummond.

The two thieves stared into the open drum. Dummond shifted his AK-47 to the opposite hand so he could reach in and run his fingers through the treasure. Almost simultaneously a staccato burst of gunfire ripped the air, and his neck exploded in a spray of blood.

Brian and Sharon dove for the dirt. Philipe dropped to the ground and started rolling down the hill. A trail of bullets stitched the ground after him.

Morris went down on one knee, hiding behind a drum. In one quick movement he swung up his assault rifle, aiming along the cliff face and firing from the hip. The shooter at top let a fusillade of bullets rain down on the barrel. The dive shop owner stuck his head out from the drum and fired a salvo in return.

Brian and Sharon were exposed on the rocky escarpment. Sharon lay flat on her stomach, Brian covering her with his own body. "We can't stay here," he hollered over the gunfire. "Any second one of them is going to turn on us."

"There!" Sharon pointed.

Nearby was a boulder that years back must have broken loose and slid down the hill. It wasn't much, but the only other refuge was a tangle of rainforest a hundred yards away, and Brian knew they would be cut down before they got halfway there.

"Go for it!" he said.

Sharon needed no further urging. They both took off running at a crouch while the battle raged around them. Sharon was the first to reach the rock and dive behind it. Brian slid in next to her.

The gunfire continued unabated. Cautiously Brian raised his head. Someone on the hilltop was also armed with an automatic weapon and, judging from the amount of shooting, apparently had an unlimited supply of ammunition.

Morris pulled another clip out of his pocket, snapped it into his weapon, and loosed another burst. In a quick movement he reached out from behind his barrel to grab the other Ak-47 from the dead Dummond and pull it toward him. More shots rained down.

Brian watched with terrified fascination. It was obvious what the man was going to do. His only cover was behind the drum, but he now had twice as much firepower as the solitary gunman on the hilltop. The dive shop owner was going to make a run for it.

This could be Brian and Sharon's only chance. Maybe the shooter up above would be too busy to notice them. "Now, Sharon. We've got to get out of here!"

They rose to all fours, but before they could flee, a figure emerged from the edge of the rainforest, running toward them. They were trapped and could only drop to the ground, praying they would be spared. The man wore a gray uniform, and he, like apparently every one else in Haiti, had an assault rifle. But it was not pointing at Brian and Sharon. The man was rapidly advancing, unseen, on the dive shop owner.

Brian quickly analyzed the situation. Clearly, the man on the hilltop was not alone. He, too, had a partner, and, unnoticed, the second man had circled around in a flanking maneuver.

Morris jumped from behind the barrel with weapons firing. He started charging up the hill, an AK-47 in each hand, and before he had gone five yards, there was a scream from the hilltop. He had hit the hilltop shooter. However, in his excitement he was oblivious to what was happening behind him. The second Haitian policeman was only a few yards away when a fusillade of gunfire erupted from his weapon. Brian saw the dive shop owner hit in the side and chest. The man was knocked sideways, screaming, and the policeman charged the falling man, emptying his weapon as he ran.

It was over in an instant. Morris' body lay in a crumpled heap, blood flowing from a dozen wounds.

The Haitian policeman hollered to the hilltop. "Merleau, Merleau. Are you hurt?" No answer.

Brian and Sharon cowered only a short distance away behind the boulder. The policeman turned his deadly gaze in their direction. His eyes cold, he popped out his empty ammo clip, reached into the leather pouch on his belt for another, and expertly snapped it into the gun. Pointing the weapon at Brian, he gestured with his head for Brian to rise. "Get up," he said.

Brian slowly rose.

"The lady, too," the Haitian said.

Sharon stood up, too, as the policeman moved closer.

He stared at her. "I did not think you would be foolish enough to return here after such a narrow escape the last time. But the alert from your own police to be on the lookout for two Americans who might be engaged in some questionable activities in Haiti made us decide to keep a close eye out--just in case." He broke into a malevolent grin. "It seems those American police would like to question you, too. I am all for international cooperation. However, in this case, the suspects are unfortunately going to be killed trying to evade the authorities." The grin widened. "Unless"--he pointed his gun toward the treasure--"that is what I think it is, and there is still more that you can recover."

"He was one of the men in the cave," Sharon said to Brian. "And that must have been his partner at the top of the hill."

"It is unfortunate that after all the waiting and watching we have done together, poor Merleau is unable to share in the success." The policeman's smile said he was not especially disturbed over that turn of events.

"Let me have a better look." He took a step toward the bullet-riddled drum, and a shot rang out. The policeman screamed in pain as he was knocked forward. He grabbed the open lip of the drum to keep from falling. Philipe appeared behind him, in his hand, Sharon's nine-millimeter Smith and Wesson. With one more shot the policeman tumbled to the ground, pulling the drum over with him. A fortune in ancient treasure spilled out on his corpse.

"He killed my brother," said Philipe simply, standing over him.

Sharon threw her arms around Brian, and they rocked from side to side, each hungrily clutching the other. Gradually Brian felt her anxious respirations slow. Looking over Sharon's shoulder, Brian saw Philipe still holding the pistol and glaring at the dead policeman. "Thank you, Philipe," Brian said.

Still clinging to Brian, Sharon added, in French, "You saved our lives."

Brian turned to gaze up the steep hillside, then said to Sharon, "But if Philipe hadn't been so quick on the trigger, we might have made your old friend here"--he nodded toward the policeman on the ground--"help us lug these barrels up that damn hill."

Chapter 46

The truck bounced over a pothole, and only the slatted wooden sides kept the drums from being catapulted out. With Brian driving, Sharon in the middle, and Philipe on the passenger side, exhaustion and disappointment had kept them mostly silent for the past hour.

After the gunfight, there was the problem of the bodies. Sharon was in despair at seeing death all around her. But she still insisted that the bodies be moved to avoid attracting attention to the mouth of the cave. So Brian and Philipe had carried the bodies of Dummond, Morris, and the two slain policemen up to the roadway, leaving them and their weapons as if the battle had occurred there. *La police de province* were well-known to shake down outsiders, especially other Haitians who might have a little money and no embassy to inquire into their welfare. Philipe believed that when the bodies were found, it would be presumed these policemen had the bad luck to pick on a couple of men as well-armed as they were.

Brian was called upon to stuff his remaining cash into the pockets of the men from Port-au-Prince to give the impression that they were up to something they didn't want the police to take an interest in. Philipe offered the opinion that the local authorities wanted no attention from the central government, and most probably, the bodies as well as the entire matter would be quickly and quietly swept away.

That matter disposed of, the trio had returned to Philipe's village, but there Sharon's plan to spirit the treasure out of the country had fallen apart. The fisherman had not arrived who were supposed to meet them and transport them and their drums by boat to the U.S. Virgin Islands. Two days to St. Croix and there, Dr. Ethel Stern, a long-time friend and colleague from Houston was supervising a dig. Ethel would go bananas when she saw what was in the drums, and Sharon had no doubt that the archaeologist would do everything within her power to get the priceless artifacts back into the country. It shouldn't be that difficult to disguise and spread the Columbus treasure among their own returning artifacts. And if something did go wrong, well at least the Virgin Islands were American soil.

But the fishermen were not there. Philipe was angry they did not show up. He had thought them reliable, and he had given them four of the five hundred dollars as partial payment. Maybe they decided they didn't want to risk everything for more money. Maybe they had ventured to close to Cuba with something besides just fish in the hold of their boat. Philipe could only shrug. Their only hope now, to seek asylum from Baptiste. That suited Brian. All along he had intended to get to Doúbe and question the doctor, but with their tight schedule he didn't know when he could manage it. Now he would have his chance.

Entering the Doúbe medical compound the dirt road smoothed out and the trio offered up a collective moan of relief. Brian commented that he should order kidney X-rays for all of them to see how much damage the violent jostling had done.

"This is all so familiar," said Sharon softly. "I remember this circle of huts." She pointed to a tin-roofed structure at least three times longer than the others. "I think I stayed there."

Brian brought the truck to a stop. The drums in back gave one last rattle, then came to rest. The three passengers climbed out and stretched their legs.

A few shabbily dressed people stood or sat around the compound. One man, Sharon noticed, was on crutches. Another, with a dressing on his arm, reclined against a porch post.

While Sharon looked around, trying to coax other memories out of her subconscious, a woman dressed in white came out of the long building and began to beckon the man on crutches, but she paused to stare at the newcomers. Then, as recognition dawned, she hurried over to Sharon.

"You are the lady from America."

The woman's coffee-colored skin and concerned expression was instantly familiar to Sharon. It was the nurse named Martina.

"Yes, Martina. And my friend and I need to see Dr. Baptiste," Sharon replied.

The woman led them to the doctor's bungalow where Philipe chose to wait outside.

Brian and Sharon were standing when the doctor entered. The Frenchman waved them in the direction of two bamboo chairs.

"It is so good to see you well," said the missionary with genuine pleasure.

"Thank you, Dr. Baptiste," Sharon said. I owe my life to you."

"I am glad I was able to assist."

"This is Dr. Brian Richards."

Dr. Baptiste arched his eyebrows. "A physician?"

Brian spoke up. "Yes, sir. A general surgeon, trauma specialist."

Dr. Baptiste looked interested. "We do have the occasional trauma case, to be sure, but mostly what we deal with here are simpler problems-- infections, immunizations, childhood illnesses, difficult childbirth. We do have an obstetrician, but"--he shrugged--"he is not working out." He looked at Sharon. "But tell me, what brings you back here?"

"We wanted to see you because Dr. Richards had some questions to ask you about... my condition and the treatment you gave me."

Baptiste looked down and nodded as if the long anticipated end to a game of charades had finally arrived.

"But now we have an even more pressing problem. We need your help to get out of the country," said Sharon, "immediately."

Baptiste's crestfallen appearance dissolved away, as concern wrinkled his features. "Are you in trouble?"

"Yes," she said simply. "And our departure must be in secret." She hesitated. The man she was seeking help from deserved to know more. "We have found something a lot of people want--something people have killed and died for."

"Does it have to do with those objects you had when you were here last?" Baptiste asked.

"Yes." She had trusted this man with her life before, and she had nowhere else to turn now. She took a deep breath. "They were rare artifacts. From Christopher Columbus' voyages. He hid the treasure in 1498, not ten kilometers from here. I found it."

"Astonishing! But are you certain it was Columbus? There have been shipwrecks and tales of buried treasure in these islands almost since they were discovered."

"It was him, all right. I found journals, logs. He hid a fortune in jewels and gold, but their historical value is far more important. The treasure belongs in museums where it can be studied and appreciated by everyone, not plundered for private collections."

"I must believe you. I saw the necklace with my own eyes. So how do you plan to safeguard this treasure?" he asked.

"I had planned to secretly get it to a fellow archaeologist in the Virgin Islands by boat and then on to the States. But that fell through. Of course, the treasure really belongs to the people of Haiti, but once I'm sure it's safe, then proper arrangements can be made for its protection and return."

Baptiste rubbed his chin while he pondered what Sharon just told him. "This treasure--how large is it? I mean, would it fit in a suitcase? A trunk?"

Sharon shook her head and smiled. "Not by a long shot." Sharon pointed out the door. "It's in those blue drums on the back of the truck."

Baptiste's eyes widened. "A load of that size will not be easy to ship, that is if you want to avoid the scrutiny of the officials."

"But we have even more to ask," said Sharon. "We need a way out quickly for ourselves, too. The two police who had attacked me last time came after me again. We only barely escaped with our lives--but"--she paused--"they did not."

Sharon's eyes searched Baptiste's face, but she saw not even a flicker of reproof. "Those were violent and dangerous men."

"They said the authorities both here and in the U.S. are hunting for us, accusing us of crimes we did not commit. If they detain us, or the artifacts, now, all will be lost."

Baptiste was silent while his gaze went from her face to Brian's, then back again. Then, as if he had searched their soul and was satisfied at what he had found, he announced, "There was a spy in my midst, a supply officer, who liked to report to..." Baptiste trailed off. "In any case, I ferreted him out and dispatched him back to his home village. So for the moment, you are safe here. Getting you two out of the country is no problem. There is a man who can help. I, with God's hand on mine, saved his child, and he will do anything I ask. He has an airplane, a small one, and makes part of his living ferrying people to the U.S., even if they do not have the proper papers. He can get across your border, but can do no more than that."

"Thank you," said Sharon, reaching out to grasp the priest's hand. Then she turned to Brian. "I can call Darcy to pick us up. She should be back in New Orleans by now." Switching back to Dr. Baptiste, she asked, "So he can take us and the treasure?"

"That is the problem. His airplane is small, and your drums are large." Baptiste's brow furrowed and he fell silent as he studied the difficulty. "But for that, too, there may be a solution. I have a supplier who brings in new shipments and takes back medical records and equipment that needs repairs. I could place a red biohazard warning on those drums and label them as: used medical equipment, blood contaminated--and indicate they should be held for decontamination. Airport and customs officials are used to these frequent shipments. I suspect your treasure would escape inspection and be safe for some time. You would already be in the U. S. and in a position to recover your items. The truck to the airport is due here tomorrow morning. Have you, by chance, heard of a company called Durbane Pharmaceuticals?"

"It just so happens, sir, that we have," said Brian. He turned to Sharon as a grin spread across his face.

"Yes," she said, returning the smile. "And under the circumstances, I think it would be a nice, even if unknowing, gesture on their part." With an air of immense satisfaction, she stood and straightened her clothing. "Thank you again, Dr. Baptiste." She held out her hand. The missionary took it. "I'd best get busy and secure the contents of those drums for air travel. And Philipe will likely be glad to have the truck emptied so he can take off."

"Perhaps, sir," said Brian. "After I help Sharon, could you and I could talk a little more? Lately I've developed considerable interest in artificial blood, and maybe you could answer some questions for me."

* * * * *

They had to wait two anxious days until their departure arrangements were complete. Brian passed the time by helping to treat Baptiste's never-ending supply of patients. Brian met the new obstetrician only once. For reasons Brian could only speculate, Baptiste had banished the man from treating pregnant females and the ob-gyn physician was relegated to handling only the most minor of afflictions.

On the matter of greatest importance to Brian, Baptiste had assured him that Durbane's U.B.S. was not only harmless but had already saved hundreds of lives, providing the recipient was not pregnant. Pregnant patients had shown a pronounced tendency to spontaneously abort after receiving the intravenous solution.

When the time came to leave, Brian had come to understand Jean Baptiste's mixed emotions about allowing Durbane's experimentation to be carried out here. Under normal circumstances, all medical test subjects should be fully informed about the risks and benefits of their participation in a study. But many of Baptiste's patients would not have understood the implications no matter how well explained, and given the region's paucity of medical care, what choice did they really have? No blood guaranteed to be safe was available to them. Baptiste had made a trade-off, and in the final analysis, far more people had been helped than potentially harmed.

Brian left Doúbe knowing that if it were ever in his power to help the medical missionary, he would.

Chapter 47

The sun was rapidly sinking as the twin-engine Cessna turned into its final approach. The pilot adjusted the flaps, throttled back the engine, and glided to a gentle touchdown on the runway. He pulled up to the private deplaning area, spoke briefly into the microphone, then, without ceremony, reached across Sharon and opened the passenger door.

She wanted to do something special for this man who had risked much to get them here, but he had refused their offer of payment, and all she could say was, "Thank you very much."

The pilot had spoken very little from the time of their first meeting, seeming taciturn, even resentful. The long flight in a cramped cockpit had not improved his disposition.

"I did this for Dr. Baptiste," he growled.

Sharon nodded, then ducked her head to climb out the small cockpit door. The pilot pushed her empty seat forward and allowed Brian to crawl out.

"Are you sure? Can't I later send you some money by way of Dr. Baptiste?" Brian hollered over the sound of the engine, which was already accelerating.

The pilot waved off the offer. "Forget you ever saw me." He slammed the door, latched it, and the plane pulled away. Brian and Sharon were left standing alone on the tarmac.

Sharon looked around and spotted a small sign. *Welcome to Houma, LA.* Below it was a plain door marked *General Aviation.* "I guess that's where we go," she said.

They entered a short corridor, which opened into the terminal's tiny waiting area. The only time Sharon had seen an airport this small was in the islands. Fewer than a half dozen people sat reading or idly eating snacks. The metal detector that led to the one departure gate had a sign across it that read *closed.*

"I don't see Darcy anywhere," she said.

"You made it plain when and where to meet us, didn't you?"

"I told you, Baptiste's phone had a bad connection, and I wasn't sure of our exact arrival time, but--"

Sharon's explanation was cut short as Brian grabbed her arm and abruptly pulled her back into the passageway.

"Did you see those two men who just came in?"

His fingers dug into her arm so tightly, it hurt. Sharon could see the alarm in his eyes. "Which two?" She cautiously peered into the corridor. Two men stood ten feet away, their backs partly turned. They were studying a flickering computer terminal that listed flight information. One of the men was tall, well-dressed, black. The other was short, squat, and swarthy.

"The black man--he looks like the one that offered me the money, or else, outside the Archaeology office.

Brian pulled her back again. "Well, they do get around. Those are the men I saw outside my office in New Orleans, and Mrs. Thompson described them as the same two who questioned her the day before she was murdered."

"How could they know we'd be here?" said Sharon. But even as she spoke, she guessed the answer. Only one person, besides Dr. Baptiste and the pilot, knew they were arriving here, and the pilot would never jeopardize his clandestine activities. "Darcy!"

"You told her to tell no one, didn't you?" questioned Brian, his voice incredulous. Sharon nodded. "Then why would she betray us?"

"I don't think she would willingly," Sharon said anxiously.

"Did you tell her we were coming in by private plane?"

"No. The pilot insisted I give out as little information as possible."

"Then those two goons are expecting us on a commercial flight. That's why they're checking the monitor."

Brian looked back down the corridor the way they had come. "Let's get out of here."

They headed back down the hallway and out to the tarmac. It was now night outside, but there was still enough light to see the six-foot cyclone fence that stood between them and the parking lot.

"Now what?" Sharon asked.

Brian pointed to where the fence disappeared into the darkness. "We'll work our way along the fence. Somewhere we'll find a way out."

"Then what?" said Sharon.

"Those toughs who keep following us around have to be from Durbane, and we've got to make sure they get caught."

"What about Darcy?" asked Sharon, nervously wiping her hair away from her eyes. "I can't imagine why she'd give us away. What if she's in danger... or worse."

"Now is the time to go to the police--with everything!"

"Except that the damn treasure won't be in the country until tomorrow. We've got to hang tough just a little longer," Sharon pleaded.

"I suppose we've waited this long," said Brian, breathing out a sigh of exasperation. He patted for his money belt, now so flat he could barely feel it. "Well, I've got just about enough cash left for a taxi out of here, supper, and a cheap motel."

Sharon's voice sounded as drained as she looked. "A cheap motel it is."

* * * * *

"Will you accept a collect call from Dr. Brian Richards?" asked the operator.

Brian waited while the sleepy person on the other end of the line processed the request.

"Yeah," said Dale Blevins, yawning. Then, more alertly, "Brian? Where the hell are you? What's going on?"

"Go ahead," said the operator.

"I've been out of the country," Brian began.

"People have been going crazy around here wondering what happened to you. The police have come by the hospital more than once and must have called a dozen times."

"Are there any charges against me?"

"Charges? Brian, what kind of trouble are you in? The detective I spoke with was pretty vague. I thought it was some kind of missing-person thing."

"I wish it were. Dale, I need you to come get us."

"There was a hesitation while Dale apparently consulted a timepiece. "It's five A.M., and I've got to be in the O.R. by six-thirty."

"You may be late."

"Where are you?"

"Houma."

"Houma, Louisiana? That's almost two hours away."

"That's why I said you'd be late."

"I don't mean to sound unhelpful, old buddy; but couldn't you just rent a car and drive here yourself?"

"I'm out of cash and we don't want to use any credit cards. They might be used to trace us."

"What are you doing there, and, by the way, who is 'us'?"

"It's a long story," Brian said, "But we've just gotten back into the U.S. by small plane. The pilot slipped us in last night pretending to be a spotter plane returning from a fishing fleet off the Louisiana coast. We wanted to avoid customs, in case someone had notified them to be on the lookout for us. I'm with a friend, Sharon."

"What's this all about, Brian?"

"Dale, there's something big and really bad going on, and we're right in the middle of it. Don't tell anybody about this call or you'll be in danger, too."

"Does this have anything to do with spongiform encephalopathy or a Dr. Peter Obrien?" asked Dale.

"What are you talking about?" Brian asked.

"That rare disease, Creutzfeldt-Jakob disease."

"I've heard of it, sure; but a Dr. Peter Obrien? Never," said Brian.

"Same here," said Dale, "but according to the information Jeanette Edwards put together, he's some bigwig in infectious-disease research, a consultant to the British government. Dr. Edwards seemed to think it was pretty important that you get this information."

"I didn't realize you knew Jeanette Edwards."

"I didn't, until she called me," Dale said. "She was trying to find you. The hospital operator put her through to me. These switchboard operators know everything," he added as an aside. "Anyway, Dr. Edwards wanted me to get some information to you in case I saw you before she did. She sent a large folder over by courier. She said it was very important that I give it to you, and I shouldn't let anybody else know. It was only after the laboratory explosion and she came up missing that I realized there might be more to this and I opened the envelope even though it was addressed to you. Inside were reprints of scientific journals and copies of some e-mail messages."

"Missing? Explosion? What do you mean?"

"You *have* been out of it. The story was in all the papers. The day after she sent me the envelope, there was a chemical explosion and fire in her laboratory at L.S.U. Medical Center. She hasn't been heard from since. The

272

police doubt the fire was accidental, but she's missing, and they don't know if she's the perpetrator or the victim."

"I'll tell you," said Brian emphatically. "She was murdered."

"How do you know?"

"Believe me, I know," Brian said, feeling sick. "She was looking into something for me, something that some pretty vicious people didn't want investigated." Brian paused, overcome with sadness as he thought back about the hours he had spent with Jeanette Edwards and the many things she had taught him.

"I didn't see anything like that in the information she sent," said Dale. "Everything had to do with spongiform encephalopathy and prions. Except for the copies of some e-mails sent to the Ministry of Health in England and a few other places about this Dr. Obrien."

"I've got to see this stuff right away."

"I'll bring it with me. One other thing," Dale added. "The credentials committee met, and Fendley had all his sycophants there. I was the only one who vouched for your good side. It wasn't enough. They rescinded your staff privileges."

Brian was quiet for a moment. "I'll worry about that later." Then he gave Dale the name and location of a small motel outside Houma, Louisiana, and hung up.

* * * * *

The car hurtled down highway 90. Brian had been quiet for about thirty minutes while he read and reread the documents from Dr. Edwards. Dale drove, while Sharon, reluctant to discuss the Columbus treasure with any stranger, including Dr. Dale Blevins, made only desultory conversation about Haiti. Dale was thoroughly confused.

At last Brian let the papers fall to his lap and stared out the car window at the pine forests and sugarcane fields they passed. Dale finally broke the silence. "Well, old buddy, since I got up before the crack of dawn, called in sick to the O.R., then drove halfway across the state of Louisiana and back again, perhaps a little explanation would be in order?"

When Brian turned his head, his face was tight and drawn. He held up the papers for the others to see. "Prion disease, Bovine Spongiform Encephalopathy, better known as Mad Cow disease," he mused.

Sharon's brow wrinkled. "Don't know anything about it."

"It's one of an invariably fatal group of diseases caused by a small, probably crystalline, particle," Dale explained. It occurs mostly in animals. It's called Scrappie in sheep, Mad Cow disease or Bovine Spongiform Encephalopathy, in cattle. There's no preventative vaccine and no treatment, so when an infected case appears, the entire herd is destroyed. Experts used to guess the cause might be something they called a 'slow virus,' one with an incubation period of months to years instead of a few days, like influenza or mumps, but there's now a lot of controversy on that point. Anyway, there's a form of Mad Cow called Creutzfeldt-Jakob, or C.J., disease, that attacks the human brain just as lethally."

Brian took over the narrative. "A few years ago there was an outbreak in England of the bovine form. Then cases of C.J. disease started showing up in people who had contact with cattle." Brian held up the papers. "Most of these reprints are from British publications, suggesting the disease had mutated to a much more virulent form, which not only had a shorter incubation period, but could more readily spread to humans. The big problem is there's no diagnostic test for the disease, until the affected person's brain starts to deteriorate."

"Sounds horrible," said Sharon.

"A lot of diseases are horrible," said Dale. "But what does any of this have to do with you and Dr. Edwards?"

"It looks as if one of the principle researchers is a Dr. Peter Obrien," said Brian. "He also did some work suggesting that the rapid variant of C.J. disease could be transmitted via blood." Brian brandished a paper from the packet. "But this is what really put Dr. Edwards on Obrien's trail. Her computerized search of the literature on artificial blood turned up this essay article from *Lancet*, the well-known British medical journal. It's entitled *Artificial Blood: Theoretical Solution for an Emerging Problem*, by Dr. Peter Obrien. Dr. Edwards has filled it with notes and underlining."

"Did she talk with him?" asked Sharon.

"It doesn't appear that way. She attempted, unsuccessfully, to correspond with him by e-mail. This one is dated last Thursday."

"That's the day before her laboratory caught fire and she came up missing," interjected Dale.

"The British Ministry of Health confirmed that he had taken a leave of absence to go to the United States. Specifically, New Orleans."

"So, what's the connection? Why did Dr. Edwards feel it so important to pass on information about this Dr. Peter Obrien?" Sharon asked.

"Dr. Peter Obrien is not just any old researcher," Brian said. "He has degrees in both biochemistry and medicine, with his original medical specialty being hematology, until he turned to infectious disease. According to this, he's the most knowledgeable person in the world about prion disease, particularly the transmissibility of the agent. And"--Brian dug through papers again until he found what he was looking for--"this is a list of his credentials. Dr. Edwards has underlined one three times, with arrows and exclamation points--*consultant to Durbane Pharmaceuticals Corporation.*"

"Wow," Sharon breathed, then a perplexed expression crossed her face. "But don't pharmaceutical companies have hundreds of physicians as consultants?"

"So far, you've only convinced me he's real smart," Dale agreed, taking his eyes off the road for a second to glance at Brian.

"O.K.," said Brian. "Look at it from another vantage point. Durbane has developed artificial blood, and--"

Dale cut his gaze back to Brian. "I haven't heard--"

Brian held up a hand, silencing his friend. "For now, just accept it. There is a rare ailment, rapid variant C.J. disease, which is spread by human blood, and it can't be detected until it's too late. The man who knows more about this disease than anyone else in the world is brought in to work for the company with the only means of preventing its spread by blood transfusion."

"So?" said Dale.

"So what would happen to that company if C.J. disease wasn't so rare, if it became widespread in the human blood supply?"

"It's product, artificial blood, would sell at any price. The company's stock would go ballistic," Dale reasoned.

"Surely they wouldn't go that far!" Sharon gasped.

Brian spoke in somber tones. "We know they've killed before--now it's only a matter of numbers." He angrily slammed his fist onto the dash; making everyone jump. "We've got to get into that plant, and see if that's really about to happen. Now! Before they have a chance to pull off their plan."

"Brian," Sharon said, clutching his arm. "I'm beginning to think you're right. We need to go to the police with this--immediately."

"No," he said, shaking his head. "There may not be time. We still have no proof of any actual wrongdoing; e-mails, reprints, artificial blood research in Haiti--great! Who gives a shit? If we show this to the authorities, I doubt they could even get a search warrant--and then, would they even know what to look for? That detective who came to see us wouldn't be able to tell the difference between a prion culture and yesterday's leftover coffee." Brian looked down at his rumpled khaki shorts and short-sleeved shirt. "I know what to do. Our next stop will be at the hospital to pick up a few things. After that, we go to New Orleans Industrial Park."

"No," said Sharon. "First we go see Darcy and find out why she gave us away."

"I'm really confused," said Dale.

Chapter 48

"You have done extremely well, doctor," said Thurston Walker.

Peter Obrien beamed with pleasure. The two of them, along with Karl Dietrich, stood looking through the glass observation wall at the three stainless steel tanks on the other side. Three men dressed in environmental isolation suits moved about the room monitoring instruments, checking gauges, and adjusting valves. Two other technicians were in the airlock suiting up.

"Your original estimate was three weeks before the cultures were complete. You have accomplished it in one-third the time. I wish other branches of this company could be so efficient."

"Thank you, Dr. Walker. As a biochemist you can appreciate some of the challenges we were up against, but the chemistry of those beasties was what helped the most."

"Excuse me," said Karl Dietrich. "I have to check on our aircraft. I will be back momentarily."

"Fine, Dietrich," said Walker.

Dr. Obrien lectured on, oblivious to the fact that he had lost half his audience. "Everything we have been able to determine from worldwide research suggest that these infectious particles, so small they can only be seen with the electron microscope, are crystals of abnormal protein."

"I'm familiar with much of that research. The experiments coming out of that Brussels lab seem to be the most revealing."

"That is Vanmeter's work. His is second to none. But, to continue, traditional culture methods involve inoculating a suitable growth medium with the organism, maintaining the mixture at the proper temperature, then allowing sufficient time for the bacterium, virus, or whatever..."

"Whatever in this case," said Walker.

Dr. Obrien laughed. "Yes, whatever. It takes time for the little whatevers to replicate themselves. Based on the usual viral replication rates, for incubation vats the size of these, I estimated three weeks." Obrien's face gleamed with excitement. "But if we consider the theory that these little buggers are crystalline, rather than biological--wait let me illustrate." He held out a hand, cupped in a semicircle, as if holding an invisible container. "I have a glass of iced tea." He frowned. "I don't know how you Americans can ruin good tea by putting ice in it, but if I had a glass of tea that was supersaturated with sugar--you know, heated so as much sugar as possible dissolved in it, then cooled--"

"Peter, I know what supersaturation is," said Dr. Walker.

"Pardon me. I am used to talking to imbeciles." He resumed holding his glass of invisible tea. "Now into that supersaturated solution, I dropped a tiny bit of sugar, instantly crystallization would occur, and a comparatively large amount of sugar would precipitate out." The scientist spread his hands wide. "Replication by living processes is comparatively slow, but by chemical processes--virtually instantaneous. And although it did take us a week," conceded Obrien, "most of that time was spent preparing the medium. The vats were inoculated with my cultures only three days ago."

"Amazing," said Walker.

"Let me show you this." Peter Obrien led him into the small electron microscope room. Designed as a work space for only one person, it was barely more than a cubicle. In these close confines the smell of the unwashed Dr. Obrien was nearly overpowering, and Thurston Walker wished he had installed a shower along with the sleeper couch in the man's laboratory office. But, he decided, Obrien was on such a roll that he probably wouldn't have paused in his work long enough to use it anyway.

Obrien began rifling through folders filled with photographs. Walker breathed a sigh of relief as he realized they would not be closing the door and activating the e.m. He stayed near the entrance to inhale fresher air.

"Here," said Obrien, handing him a black-and-white glossy. If Walker had not seen many such photos in the past, he would have thought it a picture of a dozen matchsticks spread on a carpet. "One to one-point-two million magnification," said Obrien. "That is a blood sample from a young boy--the last case I saw before I left the U.K. As soon as I got here I did an ether extraction and spun down the residue," he explained. "Now, look at this." He handed a second photo to Dr. Walker.

Instead of a dozen matches, it looked as if the contents of a hundred matchboxes had been upended. Thousands of prion particles covered the photo. The "carpet" was no longer even visible, the entire field covered by a thick layer of prions. "This is from your vats in just three day's time?"

Dr. Obrien beamed with accomplishment. "I estimate the material we have here is at least ten thousand times more infectious than any naturally occurring biological organism. So you must exercise extreme caution--" Obrien stopped his narration. "Are you absolutely sure you want to transport these cultures for storage elsewhere?"

"Yes," said Walker who had continued to polish his plan and his lie until both was now rolling perfectly. "We're working on several drugs that may be useful against prions. If a fire or some other calamity struck our main facility here, we would have to start over from scratch. That's why we have other sites to store back-ups of our test materials, our drugs under development, our computer files, everything."

"Well, in any case, do be careful. If this material were released into the biosphere it would be undetectable for at least a month until the first symptoms started appearing, and it is still untreatable with current technology."

Walker led the scientist back out into the open air of the laboratory. "I am well aware of all that, Dr. Obrien."

With renewed enthusiasm, Obrien produced an object from his pocket. "This is a little device I've come up with to make for safer transport of hazardous biologicals." He handed it to Walker.

The object looked to be nothing more spectacular than a rather large test tube, but it was made of stainless steel with a rubber seal at one end.

"Basically it is an unbreakable specimen container for virulent micro-organisms, but the real genius is the mechanism that allows for safe withdrawal of its contents. The stopper is made of two layers of rubber separated by a vacuum. As a needle is withdrawn through the stopper, the inner rubber seal wipes the outside clean and the vacuum retains any microdroplets from inside the bore of the needle. I've attached a similar mechanism to the incubation vats, which will allow your technicians to withdraw samples in the same safe fashion."

"You are truly amazing," said Walker with genuine admiration. "And for your splendid performance, here's a little something extra as a bonus." He withdrew a check from an envelope and handed both to the scientist.

Obrien went bug-eyed when he saw the amount on the bank draft.

"I've also enclosed a ticket back to London--by commercial air but first class, of course," Walker said. "I'm afraid our company jets will be tied up for a while. Your work here is done, and I'm sure you are eager to be home"--he paused--"I trust that you understand that this project falls under our corporate secrecy policy. As much as I hate to bring it up, I must remind you that any disclosure of the work you did here will require you to repay your bonus"-- Walker indicated the check--"as well as open you to legal action."

"I understand," said Obrien. "You needn't worry." He gestured to the transport test tube still in Walker's hand and spoke with a smile on his face. "In turn, I must remind you, lest your engineers get any sneaky ideas about copying my invention, I have already applied for patents on every conceivable variation of my design."

"We wouldn't think of it," said Walker, extending his hand to shake.

"Your flight is scheduled to leave at two o'clock, Dr. Obrien," interjected Dietrich, who had silently returned. "You had best begin your packing."

"That will be no problem. I have been staying here in my office, and I brought only one bag," said the ecstatic Dr. Obrien as he headed toward his cubicle, clutching his check and airplane ticket.

"One-month incubation period," said Walker, as much to himself as the security chief, as he resumed watching the technicians working on the other side of the glass isolation barrier. "That should be just about right. By then our regional warehouses will be fully stocked with U.B.S. Although, once word of the new plague becomes public, the supplies will be rapidly depleted--until our production capacity catches up." He inhaled sharply in anticipation of Durbane's meteoric rise to worldwide prominence--and huge profits. "A transient shortage should shoot the price even higher."

He turned to face Dietrich. "Can we count on the people you've placed at the regional blood centers to go ahead and perform the inoculations and not back out?"

"There is no cause to worry. For one thing all the locations you specified, with the exception of Beauvoir Hospital, are in underdeveloped or war-torn countries, where a few thousand dollars and an airplane ticket out will buy someone not only a new life, but also their lifelong silence. Our dealings with the operatives in the blood banks have all been handled through intermediaries, who made it clear what would happen if..."

Walker held up a hand and shook his head. "Spare me the details. Just take care of it, Karl."

Dietrich nodded. "Despite the recent crash, we still have our remaining MD-101 cargo jet and the Gulfstream. The specimens should all be distributed within twenty-four hours."

"Good." Walker looked at his Rolex. "Get Fendley here. We'll meet back in one hour to begin transferring the cultures. Once that's properly under way you can dispatch Obrien to the airport."

"Fendley is already here," said the ever-efficient Dietrich.

* * * * *

It was midmorning when Dale and his passengers pulled up across from Darcy's apartment. Sharon's call from the car phone a short while earlier had confirmed that she was at home and in no danger. Darcy's reticence was unusual and Sharon knew without asking that her confidence had been violated.

"Are we all going in?" Dale asked.

"No. I need to do this myself," said Sharon. "She's more likely to talk openly to me. There must be some explanation of her seeming to be involved in such dangerous stuff. She and I are friends, and I have to know why she did this."

Sharon got out of the car and headed up the front stairs. The woman Brian had met at the hospital appeared at the door. It was difficult to tell from a distance, but Brian thought he saw a moment's hesitation before the door swung wide enough for Sharon to enter.

Now that Brian was alone with Dale, it was time to bring his friend up to date. Since Brian had now dragged his friend into their dangerous crusade, he felt he owed him as complete an explanation as possible. Yet, without Sharon's go-ahead to talk openly about the Columbus discovery, Brian had to leave out many important details and connections. And he feared that his tale about artificial blood, a team of hit men, and what he believed was Durbane's deadly agenda sounded about as believable as the tale of Hansel, Gretel, and the witch.

Dale had just asked Brian to begin his explanation at the beginning for the third time when Sharon came out of Darcy's building, hurried down the steps, and climbed into the car to sit silently in the back seat.

"Well?" Brian said when she failed to volunteer any information about what Darcy had told her.

"A black guy and a heavy-set Cajun fellow visited her and made an offer she couldn't refuse. Sound familiar?"

Sharon grimaced and nodded. "And the offer?"

"A whole lot of money and a promise not to tell the authorities about her criminal activities, if she told them where I could be found. Of course, she never knew exactly where I was, but she agreed to the next best thing--to tell them when I contacted her."

"And when and where we would be arriving, so they could be there to meet us," finished Brian. "But what do you mean about her criminal activities? What was she up to? What did they have on her?"

Sharon sat stony-faced for a moment, her emotions seemingly buried under an avalanche of disappointment and betrayal. "Illegal sale of antiquities," said Sharon. "Her finds were supposed to go to *Il Museo di Firenze*. Apparently she had found a way to divert some of the artifacts to private brokers. Genuine Etruscan antiquities command an exorbitant price." Sharon shook her head. "All these years, and I never suspected."

"Then how did these men find out something like that?" Brian asked.

"I don't know, but the two goons claimed to work for a rival artifact broker, and they said they wanted to talk to me about going to work for them doing the same thing Darcy did." She shook her head again. "She actually thought I might be interested. When I told her those men were out to kill me, she freaked. Cried her eyes out. But it seems a little too late for tears."

"So she sold you out."

Sharon nodded her head.

Brian gazed at her over the seat back, trying to choose his words carefully. "Uh, mightn't our recent recovery efforts also prove illegal."

"Of course. Antiquities can't be imported into the United States without a permit from the host country. Naturally, that would apply to a fortune in gold, jewels, and historical relics. I'll have to explain to the authorities why I had to do it before returning it all to the University of the Caribbean in Port-au-Prince—once proper safeguards are established."

"What fortune? What jewels? What gold?" Dale sputtered.

"We'll tell you later," Brian said grimly. "But if Durbane does have a plan to release prions into the blood supply, we haven't got any more time to waste." With a gesture that would have done a Civil War general proud, he pointed down the road ahead of them. "Now! Forward!"

"I'm confused," said Dale, peeling out with a squeal of rubber.

Chapter 49

Outside the isolation room, stood three men--the chief executive officer of Durbane Pharmaceuticals, his chief of security, and the Special Projects director, a man named Warren Holton. Some workers across the room paid them no heed; all attention was focused on the opposite side of the glass wall. There, five technicians in environmental protection suits attended the stainless steel vats. The suited figures moved with deliberation to fill many small cylindrical tubes, then carefully place them in what appeared to be a large metal briefcase filled with a spongy material that contained carefully molded indentations for the tubes.

Warren Holton gave the impression of a terrier with glasses. He was small, with a voice like a yip, and he darted about quickly. He also had a terrier's tenacity. Prior to his assignment overseeing the Special Projects lab Holton had dealt with other important tasks for Durbane--tasks that fell in that difficult to fill niche between the medical expertise of Dr. Diane Gilmore and scientific knowledge of Dr. Thurston Walker on the one hand and the clandestine activities of Karl Dietrich on the other.

Holton briefed the other two men. "The transport tubes designed by Dr. Obrien are being placed in carriers designed by the American military as portable biohazard containers primarily for Ebola virus, anthrax, and the botulism bacillus. These valises are made of reinforced lightweight titanium, and the rubber gasket that seals them is of the same material used on the space shuttle--*after* the Challenger accident. Each can be easily carried by one man, yet is sturdy enough to resist a plane crash."

As long as it worked, Dietrich could not care less about the beauty of the system's design. His thoughts had already turned to the next step, and then the next. Only he and Dr. Walker knew the entire picture. Each person who played a role knew only his own job and little more.

He interrupted Holton. "How soon can we ship?"

"The technicians must work slowly, carefully. If a spill occurred in the isolation room, work would have to stop until decontamination was complete."

"How long?" asked Dietrich, his voice as sharp as an assassin's knife. Over his usual dark sweater and trousers, Dietrich now wore a gray sports coat, which only partly helped to disguise the weapons under each arm in a double shoulder holster.

Holton opened his mouth to further argue the need for precision over speed, but one look at the steely-eyed security man and his will withered. "We're making the final adjustments now. Perhaps two and one-half hours to complete the work. After that, the cultures are yours."

Dietrich nodded, accepting the time estimate. "Then, unless Dr. Walker has something to add, go to Dr. Obrien's office and keep him there for a while." To Walker he added, "the less Obrien sees beyond this point, the better."

"I agree," said Walker, "but I don't want him out of here until we're sure there are no glitches."

After a quick glance in Walker's direction, Holton scurried toward Obrien's chamber.

"The Gulfstream is fueled and waiting," said Dietrich, "but the MD-101 has only just now arrived from Haiti. Some of Doúbe's malfunctioning laboratory equipment must be removed from the cargo hold and brought here before the plane is ready. Three hours should be just about right."

"Are the cultures still going to the airport by one of our trucks?" asked Walker.

"Yes, sir," answered Dietrich. "We attract less attention if we maintain our usual delivery routine. Of course, I will accompany them there."

"Any personnel problems, people backing out?"

"None that I've identified," said Dietrich. He nodded his head in the direction of the technicians on the other side of the glass wall. "All the people in this facility believe they are working on secret government-sponsored biological research. I have a little more concern about the persons chosen to actually inject the prion cultures into the blood packs in the twelve regional blood banks, but they've all been carefully chosen, know no details, and handsomely paid. In any event, there are enough cut-outs and go-betweens that no one will be able to trace it back to us."

"And the shipment to Beauvoir?"

"That actually should be the easiest one. However,"--Dietrich shifted his gaze--"I'm not totally convinced of Fendley's reliability."

"Then now is the time to settle that issue. He's waiting?"

"In the lobby."

"Get him."

The security man used the nearby phone to make a short call. Then both watched a monitor while they waited. In short order a security camera revealed the administrator's distinctive bald head and moderate paunch enter the Research C laboratory. He crossed it to stop at the security door and press the intercom button. Dietrich punched the keypad, and the metal door slid open.

Darrell Fendley, despite his unprepossessing appearance, had functioned effectively for years in the complex and high-tension atmosphere of a large hospital. But this was a different kind of pressure situation, and he was visibly nervous. After one furtive glance at what was going on in the isolation room, he refused to look at the glass wall again.

"Preparations are almost complete," said Walker.

"I've been wanting to talk to you about that," said Fendley, his voice quavering. "I really think it would be better if somebody else--"

"Somebody else!" Walker barked. He glanced at the technicians, but the ones on this side of the glass wall pretended to hear nothing. The ones on the other side were in their own world. "Follow me," said Walker. He reached up and flicked off the switch on the overhead video monitor, then slapped his hand against the palm-print recognition panel, and the door slid open. Walker stepped out into the now empty main lab, followed by Fendley with Dietrich bringing up the rear.

Fendley stood almost at attention. "I didn't sign on for anything like this," whined the administrator. He scowled as if tasting something bitter. "Deliberately infecting people. It's immoral. It's criminal."

Walker's face flushed with rage. This had already been decided, and now, for the worm to back out, it would be a setback--but if the man cracked, and went to the authorities, that could be disastrous. He watched as Fendley writhed with his sudden attack of conscience. After a moment's hesitation, Walker decided to use a softer, rational approach.

"What we are doing will save more lives than will ever be lost," he explained again. "Hepatitis, HIV—a thousand diseases lurk out there to ravage human life? What we are doing is like cutting off a gangrenous limb to save a sick patient."

"I, I just don't know," stammered Fendley.

"Look, Fendley, let me explain it one more time, just like Warren Holton told you." Walker's voice dropped to a reassuring tone. He spoke slowly, repeating the basics. "Use the hospital computers to identify someone with a diagnosis of recurrent nonprescription drug addiction. You've already said that at any given time there are twenty or more inpatients like that. Then search the databank for those who are receiving serial blood transfusions—those with bleeding ulcers, chronic anemia. Once typing and crossing of the blood is done, and blood is earmarked for that specific patient, it will be a simple matter to inoculate the addict's next blood pack with what we give you."

Fendley started shaking his head. "I don't--"

"Listen!" barked Walker. Fendley cowered like a man facing the guillotine. Satisfied, Walker resumed his monologue. "If you can't do it, get your buddy, what's her name--"

"Leathers," offered Dietrich.

"Yes, make her do it. There's lot of ways. Call for an inspection of the blood bank. Send all the employees out while you do it. Claim you're looking for contraband. Or have Leathers go into the patient's room when no other nurse is present and pretend she's giving an injection of something the doctor ordered. You decide how, but you do it."

Fendley's head hung lower.

Walker took a deep breath, then moved to the conclusion. "Those addicts share needles, share the same squalid living quarters, the same filthy women. The prions will spread through those worthless addicts like judgment fire from God. You will be doing the world a favor. Good people will never be harmed--and no one will ever know how it got started."

Fendley slowly raised his head to look Walker in the face. "I just can't. I'm a hospital administrator. You need someone else to be your bag man."

Walker had had it. He slammed his hand palm down on the counter. "God damn it, Fendley, you didn't seem to have any problem taking cash from us once a month. You didn't have difficulty accepting your current position after your predecessor was caught screwing his married secretary and paying for their little love trips with hospital funds. Do you think it was a coincidence that your job became available immediately after you decided to work with us?"

Fendley stretched himself to his full five-foot-eight-inch height. "I was the assistant administrator, and I had done an excellent job for ten years. I would have been chosen as the next hospital administrator even without Durbane's help."

A twisted grin crossed Thurston Walker's face. "Perhaps, but when do you think the position would have become available without Durbane's investigators on the case." Walker paused and looked upward as if just remembering something, then came a sadistic smile. "Speaking of the previous administrator and his dalliances, it is so easy to forget about one's spouse at the conventions isn't it? And won't she and the kids be heartbroken to find out about the partying and the hookers? Mr. Dietrich, you know, is very conscientious about collecting snapshots for the Durbane family album." Walker shook his head. "No, Mr. Fendley, I think you're in. In fact, I would say you are the bag man of my dreams."

The administrator's body suddenly resembled a deflated balloon. Walker thought the man was actually going to cry. "You bastard. You evil bastard."

"I prefer to think of myself as a businessman, a very effective businessman." He looked at his watch in mock surprise. "Look at the time. We need to get this program under way. If you would, please wait back in the lobby. Our Special Projects director is getting a package ready for you, then Karl will run you over to your hospital."

A broken Darrell Fendley retreated out the door.

"What do you think, Karl?" Walker asked.

"He's too weak."

"What about Leathers?"

Dietrich's cheeks sucked in while he thought. "I only met her once, but she would probably be a better choice."

Thurston Walker stood rigid, his hands behind his back. He did not look at his security chief, but instead studied the now empty doorway. He made his decision. "Okay, Karl."

"I'll get to work on it, sir."

Walker turned to leave the room and without looking back said, "I'll be in my office."

Chapter 50

"Put on your game face," said Brian, as Dale slowed to a stop at the guardhouse.

"There's two of them," said Dale, apprehension filling his voice.

"Crap," said Brian. "We'll play it the same anyway. Remember, keep pushing. We're federal agents. We don't ask. We tell."

As Dale braked to a halt, a guard dressed in a blue uniform complete with sidearm stepped out of the sentry house and approached the driver's window. He appeared barely more than twenty years old. Dale pushed a button, and the window slid down.

From his vantage point in the back seat, Brian swept his eyes over the car to see if anything had been overlooked. The vehicle had to look official. Earlier Dale had balked at removing the Beauvoir Memorial Hospital parking sticker from the windshield, complaining that he couldn't get back into the parking lot tomorrow without going through the rigmarole of getting another sticker from the hospital front office. But Brian had reminded him that there was a fair chance that he'd be looking for a lot more than just a parking sticker. Most likely they would both need a battery of criminal attorneys for the trouble they were getting ready to cause at Durbane. And Dale might get to join the ranks of the unemployed, too, since most hospitals frowned on physicians with felony records. *And* that was only if they were lucky. If they were unlucky, Durbane's security personnel might save the police and courts the trouble. After Brian's detailed explanation, Dale went ahead and removed the windshield sticker, but his effort was considerably less than enthusiastic.

Brian did a once-over of their clothing. The attire was not the perfect costume for a team of medical inspectors but the best they could come up with on short notice. He and Sharon wore scrub suits and long white coats appropriated from the hospital, where, amazingly, Dale kept a tie and jacket in his locker. So Dale became the head honcho; Brian and Sharon the techies. Piled on the front seat between Dale and Sharon were clipboards and a black medical bag filled with a hodgepodge of items taken from an unguarded cabinet in the emergency room.

"Can I help you?" asked the guard with youthful eagerness.

"I'm Dr. Trapper. This is Dr. Pierce"--he gestured over his shoulder at Brian and lowered his voice to a mumble--"and Dr. Hoolihan," indicating Sharon. Brian held up his B.M.H. I.D. card, which after one nanosecond he stuck back into the breast pocket of his jacket. "We're special investigators from the FDA. And your name?"

"Jeff."

"Is that all?" Dale asked brusquely.

"Jeffrey Shannon."

"Make a note of that," said Dale to Sharon, who dutifully recorded the guard's name on her clipboard.

"This is a semiannual unannounced inspection by our bacterial pathogen division," said Dale. Brian raised his eyebrows at Sharon who shrugged her shoulders, unable to anticipate what ad libbing their new partner might come up with next. "We'll start the survey in Dr. Peter Obrien's lab," Dale added, "but don't inform him we're coming."

The young guard looked puzzled. "I don't know a Dr. Obrien. One moment." He stepped back into the guardhouse.

"Trapper? Pierce? Hoolihan?" groaned Brian, rolling his eyes. "It's a good thing this kid's not a M.A.S.H. fan. Couldn't you come up with something better?"

"My mind went blank," snapped Dale. "Look, you want this job?" he added, stabbing a finger emphatically at his own chest.

"The suit would be too big," Brian retorted.

"Shut up, you two," Sharon commanded. "Oh, double crap," she said looking at the guardhouse. "Now both guards are coming out."

The second man looked to be twenty years older and a whole lot meaner than the first guard. He thrust his face almost through the window opening. Even Brian in the back seat could smell the onions from the man's lunch. "Inspectors? We always know about something like that days in advance. Let me see your I.D."

"New program," said Brian, opening the rear door and stepping out. If they were detained here, the odds seemed pretty good they might wind up dead, and the evil business this company was up to would continue unchecked to its disastrous consequences. He glared at the older guard. "I wouldn't hamper this investigation, mister, or you'll find the government slapping fines on your employer the company won't be able to pay off in a hundred years." Brian looked at the man's breast pocket. The stitched name tag read *Williams*. "In which case I seriously doubt you will get the employee of the year award, Mr. Williams. As a matter of fact, I doubt you will *be* an employee after they get our report." Brian turned to Dale, who had followed his lead and was now out of the car, too. "That's Williams, security guard, for the report," Brian said into the car.

"Got it," answered Sharon.

"We might as well start here." Brian pushed between the two guards and stepped into the guardhouse. The inside was a simple affair: telephone, alarm panel, and some procedure manuals lying about. Through a partly open door he could see a toilet.

Brian's quick move caught the two guards by surprise. By the time they followed him into their own booth, the older guard had recovered his equilibrium. "Hey, asshole, what do you think you're doing?" He reached out and grabbed Brian by the shoulder.

Brian's senses, already hyperacute with excitement, received a jolt of adrenaline. Maybe it was being called asshole. Maybe it was the bastard's nails biting into his flesh. Or maybe he was just tired of being shot at, chased, and knowing that people around him were being murdered. Whatever it was, Brian spun and, with more violence than he had ever mustered in his life, swung a crushing blow upward into the older guard's stomach. With a giant rush of air and a gut wrenching groan, the man crumpled. Brian came down with a second blow across the guard's upper back, then pinned him with one knee as the man struck the floor. The effect was devastating. There was no air left to come out. Quickly Brian unsnapped the flap on the guard's holster and pulled out his automatic.

Dale hadn't anticipated Brian's attack, but he knew the stakes. While the younger gate guard stood paralyzed by the suddenness of Brian's assault on his partner, Dale slammed into him from behind with both hands. Jeffrey Shannon was slight and unprepared. Dale was six feet tall and had picked up more than a few extra pounds from too little exercise and a steady diet of high-carbohydrate hospital food. The effect was like that of a fully loaded moving van plowing into a motorcycle. The younger guard was catapulted to land in a crumpled heap on the far side of the cubicle. It took only a moment for Dale to disarm him, too.

Both doctors stood there, stunned, holding pistols and looking as if they couldn't believe what they'd just done.

"Now what?" Dale said. "I didn't know we were taking prisoners."

Brian stuck his head out the guardhouse door. "Sharon--the bag." She moved to the driver's side of the car, and tossed him the medical bag. Brian had thrown in odds and ends from the E.R.: blood tubes, specimen containers, anything medical-looking that might convince a suspicious Durbane employee that they were authentic federal inspectors who had come prepared to take samples of anything biological or pharmaceutical that caught their interest. He dug into the bag and came up with a roll of two-inch adhesive tape. While Dale kept the gun on the younger guard, Brian rapidly taped the older man's hands and feet. After a few more turns of tape around his mouth, Brian dragged him into the tiny bathroom and deposited him on the floor.

"Tape him, too," said Brian, tossing the roll to Dale who caught it one-handed. Dale quickly wrapped the younger guard's wrists, but something outside caught his eye.

"Truck coming," he said, hiding the pistol in his pocket, then taking a quick turn of the tape across the man's mouth and around the back of his head.

Brian shoved the older guard's feet into the small lavatory and pulled the door shut behind him. A delivery truck was slowing at the guardhouse. Dale's car had disappeared, and Brian assumed Sharon had moved it behind the little building.

Dale stuck an arm out of the guardhouse and waved the truck through. It picked up speed and went through the gate without stopping. "Hell, it's easy to be a security guard," he announced.

"I doubt if these two fellows would agree," said Brian, gesturing in the general direction of the bathroom and the other trussed guard.

"Hey, they were outclassed," responded Dale, throwing his shoulders back and grinning.

Brian crouched beside the young guard who was propped, half sitting, against the wall. "Okay, Jeff. I'm going to untape your mouth." After a moment, that was done. "Now, where's Dr. Peter Obrien's lab?"

"I don't know." The young man screwed up his courage and said, "And I wouldn't tell terrorists, even if I did."

For a moment, Brian was taken back. Then he laughed. "I guess it does look that way."

"Shh," said Dale. "Another truck."

Brian, gun in one hand, placed the other over the guard's mouth.

Dale waved the second truck through.

As soon as Brian heard it safely pass, he dropped his hand and said, "Let me show you something, Jeff." He dug into his pocket and came out with his driver's license. "I live right here, just outside New Orleans." He held out his B.M.H. I.D. card for close inspection. "I am a doctor--and that mean looking character over there"--Dale flashed his teeth--"is an anesthesiologist. Usually he doesn't do much, just puts people to sleep and wake them up." Dale's face fell. "And our gun moll in the car outside is actually a professor of archaeology at Tulane." Brian could see that the guard, though frightened, was listening. "You worked here long?" Brian asked.

"Four months."

Brian stared into his captive's eyes, as if by force of sheer willpower he could make the young man believe what he was saying. "This is a bad place, Jeff. They're endangering a lot of lives--maybe even producing a deadly disease here."

"That's not so. This is a pharmaceutical company. They make medicines."

Brian thought for a moment. Clearly, they needed help, somebody who knew he layout and could get them where they needed to go. Hell, waltzing in like an inspection team hadn't even gotten them past the front gate without a fight. "Listen, Jeff, you ever worked the night shift?"

"Yes, sir."

"You ever see any company trucks go out at night?"

"A few."

"Very many?"

"No."

"Where do they go?"

"Airport."

"Anything unusual about those nighttime shipments?"

The boy thought about it a bit. "There's always a man from security with the truck. I don't mean guard like us. I mean internal security--the plain-clothes people."

"You ever wonder about that? A few shipments going out at night--secret, guarded shipments--when the majority of the company's business takes place during the daytime?"

The boy shrugged.

"I'll tell you what they're doing at night," said Brian, crouching closer. "They've developed a new product. They experiment with it, using poor people in another country as guinea pigs. That lady"--he pointed in the direction of Sharon, outside--"had it used it on her while she was unconscious. That's how we know about it." Brian could see he was slowly winning the battle--maybe because the story was too outlandish to be anything but true.

Brian reached out and pulled the kid to a full sitting position, then started unwrapping the tape on his hands. "What I've told you is God's truth. All I want you to do is help us find a man named Dr. Obrien, a disease expert from England."

"From England?" the young man said, a flash of recognition crossing his face.

"The company brought him here to make deadly micro-organisms-- germs, not cures. Once they spread their disease, Durbane can sell their new medicine at an even higher price." Brian had finished his unwrapping and stood up. "You can call the police if you want to." He pointed to the phone. "After we're arrested, they'll search the plant but most likely find nothing. Durbane has probably become pretty good at hiding things over the years. Or, you can help us find Dr. Obrien's lab and then, when we have the evidence we need, I'll even help you make that call."

The boy slowly crawled to his feet, and Brian held out his gun.

Dale watched from his position at the guardhouse door. His arms hung slackly, his mouth agape, and he appeared thoroughly convinced that Brian had lost his mind.

The guard looked around, uncertain, then reached to take the weapon. He held it for a moment, pondering what to do, then slipped it into his holster. "There's a new off-limits area inside the Research C lab--Special Projects, I think they call it. I'm not allowed in, but there was a man with a British accent standing outside there talking with a couple of company bigwigs."

Brian looked to Sharon, then Dale. "Special Projects. Let's go!"

The guard looked around the security cubicle. "You know, I never did like this job." His eyes stopped on the closed bathroom door. "And I particularly didn't like him."

Chapter 51

With Jeffrey Shannon, the gate guard, leading the way, the FDA inspection team looked more official. They encountered no resistance as they wound through a maze of hallways.

Jeff slowed and spoke in a low voice. "One more turn and we'll be at Research C. It's a large laboratory. We walk through it, and in the back there'll be a security door. I don't think I can get you any farther than that."

"You've done great. Remember--Dr. Peter Obrien and FDA. That should do it."

The troop marched into the large laboratory Jeff had referred to, but he suddenly halted. "It's empty," he exclaimed. "But there's always people at work in here."

Three long parallel counters covered with glassware and electronic instrumentation ran the length of the empty room. To Brian it looked like an evacuation, perhaps in the face of some imminent cataclysm, had been ordered. An open bag of potato chips appeared to have been dropped in mid-snack. A blinking message on the computer screen went unanswered. A beaker of liquid still simmered beneath the forgotten flame of a Fisher burner.

"Something big must be going on," Jeffrey said, almost unnecessarily.

"How much farther?" asked Brian, his voice tense.

"There," Jeffrey pointed.

In the back of the large room was a polished steel door that looked as if it belonged more properly in a science-fiction movie than an industrial plant. Next to it was a wall panel keypad, and just above it, a small remote camera.

They stood in a semicircle while Jeffrey pressed a button. "Yes?" said a voice through an intercom.

"Dr. Peter Obrien, please," Jeffrey announced. "There are some people here from the FDA to talk with him."

There was a pause, then the German-accented voice reported, "He is in his quarters. It will take some time to get him. Please wait."

The wait seemed interminable, and all the while the glowing red light on the surveillance camera reminded the fake inspection team they were under constant scrutiny. Conversation remained almost nonexistent.

"Hullo?" a voice finally said from the intercom, the British accent unmistakable.

"Dr. Obrien, we need to see you," said Brian in his most commanding voice.

"Sorry, but I am very busy. Perhaps if you return in a few hours."

"If you come out now and answer a few questions, I'm sure this matter can be cleared up without summoning the police."

Silence. Brian looked at Sharon, unsure what their next step would be. Then the steel door glided opened.

A figure with a short beard and in a rumpled white coat stepped forward, and the door slid silently shut behind him, but in that time Brian saw plenty. Unlike the vacant Research C laboratory in which they now stood, the inside of this one behind the steel door was a beehive of activity. He caught a glimpse of a glass wall and technicians wearing environmental isolation suits. That meant they were working around hazardous substances, and he could think of nothing more deadly than cultures of a lethal organism for which there was no known cure. It was enough to go on, he decided. All they had to do was call the police and manage to stay alive long enough for the authorities to arrive.

"What can I do for you?"

"Are you *the* Dr. Peter Obrien from England, the expert on prion disease?" asked Brian.

"Yes," answered Obrien, standing taller. "And to whom am I speaking?"

Then Brian heard a familiar voice behind him, saying, "Dr. Richards?" Brian turned. "And Dr. Blevins, no less." It was Darrell Fendley, Beauvoir's administrator.

"You know these people?" said Obrien.

"They're a couple of troublesome doctors from Beauvoir Memorial Hospital," said Fendley.

"And *not* from the FDA?" said Obrien, his brow wrinkled in confusion.

The red light on the overhead camera blinked off, and a moment later, the steel door slid open once again revealing a dark-haired man with a wicked-looking Beretta in his hand. He stepped out, and the door automatically closed behind him.

"Dietrich?" Fendley was visibly shaken by the sudden appearance of the man with the pistol. He took a step backwards and began to speak rapidly. "I--I got to thinking things over, Mr. Dietrich. I want to help. I want to stay on Durbane's team."

The other man's lips twisted in a malicious smile. "The correct decision--but a bit too late," Dietrich said. With that, he turned and fired his weapon twice, then once more. The roar of the gunshots was deafening. But the bullets had not gone into Fendley; the young guard crumpled over. Quickly Dietrich bent over him, pulled the pistol from his holster, then coolly pointed it at Fendley.

"No!" screamed Darrell Fendley, backing away. He threw his hands up as a shield, but it was a futile gesture. This time Fendley was the target. There were two shots from the guard's pistol, and Fendley was knocked backward. The German put a third bullet in him before Fendley's body hit the floor. "Someone else will make your delivery at the hospital," he said to the dead man, while the others, stunned by the violence, looked on.

For a moment Brian hoped the technicians on the other side of the steel security door would summon help. He looked up, but the red light on the surveillance camera was still off, and below it a display panel flashed the message: *Containment on Internal Systems.*

The man with the gun must have switched off the video monitor and activated the containment system just before he stepped out. The people inside the unit, now totally isolated from the outside world, probably had no idea what was happening right beyond their door.

The others watched, frozen with horror as Dietrich stooped over the body of Jeffrey Shannon. The guard's shirttail had come dislodged from beneath his belt, and Dietrich used it to carefully wipe his fingerprints from the young man's pistol. Then, with the cloth still wrapped around the pistol, he pressed the weapon into the guard's lifeless hand. "Two problems solved. An unfortunate accident between a visitor who failed to identify himself and an inexperienced guard," he said.

Brian watched Dale reach slowly into his pocket. Dietrich's back was partly turned; the thought apparently never occurred to him that a group of doctors could be armed and dangerous. Dale rapidly brought out the gun he had taken from the older security guard.

Dietrich's instinct for survival saved him. As Dale leveled the gun, Dietrich sprang from the squatting position, twisting sideways at the very instant Dale fired. The 0.38 caliber projectile nicked his shoulder but continued on to lodge in Dr. Peter Obrien's neck. The British researcher let out a hideous gurgle, and slid to the floor, leaving a smear of bloodstains down the stainless steel door.

297

Dietrich fired at Dale only a split second later. The bullet struck the anesthesiologist in the chest, and he catapulted backward to crash into a counter, shattering beakers of chemicals. But the security man was unable to loose further shots. The bullet to the shoulder had thrown him off balance and he staggered sideways.

At Dale's gunshot, Brian grabbed Sharon and ducked for cover behind one of the laboratory benches that ran the length of the large room.

Regaining his equilibrium, Dietrich began stalking them, like a hunter closing on a cornered animal. Moving at a crouch, Brian and Sharon worked their way along the benches. Momentarily he caught a glimpse of a scrub suit. He fired, but Sharon was too quick. Another glimpse, more shots. A bullet, ricocheted off a metal sink, shattering glassware on another counter. A flame sprang up, then raced across the countertop to find new fuel from the burst beakers near Dale's body. With a horrifying roar, the fire exploded toward the ceiling, engulfing Dale's body in flame. A shrill alarm began ringing, and overhead sprinklers automatically sprang to life, ineffectually dumping water on the rapidly spreading chemical blaze.

For Brian, the sight of his friend shot, and now set on fire, was too much. Signaling Sharon to stay down, Brian leaped the distance to his friend, rolled the body over and vigorously beat at the flaming clothes. His hands came up bloody, but on the floor beside Dale he spotted the gun. Bellowing in rage, Brian stood and fired at Dietrich who was popping another clip into his Beretta. He missed, and the man, running in a crouch, made for the door to escape.

The room was enveloped in flame. Too many flammable chemicals were burning too hot for the sprinklers to extinguish them. Brian screamed, "Sharon! Get out! This whole place will explode."

Her head popped up from behind a counter. "I'm not leaving without you!"

"I've still got one thing to do"--Brian now had to yell to be heard over the sound of the fire and the alarm--"then I'll be right behind you. Now go! For God's sake, Go!"

The heat was intense, and for once Sharon put up no argument. She ran for the hallway.

Chapter 52

Outside the lab was bedlam, employees running everywhere down identical-looking hallways. Smoke was now coming out of the ventilators, and Sharon ran as fast as she could, dodging people, turning corners.

She came to a sudden stop realizing she must have made a wrong turn. This corridor had plush carpeting, and expensive paintings lined the wall. The din of the fire was far behind her, replaced by only a distant clanging of the alarm. The hallway was empty. Far ahead she saw an exit sign. She started to run for it, then heard the sound of a violent argument. She moved cautiously, the thick carpet and the distant clanging deadening her footfalls. Suddenly a man backed from an office into the hallway. She recognized him as the killer from outside the lab. He was bloodied by Dale's shot but apparently not incapacitated. In one hand he still held his gun. The other hung limply at his side. She ducked into an open office.

"We can still salvage the project!" cried an unfamiliar male voice. "We can say that--"

"No. It is over," said Dietrich. And with that Sharon heard three gunshots.

Smoke began to seep from the ventilators in the office where she hid, but she remained crouched in fear, afraid of another encounter with the gunman. She could hear explosions as chemicals in laboratories and stores of volatile substances detonated. The air grew thick with noxious smoke and fumes. She knew that to stay was to die. Cautiously, she peeked out into the hall. The smoke-filled corridor was deserted except for the body of a man lying on the floor. As she crept by Sharon saw the nameplate on the open door behind the dead man. *Thurston Walker, C.E.O.* She ran for her life.

* * * * *

Brian stood locked out of the Special Projects laboratory, a spray of water from the sprinklers raining down on him. Brian wiped the water from his eyes as he studied the steel door. He had no doubt it sealed off a biohazard laboratory, keeping it as isolated as if it were on another world. There was no sign that anyone inside knew of the fight that had occurred, much less that the building was burning down around them.

There wasn't much time; it was getting hard to breathe. He examined the electronic handprint keypad. It seemed foolproof. He looked at the remote camera; its red light was still off. Unsuccessfully he felt around the steel doorframe searching for some weakness that he could exploit to gain entry.

Suddenly his gaze landed on the body of Peter Obrien lying nearby on the floor. Brian looked back at the handprint keypad. He reached down, grabbed the corpse by the collar, and hauled it to an upright position. With one knee in the small of the back, he pinned the late Dr. Obrien to the door, then grabbed the man's lifeless hand and slapped it to the keypad. The panel announced: *Peter Obrien, Ph.D. M.D., 17:05.* The steel door slid open.

Workers inside the lab, turned to see the dead researcher standing there like a zombie, silhouetted by a solid wall of flame and smoke.

Brian let go of the body, and it tumbled to the floor, blocking the automatic door. "Everybody out!" he yelled.

No further encouragement was necessary. There was a stampede. Someone stopped long enough to rap on the glass wall that separated them from the inner isolation room. Technicians in environmental suits looked up and instantly saw their lives about to end. They fought to get into the airlock chamber, which was designed for no more than two people at a time. Somehow all five piled in, pushing shoving, and knocking empty isolation suits from their racks and onto the floor. The instant the outer airlock door opened, they tore past Brian still in their protective clothing and disappeared into the inferno.

Standing alone, Brian surveyed the laboratory. The fire hadn't got into this room yet, but it was only a matter of time. He stared at three steel spheres surrounded by transport containers, doubtless filled with the deadly organism. He stepped back, raised the pistol, and pulled the trigger again and again. The glass wall shattered. He grabbed a container labeled *Acetone-caution-flammable*. He flung it into the isolation room, where it shattered against one of the stainless steel vats. He grabbed another and flung it, and another, and another.

With a crash behind him, a section of burning ceiling panel fell into the doorway. He grabbed it by an end that was not yet on fire. Holding it like a torch, he hurled the flaming debris into the isolation room. The spilled acetone ignited with a roar, and the vats were engulfed in flame.

Chapter 53

"It's still too hot, chief," said the fireman. He had pulled his respirator down to talk, and he seemed on the verge of collapse. He was breathing rapidly, and his protective rubber coat, still hot from the flames, steamed in the cool evening air.

"That's fine. You tried," said the battalion fire chief.

Night had just fallen, but there was still plenty of light--a bonfire of what was once Durbane Pharmaceuticals illuminated the entire northern sky. Sharon stood and watched, her face tear-streaked, her heart broken.

The battalion fire chief turned his attention to her. "The police detective wants to ask you some more questions." He indicated Touchett and his partner standing nearby. "After that, you need to go home and get some rest."

Sharon pulled her gaze from the fire. "Isn't there something else you can do?" she pleaded.

"No, ma'am." He pointed to the inferno. "That place is a cauldron. The fire in the main building was out of control when we got here. Too many chemicals, too hot and hazardous." His hand swept the scene. "The warehouse, the outbuildings, they'll all go soon."

She gazed numbly where the chief had just pointed. Suddenly she thought she saw something. But it was hard to tell. Twilight played visual tricks enough, and the flames leaping skyward added to the distortion. She squinted. "Do you see?"

From the direction of the warehouse, something was moving. Something was rolling through the flames. It was orange--a forklift, with a load on the front. Sharon took off at a run. "Hey, lady! Wait!" But she was running too fast for the fire chief's grab to catch her. She jumped over fire hoses, she ducked under the barricade, and she kept on running.

Out of the flames but still smoking, the forklift jerked to a stop fifty yards in front of the line of firemen. Lashed to a pallet on its blades were three blue drums. Each carried a bright red biohazard sticker and was labeled: *used medical equipment – blood contaminated – hold for decontamination.* The driver wore an environmental protection suit. He climbed down and unlatched the helmet. Sharon ran into him with such force that he was knocked a half step backward. They kissed, long and hard.

The fire chief, accompanied by a small phalanx of men, outdistanced by Sharon's sprint, arrived panting a few moments later.

"I need some help with an injured man," Brian told them. Only then did Sharon see there was an object lying sideways on the bench seat of the forklift. Brian stepped back up on the conveyance and threw off a protective blanket. Slumped beneath it was someone else clad in an environmental isolation suit. One fireman used a handheld radio to call for an ambulance while Brian eased the figure down to the helping hands of the other firemen.

Finally he turned back to Sharon, and his grin stretched from ear to ear. "Thank God they had a few extra of these suits. They make for pretty good fire protection." He sighed in mock irritation as he looked at the fireman gently placing Dale on a litter for the approaching ambulance. "But that Dale is nothing but trouble. Have you ever tried stuffing an unconscious, and modestly overweight six-footer into one of these damned apace suits?"

"I thought he was dead!" exclaimed Sharon through mixed tears of joy and surprise.

"Gunshot wound to the right chest wall--no pneumothorax," he said to both her and the paramedics readying Dale for transport. "I think a rib deflected the bullet away from the lung. He's unconscious, but his pulse and respiration are fine. Not even too much blood loss. He'll survive to torment me in the O.R. again," added Brian, with obvious affection.

* * * * *

Brian and Sharon stood together, his arm draped over her shoulder, hers around his waist. He gazed at his recent conveyance. "You know, I always wanted to drive one of those things," he said.

"Well, you got your chance. Now go park our 'used medical equipment' over there. I've explained to the police captain that it really belongs to the people of Haiti. I've put a call into their embassy and guaranteed its safekeeping until proper arrangements can be made."

"So you're just going to keep it under your bed for a while?"

"One of my grad students is bringing out a truck. The department has a locked vault where other valuable artifacts are stored, and Tulane security keeps a close eye on it. It'll be safe enough there."

"What about that bastard, what was his name, Dietrich?"

"The police captain thinks he got caught up in the fire. When the alarms went off, all gates went on high security, and since there's a barbed-wire fence around the compound's outer perimeter, he couldn't get away. As soon as the police and firemen arrived, they searched everything that wasn't blazing and found no sign of him. They think he may have been hiding in one of the storage areas that exploded."

"What about the two fellows who were trailing us?"

"The detective says it's just a matter of time until he gets them.

"So," said Brian, "there's nobody left to bother you."

"Only you," she said with a hug.

"All right, as soon as your truck gets here I'm ready to leave. I've got a dog I haven't petted in quite a while.

Sharon took her arm from around his waist and whacked his rump with her hand. "Just the dog?" she asked.

"No, not by a long shot," Brian answered, and he returned her hug. "And after we take care of our own pressing needs, I have a few plans for the future..."

"For yourself, Dr. Richards"--her eyes cut to him in a tease--"or for the both of us?"

"Well, I was thinking about maybe a little rural practice south of here. And while I'm at work you could excavate your little heart out looking for pirate bones or whatever. Just be sure you're home in time for supper."

"I don't cook, remember?" she said.

"I'll have it ready for you," he answered.

* * * * *

"Dr. Baptiste, we need you! Please come quick. It is Dr. Taylor," pleaded the young nurse's aide.

With a sigh he set aside the otoscope he was using to peer inside a child's ear canal and followed the nurse outside. A small crowd was gathered in the central courtyard of the hospital compound. He pushed his way through it. Dr. Robert Taylor lay on one of the hospital's portable litters. Baptiste knelt down, but in this case it was just a formality to feel for a pulse. Taylor was obviously dead. His skin was white and his face contorted in an expression seen only in death. The hand was stiff to his touch. Rigor mortis had already developed.

"What happened?" Baptiste's question was met only with blank stares on the faces of the gathered Haitians. "Where did you find him?"

"On the trail to town, where it crosses the stream," said one of the men.

Baptiste knew the place, within easy walking distance even for a drunk out on a nocturnal stroll. "Go! Leave him!" Baptiste said to those standing and gawking at the body. The crowd started to move away.

Baptiste pulled off his white jacket and lay it over the dead man's face. "You there. Wait," he said to the man who told him where the body had been found. The Haitian stopped. "Did you find anything with him? A bottle?"

The native said nothing.

Sometimes Baptiste still was poorly understood. "Did he have a bottle of rum nearby?" Baptiste asked, enunciating carefully. .

"No rum," said the native. He seemed to want to say more. "Only... there was one thing."

"Show me," Baptiste said.

It was a short walk to where the body had been found. Just off the edge of the trail the native pointed to some trampled grass. "There." Baptiste looked. He saw footprints and matted grasses where he guessed the body had lain. And there was something else. "No one would touch it," cautioned the native.

Dr. Baptiste squatted for a closer look. It was a figure made of straw lying in a small miniature coffin. He looked closer. Was that twisted wire around its neck supposed to look like a stethoscope? And the hair on the straw figure--it looked real.

"He was a bad doctor," said the Haitian. "He had the touch of death. The babies of his patients die, while yours live." The man turned to walk down the path toward his village.

Baptiste sighed. He would not touch this object. It was probably best to just leave it here. He would go back to the clinic and do the paperwork now; even out here in the remote tropics there was paperwork. He would have to fill out the death certificate.

In the blank for cause of death he supposed he must write a natural cause; *Coronary occlusion* should satisfy the authorities.

* * * * *

Detective Bennie Touchett took a sip of coffee from the Styrofoam cup while his eyes went back to the large diamond and expensive clothing on the female in front of him. She was attractive, but in the harsh lighting of the interrogation room he noticed more worry lines than he would have expected in a woman her age. His gaze dropped down to the yellow pad in front of him, and he ticked off the last two items on the list.

"That's all I have, Dr. Gilmore." He turned to his partner to see if the man had anything to add.

The other man gave a barely perceptible shake of the head.

Touchett backed his chair away from the table. "Thank you for coming down."

Gilmore nervously fingered her bracelet and without looking up asked, "Are there going to be any charges against me? Do I need a lawyer?"

Touchett pondered the question. "I don't see that you have violated any laws, at least of this country. Whether your medical boards will want to review your situation"--he shrugged--"that will be up to them. Otherwise, you're free to go."

"I see," she said, then slowly rose.

"Of course, we may have some follow-up questions, so please keep us informed of your whereabouts," he added.

"There's a body still unaccounted for," said Touchett as soon as Gilmore had left the room.

"Well, it's only been two days, and the fire inspectors haven't finished sifting through the ashes yet," said the partner. "But that black guy and the Cajun..."

"The National Crime Information Center is running a search now. But even if N.C.I.C. comes up with nothing I suspect we'll find them sooner or later, particularly if they stick together. They're brazen and much too conspicuous as a pair."

The partner nodded and went back to studying his yellow pad.

* * * * *

At 32,000 feet the only sensation of movement came from watching the small patches of green crawl past on the blue velvet sea. One man sat alone in the first-class cabin staring out the aircraft window as a larger island began to slip under the wing.

The flight attendant studied him with approval: tall, muscular, exotic-looking; wearing a dark sweater and trousers that gave him a certain dangerous attractiveness. The man paid no attention to her. He seemed absorbed with looking out the window.

To get his attention, the flight attendant lightly touched his shoulder. He winced, and she realized he was holding that arm stiffly. "I'm sorry, sir."

"That's all right. A minor scrape," he said in a German accent.

"Would you like a cocktail?"

"Yes, please. Rum, Barbancourt if you have it, and with a twist of lime." Then he turned to look back out the window.

Shortly she brought his drink. "You will be staying in Rio?"

"Perhaps." He returned his gaze out the window. "It depends on the employment prospects," he added, more to himself than her.

"That large island we're just now passing, it's Hispaniola," she said.

"I know," he answered.

Epilogue

Martina cracked the door. "Dr. Richards, someone is here for you." Her smile told him he would not mind being interrupted.

Brian gently released the boy's leg he was examining. The machete wound of four days ago was healing nicely. No infection. "*Très bon*, very good," he said, smiling with pleasure at his command of the French language after only six months.

Martina shook her head and frowned. "Your accent--*est terrible*." But instantly her professional manner returned. "Does he need more antibiotics, doctor?"

"No."

"Then I will finish up. You would not want to keep your wife waiting. She said something about an anniversary dinner."

"We've got a long drive into Port-au-Prince, then a late dinner at our favorite hotel. But, I'll be back Monday."

"Enjoy yourselves."

* * * * *

The road was bouncy and afternoon sun hot, but inside their Lexus SUV the ride was almost comfortable.

"Are you sure Cecil will be okay?"

"The dog is perfectly happy," said Sharon with more than a hint of annoyance. "I told you Dr. Baptiste was more than glad to look after him-- said he hadn't had a dog since he was a kid. When I last saw them, Baptiste was trying to convince Cecil to dig a hole to lay in somewhere besides directly outside the back door of his bungalow."

"He does like to dig holes," said Brian mostly to himself, and still harboring some concern that the dog wouldn't receive quite the same attention as if he had been there.

"I've got enough things planned to keep you busy this week-end," Sharon said with a smile as she changed the subject.

"That I don't doubt. I thought we were celebrating our first anniversary."

"We are, at night. Tomorrow you can help me with some finishing touches at the museum. It's only three weeks until it's open to the public.

307

The Bureau of Tourism has already got it listed on their brochures as a 'must see' spot."

"Okay, but I thought there was a full-time staff, that's why you had to be there only occasionally."

"That's true. Contributions from historical societies all over the world have been outstanding, and establishing the museum as an extension of both Caribbean University and Tulane gave me access to their graduate students as well as more sources of grants. Still, though, there's plenty for the director--" She smiled happily as she looked at Brian, "and her husband to do."

Brian smiled back. "It will be my pleasure. Say," he said, as he suddenly remembered, "speaking of grants, research grants that is, Diane Gilmore called today."

"Who?"

"Dr. Diane Gilmore. She was the medical director of the U.B.S. project."

"Oh, yes," said Sharon. "I saw her in one of those news photos."

"She wants to come visit, maybe stay awhile, work with Dr. Baptiste. She feels like she owes him a debt."

"Stay awhile?" Sharon narrowed her eyes. "As I recall she was quite good-looking in that photograph."

"Nah," said Brian. "An old hag compared to you."

"How old?"

"Thirty-five, I think. Anyway, she's now working for the conglomerate that bought out the Durbane patents when they went bankrupt."

"I would suppose the new organization has got enough money to pay any salary she wants."

"No doubt about it. U.B.S. was too important a project to be delayed, especially with the occasional case of rapid variant C.J. disease still popping up. The conglomerate seems to have unlimited funds at their disposal."

"Well, I've certainly seen the change at Doúbe: paved roads, air conditioning, and that new building. It looks like one of those minihospitals back in the States." Sharon reached forward and patted the dash. "And I don't mind this nice little vehicle for Doúbe's chief surgeon to drive."

"When his wife lets him," said Brian. "But the real change is in Dr. Baptiste. He's positively ecstatic. The U.B.S. research is now overseen by the World Health Organization Council on Human Experimentation, and the latest formula change seems perfectly safe. Anything Baptiste wants he gets, regardless of whether it's related to the research or not. Baptiste has asked for two more doctors and is even thinking of opening a satellite clinic about twenty miles away." Brian took his eyes off the road to glance at Sharon. "But enough about work, when do we start celebrating our anniversary."

"As soon as we get to the hotel room," said Sharon.

The End